VANDERLYN'S KINGDOM

VANDERLYN'S KINGDOM

by

J. I. M. STEWART

W·W·Norton & Company·Inc·

NEW YORK

GREAT ANARCH

Young men unmanned by radiation
Inimical to procreation;
Women unchilded in the womb
By percolating strontium;
The feathered songsters of the grove
Mutant and mute; the fish that rove
The glassy wave by nuclear fission
Un-fished on a *Polaris* mission:

For these, O Lord, we offer praise,
Samples of Thy mysterious ways.

Reduce, resolve in cosmic rays
The Abundance of Thy Seven Days!

Neutron and Proton hymn thy whim,
Since, atomised, the Cherubim
And Seraphim remotely swim,
Galactic debris . . . dim . . . dim . . . *dim*.

Thy Heavenly Gates plutonium turn,
Thy Hell, a 'slow' reactor burn,
Thy Universe, first moved by Love,
Yield to mechanic heave and shove:

Lucretian atomies again,
A rudimentary meson-*scène*.

Mark Varley (Modern Languages Sixth)
in *The Nesfield Grammar School Magazine*,
Summer Term, 1961.

PART I

Chapter 1

'EXCUSE ME!'

The voice was a woman's, and the accent American. Jeremy Shefford, who had believed himself to be walking in rural solitude, turned round surprised. His surprise was increased when he found himself distanced from the speaker by the bonnet of a large car. Or rather, he thought, by the hood, for the car was American too, and had glided with an impressive noiselessness to a halt behind him: a black, discreetly opulent Cadillac, doing its best not to look out of place in this narrow Berkshire lane.

The woman in the car had lowered the window by which she sat. She wasn't young. Her complexion had the grey pallor which, on the North American continent, doesn't necessarily speak of ill health. Nevertheless she looked frail, chiefly because her skin was drawn tight over a fine-boned skull. Shefford judged her rather distinguished. She was well-dressed in good tweeds that were not too new. From the top eighteen inches of her he could guess the look of her shoes. Beside her, a slightly older man—presumably her husband—sat at the wheel. He had the same complexion, but not the same sort of clothes. He didn't look as if he gave time to matching clothes to occasions. He was the typical top executive in a large corporation, Shefford told himself knowledgeably—and at once went on to a fanciful elaboration of this. He's out of the real American dream: eight grades in a one-room country school, and now an enormously rich manufacturer of paper cartons or tin cans.

'Good morning,' Shefford said, managing to cut short his own impertinent reflections. 'Can I help you at all?'

'You are very kind. Can *you* tell *me*'—the lady stressed the pronouns as if to make it clear that *she* didn't propose to tell anything to *him*—'if we are near a building called the Red House?'

'I'm afraid I can't,' Shefford had been conscious of a certain brisk impersonality in the lady's application, which made him feel like a failed work of reference.

'It's *known* as the Red House.' The man now spoke, and with a faint and friendly amusement which had an effect of relaxing the pace. 'But it may be something more like a barn.'

'A weather-beaten old barn of reddish-grey brick and tile,' the lady amplified. 'Maybe there's a house *and* a barn.'

'I'm afraid I don't know. But I have a map.' Shefford swung his rucksack from his back. 'I have the two-and-a-half inch maps for this part of the down. They're the only ones that are any good for walking.'

'And here we are, just making a lot of dust in an automobile,' the man said. 'Do the large-scale maps have all the farms by name?'

'Yes—or nearly all.' Shefford had spread out his map on the Cadillac's enamel—casually, but with a sense that he mustn't scratch the thing with a finger-nail. 'Some names get changed in a surprisingly short time.'

'Like boulevards in continental cities?' the man asked. Again he spoke with a gentle amusement which wasn't at all patronising. 'Sometimes President This and sometimes General That, according to who's in?'

'Not quite with that speed. But there are farms round about here that had different names in, say, the earlier nineteenth century.'

'I think it would still have been the Red House in the eighteen-seventies,' the lady said. 'After that, one can't be sure.'

'There's Black Bushes Barn, at the northern end of a spinney called Upper Black Bushes.' Shefford was running a practiced finger across his map. 'But it looks as if it belongs to Angeldown Farm.'

'*Angel*down?' The American lady leant out of her window sharply attentive. 'Now, I find that very interesting.'

'Angeldown certainly isn't a modern name. And it has nothing to do with the heavenly host.' Shefford supposed that it was this possibility which had caught the lady's attention. 'It just means the down, or hill, of somebody called Anlaf. That's an Anglo-Saxon name. But I rather think'—Shefford still had a youthful weakness for venturing on territories he didn't very certainly command—'it derives ultimately from Old Norse.'

'That's very interesting too.' The lady looked attentively at Shefford. 'Don't you have a place called Anglezark in Lancashire? The erg, or shieling, of Anlaf. But would you expect Danish influence to be apparent in the place-names of North Wessex?'

Shefford wasn't sure that he could tackle this. The lady, he saw, must represent the fine flower of Vassar or Smith, and be in consequence well-armed to pursue any sufficiently cultural topic at the drop of a hat.

'Hardly at all, I suppose,' he said hastily. 'But about the Red House. Have you any idea of how it lies in relation to other places around here?'

'We know that one walks about a mile north from Great Fawley. We've just come from there.'

'We saw the school-house,' the man at the wheel said. 'We looked for the old well. There wasn't much else to look for. If there's a Small Fawley, it can be visible only ·under a glass.'

'Bernard, will you please get out the book?' The lady had addressed her husband on a forbearing note. She turned back to Shefford. 'The Red House should be on the brow of the hill, or a little over it. It commands a very extensive view over the whole Vale of White Horse. And it must be close to the intersection of this road with the Ridgeway— which is the *Via Iceniana* of the Romans, isn't it?'

'Yes—although, of course, it's much older than that.' Shefford scanned his map again. 'There's Whitehouse Farm just off to the north, and Pewit Farm to the south. I think I'd put my money on Pewit Farm. It's at about 720 feet, and the view should be pretty good. You could find out if it was ever called the Red House, or ever had a red barn.'

'Thank you very much. If you will add to your kindness by pointing the way, my husband and I will walk there now.'

'Yes, of course. But might I come along with you?' Shefford was not, as a rule, forthcoming on casual contacts. But he felt curious about these people. For example, he wanted to discover if they *could* walk. According to his best information, walking no longer much happened in the United States, and in places like Los Angeles was actually forbidden as dangerous. So it would be interesting to set a brisk pace and see the result. But—and more intriguing than this—he felt that he now knew what the couple in the Cadillac were about. They were returning in affluence to the humble spot from which some ancestor of one or another of them had set off to try his fortune in the New World. It was significant that the Red House might possibly be a barn. They probably said 'barn' where one would oneself say 'outbuilding' or even 'hovel'. The pilgrimage undertaken in this large car was to something quite unassuming. This made it rather nice.

'We'll be delighted if you care to join us.' The lady had got out of the Cadillac—as had her husband, carrying a book in a shabby brown binding. They advanced with a cordiality, an open benevolence, which no English people would have thought decent. About the man there was even a hint of the paternal which Shefford was to recall long afterwards. Shefford had a wholesome wish to say the right thing. He managed this.

'My name's Jeremy Shefford,' he said.

'I'm very pleased to meet you, Mr Shefford. I am Bernard Vanderlyn. This is my wife.'

Shefford shook hands. Nobody could ever have emigrated from England with a name like Vanderlyn, so it was probably Mrs Vanderlyn who was seeking her ancient places. She had been making most of the running in the matter of the Red House. Not that Vanderlyn himself could be said merely to be humouring her. He had the habit, surely, of highly approving whatever his wife did—a disposition frequently assuming the dimension of moral weakness, one was given to understand, in the American male. Still, they seemed pleasant people, and Vanderlyn was quite civilized. He had just said 'Bernard Vanderlyn', when it had been Shefford's expectation that he would add something like 'President of the Milwaukee Can Company'. Not that what he really conveyed was the heavy-metal effect of an industrial magnate. Physically, he wasn't so much heavy as large; he had shoulders that must have been an athlete's in their time. And a mere second glance at him, Shefford saw, hinted some answering largeness within.

Mrs Vanderlyn was small and spare. She didn't seem any more robust when out of her car than she had done while sitting rather dwarfed inside it. Shefford suspected that humour held no very large place in her constitution, and that quite soon he might be striking her as frivolous. She gave the impression of possessing a great deal of nervous energy, and of allowing it to drive her to the full—whereas her husband suggested himself as owning reserves of power he wouldn't often be in a hurry to draw upon.

'We can leave the car here,' Vanderlyn was saying. 'Anything short of one of your hayracks can get past it easily enough.'

'I think, Bernard, you should get it farther on the shoulder.' Mrs Vanderlyn was looking at the Cadillac with an air of noticing for the first time what she had been driving around in. 'My husband,' she said to Shefford, 'does like to have available a car that nobody drives but himself. And he has accustomed himself to this make. It is unobtrusive, and has a reputation for reliability.'

'It looks very comfortable,' Shefford said. He watched Vanderlyn obediently manoeuvring the monster a further foot off the road. Presently he added: 'I think we should climb to the top of the hill, and then follow the Ridgeway on the right.'

'I'm quite ready,' Mrs Vanderlyn turned to her husband. 'Bernard, dear, will you bring my binoculars?'

'Here they are.' Vanderlyn had dived momentarily into

the back of the car. 'But *he* didn't have binoculars, you know.'

'No—but his eyes were younger than mine. Mr Shefford, you lead the way.'

Shefford led the way. Had he been fully attending to this last exchange between the Vanderlyns he might have found it perplexing. As it happened, however, he had fallen into a kind of reverie prompted by their quest. The Red House was not going to prove quite what they supposed. Although small it was ancient and gracious, so that they were going to fall in love with it at once—and not only with the house, but with the vista of the Thames valley stretching like a county-wide parterre beyond. This last thought was prompted by the actual appearance of part of that vista in front of them as they breasted a rise and walked on a few yards to the point at which the Ridgeway ran off on their right. To Shefford the view seemed so lovely that for a moment it almost embarrassed him to be appearing as showing it off to strangers. He halted, all the same. The Vanderlyns halted too. For some moments they all stood in a proper silence before the scene.

On one side it was contracted still, the horizon being only the farther verge of a field given over to grazing sheep. The sheep moved over the green expanse with deliberation from west to east; overhead, against the blue June sky, a scatter of fleecy clouds sailed with an answering lack of haste in the same direction, so that one might have supposed oneself to be watching a magnified image of the flock in a vast concave mirror overhead. But on the other side the ground dropped away on a steep gradient modulating in the middle distance to a gentle curve which seemed to invite the eye following it to glide as lightly as a sailplane to the valley below. There, spinneys and hedgerows dividing the broad farmlands built up delusive effects of wood and forest as the gaze travelled farther into distance. Delusively too, the landscape had the appearance of something totally undisturbed for centuries; the church towers and grey stone roofs seemed set against their background with a care suggesting the age of the great English water-colourists.

Jeremy Shefford, a child of the industrial north, whose first wanderings had been through mean suburbs to the freedom of slag-heaps and abandoned quarries, had fallen much in love with all southern amenity long ago, and his present train of thought about the Vanderlyns was a good deal controlled by this circumstance. They were going to buy the Red House—an action which was to be at first little more than the whim of wealthy people, but which was in fact profoundly to affect the rest of their lives. Shefford was by profession a teacher of literature, and the more effectively so from being critically rather than creatively inclined. When fantasies of this sort appeared in his consciousness it was commonly by way of other people's imaginings. What, he was now going on to wonder, had been Mrs Vanderlyn's maiden name? Perhaps it was a name straight out of Thomas Hardy's peasant world—like Cuxom, say, or Longways or Cripplestraw. In that case she was certainly due to come across it quite soon, just decipherable upon some tombstone in a nearby churchyard. Or perhaps her English ancestors had been at one time grander folk than she realised. Bernard Vanderlyn might have married a Miss Durbeyfield—and presently they would both be contemplating with gratified astonishment a splendid D'Urbeville monument within the church itself. They would be full of curiosity. They would want to know what hatchments were, and how Latin inscriptions were to be translated. Shefford would himself provide such information with unobtrusive competence.

Captivated by this train of thought, Shefford opened his mouth to ask what could only have been an intrusive question. From this he saved himself by impulsively uttering something else.

'I am the land of their fathers,' Shefford announced. 'In me the virtue stays.'

'I beg your pardon?' Naturally enough, Mrs Vanderlyn had not caught on to this. But she was too well-mannered to sound merely surprised, and she was looking at Shefford

15

with earnest interest. He felt foolish. Still, there was nothing
foolish about the lines running in his head, although they
were on the sentimental side. He had no alternative but to
speak them with gravity. He repeated:

> 'I am the land of their fathers,
>   In me the virtue stays;
> I will bring back my children
>   After certain days.
>
> Under their feet in the grasses
>   My clinging magic runs.
> They shall return as strangers,
>   They shall remain as sons.'

'These are surely very beautiful lines,' Mrs Vanderlyn
said. 'Are they your own?'

'Oh, no!' Shefford's sense of having plunged into a foolish
exhibition grew. 'They're by Kipling.'

'Rudyard Kipling?' Vanderlyn asked. 'Well, that's very
fine. A great writer, if you can stomach the streak of brutality
in him. It frightened him, I guess, so that he had to have it
out and air it. He was a sensitive man. He used to corres-
pond at one time with a relative of mine.'

Shefford found these remarks surprising, and the information with which they concluded disconcerted him. He
had to remind himself that, after all, he had merely invented
the Milwaukee Can Company and the eight grades in the
one-room school. He was about to ask a question when
Mrs Vanderlyn prevented him. There now lay before them
a wide stretch of country, tinted and textured like a great
collage, and she had thrust out a pointing finger to the
north-east.

'Look!' she said, on a note of excitement. 'Would those
be spires and domes?'

'I don't think so.' Shefford felt that they *ought* to be spires
and domes, and was apologetic at having to defeat so legitimate a picturesque expectation. 'That's the Atomic Energy
Research Establishment at Harwell. I believe'—he was
anxious that Mrs Vanderlyn should receive something for

her money—'it's one of the most important places of the sort in Britain.'

'It certainly is.' Vanderlyn said this with a kind of musing indulgence. 'They showed me over it yesterday afternoon, Mr Shefford. It's a very efficient establishment on its own scale, very efficient indeed.'

Having nothing to reply to this measured commendation, Shefford remained silent. But it struck him that an inspection of Harwell is hardly likely to be afforded to casual tourists even of the best-accredited order, and that his picture of the Vanderlyns again stood in need of revision. Perhaps Bernard Vanderlyn was a Senator, or something of that sort. Shefford was trying to frame a fishing question—for he was a young man who believed in the uses of curiosity—when Mrs Vanderlyn again created a diversion.

'There!' she cried. 'Bernard, give me the book.'

A barn was certainly before them—built of reddish-grey brick, tiled, and of respectable although not pronounced antiquity. A hundred yards beyond it stood a modern farmhouse. Shefford was disappointed; none of the buildings struck him as holding any particular charm; he doubted whether Vanderlyn would produce his chequebook, after all. Both Vanderlyns, however, with the mysterious brown book open before them, were surveying the barn with satisfaction.

'Bernard,' Mrs Vanderlyn said, 'do you think there might be a ladder? Do you think we might ask the farmer for a ladder? Others may have asked him before us, I suppose.'

Vanderlyn, although unlike Shefford he was unsurprised by this proposal, appeared dubious. And Shefford himself, who had moved away a little to survey another aspect of the building, came back with news.

'There seem to be a couple of chaps working on the other side of the roof. Repairing the tiles, I think. And they must have got up there on——'

'Tilers! Bernard, isn't that remarkable—that there should be *that* going on the very day we visit it?'

Whatever this was about, Mrs Vanderlyn was delighted.

Her pleasure could be felt as of a serious and rational sort, as if it were coming to her in a museum or across the open pages of a guide-book. This thought had no sooner visited Shefford than he found the volume which Vanderlyn had brought from the car being thrust into his hands. 'You see?' Mrs Vanderlyn said to him. 'There can't be a doubt of it. And I am most grateful to you.'

Shefford looked at the right-hand page. It showed two small and indifferent photographs, smudgily reproduced. Under the first he read:

The Old School-House, Great Fawley ('*Marygreen*')

and under the second:

The Red House Barn ('*The Brown House*').

He looked at the top of the page, and saw that it carried the title of the book. It was *Heaths and Haunts of Thomas Hardy*.

Chapter 2

CUXOM AND CRIPPLESTRAW—Shefford realised—had drifted into his head in the off-target way typical of telepathic communication. Apart from this, it had to be admitted that he had gone astray about the Vanderlyns. Their pilgrimage —or Mrs Vanderlyn's pilgrimage, as it seemed primarily to be—had nothing to do with personal origins, and it was unsurprising that she had discovered no particular relevance in his spouting Kipling on the recall of the wandering heirs. Yet if her ancestors hadn't been raised in these parts her fancy seemed to have roamed them. Whatever Vanderlyn was, his wife was Anglophile. One couldn't describe as other than that a person setting out to follow, in a reliable Cadillac, the tracks of such humbler and bygone conveyances as Diggory Venn's reddleman's van or Michael Henchard's corn-waggons.

Literary shrines and associations held no particular interest for Shefford. He had been to Henry James's Lamb House at Rye; he had inspected the Eastwood of D. H. Lawrence; he had once dutifully conducted his parents over the birthplace of Shakespeare at Stratford-upon-Avon. He was familiar with Haworth, which lay not far from the home of his childhood, but he judged the moors adjacent to it less impressive in their reality than in Emily Brontë's imagination. Inns supposed to have been frequented by Tom Jones or David Copperfield he would be inclined to pass by as no better than other inns and probably more expensive. But if literary antiquarianism of this sort wasn't at all his territory, he was charitable enough to regard it as something pleasantly civilized in elderly people, particularly Americans who—apart from Yoknapatawpha County, perhaps—must be short of adequate places of pilgrimage at home. Moreover he was bound, when he set his mind to it, to prove well-informed on the sort of thing the Vanderlyns were after.

For example, Mrs Vanderlyn had been interested in Angeldown Farm because she had wondered whether it had given Hardy the Christian name of one of his most distressing characters, Angel Clare; he could tell her that as a personal name Angel had started in Byzantium and ended up in Cornwall. Or he could do quite a lot more on *Jude the Obscure*. Only a little imagination would be required to find the spot at which Arabella, Jude's disagreeable bride-to-be, had introduced herself to the chaste youth by way of a slap from a pig's pizzle. Shefford got a moment's juvenile amusement from the notion of confronting Mrs Vanderlyn with such a *locus*. More respectably, there was the small thatched house at Letcombe Bassett—the one down among the watercress beds where they kept the tame hares. Bookish people had called it Arabella's Cottage, and the name had stuck. Shefford turned to give Mrs Vanderlyn the benefit of this information. But Mrs Vanderlyn had disappeared.

She wasn't invisible for long. He had only to let his glance follow Vanderlyn's to recover her whereabouts. The men working on the roof were now both visible; they had climbed to its long, sagging ridge, and were taking their ease astride it. One was mopping his brow with a red handkerchief. The other had unhitched a bottle from his belt and tilted back his head the more readily to pour its contents down his throat. These were sights entirely right in the rural scene. But now, risen up between them like some Goddess of Learning in an Elizabethan masque, the spare figure and intent regard of Mrs Vanderlyn had appeared against the skyline. She had climbed whatever system of ladders the men had rigged for themselves to reach their present perch.

'Mrs Vanderlyn oughtn't to have done that.' Shefford was alarmed. 'If there are loose tiles up there it's really a bit dangerous.'

'She won't be careless.' Vanderlyn, although he spoke without discernible perturbation, didn't take his eyes off his wife. 'Mr Shefford, have you read this book?'

'*Jude the Obscure*? Yes—and I think I remember it fairly well.'

'The hero is denied education. He is a poor boy, and he teaches himself Greek and Latin. But the professors of the university refuse to admit him to their classes, and in the end he takes to drink and dies in misery. Would you say that was a fair account of the novel?'

'Well, yes—at least, it covers a large part of it.'

'And would you call it a good novel?'

'Hardly that. There's altogether too much Crass Casualty. I think that's Hardy's phrase. Jude keeps on getting clobbered—just by sheer chance—far more often than is natural or credible.'

'Clobbered.' Vanderlyn appeared to give a moment to defining this word in the light of the context in which it had been offered to him. 'Maybe it's to wake us up. Each of us has a sneaking belief, I believe, that chance—or Crass Casualty, if you like—has a soft spot for just him. But it would be as reasonable to believe precisely the contrary, and the spectacle of Jude's misfortunes is designed to tell us so. Or that's my reading of the book.'

'I suppose that's right. But don't you think that all those

tragic writers are asking us to eat our cake and have it? They show that mere chance bludgeons us, but they fix it so that we can feel in a muzzy and primitive way that chance is up to something morally, or at least aesthetically, acceptable. It's a kind of fraud really.' Shefford became conscious that he was treating Vanderlyn to one of those large speculations, hopefully thought of as 'stimulating', which he was accustomed to pitch at his pupils. 'Not,' he concluded hastily, 'that *Jude the Obscure* isn't a rather powerful book, all the same.'

'It's the power of it that has struck my wife, I guess.' Vanderlyn paused on this for a second. 'My wife is very interested in education. For that matter, my own family has been involved with it from time to time. We'd better get round that barn.'

They moved round the barn, and were confronted by the ladder on which Mrs Vanderlyn had made her enterprising ascent. She had now unslung her binoculars, but managed to wave to them. Shefford felt that his own sense of alarm had been unnecessary. He was inclined to be apprehensive in such matters. The pitch of the roof was shallow, and she appeared safe enough. She was in serious conversation with the workmen. It could be guessed that they had not much approved her arrival. But now, when not scratching their heads over this bewildering episode, they were pointing with stiff gestures towards one quarter of the horizon and another. The effect, held in near-silhouette, was rather like a Punch and Judy show, so that for a moment Shefford felt he must be careful not to laugh.

'It's a moving thing,' Vanderlyn said seriously. 'This child, Jude Fawley, whose life is likely to be just a hired man's about the fields, has heard of Christminster. He supposes it to be a kind of heavenly Jerusalem. He comes up here—he's never been that far from Marygreen before—and he talks to a couple of men on what might be this very roof. Then, over there on the horizon, he sees Christminster—which is Oxford. I'd guess you come from Oxford yourself, Mr Shefford?'

'Yes, I do.' Shefford couldn't decide whether or not to feel gratified by this ready identification, which struck him as being, in a foreigner, acute. 'I teach in one of the colleges there. But you're wrong, sir, about just when Jude sees Christminster. The tilers—just like those tilers, probably—can tell him where it lies, but it isn't visible. He comes back in the late afternoon, when the men have gone away. He climbs to the roof again. And there it is. Only for a few moments—but there it is.'

'You're dead right.' Vanderlyn gave Shefford a glance of approval—the kind of glance that would mark out for promotion among the Milwaukee cans (if they existed) a young man judged competent at his job. 'The city appears just for moments in the setting sun: spires, domes, and great windows flashing back the light like topaz. I doubt, at such a distance, that last touch of colour. But I like it, all the same. And then it all vanishes. That's the art of it—wouldn't you say, Mr Shefford? A brief vision, and then the boy toils for years at his books.'

'I suppose so. In fact, yes.' Shefford was again finding this literary conversation of Vanderlyn's surprising.

'In the United States we have rather come round to regarding universal education as a sacred thing. My wife feels it that way.'

'It does seem to be the basis of any sensible sort of society.'

'I wouldn't disagree with you. We've all decided, in fact, that an identical ladder should be planted in front of every child's nose. We don't want the guilt of feeling we live among unfulfilled potentialities, like Gray in his Elegy.'

'Gray's poem has a counter-argument in it, as well. A spread of education makes people discontented and acquisitive. The rich fall into shocking vices beyond the scope of the poor. Of course, it's a piece of bogus morality, put forward in the eighteenth century by the Haves to down the Havenots. I don't think Gray subscribed to it. He's touching it in almost unconsciously.'

'I'd be glad to think so.' Vanderlyn shook his head seriously. 'It isn't wholly without cogency. But, like you, I don't

22

approve of it, all the same. Which doesn't mean, Mr Shefford, that I don't sometimes get wondering whether there isn't too much concentration on the mass-produced sort of ladders now. Honest enough ladders, of course, just right for everyday use.' Vanderlyn pointed, as he said this, to the unmetaphorical ladders now on view. 'But it may be that, as a result, some more specialised ladders don't get themselves manufactured at all. Ladders for one-legged men —or, say, three-legged men—to get over awkward stretches on before, maybe, climbing pretty high.'

Vanderlyn's gaze was still directed at the roof of the barn, so that Shefford realised he was producing these curious remarks while his mind was concentrated on the safety of his wife. And now this preoccupation came through.

'You wouldn't be able to guess,' Vanderlyn said, 'that Louise hates heights. She just had to go up, and there she is. I've no fear of them myself. Perhaps the fear was there when I was a kid, and I've just gotten over it. A psychologist told me once that no fear of heights means no proper ambition. How do you feel about heights, Mr Shefford?'

Shefford found it difficult to reply. He hated heights extravagantly—but inordinate ambition didn't seem a proper passion for a young scholar, by implication, to subscribe to. His hesitation, although trivial and momentary, at once made Vanderlyn ignore his own question. He seemed to be a man sensitive to small currents of this sort.

'But to go back to *Jude*, Mr Shefford. It's a valuable book, if only because it tells us how intensely educational deprivation can be felt. The feeling seethes in Hardy as he writes. And he was already an old man, and a famous one.'

'Sexual deprivation comes through just as strongly.' It was in an experimental spirit that Shefford offered this. And for a moment he thought Vanderlyn was startled.

'That too, no doubt. I certainly know what you mean.' Vanderlyn paused, as if considering whether or not there was anything worth following up in this. He appeared to decide against it. 'But you see the attraction of the book for a person like my wife, who has the progress of education at heart. And anybody can feel the power of that image of the small boy on the roof, with Oxford far away. It's the power of a moral fable, you might say. Yet what I myself find attractive in it is just that additional dimension of art. I sometimes feel, Mr Shefford, that if I had leisure and opportunity, I should like to get more intimately acquainted with some of the arts than I've managed to do.'

Vanderlyn paused to nod encouragingly to his wife, who indicated by gesture that she had not yet completed her scanning of the horizon. When he turned back to Shefford it was with the evident intention of continuing a kind of conversation that came naturally to him. Shefford noticed how he could speak about himself without making you feel that you were being invited to poke your head through the hedge of a decent privacy.

'I suppose that education and art come together under the general head of culture. Culture's a chilly word. In England, I'd say, more than most places else, the temperature drops when you utter it. Perhaps it's like good coffee—too continental for you.' Vanderlyn smiled as he ventured on this mild joke. 'And one has to distinguish. There's culture in the anthropologist's sense: the total pattern of a folk's living. There's mass culture—by which one means, I suppose, how people at large occupy themselves in public houses and at football matches and with television sets. And then there's high culture. Mention *that*, and you create the effect of having opened the deep freeze. But it's the kind I get thinking about. I ask myself whether we've discovered yet how to do the adequate and apposite thing by it.'

'Yes,' Shefford said, and gave up the idea of the Milwaukee Cans altogether. Talk such as this—let alone a phrase like 'adequate and apposite'—couldn't be conceived of as generating itself amid their clatter.

Chapter 3

MRS VANDERLYN'S OBSERVATIONS were concluded. Perched though she was in a childish fashion on a roof-top, she shook hands with the tilers with grave transatlantic politeness—a ritual which Shefford, for the credit of his simpler countrymen, saw with relief to be well received. Then she came down the ladder, briskly and with a well-bred attitude of unconcern about her skirts.

'The air is so clean,' she said with approval. 'But Oxford is just not on the horizon, and the men say they have never set eyes on it. And they are most reliable men, I feel. One sees them to be craftsmen in the old tradition.' She paused with further satisfaction on this. 'Mr Shefford,' she asked largely, 'don't you find that a consciousness of the true dignity of labour lingers more strongly in England than in the United States?'

Shefford felt this to be improbable, but was dispensed from the necessity of judgement by the fact that he had not yet visited America. Mrs Vanderlyn at once showed signs of addressing herself in a practical spirit to remedying this deficiency, and it was a minute of two before the conversation came back to her unsuccessful reconnaissance. Mrs Vanderlyn was inclined to think that this was not the right barn, after all.

'But aren't we,' Shefford asked, 'being a little too demanding of Hardy?' It seemed undesirable that the quest for a truly authentic Red House Barn should stretch through the afternoon. 'This is the barn in the photograph. And perhaps this *Heaths and Haunts* book is right, and Hardy knew it and was thinking of it as he wrote. But he may have been stretching things a bit, mayn't he? Indeed, doesn't he hedge? I remember he says that what Jude saw may have been a mirage. I don't honestly believe that Oxford can be seen from up here—either from ground level or by climbing much higher than any building in these parts. I've been studying the map, and it seems to me that Cumnor Hill is in the way. Of course, Jude saw something else later on, didn't he? A faint glow in the sky, which was Oxford by night. It's a glow that must be much brighter now. But, even so, the lights of Abingdon will be in between. And Abingdon has become a sizable industrial and commercial place. The glow of Oxford will be drowned behind it.'

'Well, I suppose there is something symbolical about that.' Mrs Vanderlyn was putting away her binoculars as she produced this sombre thought. She didn't seem disposed to dispute Shefford's assertions, or to run the interest of little Jude Fawley and his vision to death. And Shefford found that he wasn't regarding the episode as absurd, although it could be made to sound so. Checking up on Heaths and Haunts wasn't all that different from working at establishing a text; both were labours of love; it was just that the one was an amateur and the other a professional activity. He felt, at the same time, that it might be well to take leave of Mrs Vanderlyn while he was thus amiably disposed to her. But this didn't prove easy. In fact, it was made impossible by Bernard Vanderlyn's next words.

'My dear,' he said, 'it seems that Mr Shefford is an instructor at Oxford.'

'I don't know that I ought to be credited with being that.' Shefford, inwardly offended at being called by so outlandish a title, hoped that he put adequate false modesty into the disclaimer. 'I'm what's called a college fellow.'

'Now, what would that be, I wonder, in our system?' Vanderlyn asked. He had glanced in amused comprehension at Shefford. 'Would it be about right to call you an associate professor?'

'I really don't know. More or less right, I suppose.' Shefford had very little idea whether or no this was an inordinate claim.

'Is that so?' Mrs Vanderlyn asked. She emphasised all three words in a manner that weighted her speech with equal measures of cordiality and surprise. 'Mr Shefford, you seem very young to have gone through Graduate School.'

There was a moment's silence, Shefford failing to receive these remarks well. His twenty-fifth birthday was behind him, and was memorable as having brought a realisation that he was never again going to notch up such anniversary occasions with satisfaction. Twenty-four, he had concluded, is the perfect age, just as six feet is the perfect height. But whereas if one is six feet one stays six feet (at least until shrunken and bowed by eld) the state of being twenty-four endures for three hundred and sixty-five days only. After that, one probably begins to put on weight—particularly if one is a bachelor don. This was why Shefford no longer met pupils (twenty-year-olds, whom he was beginning to refer to as 'boys') on Mondays, but came walking here on the Berkshire downs instead.

'English education,' Vanderlyn said, 'is intensive from an early stage.' He seemed to be endeavouring, although not wholly seriously, to say the tactful thing. 'And its final processes may not run on the lines familiar to us.'

'I suppose that's true.' Shefford regarded the pursuit of a Doctor's degree as the pitiful resource of earnest but untalented persons. Just after his twenty-first birthday, and in the company of a couple of hundred undergraduates of the same age, he had spent the better part of six days taking a written examination. On the strength of this, and of a reputation for being quite agreeable, he had been elected to a vacant fellowship in one of the smaller colleges of the university. Then—it was a great stroke of luck—his old tutor had dropped dead while running for a bus on the Woodstock Road, and he had returned as a fellow to his own college, one which he regarded as altogether pre-eminent upon the academic scene. All this had happened without his much thinking or planning about it, and he had told himself that when he had had enough of being a don he would go to the Bar, or write agreeably successful but nevertheless seriously esteemed novels, or enjoy a meteoric career as a politician. But now, in his darker moments, he saw himself as declining into a premature middle-age, and this was why he was discomposed by Mrs Vanderlyn's sense of a disparity

27

between his actual years and present course of life. He even found his mind going back to the most dismal stroke in Thomas Hardy's dismal novel: the apparition of the unnaturally aged small boy known as Little Father Time.

All the same, he continued to be interested in Mrs Vanderlyn, who represented a challenge he couldn't quite precisely define. An elderly lady who is very interested in education must necessarily be a great bore, but he suspected that an ability to see through or around the boredom might be an assurance that one wasn't turning a great bore oneself. He hated the thought of developing a closed mind and stereotyped reactions, and here was Mrs Vanderlyn inviting a spot judgement ('tiresome blue stocking') which might be obtuse. He had also decided that he liked her—partly, no doubt, because she seemed to like him. Not yet having arranged for him to visit America, she was now saying that she and her husband would be very pleased if he could return to their car and share their picnic lunch. Shefford, who had proposed getting himself a sandwich in a pub, accepted this invitation at once.

They retraced their path along the Ridgeway. Vanderlyn now said little. Once he stopped to pick a wild flower and study it thoughtfully—but not, it seemed to Shefford, in a spirit of informed botanical curiosity. Mrs Vanderlyn conversed with an energy punctuated only by the need to negotiate here and there a particularly awkward rut.

'Bernard,' she said, 'isn't it wonderful to think that you and I are walking on what is probably the oldest route in Britain?'

'Sure.' Vanderlyn took his gaze from the tiny flower in his hand as if withdrawing from some large vista. 'It still seems to be in some sort of use,' he said prosaically.

'The farmers use it for their heavy tractors,' Shefford explained. 'I expect it was pleasanter walking in Hardy's time.'

'You mustn't think, Mr Shefford, that I have nothing but Thomas Hardy in my head,' Mrs Vanderlyn said. 'It's simply that, when my husband and I are on vacation, we like to do a little of this sort of thing. We like to keep away from the tourist places. We like to keep away from Americans. Does that sound very bad to you?'

'Good Lord, no! I find the English abroad unbearable.'

'Have you noticed how some American men dress over here? Elderly men, quite often, from whom you might expect at least sobriety. Shirts in very large, bright checks, and jackets like truncated dressing-gowns in larger and brighter checks still. An urban notion of what looks right around a camp-fire in the untamed wild. And the hats!'

'It brightens up the scene,' Shefford suggested tactfully.

'It's inappropriate and ignorant. But don't think that I disapprove of their being here. There's now a great volume of lower-class travel, and we all stand to gain by it. I wish more people of the same sort would come to the United States. It aids understanding and breaks down prejudice.'

Not much believing this, Shefford refrained from comment. He was interested that Mrs Vanderlyn talked firmly about the lower classes, since he had imagined such expressions to be more or less *tabu* in America. But chiefly he was hungry, and he began to wonder about the picnic. Did you, if you put up at Claridge's or the Savoy, ring a bell and order a packed lunch? And what did you get, if you did? Would there be enough for three, or would awkwardness result from Mrs Vanderlyn's hospitable impulse? It was with an effort that he recalled himself from these youthful questions to the sustained conversation of his prospective hostess.

'Not,' she was saying, 'that all Americans, even when educated, are anywhere near being good ambassadors. In Paris I've seen things that make me ashamed—and in people who have been through college and should know better. Not that I'd have you think that my husband and I are not very loyal American citizens.'

'Of course not,' Shefford said. And he added, because this sounded inadequate, 'It's just because you are, that you do feel that way.' He tried, on his inward ear, to hear himself assuring a stranger that he was an Englishmen well-affected

29

to the Crown. 'One turns more critical of one's own countrymen when one goes abroad.'

'Which is a very good reason for *going* abroad. I think far more of our young people should see something of the world. That's why I am a sponsor, Mr Shefford, of Schools Afloat.'

'Schools Afloat?'

'Of course, it's happening right now in a small way. But I want to extend it. I want to take over all those useless liners. Nobody with any serious business to transact travels other than by air these days—or can conscientiously afford time to begin and end a vacation with five nights at sea. Most times now, those ships are simply being used as vacation resorts themselves—and what could be more stupid? People all more or less of the same sort, huddled together in circumstances of enervating luxury. I want to turn them into floating schools, and send American boys and girls out to see the world and learn from it before they go to college. Do you think that a good idea, Mr Shefford?'

Shefford didn't, so he found it awkward to be challenged. But Mrs Vanderlyn would always be challenging. He could imagine her challenging the whole board of a shipping company to produce a single cogent argument against her plan. He wondered how far Bernard Vanderlyn backed it. Although he seemed to have almost a dreaming side to him, he was clearly a competent man of affairs, and must know that there was a large element of airy-fairy about Schools Afloat.

'But I see it,' Mrs Vanderlyn said, 'as only part of the effort we must make to liberalise education. And let us not be afraid of the word.'

'Education?' Shefford asked.

'*Liberalise*, Mr Shefford. We must not let the liberal idea become debased, or soiled by political usage. Indeed, even in that context, I must tell you that my husband and I have a great respect for sincere liberals. Many of them have an intense commitment to the future which one must admire.'

'Yes, of course.' Shefford was conscious that this wasn't a particularly cogent response to Mrs Vanderlyn's largest

manner. He wondered whether there was something out-
moded in her vocabulary. She spoke of liberals rather as an
enlightened Victorian spoke of the good poor. He ventured
on what might be called a dig at Mrs Vanderlyn. 'By liberal-
ising education,' he said, 'do you mean making the process
easier and more attractive? Schools Afloat sounds a little
that way.'

'Certainly not. I mean that we must broaden the whole
conception.' Mrs Vanderlyn paused. 'While deepening it at
the same time,' she added. 'I attach proper importance, Mr
Shefford, to the most severe academic discipline.'

Shefford felt uncomfortable—for the first time since meeting these people. His attempt at a dig had not been a success.
Mrs Vanderlyn had touched a note of asperity.

'My wife,' Vanderlyn said on his own note—which in this
context was one of humour—'has come up that way herself.
She majored in English Philology, which is a pretty tough
programme. I'll get the lunch out.'

So that was why Mrs Vanderlyn knew about the erg or
shieling of Anlaf; she had followed some dreary and useless
course in which you mugged up that sort of thing. Shefford
had done some of it himself—and now, as he gave Bernard
Vanderlyn a hand with the picnic, he reflected on what a
queer trade he had got himself into. Most of his attention,
however, went to what was coming out of the Cadillac. It
didn't disgorge chairs and a little table, but only a rug.
Whatever the fare was to be, it was stored within an old-
fashioned hamper of modest size. He had a sudden depressed
prevision of excessive austerity; the Vanderlyn's midday
meal would consist of a choice of substances purveyed in
what are called health food shops; they would drink a vita-
minised beverage obtained by dissolving little pink tablets in
water. It had been a great mistake to accept their invitation.

'Bernard,' Mrs Vanderlyn said with severity, 'you have
forgotten the wine.'

Even in the face of these surprising words Shefford pre-
served a certain caution. The wine, after all, might be of the

sort that is made out of elderflowers or gooseberries. In fact
it proved to be Hock, and mysteriously cold; it was only a
half-bottle—but nevertheless the hamper turned out to
contain three glasses. The food was scarcely abundant, but
there was an admirable *pâté* to stuff into the middle of some
small rolls, and along with the Bath Olivers there was an
avocado-pear dip such as in England could only come out
of the most sophisticated kitchen. There was also a large
vacuum flask of iced water, a smaller one of coffee, and a
carton of cream. Yet the meal couldn't exactly be called a
festive one. Watching his companions, Shefford concluded
that Vanderlyn (though not, like himself, actually greedy)
had some capacity for enjoying what was before him, but was
rather unobtrusive about it. Mrs Vanderlyn was the sort of
person who betrayed no consciousness at all of what she ate.

This didn't mean that Mrs Vanderlyn wasn't fastidious;
indeed, she would instantly turn down, one felt, anything not
bang up to the mark. If she were an anchorite—such as one
meets in Anglo-Saxon texts while pursuing English Philology—she would take it for granted that the water should
be iced in her pitcher, and that her herbs should be packaged
by Fortnum and Masons or Harrods. But the idea of personal
gratification was foreign to her, except in what she thought
of as the sphere of the mind. She had experienced a flash of
pleasure on finding tilers at work where—according to *Heaths
and Haunts*—Jude Fawley had found them. Yet it was only
on ground of this sort that anything which might be called
imagination would visit her. And she wasn't, really and truly,
at all readily aware of you as a person. The notion that she
had taken a liking to Shefford was not quite accurate; she
was simply interested in him in his character as a young
teacher in a famous university. This spareness of instinct for
personal relations was what had put into his head the notion
of her as an anchorite. It didn't altogether fit, since she had
clearly trained herself in much earnest concern for the
general betterment of a here-and-now world around her,
whereas anchorites and their kidney had given up the whole
concern as past anything but praying for. But it fitted very

32

well with something else. Anchorites, he supposed, whether male or female, were dedicated to celibate lives. And that was how he would naturally have seen Mrs Vanderlyn. He just couldn't think of her as ever having been in bed with her husband—or with anyone else.

Shefford was startled that this thought should come to him. The Vanderlyns, although not excessively old, were past the age at which it is agreeable to think of people as making love to each other, and there was no reason why the image of them in such an employment—or failing of such an employment—should bob up even fleetingly in his mind. Yet he knew why it had done so. He had perceived that there was one personal relation which Mrs Vanderlyn *did* acknowledge. It was with her husband; it was of an intensity such as one is accustomed to think of as sexual; yet he had this strong sense of that whole side of life as something rejected by her long ago.

Shefford drank Mrs Vanderlyn's coffee, decently uncomfortable before what was running through his head. For now he was remembering a picture he had come across somewhere—it must have been in Italy—of Adam and Eve in extreme old age. He didn't clearly recall Adam, but Eve was vivid to him in all the indignity of senescence. Yet it was a great painting—had it been by Masaccio, or by Piero?—and the point was that from that shrunken flesh all mankind had sprung, that it was the same flesh that Adam had first touched in innocence in Paradise. Shefford couldn't imagine Mrs Vanderlyn in Paradise, eating the fatal apple and giving it to the youthful Bernard Vanderlyn to eat. More simply, it seemed impossible to think of her with a child at the breast.

'And then,' Vanderlyn was saying, 'we shall return to Paris—and remark our countrymen's bad conduct again, no doubt.' He reached out and touched his wife's hand in a quick gesture, at once humorous and tender, which left Shefford's conjectures standing. 'And then we shall pick up my stepdaughter, and fly home.'

33

Chapter 4

SO AGAIN SHEFFORD had got it wrong. Or almost certainly he had. It was possible that Vanderlyn had been married twice, and that his first wife had borne a daughter to a former husband. But it hadn't sounded like that. The stepdaughter was Mrs Vanderlyn's child. It was she who had been married before, and she was not the barren woman of Shefford's imagining. Perhaps she had produced children by Vanderlyn too.

The early afternoon was hot and still. High overhead a lark was singing, but there was no sound near at hand except the low hum, drowsily undulant, of insects in the wayside grass. The line of the Ridgeway, itself invisible as it skirted the prehistoric earthwork called Letcombe Castle, was marked by a fine suspension of chalky dust in the air, but the breeze raising it was so faint that one might rather have supposed it occasioned, in this numinous land, by the ghostly passing of a Roman cohort or a wandering Bronze Age tribe. Shefford realised that amid these influences his mind had taken a dreamy turn, and that his speculations about the Vanderlyns had got in the way of his fully attending to their talk.

But he had been developing during his first years as a college tutor a capacity for recovering from some unconsciously receptive area of his mind the gist of things said during such culpable lapses of attention. So he now knew that the Vanderlyns had been in Cumberland the week before—not, it seemed, in pursuit of literary associations (although that might have happened on the side) but on some business occasion of Bernard Vanderlyn's which was left unspecified. He knew that their return to America must be earlier than they had hoped: partly because Vanderlyn had in Washington a commitment which, again, neither particularised, and partly because Mrs Vanderlyn was due to attend in New York a meeting of some philanthropic body about which she was prepared to say a good deal. What was in question was the planning or building of a College of Education for Leisure. The general idea appeared to be that the former should swallow the latter; as people were going to have more and more leisure it was urgent that they should be taught to fill it with strenuous attempts upon social and intellectual betterment.

Shefford saw once more that it would be terribly easy to laugh at Mrs Vanderlyn—or, on an afternoon like this, simply to yawn at her. When he asked himself why he had no disposition to do either the only answer that came to him was in the form of a sharp visual memory of her perched on the roof of that barn. He doubted whether she had ever been athletically disposed—but up she had gone, and he came back to the conviction that a certain ardour of the spirit must preserve her from the ridicule of anybody but an oaf.

Nevertheless it was undeniable that she did rather dauntingly deal in generalities. It was a fair guess that a woman so securely of a privileged class had a tolerably tranquil history behind her—yet Shefford found himself wondering whether life in the concrete had not somehow hit out and wounded her, so armoured in abstraction did she appear. An individual to Mrs Vanderlyn was *the* Individual, complete with a capital letter; and what she was interested in was his dedication to progressive action or his relation to the social whole. The arts darted in and out of her talk a good deal—yet their bright plumage faded, somehow, as they came within the shadow of her particular sort of seriousness. It was ground upon which, in a sense, she appeared to have got ahead of her husband, but Shefford had an idea that Vanderlyn would be aware of the quality of a beautiful thing if it was placed in front of him—whereas Mrs Vanderlyn, if she didn't positively need to wait to be told, would have to bring to bear on it conscientiously acquired canons of taste and reassuring information on the identity of the artist responsible.

Still, she had strong feelings about this whole department

35

of culture—which was something a great deal more respectable than indifference. Museums, she explained, ought to be modernised and far more people conducted through them. Classical music was to be discoursed nightly on all Schools Afloat. Above all, artists of every sort must themselves be taken in hand. They must, that was to say, be encouraged —but at the same time certain large truths must be pointed out to them. In particular, they must be made aware of the need to be affirmative. Most of them, unfortunately, were quite perversely negative at the present time. It might prove possible to organise summer schools at which they would receive an improved inspiration from eminent university professors, and religious leaders of the less dogmatic persuasions.

Mrs Vanderlyn was not an intellectual woman. No amount of English Philology, and no gallantry of the spirit, could serve to make her so. Shefford was sure that Bernard Vanderlyn knew this, but it was clear that her large innocence didn't disturb him. Nor, although he must already have heard most of what she was saying, could he be detected as letting his attention wander from her. It was as if behind her words he heard other words being spoken: words wholly valid and true. Shefford remembered the moment in which he had caught Vanderlyn looking at a wild flower; gazing into it—he now realised—as if some gateway might open at the minute heart of it. There was something like this about the regard he bent upon his wife.

And perhaps, Shefford thought, it was he himself who judged superficially of talk of this kind. The desire and pursuit of impersonal purposes, although it has often enough loosed sheer hell in the world, is inherently good, and where it exercises itself in innocuous contexts it deserves attention and respect. He realised by now that the Vanderlyns were not merely prosperous. That they must be very rich had emerged from the evident scale of those Funds and Foundations, Agencies and Boards and Committees, on which both of them appeared to be lavishly at the distributing end. If either of them had owned grandparents equally wealthy,

36

the relationship of these to 'art'—back at the turn of the century—had almost certainly been purely acquisitive: a matter of competition with others of their own kind in snapping up Titians and Velasquezes, Rembrandts and Claudes. That the rich have a duty to keep living artists alive was a notion that had passed those avid collectors by, and the only flesh-and-blood artists they ever encountered were those commissioned to paint their portraits—a job for which Titian and Company were unfortunately not available. With the Vanderlyns it wasn't so. Mrs Vanderlyn had large notions of present responsibility here. Yet she had probably never been closer to an actual painter or sculptor or playwright or poet than was represented by a handshake at a cocktail party. Between Mrs Vanderlyn and the actual chap with his chisel or his palette there interposed like a golden grille, the Fund or the Foundation or whatever.

Mrs Vanderlyn had looked at her watch—a movement bringing Shefford rather too hastily to his feet.

'There's no need to hurry,' she said. 'It's very pleasant here. And I certainly am enjoying our talk.'

Shefford made a slightly awkward business of saying he was enjoying it too. Simple statements of this kind were unusual among his friends.

'But my husband and I are not quite our own masters at the moment.' Like a priestess offering libation before some shrine of Education and Leisure, Mrs Vanderlyn inverted her coffee-cup over the grass. 'We are visiting with friends in Wiltshire, and they have asked us to be back to tea. We are stopping with them until tomorrow, because this evening my husband has an engagement in Oxford. Do you know Professor Blaine?'

'Charles Blaine? Oh, yes—quite well. He's a fellow of my own college.'

'A fellow?' Mrs Vanderlyn was puzzled. 'But he *is* a professor, surely?'

'Certainly he is. A most important one, I suppose, responsible for all the atom-bashing and so forth that goes on.

37

But every professor has to be a fellow of one college or another. It's part of the sealing-wax and string by which the university and the colleges of Oxford are more or less held together.' Shefford noticed that although Mrs Vanderlyn was mystified by these remarks her husband was not. Vanderlyn would get hold of anything in the way of organisation or structure at once. 'Blaine,' Shefford continued, 'is an awfully nice chap. Of course, he's getting on. He must be in his mid-thirties, which is said to be a bit old for a top-flight physicist. But he's quite active physically. We play squash together.'

'Is that a fast game?' Mrs Vanderlyn's question seemed motivated less by genuine curiosity than by her being, for the first time, rather at a loss.

'Not so fast as real racquets,' Shefford said. 'But it's quite a strenuous one, with rather a small ball. I'm glad I don't have to play it this afternoon. After, I mean, your quite delicious lunch.'

'You were very welcome.' Mrs Vanderlyn seemed pleased by this handsome speech. 'Bernard, was it when you were first at Los Alamos that you met Mr Blaine?'

Vanderlyn agreed that this had been so. Shefford, who knew about Los Alamos, saw that Vanderlyn's visit to the nuclear crowd at Harwell was now explained—and also, probably, his trip to Cumberland. But did it mean that Vanderlyn was a physicist himself? If so, his own remark that a man was past that sort of thing by his mid-thirties had hardly been the happiest of conversational sallies. It would be tactful not to explore this further. Anyway, Mrs Vanderlyn was now winding up the picnic.

'Bernard, will you please collect the trash? Mr Shefford will fold up the steamer rug. Thank you. It goes in the trunk, Mr Shefford.'

Shefford judged it to be consciously that Mrs Vanderlyn had briskly fired off this little cluster of transatlantic expressions. Perhaps he really had made a bit of a *gaffe*.

'I took a liking to your Charles Blaine,' Vanderlyn said. It seemed to be as a matter of quick tact that he too struck this familiar note. 'He had an almighty row with somebody I have to work with for my sins.'

'Magalaner?' Mrs Vanderlyn asked.

'Sure, Magalaner.'

'I remember that.' Mrs Vanderlyn spoke sharply. 'And it wasn't an intellectual situation, Bernard, only a social one. Mr Blaine ought to have kept quiet.'

'Maybe so.' As Vanderlyn acknowledged this point of etiquette, Shefford detected him in a glance of affection at his wife. 'But Magalaner had been ribbing him, you know. I guess he deserved what he got.'

'Did he?' Surprisingly in one of her complexion, Mrs Vanderlyn had flushed faintly. Shefford supposed that she was angry, and then saw that this was wildly wrong. Mrs Vanderlyn had registered her husband's glance. It was as a wife—almost, one might say, as a young wife—that she had flushed. Momentarily, Shefford experienced a new, and surely very odd, feeling towards the Vanderlyns. It might have been called a feeling of loyalty. And then he saw that Mrs Vanderlyn had produced a silver pencil, and that he was being given an address. 'It has been a pleasure to meet you, Mr Shefford,' she said. 'When you are in the States, I certainly hope you will find time to come and see us. We have a number of friends who would be very interested to know you. At Princeton, mostly. But at Harvard, too.'

'Just call us up,' Vanderlyn said. 'Now, can we drop you somewhere?'

Shefford explained that he had his car at the top of Gramp's Hill, and that he would walk to it along the Ridgeway. As he put the address in his pocket he thought what a pity it was that the English don't take such invitations seriously. He knew that, although they are given very freely by such pilgrims as the Vanderlyns, they are given sincerely and not as a matter of convention. To discount them is a shade mean.

But now this small episode in the international comedy was over, and he had opened the door on Mrs Vanderlyn's side of the Cadillac. There was a shaking of hands, and as he

39

closed the door again on her gathered skirts he remarked the expensive click with which it went home. Bernard Vanderlyn manoeuvred the car from the grass verge; they all waved; it departed smoothly and not fast—but with a hint of the sort of power that might take it to the moon. The encounter had all been rather fun, and he must remember to find out whether Vanderlyn was really a physicist. Charles Blaine would tell him, and perhaps have some information about Mrs Vanderlyn as well. But he himself would never see either of them again.

Chapter 5

HE NEXT SAW Bernard Vanderlyn, however, at dinner that evening. He might have guessed that this would happen, simply by putting together the facts that Vanderlyn knew Charles Blaine and that Mrs Vanderlyn had mentioned her husband's having an Oxford engagement. There was no immediate opportunity of renewing contact, for Shefford had come into hall rather late, and Vanderlyn was already established between his host and the President. It was a guest night, and a crowded one, and the scene was undeniably splendid; nowhere in England were four hundred young men sitting down to an evening meal in such a setting; wealth and piety had laboured for centuries to set it up. As an expression of high culture, Shefford thought, it ought to be giving Vanderlyn considerable pleasure. Indeed, it seemed to be doing so. Vanderlyn didn't appear exactly overwhelmed, but he was looking round about him with proper appreciation.

There must have been more than thirty men at high table. Glancing round, Shefford saw that a stranger had been sat down next to him—without, so far, having been introduced by his host on his farther side. But the stranger took this matter into his own hands at once.

'Good evening, sir,' he said. 'My name is Peter Wright.'

'How do you do. I'm Jeremy Shefford.' Shefford managed a sideways handshake, for he detected that this was expected of him. He seemed to be having an all-American day. The speaker was American and very young; it was impossible that he could be more than seventeen. Shefford remembered that, somewhere about the university, there was a visiting American professor of the name of Wright, who was doubtless this boy's father. The conjecture was confirmed by the boy's next words.

'Dr Heffer invited me here.' He indicated the man on his other side. 'He and my father are both historians. It's been very kind of him. You certainly have a wonderful hall. Are those *alumni* all down the sides?'

Shefford agreed that the ranked portraits of prelates and statesmen, here and there diversified by a soldier or a man of science, were indeed of former members of the college. Peter Wright seemed to him like a Red Indian who had been caught young and sent to Eton or some similar place. He talked with the unconcern which Shefford could recall himself as once envying in the English public-school boys among his own contemporaries. Only Peter talked, perhaps, a little more than they would have done in his present situation. Nevertheless he did now seem to feel that Shefford should lead the conversation.

'What are you doing now, Mr Wright?' Shefford accordingly asked.

'I go to school here in Oxford, while my father is on the Faculty. I like it very much. Only it's a little confined.'

'I expect it is.'

'At home, you see, I've travelled around a good deal. Last summer vacation my friend Emmet Feidelson and I hitchhiked across the United States. I don't think anybody should call a kid Emmet. Do you, sir?'

'No, I don't think they should.'

'Once we went for forty hours with a man who had guard dogs in his truck. He trained them, you see, and was taking them round as samples. Emmet and I slept with the dogs, and they were shedding. I guess we looked like German shepherds in the end.'

This image rather eluded Shefford. The colleague on his right had offered some remark to him. But Heffer had become involved in an argument with a man across the table, and it might be a minute or two before he could be relied upon to give proper attention to his young guest. So Shefford didn't allow himself to be diverted.

'Were the dogs fierce?' he asked.

'Well, we got to know them. And the man, too. He'd been in Korea, back when that was where the war was. He was a special sort of Marine. There were thirteen of them with each big body of ordinary troops, and they were trained to go behind the enemy's lines. They'd cut through the nerves running to their fingers.'

'The enemy had?'

'No, sir. Their own surgeons. And grafted rough skin on their hands.'

'Why ever did they do that?' Shefford was aware that by this time the clear and pleasant voice of Peter Wright was attracting attention for some little way around. Heffer had dropped his argument and was listening with interest. So was the man who had tried to initiate a conversation a few moments before. Even some of the portraits down the hall, snug in their ruffles and powdered wigs, their ermine and lawn, had the appearance of having bent an expectant regard upon the boy.

'They were turning them into fighting machines. Sensitive hands and fingers—like you would want on a guitar—just weren't required. Those men could *club*.'

'I see.' Shefford wondered fleetingly whether there was something a little strange or eccentric about Professor Wright's good-looking son. He found that he had to conclude against this conjecture. 'I see,' he repeated. 'They were being trained for unarmed combat.'

'And then they pulled out a lot of their teeth.' Peter, although he would have been abashed had he noticed the fact, was now commanding a considerable auditory. The

42

President and Bernard Vanderlyn were listening. 'All except eight,' Peter went on.

'I'd have thought that, in unarmed combat, teeth would be rather useful.' The man on Shefford's right said this with friendly humour. 'So why pull out any of them?'

'They have to leave eight, because you can't be in the front line with less than eight teeth. But they wanted to leave them with as few as possible. You see, pulling out teeth, very slowly, was one of the tortures, and they figured a really tough Marine could stand up to eight.'

'Did your man with the guard dogs suffer these things?'

'He was caught, all right. He showed us his body, and it was covered with great scars and weals. He was in a coma for weeks, after they brought him back.'

'Was he very much marked by his experiences—mentally I mean?'

'He'd gotten over them,' Peter Wright said, rather briefly. 'They were wonderful dogs, if only they hadn't been shedding. One day, I'd like to have dogs like that.'

At this point Heffer, doing his duty, led the talk to other things. Shefford was left not quite knowing what he'd been hearing about. When schoolboys were invited to dine at high table—which was an old-established custom in the college—one did sometimes have to accommodate oneself to the reception of immature remarks. But this hadn't been quite like that. He formed a vague picture of the two boys, Peter and the unfortunately named Emmet, huddled with these great dogs in a van, and some hard-bitten man amusing himself by curdling their blood with abominable fairy-tales. Only it didn't seem as if Peter's blood had been curdled. Nor was Peter himself now consciously telling a fairy-tale. The man, however inventive, had really had that body to show. And the disposition to show it to two children.

Shefford glanced along the table, and caught Vanderlyn in a moment of silent and sombre contemplation of his plate. He had gathered, it seemed to Shefford, the gist of his lively young countryman's narrative. Shefford thought of Mrs Vanderlyn, perched on a rooftop and scanning the horizon for Jude Fawley's Christminster; of Mrs Vanderlyn, propounding plans to broaden and deepen education. For a moment he knew Mrs Vanderlyn to be so precious that any concomitant absurdity in her didn't count. He wondered whether her husband, too, saw her that way. People talked about the horror of the modern world, the particular terror of the time. Shefford was inclined to suppose that the horror was perennial, was part of the way that the world had been set on its foundations at the beginning. There had been the Golden Age of the Antonines in Rome, the Peace of the Augustans in England. In remoter places there had been similar periods one scarcely knew about: in India the era of Gupta rule before the Huns came, in China vaguely discerned centuries characterisable in the same way. But when you looked into them, when you asked the historians, you came to doubt whether the gold had been more than gilding. The horror was present always; what shifted was how and where people felt about it. The focus of consciousness, the burden of conscience: it was these that drifted around. Perhaps it was arguable that Europe was through with all that for a time; it had supped so full of horrors that it had simply signed off. It was America's turn.

Peter Wright was now talking to a man on the other side of the table. He was explaining that music was pretty well his life. He intended to go a long way with the guitar. He had met a violinist who had told him that the better you got the less good you knew you were. The truth of this had struck him strongly, and he had bought two books about musical theory. But in the main he liked improvising, which was something the best jazz musicians had a genius for. It was very difficult to build up your own jazz group, but that was what he meant to do. He was going to make money that way.

Shefford decided that Peter on music, although authentically American, was less interesting than Peter on the disasters of war, and for some time he let his attention move elsewhere. But near the end of the meal it seemed time to have some further talk with the boy, and it occurred to him to ask a question.

44

'Can you tell me anything about an American called Bernard Vanderlyn, Mr Wright? He's the man sitting on the right of the President.'

'Bernard Vanderlyn, Mr Shefford? Sure. I guess he's pretty close to the President.'

'That's what I'm saying.' Shefford felt he couldn't have been heard. 'He's sitting beside him now.'

'I meant *our* President, sir. Mr Johnson.'

'You mean,' Shefford asked, 'that Mr Vanderlyn is an important politician?'

'Something like that. I don't know whether politician is the right word.' Peter Wright seemed to feel misgivings about his ability to expound the governmental structure of the United States. 'Anyway,' he continued, 'that's where he is. Very much a personal adviser. My father could tell you about him.'

'Is he a physicist, do you know?'

'I never heard that, sir. But maybe he controls a good deal of that sort of thing.'

At this moment the President, who had for some time been eyeing bleakly a forgetful man before whom there was still an undrained wineglass, rose to his feet and uttered a couple of Latin words in a semi-clerical voice. The diners at high table proceeded to file through the empty hall. The undergraduates, more sparely dieted, had departed half-an-hour earlier.

Dessert was all university politics, as too frequently happened nowadays. In the outer world a persuasion had been growing up that Oxford stood in need of reform, and people were beginning to feel that something of the sort might really have to happen. Nearly everybody talked about it, although not everybody talked about it seriously.

'I'd have supposed,' Charles Blaine was saying, 'that a college's housekeeping, at least, might be regarded as its own business. Is some busybody going to say "Walnuts on Wednesdays" '—Blaine had reached for a nut—'or even'—he took up a decanter—' "Fonseca '34 only at feasts"?'

45

'No more feasts,' Heffer called out from down the table. 'Only that yearly garden party in the rain.'

'But it would be perfectly reasonable, Charles,' the President said. 'Our predecessors did themselves proud, when their money was all their own——'

'When it was what they could extort from tenants and their labourers.' Blaine was fond of reflections of this kind.

'Of course, of course. But now, to a substantial extent, we live off government. So the writing is on the wall. Fortunately, the intellect is said to do very well on a dish of herbs.' The President turned to Vanderlyn with the air of a man who, although competent at trifling, is impatient of it. 'Broadly,' he said, 'our position is this . . .'

The President was good at exposition—and particularly (Shefford reflected) in situations which Mrs Vanderlyn would find hard to categorise either as simply social or simply intellectual. Politics remained boring, nevertheless. So when coffee had been brought in, and people could please themselves, Shefford saw with satisfaction a young man seated far down the table pick up his coffee-spoon and absentmindedly tap his nose with it. Gavin Naylor was his particular crony, and this inelegant gesture (in which they took childish satisfaction) was a code between them. A couple of minutes later, Naylor slipped from the room. Shefford himself took a quick look round. He had managed to speak to Vanderlyn before they sat down to dessert, so he had no further duty there—nor was there anybody else with whom politeness required him to converse. He got up and went out into the quad.

It wasn't late, but for the moment Gavin Naylor's was the only figure visible. His shirt-front glimmered beside the fountain in the gathering summer dusk; he was watching the green bronze dolphins toss into the air water-jets the tips of which would soon be dancing in moonlight. It was going to be that sort of night. Already to the west the great tower of the college had become only a majestic silhouette against a soft, uniformly luminous sky, and looking eastward through the airy Ionic arcades so miraculously supporting all the

46

vastness of the New Library one saw the darkness of ancient cedar-trees cantilevered far out over ancient turf: that and broad flower-beds from which colour had drained away, so that now there would appear to be only a barrier of scent separating the garden from the water-meadows beyond. The fountain murmured, plashed—and every now and then, through some hydraulic vagary, produced a single vibrant musical note. More complex music came from the next quadrangle, where an ambitious pianist, his windows unlawfully flung open to the night, was threading his way through a piece by Schönberg. It could be overpowering at times, Shefford thought, as he joined his friend; you could fairly accuse the place of laying it on a bit thick.

'Have you ever considered,' he asked, 'what a tremendous moment this chunk of architecture constituted in the university's intellectual history? Walk round the other colleges, and you are inside a series of stone pens all the time. There's a bit of open sky on top—just to remind you that God is squinting down at you—but you can't get out. And here, at long last, somebody knocked down a wall.' He pointed at the east colonnade. 'And there was the beautiful earth—not quite ready to receive its saints, but at least offering the four winds to its sinners. Glory to Inigo Jones!'

'Even then you could only *see* out,' Naylor said. 'You couldn't *get* out. In every archway there were those iron grilles. The nymphs might be dancing in the garden, wantoning in the meadow. But you couldn't get at them. You couldn't even make an honest woman of one without having to vacate your miserable fellowship.' Naylor was spare and pale; he regarded the world seriously through gold-rimmed spectacles. But his habits were scarcely ascetic, and at the moment he was smoking a large cigar. 'Your Inigo Jones,' he went on, 'was a sadist, as all Welshmen are. Talking of sadism, whatever was that American boy prattling about at dinner?'

'Torture in Vietnam. No, in Korea. Did you notice it startling people?'

47

'It seemed to catch the attention of his elderly country-man—some sort of wandering professor, I suppose.'

'Not a professor. A chap called Bernard Vanderlyn. He's a top man in the presidential *entourage* at the White House. One of the last of the civilised ones to survive, I'd suppose. Come to my rooms, and I'll make you some coffee.'

'We'll walk round the quad first. If Vanderlyn's that sort of person, I shouldn't expect him to bother his head about a child spouting tortures. But educated Americans are sensitive about such things. They hate the violence at the roots of their society. They hate the way it bobs up in the stuff their kids are fed on in comics.'

'Whereas we were brought up on Tiger Tim and the Flopsy Bunnies and Christopher Robin.'

'And Babar and Ferdinand the Bull and the perfectly conducted Swallows and Amazons. Not that polite American nurseries aren't knee-deep in all that too. But seriously, Jeremy, the way the face of violence keeps bobbing up over the hedge at the young of this generation is frightful. America is far from having a monopoly of it. Take television. Every now and then it has a regular field-day with the stuff—and announces beforehand that perhaps the children had better be sent to bed. How do you think they react to that? But that's rather special, and will be about the Congo or Vietnam or whatever at the moment are the darker places of the earth. Much more significant is what you get quite casually in the news bulletins: the police in one centre of western civilization or another getting people—mostly young people—nicely down on the pavement and whacking them hard.' Naylor paused. 'Hard,' he repeated mildly. 'And kicking them. You can hear the boots going home.'

'But these things have always happened,' Shefford said. 'The dungeons have always been there. It's just that they get heard about more nowadays. In the nineteenth century, not even the major atrocities that kept happening in one corner of the world or another got widely known—not unless they were what was called ventilated in parliament. There

48

they were, but there was no modern system of publicity. And it's not unwholesome that we're shown horrors now and then. Look at you and me now, living and chattering amid conditions of enervating security. For if these places were built like prisons to keep scholars *in*, they were also built like fortresses to keep the marauding world *out*. . . . Good God! What's that?'

Schönberg was still coming from the distant piano. The fountain continued to plash. But suddenly no such gentle sound, congruous with the calm and cloistered place, had a chance of making itself heard. The whole quad was ringing as with the clamour of a savage tribe: trampling feet, the blast of a hunting horn, hallooing voices giving uninhibited utterance to the cries of the chase. And through an archway came the occasion of all this: a group of young men in full evening-dress, their tail-coats brilliantly faced with scarlet and blue, as if they were a rout of angry penguins incongruously splashed with the colours of birds of paradise. They belonged to the most admired of Oxford's undergraduate clubs. Shefford and his friend came to a halt in their dignified stroll, terrified and appalled.

'I think,' Shefford managed to say, 'we might slip up this staircase.' They dived into a saving near-darkness, and remained in craven silence until the sound of blood-lust died away. Presidents and Deans, Proctors and Vice-Chancellors have blanched before it, so no doubt they were to be held excused. 'They'd think nothing of chucking a couple of young ushers into the fountain,' Shefford said. 'Gavin, just think of being a bloody fox.'

'It's incredible.' Even Naylor's calm was shaken. 'It's straight out of the middle ages and Evelyn Waugh. Let's have that coffee.'

They returned to the open, and made their way to Shefford's rooms. They threw themselves into chairs and shouted with laughter. The tenor of their previous conversation required that they should do nothing less. Absurdity was something they had a relish for. They drank coffee, and listened to some scraps of music on the record-player. After

49

that, however, they didn't seem to settle down to talk. Shefford fell to prowling about the room.

'I wonder,' he asked, 'if anybody's gone up to the library? Let's go across and see.'

Chapter 6

T HE NEW LIBRARY (which the sadist Inigo Jones had built) was very much a place of seniority and security; it was inconceivable that nocturnal riot, however desperate, could intrude there. The Governing Body of the college used it for its deliberations, and recently there had grown up a habit of repairing to it late in the evening. It could be reached from the senior common room by a walk along the leads, and people would move across—perhaps with a wineglass in one hand and a decanter in the other— when they felt there would be satisfaction in a change of scene. In the library one could continue comfortably to sit around. Alternatively, by strolling up and down its remarkable length, one could soon cover half-a-mile or so before bed-time. In splendid carved and gilded presses on one's either side one would be fortifyingly aware of vast accumulations of human knowledge encased in vellum or ancient calf. Since, however, it wasn't a sort of knowledge any longer in demand (so that not within living memory, conceivably, had one of the books been taken from its place except for dusting and polishing), no inconvenience to the learned was ever caused by these purely social incursions. The college's 'working' library was elsewhere.

Despite the intimidating load of lumber it housed, the New Library was very much a feature to display to visitors. This was partly a matter of its fabric and appointments. A few generations after Inigo Jones moved out Grinling Gibbons had moved in. The ceiling, renewed by some Italian of genius in the early eighteenth century, had cost a lot of money every fifty years or so ever since. It would have been overwhelming if it hadn't hung so savingly high in air. Shefford used to think that Henry James would have been happy here. It was on record that James could stand a great deal of gold.

But over and above this there were the really respectable treasures of the place, variously available for exhibition to the informed. It was possible to observe fashions, Shefford had remarked, in bringing forward such things: one term, it would be all Old Master drawings; the next, the diaries of a Victorian notability; the next after that again, a Greek text marginally scrawled on to effects of incomprehensible wit by some acrid and forgotten scholar. For visitors un-stirred by such objects—and they did exist—there was held in reserve the prospect from one or other of the high win-dows which faced each other down the length of the cham-ber. One of these framed the great tower of the college —flanked, to its rear, as if in deferential attendance, by several of the better architectural features that other colleges could show. The other window looked out on the garden, and on the park beyond it, and on the meadows beyond that. It was the general persuasion, fortified by experience, that only a clod could fail to be pleased by these contrasting views.

There were half-a-dozen men in the library now; the President, Blaine, Vanderlyn, and three senior fellows from among what Gavin Naylor was accustomed to call the graver sort. The college's politicians had either gone to bed or remained in the common room discussing committees and statutes. The President, remarking the youth of the new arrivals, passed from cordial gestures to a careful introducing of Naylor to Blaine's guest. Then he turned to Shefford.

'Jeremy, do they keep a telephone in this splendiferous place?' Vagueness about minor college dispositions was one of the President's lines.

'Yes, President. Down in the hall.'

'Then would you—very kindly, and sooner or later—get on to the lodge, and have them send for a cab for

51

Charles's guest? Mr Vanderlyn is staying in the country and was sent down in a car. And he felt he'd like to dismiss the chap home, and be run out in a taxi later.'

'Yes, of course.' Shefford was rather pleased at being asked to run an errand for the President, since the President's tone contrived to indicate that he would himself consider it entirely natural to run an errand for Shefford at any time. He remembered, however, that Vanderlyn was staying somewhere in Wiltshire, the nearest boundary of which must be twenty miles away. And he both doubted the comfort of an Oxford taxi and reflected that Vanderlyn was an important as well as an interesting man. So he turned to the American. 'But, sir,' he said, 'might I run you out myself, when the time comes? My car's close by, and I'd love a drive on a night like this.'

'That is much too kind of you, Mr Shefford.' Vanderlyn seemed pleased, and he certainly wasn't disposed to fuss. Young men jumped to attention in his presence regularly, no doubt. So the matter of conveyance was settled. 'But first,' Vanderlyn then said, 'I'd like to know what Mr Shefford and his friend think about all this.'

Shefford and his friend looked properly interested. It was gratifying to be drawn at once in this civil way into whatever was going forward.

'It's the poet's purse,' a man called Martin said. Martin was decidedly of the graver sort: an old-fashioned scientist of some kind, who prided himself on numerous extraneous interests. ('I can give you the date of the battle of Salamis,' he liked to say. 'But can you give me the atomic weight of helium?') 'The poet, it seems, has been holding out his empty purse since time immemorial. Does it do any good to fill it?'

'Of course it does,' Shefford said. 'Unless from the standpoint that no man should be counted happy till he's dead. The poor devil holds out his purse because he wants a square meal.'

'Certainly he does—and good luck to him. But he doesn't *say* that what he wants is a square meal. Or, if he does, he goes on to claim that he has a special sort of digestion, a specially valuable way of converting energy. Like all those fiddlers and people in an orchestra. Scrape, scrape and *bang!* Any amount of friction and percussion going in at the one end, and out of the other coming divine harmony. And so with the poet. He asks for a high-protein diet and tolerable claret, in order that he may produce vigorous and pleasing verse.'

'Milton,' Naylor offered, 'appears to have written *Paradise Lost* on olives and cold water. And it's a very noisy poem.'

Vanderlyn, to whom this last piece of information was probably new, glanced curiously at the speaker. No doubt he was wondering, Shefford thought, whether Gavin was another associate professor. But when Vanderlyn spoke, it was to return crisply to the point.

'Of course the poet, or any other artist, must be supported. If we are to have any sort of civilisation, simple economic support must be conveyed to him somehow. The question is, what is the best way—and with what other kind of support it ought to be tied up, if any.'

'I'd have thought you don't want any sort of tying up.' A man called Peart, who didn't always follow argument very clearly, said this with emphasis. 'No strings attached: wouldn't that be the golden rule? It's the artist's freedom of expression that must be safeguarded all the time.'

'I wonder if that's so?' the President asked gently. 'I believe it would be reasonable—perfectly reasonable—to advance a different point of view. Must the chap have as his main stock-in-trade a self to express? I know *I* haven't a self to express. I don't believe that even Gavin has a self to express.' The President was inclined to make a favourite of Naylor, which accounted for this teasing. 'And is this poet or painter or whatever so very different? The notion that he is may be no more than a romantic fallacy.'

'I'd say the President is right—up to a point.' Blaine, who had been peering into a glass of port as if some advanced nuclear mystery lurked in the depths of it, had glanced up abruptly. 'Self-expression is bosh. An artist who's any good focuses the consciousness of his society. He expresses the conflicts to a resolution of which that society is moving. But that doesn't mean that the concept of self-expression wasn't a valid factor in the activity of art at a certain time and in a certain place. The time and the place of the rise of the individual entrepreneur.' There was a moment's silence—something that the voice of the children of Marx is inclined to produce. 'That the notion of self-expression is nonsense today,' Blaine went on easily, 'is surely evident in the mere fact that it is nonsense that it produces. I don't know how it may be with you, Bernard' —this manner of addressing Vanderlyn for some reason startled Shefford—'but I've noticed an interesting phenomenon in our public places within recent years. It's the erection in parks and so on, at the general expense, of pieces of sculpture wholly devoid of meaningful content to ninety-nine per cent of the people who look at them. As far as I know, it is something totally new in the history of the relationship of the artist and society. Mind you, I'm not saying the chap *isn't* an artist——'

'Charles is no philistine,' Shefford interjected wickedly.

'Thank you. And I don't really think that I am. But you see what has happened. The chap has been given a cheque, or the promise of a cheque, told to go away and peer into his own inside, express the result, and bring it back for the delight and edification of his fellow-citizens. The stimulus is nonsense, so naturally the response makes nonsense as well.'

'Do you mean,' Shefford asked, 'that he should have been told not to express himself, but to turn up with a decent statue of Alderman Bloggs, being careful to represent him as prosperous, dignified, kindly, and enormously reliable?'

'That's it!' The only man who had remained silent so far, a philosopher called Raggett, spoke with quick nervous energy. 'That's the nub.' He turned to Vanderlyn. 'Get right about that, and your troubles are over.'

Vanderlyn's only reply to this for a moment was a slow smile. Shefford wondered whether this casual debate had

54

really begun from any troubles of Vanderlyn's upon which he had been prompted to consult the wisdom of his hosts. He remembered how that morning something about the Vanderlyns or their talk had introduced into his own head a theme very like the present one: the relationship in which influential and well-meaning people like themselves stood to what Vanderlyn had called high culture.

'Be quite firm about it,' Raggett went on. 'Make it clear that the artist is your servant, and that he must do what you want. *You* decide what's wanted. You're fit for that, aren't you?' This question to Vanderlyn came with all the sharpness that was said to petrify Raggett's pupils.

'I could try, I suppose.' Vanderlyn certainly wasn't petrified. 'It's something I've had to do rather a lot of in some fields. It would require a background.'

'You will have something of that, if you are interested at all. And, of course, you mustn't be a fool. Jeremy, what was it the Prince Regent's librarian wanted to get out of Jane Austen?'

'An historical romance, illustrative of the history of the august House of Coburg.' Shefford, although he had given a nervous jump, reacted like a competent pupil.

'A little bit of ivory, two inches wide,' Martin said, innocently pleased with his command of this further reference. 'She said, very sensibly, that her true scope was there.'

'It's your feeling,' the President asked Raggett, 'that the artist does better under the conditions you describe? It's arguable, certainly—a perfectly reasonable theory.'

'It's nothing of the kind.' Raggett, who regarded the President as one of nature's Beta-Alphas, snapped this out. 'It's plain historical fact. The artist is no good as his own master; such a status burdens and distracts him. But just *you* be his master, and—paradoxically—*he'll* be *your* master in no time. If he's potentially a great artist, that's to say.'

'You mean,' Shefford asked, 'his Bloggs will be so terrific we'll gaze at it with reverent awe?'

'Well, yes—if you must labour Bloggs. What it's sensible to maintain is more or less what Charles was saying—or would have been saying, but for his blessed jargon. The chap has to feel that, broadly speaking, his job is socially defined for him, and socially approved. But I can see that Peart is going to say something very deep. He's going to say that all this is to degrade the artist to the condition of a mere craftsman.'

'I'm inclined to say that myself—or at least that the danger would be there.' Vanderlyn said this to the accompaniment again of his slow smile; and Shefford marked the quickness of his instinct to give some support to Peart, a dull man being pointlessly bullied. 'But the theory of what you might call the artist's straight assignment has its attractions, I admit. I'd get a big kick from giving those orders. I'd go out on my terrace after breakfast, and there across the valley would be a great mountain. "That mountain," I'd say, "looks like Bloggs to me. See that it looks like Bloggs to other people." And a whole Royal Academy of carvers and sculptors would go to work.'

'As a matter of fact, I wasn't going to say what Raggett says I was going to say.' It was one of Peart's tedious habits to hark back in this way. 'I was going to point out that what we are really talking about is patronage.' Peart looked round the company, with the comfortable air of a man who has produced light.

'I suppose that's so.' Vanderlyn took the trouble to look enlightened. He was an untiringly courteous man. 'But it's not a word that, with us in the United States, comes very naturally. Of course, the fact of it is there. We have plenty of folk who deserve to be called great patrons, I don't doubt. But, on the whole, the individual patron belongs to the past.'

'Penal taxation,' Blaine said. 'That's what you call it, when you're at the paying end. The individual patron flourished in the palmy days of finance capital, just as he flourished during the Renaissance with the coming of the great merchants and bankers. But he's a back number now.'

'I doubt whether he need be, so far as command of money is concerned. Not, I mean, in America. But perhaps confidence, or active interest, has been draining away from the people with that sort of means.' Vanderlyn paused, as if he was making a silent roll-call of actual persons to whom this might apply. 'Yes, I suppose it's like that. We tend to set up expert bodies to administer what we are calling patronage. I gather you do the same thing over here. The idea is that, in the arts and so forth, one gets a surer return in the way of public benefit that way.'

'An argument of that sort,' Raggett began, 'is the most unmitigated——'

'It's a subject upon which Mr Vanderlyn must carry weight.' The President had interrupted, smoothly but rapidly. 'The Vanderlyn Foundation is a notable instance of what he's speaking of.'

'The Vanderlyn Memorial Foundation,' Vanderlyn said gently. 'My father is commemorated. And it's for the advancement of education, chiefly, since much of his own interest outside business affairs lay there—as did his own father's before him. But we try to bring literature and the arts in.'

There was a moment's silence, as people became aware of the bricks they might have dropped. Characteristically, the President had done his home-work on Blaine's guest. Equally characteristically, he had left it at that, murmuring nothing to anybody about Vanderlyn's Foundation.

'You'd get a decay of patronage even if the tax-gatherer drowned himself,' Raggett said. 'Taste and knowledge are required, and the wealthy are now resigned to be without them. It shows a very proper humility. The acquisitive life has become a high-pressure, full-time affair, and they can no longer get up these things for themselves. Their wives can have a go, if they want to. But on the whole they let it all go by.'

'A shocking state of affairs,' Peart said.

'Nothing of the sort. In a mediocre way, the general level of taste benefits from it. There's no demand from wealthy but uninstructed persons for vulgar things of the most showy kind. That's where we differ from the Victorians and

Edwardians. Our lower classes know, in a fashion, what they like, and the harmless rubbish is purveyed to them. The prosperous know they *don't* know what they like, and I admit that they get landed with a lot of impudent absurdity as a result. Go to any expensive art show in London, and you can be left in no doubt as to that. On the whole, however, they just accept what reasonably honest professionals supply. So you get good taste of a sort all over the place. It's aesthetically negligible, of course. For the real thing is out, and will remain out until something like patronage in the grand manner comes back again. And all that *that* needs is nerve.'

Chapter 7

'I THINK IT needs more than nerve.' Gavin Naylor, whose only contribution to the talk so far had been his joke about *Paradise Lost*, looked at the dogmatic Raggett with the dispassionate severity which a mathematician might bend upon a faulty computer. 'I can imagine few more difficult relationships. The patron has wealth and the client has not—which doesn't mean that the client admires or respects the patron. Far from it. The client, on the other hand, does have something which the patron admires and respects. So some further factor has to be present, if there's to be a balanced relationship. In the past, that was supplied by rank—or it might be better to say by hierarchy. Each had his place in an appointed order; and it wasn't an order felt as drawing its validity simply from differentials in the pay-packet.'

'But it did, all the same,' Blaine interrupted. 'Any persuasion to the contrary was cooked up by priestcraft.'

'It made a large part of man's sustenance, whatever kitchen it came from. And it provided the framework into which this difficult relationship could be fitted. I don't say

58

that patronage in the full sense we are considering is impossible today. But the patron would have to command, in his own character, a kind of authority, quite distinct from that of the purse-strings, in place of what society endowed him with in former times.'

'But authority *is* nerve,' Raggett said. 'We're arguing in a circle. Charles, don't you agree?'

'My dear chap, all this isn't my sort of thing.' Blaine had finished his port, and was pushing his glass away with the air of a man who no longer has a source of wisdom to consult. 'But I'm prepared to believe a decent patron must be a man of sense, and I just don't think that, in our time, a man of sense is going to be a patron. He may appreciate the artistic inheritance of our civilisation, and so forth. But he's not going to put in time and energy holding hands with young artists and writers. He knows that if he's going to survive—if any of us is going to survive—he has other things to do, right round the clock.'

There was a moment's silence. Most of Charles Blaine's colleagues suspected him of being a haunted man. He lived, the President liked to say, deep in unfathomable mines of never failing skill—a skill which he then had to place in the hands of a society to which only an optimist would issue so much as bows and arrows. Blaine's regular recourse to the idiom of classical communism was thought to be a reflex of this unease.

'As long as he's let do them—those other and more urgent things.'

It was Vanderlyn who said this—impulsively, as it seemed to Shefford. Vanderlyn's conversation was easy; he gave no effect of weighing his words; yet one guessed him to be a man obliged to refrain from much spontaneous speech. And now he and Blaine had exchanged a brief glance.

'If one were fired,' Vanderlyn elucidated with his slow-motion smile, 'one might set up as a full-time patron of the arts.'

'It was like that with Cosimo de' Medici, I seem to recall.'

59

Martin, the scientist for whom physics had culminated in the age of Rutherford, dived happily into his historical reading. 'I think—President, you will know—it was in 1433 that they turned Cosimo out of Florence. So he went off to Venice, taking Michelozzo in his train, and set up as a patron in a big way.'

'He must have taken a good deal of hard cash, too,' Shefford said.

'Wasn't somebody saying that patronage isn't essentially a matter of hard cash?' Martin asked. 'Big results can be obtained on a small budget. Think of Federigo of Montefeltro. It's true that he became Duke of Urbino, yet that didn't make him an outstandingly wealthy prince, even by the standards of that time. But he'd been a pupil of Vittorino da Feltre, so he was qualified to be a patron by commanding pretty well universal knowledge.'

Martin was off on what his younger colleagues would have called one of his routines. At least he had a great many of these. They may have been based—as Naylor was accustomed to assert—on small books on big subjects, but they were carried by an enthusiasm which wasn't to be scoffed at. To Federigo, it seemed, art, science, war and statecraft were equally familiar; Thomas Aquinas was read to him at meals; he was constantly finding time to visit his favourite nuns of Santa Chiara, or to watch the young men of Urbino at their athletic sports; artists flocked to his little court from all over Italy and indeed Europe: Piero, Pisanello, Justus of Ghent. Vittorino Raimboldini, the master of this prize pupil, had come up the hard way, serving as footman to the professor of mathematics at Padua, setting out to learn Greek when he was forty-two. . . .

It was dark now, and at either end of the library the great windows were as black as caves. The long ceiling, its intricacies of pink and grey and gold flooded from invisible sources of soft light, floated at once lightly and massively over the austere richness of the New Library. The building had been put up in an age willing to acknowledge the dignity of learning as well as the mere utility of education, and it would have made a fit enough setting for a weightier discourse on the ideals of the Renaissance than Martin was equipped to offer. But nobody fidgeted, or did other than preserve an air of attention. Besides—Shefford told himself firmly—Martin has the root of the matter in him. A university would be no use to him without whatever kind of old-fashioned laboratory he pottered round, but he knew that a university ought to contain other things as well.

'And all these triumphs were achieved,' Martin was saying, 'in a factious and warring country, a lawless and brutal age. The position was analogous to that of the nightmare decades we are ourselves living through. There wasn't a city in Italy in which the inhabitants could be sure they wouldn't be massacred before a week was out.'

'That's a little strongly put.' The President had laughed genially. 'But, no doubt, you're right in a general way. Nasty things happened. Then as now, there was plenty of *Realpolitik* blowing around.'

'A hideous time, like our own, certainly,' Peart said. 'In a way, those wealthy people, with their little courts of poets and painters and philosophers, were retreating into ivory towers.'

'Nothing of the kind.' Raggett, who seldom gained in urbanity as an evening wore on, contradicted Peart flatly. 'They had perfectly serviceable towers of stone and brick. Often cheek by jowl, and each trying to frown down upon the other. A kind of perpendicular rat race.'

Nobody responded to this, and a slight restlessness made itself felt. The President turned to a side-table.

'A pity about that empty decanter,' he said. 'But if you would all care to adjourn to my Lodging——' He paused, with no great air of proposing to complete his sentence. And Vanderlyn was already on his feet, advancing upon him with an outstretched hand. There was a general exchange of civilities, and while Vanderlyn had a brief conversation with Blaine the others faded away. Then Shefford, now in charge of the guest, led the way down the staircase to the ground floor. The oval well in which the shallow marble steps were set owned a wholly unobtrusive elegance. Vanderlyn paused to admire it. There could be no doubt that he had an eye for things.

The Great Quadrangle was three-parts in moonlight, with a long crenellated shadow thrown across the grass. The jets of the fountain, as Shefford had known they would, glittered in a cold radiance. The air was warm; there was nobody about, and no sound except the footsteps of some of the others fading down a farther quad; night scents came through the long arcade.

'I hope you weren't terribly bored,' Shefford said, 'by old Martin's version of Robert Browning's two-pence coloured Italy.'

'Did you feel it to be like that?' There was a note of surprise in Vanderlyn's voice—and a more disconcerting note of kindness as well. Shefford was overtaken by confusion. It had been his actual sense that the talk in the library, although it had kept to a related group of topics, had been conducted in a throw-away fashion disappointing to the serious expectations of an American visitor. But this feeling—which in any case it wasn't his business to express—had tumbled him into a derogatory remark about Martin, whom in fact he was quite as willing to respect as to laugh at. Shefford, who didn't like letting himself down, found that he was about to embark on incoherent explanation.

'Before it grew dark'—Vanderlyn appeared not to have heard his scrambling for words—'I greatly admired the view over your college garden through that high window. It must be just as beautiful now, in this moonlight. Would it be too much to ask that we take one turn round it before you drive off with me?'

'Yes, of course. I think you will like it very much.' Shefford's vexation had given way to pleasure—an emotional reversal which didn't get in the way of his registering the discovery that Vanderlyn had a quick instinct for the sensibilities of young men. 'You won't get the colour, but you'll get the general effect. The nearest gate is through this way.'

For some moments they walked in silence, side by side.

'My wife is very fond of English gardens,' Vanderlyn said. 'It's one of the things I've learned from her.'

Chapter 8

THE COLLEGE NIGHTINGALE was singing in the acacia tree. It was a restricted performance, since the bird was only a thrush—the same thrush, the common-room's ornithologist said, that occasionally put on an equally clever turn as an owl. Shefford wondered whether he should embark on an explanation of this to Vanderlyn. But in America, he reflected, the birds may not have got round to imitating each other, and the subject might prove confusing. Besides which, there was no urgent occasion to talk. The garden on this summer night was very lovely—as lovely as had been that larger garden, country-wide, upon which he had looked down from the Ridgeway with the Vanderlyns that morning. Vanderlyn seemed quite content to stroll in it in silence.

Shefford did not know much about flowers. Such information as he possessed came in the main from literary sources, which are often unreliable as to what blooms when and where. He knew that many shut up shop at night, but that in a warm darkness others are prodigal of scent. There seemed to be many of the second sort around them now. A properly instructed gardener, he thought, could produce you little symphonies in scent. You would follow some appointed path—in darkness or near-darkness would be best—and this new art-form would involve you in its intricacies as you moved. This theme would be no use with Vanderlyn either. He wasn't an unsophisticated man, but there was something too weighty about him to be entertained by whimsy.

'Scented limes,' Vanderlyn said. 'Whereabouts are they?'

'Over there, sir,' Shefford said. He made a gesture that had to be detectably vague. 'But shall we go down these steps? I think it's light enough. We have a formal garden that's rather Italian in feeling: lawn and tall clipped hedges, with patches of water and chunks of marble here and there. It looks rather well under the moon—if you don't mind the suggestion of opera.'

They went down the steps. Shefford wished he hadn't added that bit about opera, which had sounded silly. But when they reached the lower level, and were moving down the main yew walk, he no longer bothered. Between the towering hedges, black as Stygian wharves, the grass seemed to flow like a silent and silvered flood. At wide intervals on either hand, like a meagre guard of honour spread out to make a decent show, miscellaneous marble objects stood ranked: urns, ancient philosophers, Victorian Presidents of the college, nymphs, boars with curly tusks, slavering hounds—an assemblage the absurdity of which was softened to fantasy by the regnant moon. Ahead, the vista closed upon the most beautiful of Oxford's spires, set against a sky powdered with faint stars.

Moved by a common impulse, Shefford and Vanderlyn came to a halt. Somewhere not far away, the great Christ Church bell began to utter midnight. Stroke followed stroke across taut interspaces of deepening solemnity, and then the silence into which the last reverberations faded was broken by another sound. It might have been a violin string snapping, and as it reached their ears they were aware of something soaring into air before their eyes—so swiftly that its form was invisible, as if one were to imagine a supersonic bird. Something made them both turn to the left, where a break in the high hedge opened upon a glimmering semicircle of clipped hornbeam. Framed in this was the figure of a young man. He held a bow in his left hand, and he was stooping to pick up something from the grass. It might have been a second arrow; one couldn't be sure, since from the knees downwards he stood in a pool of shadow. He straightened up, and his slim body in the moonlight might have been no body at all but only some ancient artificer's vision of a body, hammered out in silver or palest gold. He was naked.

The strangeness of this spectacle was for a moment its only feature. Yet Vanderlyn didn't seem notably surprised. It was as if the influences of the place and hour had so affected him as to make him expect something a little out of the way. Shefford, for his part, experienced the faintest sensation of a moment of choice. This apparition had a dream-like quality in which it would be possible, so to speak, to acquiesce. In such a garden as this, itself turned to dream by drenching moonlight, why should not such an archer appear? On the other hand, it was obvious that here was an undergraduate folly of the most tiresome sort. Shefford plumped for the other hand. Having done so, he at once went on to decide that the concept of tiresomeness didn't cover the thing at all. It was improper in this young man thus to appear naked before the guest of a senior member. If one had been giving a private dinner-party, with ladies present, it was conceivable that one would have taken them for a stroll in the garden at midnight before their departure to the domestic sanctities of Headington or North Oxford. So here was outrageous behaviour. Boys who wanted to indulge in such orgies ought to get into punts and pole themselves far up the Cherwell before starting anything of the sort.

'To invocate the moon,' the young man was saying. 'And then to shoot an arrow at a star. It's how to have a vision.'

'I see. And what will the vision do for you?'

'It may become a poem.'

Shefford realised, with an irrational feeling of exclusion, that during his interior musing the naked young man and Vanderlyn had entered into talk. But this didn't develop. The young man had again reached down into the pool of darkness in which he stood; he fumbled for something; and what he held in his hand when he straightened up was a crumpled cigarette-packet. He opened this, and it proved to be empty. He held it out to Vanderlyn, so that its emptiness could be seen.

'I say,' he said, 'can you let me have a cigarette?'

'I think I can.' Vanderlyn put a hand in a pocket, and as he did so the young man stooped down once more. With quick precision, delicately and vulnerably, first one knee and then the other rose into the full light and fell again; he gave a wriggle and had pulled on a pair of jeans; he drew up a zip, and stood with the slim-fitting garment, ghost-coloured, slung low on his hips. He would now have been just presentable to Shefford's hypothetical wandering ladies. He took Vanderlyn's cigarette, and there was a spurt of flame; in the light of this the young man's torso turned ruddy and his jeans the palest blue.

'Thanks a lot,' he said, and for a moment paused, smiling. He was tall and dark, very handsome, with a lock of dark hair hanging between his eyes, and a small scar—it might have been a birth-mark—showing as an awkward blemish on one cheek. His smile held mockery, and there had been a kind of social assertion—presumably imperceptible to Vanderlyn—in the last turn of phrase he had chosen. His accent was provincial; he hadn't, as Shefford had, picked up 'standard' English. But his voice was remarkably beautiful; it was grave and sensitive; it seemed not to join in the charade he had been concocting. And the mockery asserted that here was somebody confident of his own powers, indisposed to play ball with persons not of his own sort, seeking no help. Now he threw back his head to exhale a ring of smoke, so that his dark hair, worn long, rose towards the moon. He looked—it was for the first time—straight at Shefford. Shefford looked straight at him. It was an instant of hostility as naked as the young man's body had been a moment before, and it left Shefford astonished—the more so because he was himself contributing his full share to this primitive and unaccountable discharge. It seemed unrelated to his feeling—which he recognised as absurd—of outraged propriety. But now the young man had turned from him in a swift arrogance, and had addressed Vanderlyn. 'That was good of you,' he said with conviction. He stooped down for the last time, swept up the bow which had fallen on the grass, turned away into the darkness of some alleyway, and vanished. Nothing remained of him but a waft of tobacco-scent on the air.

'I'm sorry about that,' Shefford said.

'He appeared to be alone.' Vanderlyn showed no impulse to take up the notion of apology.

'You think he might be expected to want an audience? I quite agree.'

'It wasn't in my mind. But a young man must have some real belief in invoking—no, invocating—the moon, don't you think, to conduct such a ritual in solitude?'

'I suppose so. But he needn't do it in the college garden.'

'It seems a suitable setting to me. It's against the rules?'

'Oh, I don't know about that.' Shefford, although his own impulse had been censorious, would not have had the college judged illiberal. 'I expect the President would laugh at it. He might even call invocating the moon entirely reasonable. But then he has no concern with the day-to-day discipline of the undergraduates. The Dean would take a darker view. He has to keep about four hundred young savages in some sort of order.'

'I see. It must be difficult to get round to helping a young man like your archer when one is preoccupied with a tough assignment like that.'

'I suppose so.' Shefford found this reflection somewhat inconsequent. It wasn't one's job, after all, to go nurse-maiding after the undergraduates. But now they had turned round and were retracing their steps through the garden. Vanderlyn was silent, as if more concerned to continue savouring the enchantment of the place than to reflect upon his late encounter. When he did speak, however, it was to take up the subject once more.

'I met some of your young savages, when walking across from your common room to the library. They were in war-paint—of an expensive sort—and howling war-songs. They were also surprisingly drunk, but they decided on a detour when they spotted the President.'

'I saw them too,' Shefford said, rather grimly, remembering his ignoble fear. 'They're a pretty ghastly feature of the place.'

'You have no monopoly of that sort of exuberance—and it can be diverted, unfortunately, into lethal channels from time to time. I think I prefer young men who address themselves to the moon, even if they've mislaid their undershirt and pants.' Vanderlyn came to a halt, and looked upward. 'She's at the full, I think. It's no doubt the time for invocations.'

Shefford looked up too. It was a full moon, and a very splendid one.

'It looks no distance away,' he said.

'But it is. Just to pepper that surface with occasional scraps of hardware costs a fortune that could control all the plagues of Egypt.' Vanderlyn had spoken with a new voice. But at once he was casual again. 'Perhaps it's a hard age for invocations. We may have alienated the moon, battering at her as we do.'

'You speak of her as female, sir, which is classical enough. So probably she likes attention.'

'I've been requiring far too much of it myself. Now you must take me away.'

Chapter 9

SHEFFORD'S CAR STARTED easily. It was on its best behaviour during summer nights, and now it seemed to run with an impressive noiselessness, almost like the Cadillac. The streets were deserted. Only at Carfax there was a little knot of coloured people. They were gossiping idly. At this hour, now past midnight, they could have nothing in particular to do and nowhere in particular to go; they were simply enjoying the sensation of standing under something like a Caribbean moon. The car gathered speed, and the university city lay behind it. But the clustered towers and spires would be splendid from a little way away. Shefford resolved to pause for Vanderlyn's enjoyment of this when they reached the first rise of Hinksey Hill. He wondered whether Vanderlyn knew Matthew Arnold's *The Scholar Gipsy*. Mrs Vanderlyn would certainly have studied it, perhaps from a carefully topographical point of view.

But this last thought was unfair to Mrs Vanderlyn. He recalled that morning's mild and touching caper. The image of Hardy's hopeful boy, doomed to exclusion from learning's citadel, had been very real to her; it stood near the centre of a complex of ideas and idealisms she was devoted to. Mrs Vanderlyn was lucid and admirable. Her husband, he now admitted to himself, was far from being so readily understood. He was, of course, one now knew, a public man, a political character. He carried about with him, like a sober banner, the simplicity of bearing proper in an ambassador of the great republic. He carried an equally proper reserve. Perhaps it was some quality attaching to this that hinted at his being a man with stiff problems around him. And perhaps in the past, remote or recent, he had missed some tide, some boat. In his public character, that would presumably be. But possibly not.

'Do you know the young man with the bow and arrows?' Vanderlyn asked. He was doing no more than make conversation, but Shefford felt resentful of this recurrence to the subject of the posturing boy in the garden.

'I know a bit about him. He's an undergraduate called Varley.'

'Varley? He ought to be a painter with a name like that.'

'I suppose he should.' For a moment Shefford had been at a loss before this reference, which was an instance of Vanderlyn's having unexpected interests tucked away in him. 'John Varley was a friend of William Blake, wasn't he? They went in for having visions together. But Varley wasn't a mystical painter. Just quiet landscapes. This Varley's called Mark, I think.'

'He seems to have a hankering after visions too. Is he by way of being a poet?'

'I suppose so. He's certainly one of the college's aesthetes of the moment. But I don't know that he's been a great success with the others of that crowd. Something awkward about him. An odd man out.'

'We all had awkwardness in us at that age, don't you think?' It was with a curious effect of something like affection that Vanderlyn produced this irony. For an irony it certainly was, since the little span of years between Shefford and the tiresome Mark Varley would scarcely be apparent to him. And all through this day Shefford had no doubt been producing his own awkwardnesses every now and then. He was surprised to find himself not at all annoyed by what might almost be an amused reference to them. 'We were all awkward,' Vanderlyn repeated seriously. 'With just a bit of bad luck, we might have been odd men out as well.' He paused. 'So perhaps that was why Mr Varley was performing his mysterious conjurations alone.'

'Perhaps it was. He's not popular, as I said, with other quasi-beatnik characters.' Shefford heard himself without satisfaction as he produced this small pedantry. 'And he even got across some of the bloodies, which is unusual nowadays.'

'The bloodies?'

'Well, chaps rather like those that you met coming away from their dining-club.'

'The wealthy and arrogant?'

'Yes.' Shefford was surprised at the sharpness with which this question had come. 'They broke up his rooms, as a matter of fact. Destroyed his pictures and poured ink on his papers.'

'That *would* produce disciplinary action?'

'Oh, yes, of course. That kind of thing is intolerable. Two or three of the hulking brutes were rusticated for the remaining weeks of the term.' This information fell into a silence that Shefford found disturbing. 'Not that that was quite all. One of the chaps, the Master of Ballater——'

'Isn't that something by Robert Louis Stevenson?'

'That was Ballantrae. This was a real chap—and I suppose the heir to a Scottish peerage. Rather nice, he was said to be, as a rule. But not that night. I was there, as a matter of fact—calling myself Sub-Dean, and wearing my gown and not feeling it much protection. And this Ballater-character said to the Dean something like, "Why create, man? It's only another upstart little snot-school shit".'

'Snot-school?'

'Proletarian school, where all the boys have dirty noses. He was tight—the Master of Ballater. He'd bloodied Varley's nose, I seem to remember. Of course, the college wouldn't take that: an undergraduate being contumacious to the Dean.'

'Contumacious to the Dean? Yes, I see.'

'The President sent him down for good next morning. He was out of Oxford within twelve hours. There are limits, even for those people.'

'That's surely something.'

'Yes.' Not being sure what he was concurring in, Shefford tried a change of subject. 'Did you have any conversation,' he asked, 'with the American boy, Peter Wright?'

'I certainly did. I remembered meeting his father once.' Vanderlyn paused, and Shefford reflected that political characters have to be good at remembering that sort of thing. 'Young Peter has his head rather full of the wars.'

'He had a horrific yarn about Korea.'

'It's something all our boys have to think about. Some even judge it best to go out and meet the thing. It happened that way, a couple of years ago, with the son of an old friend of mine. He was a clever boy, but turned lazy when he went to college. His grades were a disgrace, and eventually he got so that he felt he must do something drastic to take himself in hand. He decided to enlist. And that means three years, not two.'

'He enlisted in the army?'

71

'He did. But he was a clever boy, as I said, and his languages were particularly good—which is a state of affairs not common with us. So he **thought** he might get into intelligence, and measure up to being a pretty effective agent. It just happened that he turned up with his papers on the wrong day. The intelligence tap was off, and another tap was on. He found himself a driver-clerk in Vietnam. And a driver-clerk he is still.'

'It seems bad luck.' Shefford laughed, because he saw that this anecdote, with its flat conclusion, had been offered lightly, although attached to a sombre theme. 'Has it been good for him, or bad?'

'Neither good or bad, I'd say. He just spends three years as a driver-clerk. And that's the age to which young Peter Wright must be coming up. Would you say he was seventeen?'

'Yes, or just short of it. I suppose Vietnam may still be absorbing driver-clerks when his time comes along.'

'I'm afraid it may.' Vanderlyn spoke dryly and fell silent, so that Shefford felt he ought perhaps not to have continued this theme. But in a minute Vanderlyn himself resumed it. 'Blaine may have told you,' he said, 'that I have some concern with these matters. I sometimes wish that I had sons of my own at hazard. It might make me feel better if I had a full stake in the game. You understand that?'

'Yes, sir—I think I do.'

'But I have no children. Perhaps Louise and I married just a little too late for it.'

That Vanderlyn should volunteer this information was not surprising in itself. He did have a trick of occasional impulsive speech—and Shefford was aware that for some reason Vanderlyn would speak more freely to him than to an older man. It was the tone in which Vanderlyn had spoken that was striking. Shefford was unable to interpret it, until it occurred to him that the effect intended had possibly been one of whimsical understatement. Perhaps the Vanderlyn's marriage was of quite recent date. Perhaps—it came to him fantastically—they were on their honeymoon now.

'But my wife has a daughter by a previous husband,' Vanderlyn said, with a return to his normal manner. 'She is almost grown-up. Her father died many years ago.'

They were now outside the city, and approaching the spot from which Shefford designed that his passenger should have a last view of it. Ahead of them, round a gentle curve, the road crossed a railway and a canal on a single long bridge. The site was a superb one, and the bridge, which was new, had been designed with care to be worthy of it. There was a plain parapet, perhaps four feet high, of finely dressed Bath stone. It was set off beyond this that one saw Oxford—and on a night like the present the sight could be very lovely indeed.

'Just here,' Shefford said, 'there's rather a view. I think you'll like it.' He swung the car on to a wide verge just short of the bridge, and turned it so that the enchanting prospect lay obliquely before them. And there the city was, moon-blanched and as if of another world—just such a heavenly Jerusalem as the little Jude Fawley had dreamed of. But there was something else on display, glaring at them in the dipped headlights of Shefford's car. Somebody had been at work on the parapet with a desperate brush and a great deal of red paint. The slogan, splashed in letters a yard high, ran from end to end. It read: YANK BABY BURNERS OUT OF VIETNAM.

They looked at this in silence for a moment, and at Oxford swimming in so serene a detachment beyond. Vanderlyn murmured that it was indeed a splendid view. Shefford muttered something incoherent, swung the car back on the road, and sent it roaring up Hinksey Hill. He was shocked. What shocked him was the consciousness that he didn't know what to think. He didn't know what to think, because he had never properly thought about those grim but distant matters. And probably he never would.

There were plenty of walls back in Oxford upon which the political passions could be spread, and every now and then this happened in quite a big way. On one long expanse

73

of brick out on the quiet Banbury Road you could still decipher the injunction: OPEN SECOND FRONT NOW. But it had required a certain act of imagination—or at least intelligence—to achieve this present anti-American gesture, since by its siting it somehow contrived to arraign the dreaming English city as well. Shefford responded to this. Something inside him wanted to applaud the ugly words. The manner in which he had been instrumental in hurling them at Vanderlyn, on the other hand, distressed him wildly. He was even afraid that Vanderlyn might suppose it to have been deliberate. Remembering how they had been talking about Vietnam, Shefford thought he saw that it bore absolutely that appearance. He opened his mouth to proclaim his innocence. Vanderlyn, who perhaps had an intuition of the unnecessary thing about to be said, spoke first.

'Babies do get burned,' he said quietly. 'And most of the things happen that are coming to haunt the minds of boys like Peter Wright. I've imagined myself performing acts of cruelty, Mr Shefford, and I guess most men have. But it may be that, among young people, that sort of imagination is becoming harder and harder to resist.'

'The dungeons have always been there,' Shefford said. He was still so distressed that he couldn't talk sensibly; only drag up this imperfectly intelligible remark from some earlier conversation that evening. He couldn't even remember what its context had been.

'If that is so'—Vanderlyn took up the point gravely—'and if dungeons there must always be, then our true wisdom is to build other things in disregard of them. Rival towers.' He too was recalling earlier talk. 'Which might rebuke them in the end.'

Shefford breathed more comfortably—which he was no doubt meant to do. He concluded that Vanderlyn hadn't been much affected by that brutal crack on the bridge. After all, public men—men so public as to stand close to Presidents—walked disregarding between such slogans whenever some do-gooding crowd thought fit to demonstrate. They weren't inconvenienced. If there was any sign of that, the police backed their horses deftly on people's toes. Shefford took momentary comfort from this hard-boiled way of regarding the thing. Nevertheless he still found it difficult to converse. He had driven a guest straight up to an insult.

'It was Solomon who first talked about a tower of ivory,' Vanderlyn said. 'But he didn't mean what people mean when they talk about ivory towers today. It's a phrase that has got us scared, I guess, so that all towers seem disreputable. On the whole, though, I stay anti-tower, whether ivory or not. As I see it now, it's like this. As long as a man is in and fighting, as long as a responsibility is charged upon him, he must stay in. If he is in real authority, he may stay in to turn the fight this way or that, to conduct it in one fashion or another. He may pull his country out, but he mustn't simply pull out himself. On his honour he must not do that. It gets me mad to be told there's virtue in such a thing: stopping being a man, and withdrawing into the garden to smell the flowers.' For the first time, Vanderlyn had spoken with passion, and perhaps from a troubled and divided mind. Suddenly he smiled. 'Not that you and I don't know the pleasure of doing that—but on a vacation basis, one may say. And this evening has certainly been a very pleasant one to me.'

The transition was like a practiced speaker's, yet Vanderlyn's appreciation of his entertainment didn't sound merely conventional. He had greatly enjoyed the talk, he said. His wife would be most interested in his account of it.

Shefford found this last statement surprising. It didn't seem to him that anything much in the way of fireworks had been laid on. The party hadn't included any of the university's top conversationalists, or even any out of the second flight. Shefford, whose vision of things in general was conditioned more than he realised by the notion of awarding people and occasions Firsts, Seconds or Thirds, couldn't see that there was much to pass on for Mrs Vanderlyn's entertainment. But Vanderlyn's recurring to his wife reminded Shefford that he should recur to her too. So towards the end of the drive, and when he had turned off on a side road under Vanderlyn's guidance, he said how nice it would be if both the Vanderlyns should happen to be in England again soon. The college wasn't entirely monastic in orientation. Occasions with ladies—luncheons or dinners rather than cocktail parties, which were noisy affairs —were very much enjoyed.

'Louise would greatly appreciate anything of the kind,' Vanderlyn said. 'She has a great opinion of academic life.' It was impossible to tell whether Vanderlyn had imported his occasional faint irony into this. If he had, its edge was certainly not directed towards his wife. 'And she would love your garden.'

Shefford wondered whether Mrs Vanderlyn would appreciate the aspect of academic life represented by the turn young Mark Varley had put on there that night. But the tenor of this speculation—the confrontation it called up— displeased him, and before he could say anything more Vanderlyn had directed him to turn into a private drive. There were massive gates of the heraldic and emblazoned sort, set between twin lodges. The car was suddenly in near-darkness, with its headlights probing a beech-avenue that stretched to a vanishing-point in front of them. They were tremendous trees. Only here and there did a beam of moonlight strike through.

'Louise and I have both been around the world a good deal. But when we're together—well, we feel we have it all to do.' Vanderlyn was silent for a moment; he was now hardly visible; and Shefford had an impression that it was this circumstance which had released his last speech. 'I can't say just when we may be back. She's certainly glad to have made this trip.'

There was something about this that wasn't easy to reply to. Within a couple of minutes the avenue had at last taken a turn, and before them was a terrace and a house. Shefford was unprepared for the house, even although its name had rung some bell in his head. In the moonlight it may have shown as bigger than it was, but it was a very imposing mansion indeed. There was a light in a high *porte-cochère*, and he drew up the car beneath it. There was a light, too, in a tall uncurtained window, and through this he glimpsed the figure of a manservant, who must have been keeping watch, advancing as if to open a door. Shefford scrambled out and decanted Vanderlyn, who invited him indoors: his hosts would not have stayed up for him, but it would be by no means difficult to find a drink. When Shefford had declined this, Vanderlyn repeated his wife's hope, and his own, that he would visit them in America. He shook hands, and Shefford, having said something about giving his best wishes to Mrs Vanderlyn for a pleasant journey home, got into his car and drove away.

PART II

Chapter 1

THE AEGEAN MORNING was already very hot. Jeremy Shefford dropped his rucksack on the quay with a satisfied sigh. It was a heavier affair than he was accustomed to carry around the Berkshire downs, and his ability to hump it here and there about Europe told him that he was still entirely young. He was also prosperous; he could travel abroad twice a year; sometimes he did it alone, like this, and sometimes in a car, with a friend. When he came alone, he experienced an increased sense of expectation about what might turn up. For instance, he indulged in erotic imaginings of a naïve sort which he would have been reluctant to share even with a close companion like Gavin Naylor. It was true that, in the end, the holiday always came down to ruins and museums and picture galleries, for he was a fastidious or inhibited young man with his sights raised protectively high. He kept an eye open for a beautiful, intelligent and hitherto chaste young woman with whom he would enjoy a tempestuous love-affair. So far, she had never turned up.

There had been no sign of her, certainly, on the little ferry boat from which he had just disembarked, nor was she likely to appear on this primitive waterfront. So Shefford dismissed the dream-girl from his head—he was far from being haunted by her—and looked about at what this new Greek island actually had on offer. There was a group of rickety chairs and tables nearby, which he supposed indicated a *taverna* of sorts. So he crossed over and sat down. The buildings fronting the harbour on a shallow curve seemed to mingle dwellings, warehouses, churches and outcrops of fortification. They were all solid, but they all had a protean air, as if they had been accustomed to exchange functions every century or so for rather a long time. There was a colonnade that was identifiably Graeco-Roman; there were façades so battered and eroded that only a generalised and unexpected dignity remained to them, and he had to dub them either Turkish or Venetian, leaving it at that. In front of him, across a blaze of sapphire water and beyond a tangle of masts and sails, a small and exquisite pharos marked the harbour-mouth. And away to his left, sited amid the remaining bastions of a ruined fort, was the ugly modern hotel in which he supposed he would have to spend the night.

A man came out of a church and stood beside him in a tentative manner, so that he rather expected to be engaged in religious conversation. But the man was carrying a tray, which meant that the church must be a hostelry, and Shefford asked for an *ouzo*. When this arrived it was accompanied by a plate holding two olives, two tired-looking prawns, and some small pieces of bread. He was always apprehensive about his inside on these occasions, so he ate some of the bread. He supposed it would be a rejection of hospitality entirely to ignore this bonus issue.

The *ouzo* distilled itself with amazing rapidity into enhanced contentment. For a time he watched with undisturbed composure the only activity which the quayside exhibited. An old man sat by the edge of the sea with a basket full of octopus-like creatures beside him. He was taking these out one by one and lashing the cobbles with them. Perhaps it was a tenderising process. If so, it had no doubt been in use since the time of Odysseus, and it would be foolish to be horrified. Nevertheless, as the phrenetic walloping continued, Shefford did feel that it would be nice to look at something different. He turned in another direction, and saw that somebody else had sat down at one of the little tables, only a few yards away. It was a young man.

That the young man *was* young, however, it had taken a moment to determine. This was because he had set down beside him on the table an immaculately white panama hat with a narrow black band. Shefford associated this with the elderly. But the hat went appropriately enough with the equally immaculate white linen suit the stranger was wearing. Shefford concluded, despite the English cut of this, that here was something hitherto unfamiliar to him: a young Greek dandy of a prosperous class. The young man was dark enough to be Greek. But now he turned his head, and proved to be Mark Varley.

It was two years since the episode in the college garden. But it was that episode which came first into Shefford's head, with the result that, when their eyes met, he gave Varley no more than a nod. Then he remembered something that brought him to his feet and across to the other young man's side.

Since he had last seen Varley, Varley had been in gaol.

'Hullo, Varley—what are *you* doing here?' If Shefford had stopped to think, he might have hesitated about making any approach at all—telling himself that Varley mightn't want to be recognised. But having acted on an impulse it wasn't possible to regret, he said the first thing that came into his head. The question was what he would have pitched at any colleague or contemporary encountered in this way.

'Hullo, sir.' Varley had flushed darkly as he used this unnecessary term of respect. It wasn't possible to believe he flushed with pleasure, and it was like a danger signal that the small blemish on his cheek glowed for a moment to an angry red. Then he smiled uncertainly. 'I'm trying to do some writing,' he said, as if Shefford's question had been seriously intended to elicit information. 'They didn't give me much chance to in quod.'

'I suppose not.' Shefford felt relieved there was to be no question of ducking Varley's misfortune. 'Was it absolutely ghastly?' he asked.

'Of course.' Varley had recovered his poise, and his glance was more friendly. 'But I was lucky, in a way. At least I wasn't young enough to be sent to some kids' place —an approved school or whatever they call it—where they can give you an off-the-record licking whenever they feel they want quiet fun.' He paused. 'Like *that*,' he said, and pointed to the old man exercising himself with his current octopus.

'There wasn't really anything of that sort?' Shefford was horrified.

'No—but you never knew. They'd look at you some-times——' Varley broke off. 'All these places have their methods. Humiliation is built into the theory of the thing. I hated the clothes they handed me. Pressed quite flat, and smelling of disinfectant. I think I'd have minded less if they'd just had the smell of the last poor chap who'd worn them.'

'It was a horrible thing to happen to you.' Shefford sought for some possible line. 'And just because of a rush of political feeling to the head.'

'It was nothing of the sort—or not at the start. I'm not political. I was in Grosvenor Square by accident, looking for some man who runs a poetry magazine. I didn't even know the Americans keep their rotten Embassy there.'

'But you didn't say so to the beak, did you?'

'One has one's pride, and I wasn't going to admit to just being caught up in the affair. But that's what happened. There were all these chaps—girls, too—yelling away about the bombing of North Vietnam. It wasn't my sort of thing —but of course I knew they were right. So I started yelling as well. I didn't even get in many yells. Suddenly there was a lot of scrapping, and this bloody policeman was on top of me. But not merely on top of me, you know. He was a dirty bastard, and it was his knee. I was in agony, all right, just as he'd intended. I suppose he thought I'd simply crawl away. He underestimated me.'

'You were going to get your own back?'

'If one's hurt, one must make somebody pay for it, mustn't one? That seems a matter of elementary human dignity to me.'

'I suppose I might think of it that way, if just that had happened to me.'

'You would, if you had any guts. Well, I did crawl,

84

more or less, since it was minutes before I could stand up. Only I knew where I was crawling to.'

'You'd remembered some road-mending stuff, wasn't it?'

'Yes, I'd noticed it in a side street, just before I went into the Square, and I managed to get back to it. What I took was the haft of a pickaxe. I can feel the joy of getting my hand round it at this moment. It was smooth to the palm, man, and the balance was just right.'

Shefford remained silent. Varley was putting on an act. But the thing had happened, all the same. The vengeful and ruthless image of himself he was parading had somewhere an actual existence in him. Or so it seemed necessary to believe.

'I expect you read what the magistrate said. Stuff about an element of premeditation, and forming a plan, and during a substantial period of time taking successive steps to put it into effect. He was right on the ball, wasn't he? Just as the bobby had been right on my balls. It meant I hadn't a chance in their beastly dock. It had spikes round it, as if I were a wild beast.'

'You'd done something to substantiate that impression, if you ask me.'

'Perhaps I had.' Varley seemed unoffended; he had produced a wicked grin. 'At least I did get one policeman, didn't I? And I chose the nastiest looking specimen I could see. You're going to say, Shefford, that between nasty specimens there was nothing to choose.'

'No, I'm not. I'm not buying you at your face value—quite.' Shefford fell silent, not being at all clear what more he could say. He remembered how Varley had received considerable sympathy at Oxford, and he didn't think that wrong. The President had refused to consider removing his name from the books of the college. Raggett declared that between fifteen seconds and fifteen minutes the difference was insignificant, so far as the maintaining of an evil design was concerned, and that he himself would have judged Varley's character malign only had he let a sun go down upon his policeman. An old lady of liberal views in North Oxford had offered to employ him as a gardener-chauffeur. But immediately upon his release, he had vanished. It showed—Raggett had said, dismissing the affair—that the young fool had a substratum of sense in him. His conduct hadn't earned him the right to be met by a committee and tendered a complimentary dinner.

Shefford was conscious he mustn't behave like a committee now. He mustn't be fussy, but friendly he could surely be. Their ages didn't materially differ, and the passing of two years since the episode in the garden had narrowed what gap there was, and blotted out their difference in academic status. He remembered the strangest moment in the garden; the spark of antagonism that had passed between them. Perhaps status had been involved there, and they wouldn't feel that way again.

'It's over, anyway,' Shefford said, and at once felt that this was a weak and irritating remark. And there was a grim sense in which it probably wasn't true. He had a vision of Varley—no more than a boy—in his ugly prison clothes; perhaps they were garments which, once donned, one could never again hope quite to tear from one's back. Perhaps they explained the over-elegant clothes Varley was wearing now. Something permanently maiming had happened to him, just as a result of the black quarter of an hour; had sprung into being at a mere gesture by society, a word from a magistrate on a bench. Shefford found himself trembling with anger. 'I'm so damned sorry!' he said. And the words seemed almost meaningless to him.

'Well, thanks a lot.' Varley had flushed again—but this time it might have been under some different compulsion. 'Do you remember when you last heard me say that?'

'Yes, in the college garden.' Shefford, who had brought his *ouzo* across with him, gave a moment to finishing it. 'Do you know, I think I was rather an ass that night? Not in anything I said——'

'You said nothing, as a matter of fact.'

'I suppose not. But I had feelings, and they were a bit

absurd. They were of outraged propriety. That was rot.'
Shefford paused—and risked a bid for Mark Varley's friendship. 'What you were doing was pretty silly. But that's all there was to it.'

'Bloody silly.' Varley produced this mildly intensive expression with care. 'Or put it that I was being provocative. Trailing my coat, as they say.' He gave Shefford a wry grin. 'Not that it was precisely that—was it? I had no coat. Call it trailing my arse.'

Shefford looked round for the man with the tray. He felt that his acquaintanceship with Varley was prospering, and that he wanted this. He had never himself experienced life as a really desperate affair. But it had been that for Varley, almost before he could be called a grown man. And perhaps he had been left with some devil slumbering inside him, so that it might all happen over again. Shefford felt he didn't want to turn away from Varley. And he felt that if he could even get a few more four-letter words out of him there would at least be the beginning of a relationship.

'I'd been taken quite away from how I was brought up,' Varley said. 'They would have happened anyway, things like that garden ploy, even if I'd never gone near Oxford. Because of the extent to which I seemed different from most other people. Can you understand that? Because of what I *have*, really. I was baffled, and very unhappy; and to do a freakish thing—if only something *fin-de-siècle* I'd read about somewhere—was at least a gesture. Even although I didn't expect an audience to turn up.'

There was nothing particularly wrong with any single element in this speech, yet Shefford found himself having to refuse to be put off by it. What it suggested, he supposed, was simply that Mark Varley was an abundantly self-absorbed young man.

'But there the audience was,' Varley was saying. 'It's odd that it should have been Bernard.'

'Bernard?' For a moment the name rang no bell.

'I suppose it's because of him that you're here?' Varley drained his own glass. He appeared to be drinking the local brandy—the stuff they called *metaxa*. 'You've come to visit Vanderlyn's kingdom?'

'I know nothing about Vanderlyn's kingdom.'

'I'll show it to you.' Varley got to his feet and picked up the panama hat—which he then looked at sombrely, as if he didn't much care for it. He walked off down the quay, gazing out to sea as he did so. 'The pharos hides it,' he said over his shoulder, and walked on. Then he stopped. 'About two fingers from it now,' he said. 'Can you see a cloud?'

'Yes.'

'It isn't a cloud. It's Vanderlyn's kingdom.' He paused, and regarded Shefford broodingly. He looked as if he *knew* it was broodingly. The dark lock had fallen between his eyes. 'Unless,' he said, 'Vanderlyn's kingdom *is* a cloud.'

Chapter 2

VARLEY HAD SPOKEN with the recurrent sense of theatre he seemed to indulge in. Shefford didn't like it—and the less because Varley still had the notably beautiful voice he remembered from the college garden. However silly or irritating the words the young man uttered, this sheerly aesthetic quality would accompany them still. There was something almost unfair about it. But Shefford's mind didn't pause on this. He was full of curiosity.

'It seems a long way off,' he said. 'You've come from there now?'

'Yes. Just a half-holiday, and to do a little shopping. There's a fast launch at the farther quay, with two young Phoebus Apollos to sail it. Let's have some coffee. I've acquired a taste for the Turkish kind. If you don't like it, you just say "Gallicos", and they bring you a milky variety.'

Shefford, although he rather resented this informative note, agreed to coffee. They went back and gave their order. At least for the moment, Varley had no more to say. He seemed to veer between a frankness which was entirely attractive and the embarrassment of a man beset by some lurking sense of a false position. Shefford decided to ask further questions.

'Vanderlyn has a house over there?'

'Yes. He owns the whole island. A big island called Tyros. The house is sizeable too. It was a monastery. The whole set-up is quite something. I'm only one of a crowd, I may say.' Varley had shot out this defensively. 'You'd better come back with me and see.'

'Does Vanderlyn live there much?'

'All the time, more or less. I tell you, it's his kingdom.'

'But surely he has a great many affairs to see to?' Shefford was irritated by this mystery-mongering. 'In politics, and so on?'

'My dear chap, you're just not with it.' Varley had advanced boldly upon this familiar address to a fellow of his old college. 'Bernard was sacked—just like that. It seems to have been a matter of pretty high policy. Not so much how people should be butchered, as whether they should be butchered at all. I say he was sacked, but of course he simply resigned from what had become an untenable position. It was the sort of resignation that, in England, could bring down a government. Things are different in America.'

'I see. And now he simply——?'

'He patronises the arts. In quite a big way. And including me.'

'That sounds fine. But just how did you come to contact him again?'

'Well, it was no time ago at all. I heard about what he was doing, and I wrote to him.'

'Expressing interest?'

'Yes.' Varley, although he had certainly registered an irony which Shefford regretted as soon as he had uttered it, seemed unoffended. 'And then I went to see him. We recognised each other at once—from that bow-and-arrow business, I mean. It was rather fun, really. I felt awkward for a moment, because it had been bloody stupid, as you say. But he said, "I guess it was you who held out the empty cigarette package." He's not an artist, you know—but I saw that he was like an artist in understanding what things can mean. So I told him I was a naked beggar again now, and about those awful three months, and what I wanted to do. He was marvellous!'

'Vanderlyn signed you on? Was it on a basis of political sympathy—your having been the victim of generous protest against the horrors of war? I know he has feelings about that.'

Shefford had come out with this—it was a further irony—upon an impulse he couldn't quite identify. Perhaps he felt that, if he were to make headway with Varley, there would be no harm in a testingly astringent note. And, this time, Varley was held up. He flushed faintly.

'It was an element,' he said. 'I was to discover it was an element. But I didn't plug it. It wasn't even in my head. I give you my word on that. I'm a poet, and I said so. There aren't many men one *could* say just that to. Or that *I* could. And I repeat that he was marvellous. He has been marvellous. Nothing that ever happens can cancel that.' Varley's voice had rung out on this, and for a moment he looked gravely at Shefford. Then, suddenly, he was looking down at his finely laundered linen trousers. The gesture carried a baffling suggestion of a rapid change of mood. 'But perhaps,' he said, 'there's more enterprise in going naked. I must have thought so in that damned garden.'

This tag from the poet Yeats gave Shefford a jolt. Varley—whether talented or not, he didn't know—had found a patron. He had just acknowledged this, and said something generous about it. But now he had added—if the tag meant what it seemed to mean—that the situation was one in which he felt himself caught and caged. Probably such an ambivalence of feeling was common enough in the artist-and-patron relationship. But it was curious, Shefford thought, that Varley should pitch it at him within ten minutes of this casual meeting. Varley seemed, in fact, to be a young man incapable of any settled attitude for very long.

'I think you really *should* come across,' Varley was saying. 'I'll have to tell Bernard we met, and he'd be hurt to think you passed by disregarding. He's spoken of you sometimes, Jeremy.' Varley appeared to be unaware of surprising Shefford by this grab at his Christian name, which carried an obscure suggestion of appeal. 'And I'd like you to see it, too. It really is rather good. I don't know what I can produce to live up to it. Although I have got a small book in the press now.' Varley paused, clearly for an expression of interest. 'But that'—he went on, when Shefford had produced a decent murmur—'is nothing but some of the poems I was writing at school and as an undergraduate. I've got to do something bigger now. Bernard has some ideas, as a matter of fact. I just wish——'

'Ideas about what sort of poetry you should write?' Shefford asked this only because Varley had broken off awkwardly in mid-sentence.

'Well, yes—among other things.' Varley was frowning now. 'Bernard has lots of ideas. He's a remarkable man.'

'Does he have the idea that it's an artist's duty to be positive, and not negative?'

'Yes, he has.' Varley looked startled. 'How on earth do you come to know that?'

'I was just remembering something.'

'I don't pretend it isn't difficult. Sometimes I'm just not on his wave-length. He has some rather old-fashioned notions, of course. And rather wants to sell them—which might be the real trouble. It's being an American, I think. And having had enormous power in a totally different kind of set-up over there. By the way, I'm called Mark, please.' Varley looked straight at Shefford—and Shefford felt that, for a moment at least, they had come quite close together. He couldn't remember what sort of a degree Varley had collected. Probably a thoroughly bad one; a Fourth Class, as likely as not. But Varley was not less intelligent than he was himself, and it was shared intelligence which—perhaps delusively—was bringing them into a relation of friendship now. 'You see, Jeremy, hardly anybody's interested in poetry. Hardly anybody cares. What about you? You teach Eng. Lit. Do you care? I mean, in poetry as something happening, or trying to happen, today? For example, will you buy this small book of mine?'

'Yes.'

'But only because of our happening to have met again like this?'

'Yes.' Truthfulness—Gavin Naylor had once told his friend—appeared to be the only virtue he had little difficulty in commanding.

'So you can see how good it is to have a mature and informed person with a powerful mind—a mind, just *qua* mind, much more powerful than one's own—not merely caring and sympathising, but actually casting around? You *do* see?'

'I suppose I do.' There was something perverse and comical, Shefford was thinking, in Varley's belated subscription, on the island of Tyros, to the classical virtues of the tutorial system. At Oxford, perhaps, some colleague of Shefford's had fallen down on the job. Varley must have been a trying pupil, after all. Of course, the submission to Vanderlyn—if it was to be called that—didn't sound altogether untroubled. The urgency that had gone into asking Shefford if he *saw* suggested that Varley's own vision wasn't entirely unfaltering. Tyros held its problems for him.

'Mrs Vanderlyn should be back by this time,' Varley said. 'She was only going to the *pharmakeion*.'

'Mrs Vanderlyn?' Shefford was surprised at the pleasure with which he repeated the name. 'Mrs Vanderlyn is here?'

'Oh, yes—and she and I are to join up again on the quay. She'll certainly invite you to come across. I don't know what she wants at the *pharmakeion*, anyway. We've everything laid on over there: even a whole small town of our own. Perhaps she rather wanted a half-holiday too.'

Shefford turned to scan the quay—but it wasn't before he had caught on Varley's face an expression which, for the moment at least, he found uncomfortably alienating. Not that 'caught' was the right word. For what Varley had pro-

92

duced could only be called a secret smile which he intended
should be observed. He wanted Shefford to mark his amused
comprehension of Mrs Vanderlyn's feeling the need of a
half-holiday from Vanderlyn. The smile even contrived to
lend his words an obscure sexual connotation. What was
chiefly offensive about this was its plain lack of sense. Varley,
however clever, must be quite obtuse about the Vanderlyns
as husband and wife.

The quay was empty, or almost so. The old man was still
beating the cobbles with the octopuses, or the octopuses with
the cobbles. Beyond him, some children had secured an
abandoned octopus, and were taking it in turn to put on a
show of their own. Nearer at hand, from a dark and jagged
cavity—seemingly blasted out by shell-fire—which showed
like a missing tooth in the gleaming façade of an ancient and
marble-sheathed public edifice, another old man had crept
to sit in the sun; his *komboloyi*—his worry beads—glinted
glassily as he fumbled them. Across the harbour, and turning to a slow tumble of jewels the silken surface of incredible
blue, a fishing-vessel was gliding towards the water-front;
in its prow, splendid as Palinurus, a young man in a ragged
shirt and sea-bleached trousers frayed away to above his
knees stood poised, coiled rope in hand, to leap on shore.
And it seemed to be no longer simply that the sun shone;
Helios was driving through the heavens his four-horsed
flaming chariot. For Shefford—as for Breughel when he
saw Icarus fall beyond the homely ploughland—it was a
moment in which a remote and timeless wonder flashed
across the familiar world. He glanced farther along the
quay. The figure of a woman was advancing towards them.

For a second he thought it was Mrs Vanderlyn. Then he
saw that it was a much younger woman. She might almost be
his dream-girl, for even at this distance he could see that she
had notable beauty, and carried herself in a manner inde-
finably suggesting some other sort of distinction too. Yet she
wasn't quite the dream-girl; she was older than that, though
she wasn't at all old. It was clear she didn't belong to this

93

simple place, and he hadn't seen her on the ferry boat. She must be off some foreign yacht, luxuriously cruising. There were plenty of these around.

The woman was now too close for him to continue looking at her with politeness, and he turned away. It was to see Varley getting rather elaborately to his feet.

'Gemma,' Varley was saying with formality, 'may I introduce Mr Shefford? He is a friend of Bernard's, and a kind of professor of mine.' He turned to Shefford. 'Mrs Vanderlyn,' he said.

Shefford recalled something about a stepdaughter—a stepdaughter who was to have been picked up in Paris. This was the kind of woman you might well—in a wholly respectable sense—pick up there. She was dressed that way. Yet it didn't seem possible that a stepdaughter of either of the Vanderlyns could be called Mrs Vanderlyn.

'I'm happy to meet you, Mr Shefford,' the woman called Mrs Vanderlyn said. The idiom was American, but the accent was not; somehow it suggested to Shefford international cookery in an expensive place. They shook hands over the tiny drained coffee-cups, and the woman sat down on a third rickety chair reached for by Varley. 'It's pleasant,' she said, 'to get to know more of my husband's friends.'

Before the unexpectedness of this, Shefford completely betrayed himself. There was a stammer in his reply. But Gemma Vanderlyn was not discomposed. No doubt it was a situation that still occurred from time to time.

'I think you may not have known,' she said quietly, 'Louise Vanderlyn died eighteen months ago. And Bernard and I were married in May.'

Chapter 3

TYROS—VANDERLYN'S KINGDOM—was, like Odysseus's kingdom of Ithaca, infertile ground: a skin of earth everywhere splitting and falling away beneath the upward thrust of earth-coloured rock.

Or it was thus, at least, that the island showed as it rose out of the sea, a terrain austerely beautiful and forlornly arid—almost waterless, one would have said at a guess, so that it appeared a wonder that anything could be grown on the frail terraces scraped across its slopes, or that, beyond these, even the wild goats could find their sustenance. There was a southward-facing, sun-baked village, straitened between the sea—from which it gained its livelihood—and a savage precipice: a place so humble and low-roofed that it might be mistaken, from a little way out, for a marine cemetery, or even for a scatter of bathing-huts attached to some invisible resort. The houses or hovels, when one realised them to be such, seemed beaten down by light as brutal as a lash; some were at bay behind the dark reticulations of fishing-nets stretched on poles to dry; others had thrust out uncertain awnings of patched and tattered rust-coloured canvas. In the midst of them stood a church: a white-domed building on a scale so minute as to suggest a puffball, or something contrived by birds or insects of an architectural turn. Everything human here spoke at once of timelessness and of evanescence; of generations perpetually the same, and perpetually passing from darkness to darkness through this endless blaze of noon. Only on a promontory to the east, sufficiently dominant to have once, perhaps, aspired to the condition of an acropolis, stood something firmly temporal: a row of broken columns—yet one of them rising intact to a Corinthian capital—which asserted that, after all, history happened, and was full of perfectly distinguishable phenomena.

But again like Ithaca, Shefford supposed, Tyros was to be of forward youths a nurse of name. Mark Varley was to be one of them. Shefford wondered whether there would prove to be forward maidens as well, or whether Vanderlyn had sited his venture in a monastery because it was something like a monastic idea that he was following out. Or perhaps —he fleetingly recalled the evening's talk in the New

95

Library about Cosimo de' Medici and Federigo of Monte-feltro—perhaps it was a little Renaissance court that Vanderlyn had set up. Or, again, he might be discovered living like a mediaeval nobleman in his castle, and the forward youths would be well-born retainers, troubadours, persons of that sort. In this last event, the second Mrs Vanderlyn's position would be odd. She would be more or less the only lady on the premises. And the forward youths, followers of *amour courtois*, would put in their time celebrating her in verse and planning to go to bed with her.

This fancy set Shefford cautiously studying Gemma Vanderlyn. He couldn't tell quite what it was that called for caution. If you disregarded her looks—which might be hard to do, once you got thinking of them—your chief impression was likely to be of a slightly chilly social competence. She had asked just the number of questions necessary to get her bearings with this new young man, and now, as if she had been aware of the speculations going through his head, she turned to the subject of what her husband was hoping to achieve. The experiment, she insisted, was on a modest scale, and wholly a private affair. In the past, Bernard had been a good deal involved with various cultural agencies corporately organised and in the public sphere. Now he was working quietly and on his own.

Shefford listened respectfully. Sometimes, when he felt that his glance at Gemma wasn't perhaps equally respectful, he looked away hastily at the sea, and thought about her husband instead. If Vanderlyn's experiment was private, it at least didn't look as if shaping to be very privately conducted. Even in this remote place, that would hardly be possible. To call Tyros Vanderlyn's kingdom had been a joke of Varley's which chiefly hinted something equivocal or uncomfortable in the young man's attitude to his patron. Yet it seemed apt enough, in a way. Actual princes had held court in territories not much larger than this island. Even in the age of Goethe there had been such grandees: some of them concerned to attract around them people of distinction or promise in learning and the arts. By taking a whole island to himself Vanderlyn had declared a sort of autonomy recalling this. And if his venture wasn't yet on a large scale, it sounded scarcely so small as to be unobtrusive. He had, after all, held his place in the counsels of a nation long denied the blessing of unobtrusiveness, and over against his personal modesty there had to be set the habitual assumption that new ventures, if to be floated at all, are best floated in a large way. What Shefford had heard of only from Varley this morning was something the bruit of which must in fact be getting substantially around. Varley himself, for instance, had heard of it some time ago, and had got in on it. There was nothing discreditable in that. If it worked out well for Mark Varley, good luck to it.

This, along with some speculation as to what actually lay ahead, ran through Shefford's mind as the motor launch—certainly a fast one—flung a long wake of foam across the Aegean. Of the two Phoebus Apollos attending it, only the dark and silent Stepho seemed to have any present nautical function. Dionysios—fair and with hair as curly as a statue's—had the role of personal attendant to the *archontissa*, although there seemed no pressing reason why Gemma Vanderlyn need be so accommodated. Both the boys were in trim white clothes which they obviously enjoyed wearing, but Shefford thought they would have looked better if dressed like the young Palinurus of the fishing-boat. The launch was all white paint and glittering brass.

It was perhaps these things that had made Shefford uneasy during the crossing—unless it was the motion of the launch, which put him in mind of having ventured on a fast gallop. There was also the fact that he was very hungry; he was almost sorry that he had refrained from eating the two tired prawns. That he had embarked at all was surprising, since he had felt that he might not be a wholly welcome guest, so far as Bernard Vanderlyn himself was concerned. But he had once accepted an invitation from the first Mrs Vanderlyn to luncheon, and there might be something a little offensive in rejecting an invitation from the second. So he had boarded the launch, rucksack and all.

As far as the size of the craft permitted, Varley had withdrawn himself from the others. Perched with some show of hazard on the covered deck of its rising and falling prow, he seemed to take satisfaction in being whipped by the light spray which the motion every now and then sent high in the air. It wasn't good for his immaculate suit, and perhaps it wasn't meant to be. Yet Shefford couldn't believe that he had been directed to dress nicely, or been absolutely provided with a livery, as the young servants Stepho and Dionysios had presumably been. Gemma Vanderlyn, indeed, was an unknown factor in the set-up he was being drawn into investigating. But her husband—although, Shefford glimmeringly saw, he might be prone to errors answering to his own essential largeness—was surely not a man to make small mistakes in tact. One had to come back to the view that Varley was constantly not at ease with himself. Perhaps he should still be thought of in terms of the pains of adolescence and the awkwardness of self knowledge unachieved. That was probably how he must be viewed from the standpoint of maturity—from Vanderlyn's standpoint, say. Oddly enough, Shefford didn't himself feel drawn to this distancing of Varley as a younger person. In their short acquaintance Varley had exhibited little that was particularly amiable, but Shefford was experiencing a rapidly growing sympathy with him, all the same. It was even a kind of admiration or envy. Varley, if he didn't founder, might achieve things Shefford could never achieve. It was partly that. And it was partly—the two things were mixed up—that Varley was a more readily enjoying and suffering creature than he was. At this moment, it would be rather nice to be out there with him, feeling the spray: that rather than sitting in the cushioned stern, with Gemma Vanderlyn talking politely beside him, and just in front of him the silent Stepho upright at the small wheel. It would even be fun if he and Varley—whom he might as well begin thinking of as Mark—could have the launch to themselves to fool around with.

This honest thought had come to him during the last

98

stage of the passage to Tyros. They had headed, at what appeared a reckless pace, straight towards the strip of shore in front of the little village. It was called Trianta, Gemma said, following her informative bent. Such small craft as were visible were either at anchor within a few yards of land or had been drawn up on the shingle and let heel over where they lay. There was no sign of a jetty, and Shefford was envisaging some awkward disembarkation, followed by a trudge through gritty Aegean sand, when the launch swung to the left with a speed which shot the small spectacle in a dizzy arc past their starboard bow. The deck canted over as the immobile Stepho twirled his wheel. Mark, apparently accustomed to the manoeuvre, balanced himself nonchalantly upon his hips. Shefford, who had grabbed the gunwhale, received without resentment a flashing and reassuring smile from the curly-headed Dionysios, who had hitherto distinguished himself only by a surprising ability to sit or lie staring straight up into the blazing heaven. The turn, it was to be supposed, had avoided rocks or a sandbank, and their actual destination lay somewhere farther along the coast.

They rounded the promontory with its ruined shrine, and Gemma provided archaeological information. She appeared to have in common with her predecessor a rather extensively educated mind. The resemblance probably ended there, and the difference was something that Shefford hadn't begun to try to take the measure of. Gemma still alarmed him. There was nothing lascivious about her; she wasn't going to grab; but he increasingly saw her as the kind of woman who, if you once got round to thinking of her in an unguarded way, would have the blood hammering painfully in your temples in no time. It struck him that this ought at least to make sense of Vanderlyn's marrying her. Yet in some unaccountable way it didn't. Vanderlyn's first marriage had worried him as sexless, and it seemed perverse to be baffled again now. It wasn't as if Gemma were disposed to make an enigma of herself. Her talk was straightfoward enough. Yet the effect—it was almost a premonition—of something unaccountable remained.

She had told him quite a lot about herself, in a brief way. She was Greek, but her mother had been Italian, and this latter fact accounted for her Christian name. She had learnt her English in England, because her father had been Chancellor at the Greek Embassy there. Then she had lived rather longer in America, her father having become Ambassador in Washington. Since this had been after her mother's death, she had been obliged to shoulder numerous social duties. She could hardly imagine in the whole world a less favourable position in which to continue a career as a professional musician. Nobody gave you any time; nobody took you seriously; nobody—except the most eminent teachers, of course—ever offered you anything except meaningless praise. But she had persevered, since it just so chanced that perseverance was a quality she possessed. She could now, she supposed, account herself a composer of sorts.

Gemma appeared to have provided all this information out of an unembarrassed sense that an acquaintance of her husband's during the period of his first marriage should at once be put in the picture in regard to his second. Viewed this way, her account of herself became quite reticent. But at least—if one really felt the second marriage to need accounting for—it afforded a basis for conjecture. As one possibility, Shefford thought, you could see through it the outline of a political alliance. A beautiful and intelligent woman in her first maturity—for it was as in her early thirties that one had to think of her—who had been born into a ruling-class world, earned some position in that of music, and achieved the freedom of several languages and several of the great capitals of the globe: a woman with these qualifications (to use a sober and even faintly commercial word) was eminently well equipped to be the consort, if not of Bernard Vanderlyn, at least—so to speak—of Bernard Vanderlyn's new enterprise.

Shefford didn't in the least like this. He had read most of the great novels of Europe, and some of these had no doubt contributed to broadening his theoretical grasp of the varieties of sexual experience. But they hadn't in the least affected

those notions of marriage which are unconsciously axio-
matic in any respectably brought up English boy. It was
supremely the area in which nobody must simply use anybody else. The archetypal disaster (he would have said,
pointing straight at one of the great novels) was Adam
Verver's marriage to Charlotte Stant. Probably, he told
himself, there was a vast deal in the diversity of human
needs that he just didn't know about, and out of these all
sorts of curious relations could, so to speak, be legitimated.
But he remained in the dark about this Vanderlyn business,
all the same.

The launch had rounded a further promontory; Stepho
cut down to half speed; Shefford saw that the voyage—for
it had been almost that—was ended. In front of them was a
much smaller bay, surrounded for the most part by sheer
rock, but with a gently sloping beach at its western extremity.
The beach was flanked by two jetties, one old and crumbling and the other new. Above one end of it impended a
perilous-seeming tumble of loose rock and scree. But beyond
the other end the precipitous slope swung back in a wide
arc. Within this, quite unexpectedly, lay a garden.

It was a forsaken garden, although with an air of having
been recently tidied up, and any house that had stood within it had vanished. Apart from a boat-shed, there wasn't a
building in sight. The only other man-made thing was a
road. This started as a mere track from the old jetty, and
became broader and metalled where it reached the new. It
then ran through the garden and wound upwards among
the rocks. Then it turned northward and vanished into distance. Here and there it could be seen as a mere line, apparently etched across the face of a precipice.

The scale of the island which this prospect suggested,
and the apparent further remoteness of Vanderlyn's dwell-
ing, both took Shefford by surprise. And he didn't like the
look of the road at all. There was a car waiting at the new
jetty, and it seemed certain that he was going to spend a
terrifying twenty minutes in it. He had no reason to suppose
himself cowardly in a general way. But he did have a thing

about heights. Motor-roads of the *corniche* sort were his particular aversion. Perhaps he had actually gone pale. Dionysios was turning on his encouraging smile again.

The engine had cut out altogether; for a moment there was only the slap of water against the bows; and then, from somewhere in the garden, there came what must be the song of a nightingale. For a moment it pierced and filled the air, and then fell silent. The bird, perhaps, had taken alarm and departed.

Chapter 4

'SHALL I DRIVE?' Mark asked.

Stepho had been left behind with the launch, and Dionysios had been moving towards the wheel of the car. At Mark's question he halted, and he and Mark looked at each other with what Shefford was aware of as swift, hard challenge. They both wanted to drive. Or perhaps it was that they both wanted to drive Gemma Vanderlyn. Shefford wondered whether Stepho and Dionysios were, after all, exactly servants. Perhaps they ought to be thought of as pages at Vanderlyn's Renaissance court. It struck him that in the isolated community which he was about to visit there must be plenty of occasion for all sorts of jealousy.

'No, Mark, not you,' Gemma said. 'I think——' She broke off, for Mark's dark flush had appeared, and he had uttered an impatient sound, made a small angry gesture. Shefford waited to see if Gemma would let this pass. She didn't. She checked it—firmly, but within a convention of humour. 'What can you do with such a man?' she asked Shefford resignedly. As she spoke, she touched Mark on the arm, as if to soften the small rebuke. Then she turned to Dionysios, who had triumphantly renewed his movement towards the driver's seat. 'I will drive myself, *Dionysi mou*. And you shall sit in the back with Mark.'

Shefford noticed the diminutive, and that she hadn't said 'with Mr Varley'. He thought he noticed, too, that for a fraction of a second the eyes of the Greek youth held Gemma's before he dropped his glance modestly to the ground.

'*Kyria*,' Dionysios murmured submissively, and helped Gemma to her seat.

The car was a big open Mercedes, and its colour much that of the dust which it would presently be raising behind it. As Shefford climbed in beside Gemma he felt a sense of relief. On the alarming road ahead either of the young men now relegated to the back seat might well have been tempted to show off. Gemma was unlikely to do that. She hadn't, he supposed, any need to draw attention to herself. She showed no disposition to do this in any way. It had been an absurd irrelevance, he now saw, to tell himself there was nothing lascivious about her. Why on earth should there be, just because she was startlingly beautiful—and because her marriage (he saw that this thought had been in his mind) was a January and May affair, of the kind with which mediaeval story-tellers liked to start off a romance of adultery? Physically, Gemma was quite remote. Very lovely women learnt, perhaps, to live behind a faint protective chilliness, against which they balanced a purely social approachability. Gemma was like that. But this told him nothing at all, he realised, about her underlying temperament. He sat back as the car moved away from the new jetty, accelerating swiftly.

'It's very forlorn, right here,' Gemma said. 'But all through the spring it becomes a garden again—although the flowers are wild flowers. *Silene colorata* towards the sea, making a great sheet of pink. And on the other side Corn Marigold, which last longer. It makes a mass of colour too —a deep buttercup yellow. It's like driving between two stripes of a strange national flag. And although it's a marvellous part of the world for wild flowers, you don't often get whole carpets of them. Although sometimes one gets the Bermuda Buttercup that way. *Oxalis Cernua.*'

Shefford decided he would never know much about the

second Mrs Vanderlyn. This degree of informativeness on an old wives' topic such as he felt botany to be seemed far from presaging any intimacy. He glanced round the deserted garden—it was large, so that they had not yet emerged from it—and found it, if not forlorn, at least uninteresting. There appeared to have been at one time many formal beds, which could never have had much character. And goodness knew how they'd got watered. He was aware of a strong odour in the air—so that he found himself recalling another garden, and Bernard Vanderlyn's voice saying, 'Scented limes—whereabouts are they?' But this was a different scent, and his mind switched to a more distant memory, to an image of himself kept away from school, and with a towel round his head, bent over a steaming bowl.

'I say,' he said, 'are those gum trees?'

'Yes—all along that side. Of course, eucalypts are not indigenous. When you find them on the islands, it means that an enterprising Turkish landowner put them there. What seems to me strange about them is their giving so little shade. You notice that? It's because they turn their leaves blade-wise to the sun.'

Shefford lapsed into silence. The waft of scent, with its childhood association, had been curiously exciting, but the same couldn't be said of the conversation of Gemma Vanderlyn. She was maintaining the note of polite *cicerone* to an extent which almost hinted that she found her casual guest a bore. Or so Shefford thought, not unresentfully, for a time. At least he had to give her credit for good driving. The road was as hair-raising as he had feared, for within minutes they had climbed high above the sea and were looking perpendicularly down upon the bay with its two jetties where they had landed: a scene now so rapidly miniatured that it might have been flicked into focus through the wrong end of a telescope. The sea, at sea-level uniformly blue, showed from here like a subtly kinetic action-painting in many blues and greens, indigos and violets. It was dizzying to gaze at and impossible to look away from, and as it circled and slanted with the movement of the car Shefford found it hard to conceal his impulse to grab something. He felt as frightened as if he had been in one of those abominable tourist coaches which, having a total length much greater than their wheel-base, can actually suspend one over nothingness as the driver swings unconcernedly round a bend. Gemma had no air of unconcern, nor on the other hand did she seem tense and anxious. Within ten minutes the coast had disappeared, and other aspects of the island of Tyros were opening up.

They were among upland valleys, amid pasturing goats —and here and there wild flowers had survived the spring. There were first strips and patches, and then more substantial tracts, under cultivation: small olive groves, with trunks and branches gnarled and striving like old peasants inured to toil; a brave splatter of vines on a terrace; contrastingly unevocative maize, browning within its rushy leaves. High up above a wilderness of boulders a tiny sunblanched village showed as no more than the casual droppings of birds on the brown rock. Here and there they passed a child leading a kid, an old man huddled amid shapeless bundles on an almost invisible donkey, an old woman acting as her own donkey, and so burdened with faggots that she might have been Birnam wood closing in on Dunsinane. There was a ruined and deserted hamlet, with flat-roofed little hovels such as might have been run up for rodents in a third-rate zoo. There was a similar hamlet, in part rebuilt and in part with new dwellings more human in suggestion, and with a smithy or primitive engineering shop in which a young man could be glimpsed tinkering with the engine of a piece of agricultural machinery. There was a tiny school, announcing in a Greek which Shefford could understand its resolve to provide only a plebeian education—yet with some show of fresh paint and a recently laid-out playground with swings and seesaws and a few more up-to-date contraptions for juvenile amusement. It seemed possible to sense the hand of Bernard Vanderlyn beginning to extend itself over these further reaches of his domain.

'Was Mark thought much of at Oxford, Mr Shefford?'

Shefford was startled by Gemma's sudden question—both because it suggested a new level of conversation and because Mark himself was surely within hearing. On this last point he turned round involuntarily to satisfy himself. He saw that the two youths had raised a large glass windscreen in front of them, and that in this big car they were in consequence entirely out of earshot. Mark, who seemed to have recovered his good humour, was talking to Dionysios, no doubt by way of practicing his Greek. Shefford noticed, for the first time, that these two had something in common. This was simply good looks, in part blemished. Mark was dark and handsome, but he had that mark which could show like a danger-signal on his cheek. Dionysios was handsome too: fair-complexioned, and with features—which surely one scarcely expected to find in Greece—that were classically Hellenic. His nose was beautifully on a line with his forehead—as beautifully as in the Hermes of Praxiteles. Only Dionysios, unlike Hermes, seemed to have been in a punch-up. Somebody had given his nose a bash; it had been a little deflected from the plumb line down the hitherto perfect symmetry of his face. This misadventure had achieved the happy consequence of making Dionysios a good deal more attractive than Hermes. And this, in its way, distinguished him from Mark—whose small blemish was simply that.

Shefford turned away hastily from this inspection. It hadn't been mannerly to look back at all, since the action questioned the propriety of Gemma's having asked her question. He was also rather disturbed at having lingered over the comparative good looks of these two youths—since it wasn't a department of aesthetics that was at all his line. He didn't suppose it was Bernard Vanderlyn's either—but he glimpsed, nevertheless, a possible function for Gemma which hadn't previously occurred to him. Scattered about this Mediterranean world one could find plenty of elderly and wealthy men with an entourage of personable youths more or less artistically oriented, and on Tyros there was the potentiality of some imputation which might be vexatious to Vanderlyn and prejudicial to what he was seriously about. It would be unreasonable to suppose that he had remarried with anything of the kind consciously in his head. Still, Gemma must be, so to speak, a spoke in the wheel of any vulgar chatter.

This train of thought—although he felt it to be a tribute to his own enlarging knowledge of the world—didn't employ Shefford for long. And now he had to fish up a reply to Gemma's question.

'I don't know a great deal about Mark,' he began. 'He was only making a joke about my having been one of his professors. He didn't study the subject I teach. I think he was rather notable, in a lone-wolf way. And, of course, the business of his being sent to gaol lent him a certain prominence. It was——' He broke off, thinking with dismay that Gemma might have been told nothing about this.

'Yes, of course.' Gemma's response dismissed this apprehension at once. She even sounded impatient. 'But as a poet. I know Mark hasn't published his first volume yet. But he has printed poems in magazines or journals. What has been thought of them?'

'I'm afraid I just don't know—and I haven't even seen any myself. For two or three years I've rather missed out on that sort of thing.' Shefford found he was being apologetic. 'I suppose because I've been learning my job. And at Oxford, as far as any sort of syllabus goes, English poetry is always thought of as something that stopped off decades or generations ago.'

'I see.' Gemma was silent for some moments, steering the car at a good speed but with adequate care through another scatter of humble dwellings. Shefford felt that he hadn't raised Oxford in her esteem. 'I have,' she said.

'I beg you pardon?' For a moment Shefford was at sea.

'Of course I've read anything of Mark's that I could. I think he is a poet, for what the opinion is worth. English isn't my nursery language, you know.'

'It's Mr Vanderlyn's nursery language. If he thinks Mark

is really good, he's probably right, I'd say. It would be my guess that, even on rather unfamiliar ground, his taste would be very exact.'

Again Gemma was silent. Shefford wondered if his commendatory word on Bernard Vanderlyn had been impertinent. The car braked, and he saw that they were about to go steeply downhill. The sea was in front of them again, although at present only a narrow curving inlet of it was visible, gleaming like a great scimitar cutting into the reddy-gray recumbent land. There was a glimpse, too, of white buildings set, with an Italian look, behind the dark columns of cypresses. Then this disappeared beyond a stony hillside.

'It's a question of scale, isn't it?' Gemma asked. She gave Shefford a swift glance, something she had scarcely done since they set out. 'Or is "weight" the proper word? You know what I mean.'

'Mark might be quite good—but too much might be expected of him, all the same?' Shefford looked quickly behind him again. He continued to feel an awkwardness in this conversation going on more or less under Mark's nose. It couldn't be other than inaudible—he reassured himself, as he gave Mark a grin—but it was surprising that Gemma should have entered upon it, all the same. Perhaps, it came to him, there were things she wanted got clear before he arrived in the presence of her husband. 'There might,' he amplified, 'be a kind of burden on Mark?'

'On Mark? Something like that, perhaps.' Again she glanced at him. Her attitude had changed, and he guessed that she would not again produce archaeological or botanical small-talk. 'Mark is coming to occupy rather a special position in Bernard's regard. I think Bernard has always very much wanted a son.'

Shefford stopped himself from saying, 'And he may still have one.' It was Gemma's own affair, that. Instead, he said firmly, 'Then he won't find a trouble-free buy in Mark Varley.'

'Of course not.' She was amused. 'I don't feel frightened of that. Remember that I'm a musician. I've seen all sorts of prima-donnas in my time. And I think it's probably possible to like Mark very much.'

'Well, yes—I agree.' His agreement, he noticed, was with a verdict markedly provisional. 'But if it's a matter of a big build-up and the choosing of a principal *protégé*'—he glanced at Gemma in an attempt to make sure this wouldn't offend her—'then, dash it all, why pick on Mark?'

'He is one sort of person—a young artist with no position or influence—that Bernard is setting out to help. And society has been hard on him, I suppose. There's a lot of social conscience in Bernard. Social passion, perhaps it should be called. It may be deeper in him than any championship of the arts.'

'Yes.' Shefford remembered how stiffly Vanderlyn had responded to his telling him about the bloodies wrecking Mark's rooms. 'As for the arts, Mark himself told me he is only one of a crowd. He seemed anxious to establish that.'

'It's true that Bernard has gathered other *protégés*, as you call them, around him. I've even done a little of it myself. But, for good or ill, Mark's position is—or is going to be —special.' Gemma Vanderlyn's tone might have been taking on an extra dispassionateness. 'There was Louise's interest in him, too.'

'But that's not possible! Mrs . . . Louise Vanderlyn can never have set eyes on Mark.'

'She heard about Bernard's encountering him. It impressed her. Everything that Bernard told her about that Oxford night appears to have impressed her. Perhaps her picture wasn't quite right. She thought the young poet should be rescued from the coarse college boys who were bullying him in the dormitory. She recurred to the subject from time to time. Not long before her death, she had some plan for contacting Mark. She was on a committee which could nominate him for a travelling scholarship to take him to an American university where he could study American literature for a time. Later he might be allowed to teach a course: Freshman English, I guess, and even become a professor in the end.'

109

Shefford had no difficulty in accepting this account, for the first Mrs Vanderlyn sounded in it authentically enough. Even if she had met the real Mark, she would have been capable of planning just such an inept species of aid for him. What seemed to have happened was that Mark had become a bequest—or that Vanderlyn saw it like that. Vanderlyn had started his scheme; Mark had reappeared out of the blue, a hopeful applicant; and what Gemma was calling his special position had grown inevitably from that moment.

The car turned a corner, and Shefford had a surprised impression of looking down on a complex of abandoned asphalt tennis-courts, cracked and with a thin grass growing out of them, such as one might come across in the derelict public park of a bombed-out city. One could have supposed, too, that some surviving inhabitants were keeping themselves alive by rearing a wretched poultry, for scattered at random over these crumbling surfaces were innumerable small turreted structures, dark-holed like hen-roosts or miniature dovecots. Like real dovecots, they were built of stone. In fact they were chimneys, and the whole area was an aggregation of flat roofs, suspended through the exercise of some primitive architectural mystery over a system of piled-up cubical buildings such as a child might construct with the most old-fashioned sort of nursery bricks. That the building had been a monastery was attested by a belfry in which two big bronze bells still hung.

It was a monastery remote from the conception of such a structure evolved in distant centuries within the Roman Catholic Church. The place had been conceived without grace or amenity; you could nowhere point to fine proportions, a calculated line, the basic notion that man owes his command of sensuous beauty to God's service. It had a tough integrity of structure, a straight adherence to its own governing idea, not much else. One soon saw, of course, that it wasn't a monastery any longer; that in fact the paint and plaster were virtually still damp on much that had been done to it in an unobtrusive way. But Shefford was impressed by a certain unexpectedness, an imaginative quality, in Vanderlyn's having pitched his venture in such a place. It seemed absurd to think of the plan as having any origin in that casual talk about Federigo of Urbino and goodness knew what else in the New Library. But if it had, then one might have expected Vanderlyn to have equipped himself with a French château on the grandest scale, a mediaeval Italian castle, a Palladian villa of post-Palladio size, a vast palazzo in Rome. This abandoned tenement of the Orthodox Church on Tyros might be a little mad, but at least it hadn't been obvious.

'It isn't at all like an ivory tower,' Shefford said.

Gemma Vanderlyn turned to him, and for the first time it was something other than what would have to be called a social smile.

'An ivory tower? No, Bernard doesn't want that—or even a mere stronghold. He's an ambitious man, Mr Shefford, and he sees Tyros as a lighthouse.'

Chapter 5

THE CAR TURNED a further corner before coming to a stop, and a new aspect of the monastery was revealed. If much had been done to the place recently a great deal more had been done not long ago. For here, merging into the ancient buildings only at the back and on one side, was a large modern house, entirely simple yet notably elegant. It couldn't have been built in a hurry. Its stone appeared to have come from the same quarry as that of the old fabric: only it remained lighter in colour, and was finely dressed instead of rough-hewn. Although generously arcaded against the heat, its predominant effect was of a uniform lustre, only softly shadowed. Shefford thought of a pearl, still half buried in its shell. Then he thought of some costly architectural ornament, in part chiselled from its contrasting and

III

still enfolding matrix, like a statue which the sculptor has chosen to leave engaged in its bed. He now saw how it had been possible for Vanderlyn's kingdom to become, in little over a year, a going concern. Somebody had been here before him. It would be a Greek shipping millionaire— Shefford decided with a dip into his knowledgeable manner —who had done himself this more than commodious island hide-out. Vanderlyn had needed only to adapt and augment what already existed.

Vanderlyn was on his doorstep—if one might so describe a broad flight of marble steps which led up to a terrace smothered in vines. It could be seen at a glance that he hadn't changed—except that he no longer wore a business suit. He had paused on the terrace as if made aware, while going about his affairs, that a guest had turned up. Beside him was a woman, conveying the same suggestion of arrested movement. Both came down the steps as Shefford jumped from the car. The woman was young—and Shefford found himself feeling that this was absurd. Perhaps the bright light striking back from the pristine stone had confused his wits as he told himself of the absurdity of Mrs Vanderlyn's looking so young. He recovered and saw the truth. Mrs Vanderlyn—*his* Mrs Vanderlyn—was dead. And here was her daughter—authentically, this time. She was the image of her mother.

'Mr Shefford, this is a delightful surprise.' Vanderlyn hadn't lost his ability to remember people. He shook hands. 'Gemma, what a splendid catch! Marion, this is Mr Shefford from Oxford—Jeremy, I think, among his colleagues. Jeremy —if I may call you so—this is my stepdaughter, Marion Causland. Dionysios, please take charge of Mr Shefford's bags.'

'I haven't any bags.' Shefford was laughing, pleased by the warmth of his welcome. 'I'm a day tripper, sir, with just a rucksack.'

'Then, if we hold banquet in your honour, Mark must lend you some of his notable clothes.'

'No good,' Mark said. 'I'm taller—and not nearly so

112

tubby. Don't dons put on weight like anything! Jeremy's a kind of college Hamlet, fat and scant of breath.'

'We'll make a Horatio of him, and teach him to drink deep ere he departs,' Vanderlyn said. 'But we'll start with a tolerable seafood lunch.'

Shefford found this gay talk unexpected. As it continued for a minute or two he noticed that Gemma Vanderlyn took part in it competently, and that the girl named Marion Causland didn't take part in it at all. He had a sense—which was surely extravagant—that in this she was bearing, so to speak, the standard of her mother, who hadn't lightly inclined to merriment. He had a sense too, and this more substantially, that Bernard Vanderlyn *had* changed, although it mightn't be easy to decide just how. One was prepared to find a man from whose shoulders a burden had been lifted —since his venture on Tyros, however much a matter of his deep concern, could involve none of the grim confrontations of the power-game between nations. And something of the sort did seem evident; it was possible to see Vanderlyn as a man reaching out in directions he'd only dreamed of. Yet an unsympathetic observer—it just brushed Shefford's consciousness—might contrive a different view. Here, he might say, was merely a cultivated and affluent gentleman living *en prince*, like a Bernard Berenson at I Tatti. Or he might say that the Federigo of Urbino image had really taken hold, and that Vanderlyn was in danger of showing as diminished in consequence; that he might have parted with more than he was yet aware of in exchanging Washington for Tyros.

This second and disenchanted voice gave Shefford no pleasure. But he guessed that such speculation would continue to occupy his mind, all the same. If there was no leisure for it now it was evident that there would be later. For a day trip to Tyros was an obvious absurdity. Dionysios had already disappeared with the rucksack—which it turned out, however, he hadn't thought proper to do other than hand on to a maidservant. For when Gemma led Shefford off to his room, there was Dionysios, lording it over a young

113

woman in the matter of unpacking and disposing of Shefford's scanty possessions. The maid was called Vangelio—which it seemed to Shefford ought to be a man's name—and she was so pretty that, for a few moments, he noticed nothing else round about him. Then he became aware of Gemma dismissing Dionysios with a touch of impatience, and of Dionysios saying '*Kyria*', as he had done before. Shefford supposed that it meant 'Madam', or something like that. Dionysios uttered it with what wasn't exactly insolence, but wasn't the mere impersonality of a servant either. And again his glance seemed first to meet Gemma's, and then drop in what was almost a ritual way. Shefford again thought of the conventions of Courtly Love; of privileged squires adoring with discretion and according to the most complicated rules—but with an eye to the possibility of actually seducing their liege-lady, all the same. As rather frequently happened, Shefford found himself disapproving of his own thoughts. When he recovered from this, he found he had been left alone to wash. He washed in a hurry. He was famished by this time.

But he was still able to notice that he washed in his own bathroom, and that this matched his bedroom in a reticent but pervasive luxury. That, of course, would be the shipping millionaire. All the same, it left him uneasy as he went downstairs again in search of his now madly craved-for meal. Mark was waiting for him at the foot of the staircase, and it occurred to him that his new friend wouldn't normally be an attentive and mannerly young man in small matters of this sort. Perhaps he had been told off by Vanderlyn or Gemma to perform his duty. Or could it be that Mark was lurkingly home-sick, so that he had an instinct to gravitate towards a contemporary from Oxford? Shefford recalled Mark's making that joke about a college Hamlet. He didn't have to know Mark all that well to be aware that that hadn't quite *been* Mark. The joke was like his panama hat, belonging with new clothes that he felt it due to his position on Tyros to wriggle into. His motive might be creditable; it might be loyalty to Vanderlyn; yet it carried the hint of a false situation. Federigo's Urbino, Shefford seemed to remember, had overflowed with good-humour; even the ceaselessly pedagogic Vittorino da Feltre —who would surely have commanded the approval of the first Mrs Vanderlyn herself—had been very gay. Shefford felt he too was prepared to be reasonably gay—just as soon as he had a solid meal inside him.

Such a meal was provided. He wasn't sure of the circumstances in which he had envisaged it. Perhaps he had imagined something like a refectory, with Bernard Vanderlyn on a dais, and ranks of young geniuses—literary, artistic, or whatever—in files below. Mark's insistence that he was only one of a crowd may have prompted such a picture. But the occasion turned out to be domestic. The meal was served on the terrace, and besides himself there were only the Vanderlyns, Marion, Mark, and a middle-aged man called Andreas. Andreas was an architect, and he appeared to be engaged in building a hospital.

This disposition of things pointed sharply enough Gemma Vanderlyn's oddly abrupt intimation of her sense that Mark Varley was coming to occupy a special place in Vanderlyn's kingdom. It might almost be called the place of heir apparent. Or at least—Shefford added to himself as he glanced at Gemma now—of heir presumptive. But this notion could, of course, be delusory. Perhaps the *protégés* were summoned to a meal one or two at a time, like undergraduates obliged to go to tea with their tutors' wives in North Oxford. Andreas himself was identifiable as a *protégé*, if in an elderly way. His career hadn't been prospering, and Vanderlyn had taken him up. He had designed, for the government of some emerging African state in the neighbourhood of the equator, an entire capital city constructed mainly of glass. A good deal of air-conditioning had naturally been required, but this had never materialised—the funds for it having been appropriated by the Prime Minister for some private purpose. So a large number of people had died of heat-stroke, a fatality unusual among the natives of the continent. This had made it awkward for Andreas elsewhere.

115

Andreas himself was the source of this information, which he retailed to Shefford with an abundance of wit. It was a cynical wit, and of a hard-bitten rather than a merely flippant order. Shefford thought that it would be impossible to imagine Andreas in conversation with the first Mrs Vanderlyn, and he was surprised to find him living on terms of familiarity with her husband now. In fact, he disliked Andreas, although he hadn't known him for half-an-hour. Perhaps it was simply because the chap was outside his range. He talked perfect English, but you felt he might be of any nationality under the sun. He was small and dark, with a little clipped moustache, like the villain's in a movie; and his eyes were liquid and prominent in a fashion that seemed to clash disturbingly with his temperament. He was well-groomed to the last millimetre of fingernail, and as cold as a coelacanth, and his manners were those of an old, rather than a new, cosmopolitan society. Or so Shefford told himself. Certainly the man was mysterious to him— such types being of infrequent appearance in Oxford common rooms. But it seemed that he and Vanderlyn had been friends for many years.

The meal was a good one, although not in a grand way. The seafood promised by Vanderlyn was abundant; there were *dolmadakia* stuffed more cunningly than any Shefford had come across in restaurants; they drank *retsina* in noticeably temperate quantity. A hideous old woman whose name turned out to be Aphrodite presided over the service; she was in the nature, Shefford thought, of an indigenous showpiece, and assertive of a simplicity which wasn't entirely authentic to the establishment. There was a good deal of expert housemaiding, he felt, going on behind the scenes.

Vanderlyn inquired about Charles Blaine, and about the President, and even about Gavin Naylor. He certainly had the memory of a diplomat. He recalled the alarming conversation of the American boy named Peter Wright—and almost as if it had held some significance for him. But he also recalled the hunt for Jude Fawley's barn, and Shefford saw that he was going to show no disinclination to talk about his first wife. What he didn't refer to were the circumstances that had taken him out of American politics.

Marion Causland was less conversable. Applied to for an account of herself, she replied with downcast eyes that she studied sociology with a private tutor. Shefford wondered where this person was stowed away. And sometimes, she went on, when they spent some time in Athens, she audited a course at the university in order to improve her Greek. Shefford found this hard going, and had to tell himself that he wasn't good with girls, anyway. Marion certainly wasn't the dream-girl; a general dimness was the physical and superficial fact about her, although it was impossible to be confident that this went, as it were, all through. For a time he wondered whether, unlike her mother, she added intellect to earnestness, and was all set to be a sociologist in a high-powered way. But in that event it was unlikely that she would be perched in this fashion on Tyros; she would now simply be on vacation from some place like Wellesley or Radcliffe. And the intensity in her—for there was an intensity—was perhaps not intellectual at all. In which case he didn't know what it was. It seemed to him that she overdid a routine of flushing faintly and obstinately studying her plate when spoken to. 'Shamefast' was the old bookish word for that sort of thing. It could be sexually exciting, he supposed, but he didn't find it excited him. And it certainly didn't excite Mark, who sometimes ignored Marion and sometimes was too attentive to her, as if she were a neglected guest at a party in a strange house. Shefford wondered, as he often did in fresh company, how uncertain his own manners were. As they now stood, he supposed, they would remain.

Shefford's drift into self-consciousness made him awkward with Gemma, who had returned to her distancing social chat. It was a faint discomfiture, but Vanderlyn noticed it. The flair was one that Shefford remembered in him. Now, at the end of the meal, he took Shefford for a moment by the arm as he suggested accompanying him on a stroll round the monastery.

117

Chapter 6

'I HOPE YOU can stay for two or three days, at least,' Vanderlyn said, as soon as they were alone. 'I want you to see everything—not that there's all that to see; and I wouldn't have
you think we're trying to operate on a grand scale. I want your
criticisms. I know I'm likely enough to be making errors,
I want to get past that stage. It's already more than a year
that I've been on the project. So the time's running out in
which I can plead the baby act.' His smile showed that it
was consciously he produced this mysterious expression.
'And I haven't all that time, absolutely. I won't name the
birthday that's ahead of me. But it's a bleak promontory.'

Shefford was surprised and a little flattered. Although
not portentous, this had been an appeal, and he knew that
he was committed to taking a straight look at Tyros and
speaking the truth as he saw it. He wanted to start by
saying something like, 'At least, you got quickly off the
mark'. But that might be too abrupt a truth to begin with.
It could refer to the speed with which Vanderlyn had
switched from a public to a private sphere of activity. But
it could also—which wouldn't do at all—refer to his rather
rapid acquisition of Gemma. About that, Shefford had a
feeling that something would sooner or later be said by
somebody.

'You see,' Vanderlyn went on—and it was as if he had
in part read Shefford's mind—'Louise and I planned this
together. But it was in the last months of her life. She had
her condition, and the truth was known to us.' He paused,
and continued for some moments in silence. He had led
the way to a shaded walk at some distance from the main
building. Here and there this had been cut through rock,
and there was the sound of water trickling sparely down
hidden channels; beneath small overhangs dark purple
shadows swam, and within them a few irises, a darker purple
still, hovered like the last exhalations of spring. 'It wasn't

wholly uninfluenced, I should say, by the visit to your college, and one or two impressions I gathered then. Which is why, no doubt, I speak to you in this way—and have the "cheek", as I think you'd say, to call you Jeremy. Of course I know that you're not really Mark's contemporary. You're his senior—or you were, on that night.'

'That was all rot—and of course you must call me Jeremy.' Shefford wasn't happy at Vanderlyn's making a business of this small matter. He had seen that Mark Varley was a young man not at ease with himself. But Bernard Vanderlyn had come to exist in his mind almost as the type of masculine maturity and clarity of purpose; he would be disturbed if he found himself stumbling on ground upon which even the narrowest cracks in this image were perceptible. But any apprehensiveness of this sort vanished as it came. Vanderlyn had lightly sketched a reason for giving Shefford his confidence; and he now continued seriously.

'You probably know how it started. I lost my job.'

'Were you in a position just to lose a job?'

'Well, I ceased to see eye to eye with more powerful men. I might have gone into opposition, as you'd say; and we talked about doing that. Do you remember my saying something to you—in your car, I think—about staying in a fight? I thought about that, and I can conscientiously say it didn't seem the answer. It might have been the answer from the point of view of my own private conscience. But it wasn't the answer, as soon as you took a wider view. Too many people horsing round with their own delicate consciences already.'

Shefford was silent. He couldn't have said that this was clear to him. But he had a momentary vision of the first Mrs Vanderlyn in conference with her husband during the crisis, and he had no notion that it all hadn't been very much a matter of integrity.

'So it was fresh woods and pastures new. And really that. We were both involved, as you know, with education projects. But, with us, it's hard to disentangle these from other things. What would you say Mandarin Chinese is?'

'Mandarin Chinese?' The sense of this eluded Shefford.

'It might be defined as what we started a crash programme in at the time of Korea. The Korea of the man with the guard dogs in his truck.'

'Tyros is a long way from all that.'

'I wouldn't deny the geographical fact. It's too early to say whether certain small islands—metaphorically, you know, but perhaps geographically too—may have a part in preserving a few things through rather desperate times.'

'I think they well may,' Shefford said. He looked at Vanderlyn soberly—for he was seeing him for what, of course, he'd always been: a man who had been constrained to look hard at very frightening things. He even wondered for a moment whether the Tyros project included the digging of deep shelters and the stocking up of uncontaminated food. But this was a fantastic idea, although Vanderlyn's next words might have been taken as not wholly discounting it.

'Perhaps it's only a dream,' he said, 'the notion of preserving, in mere enclaves, a few traditional values of one sort or another. Or perhaps it's a dream that *could* be actualised, but I'm not the right man for the job. One thing's clear: one can only begin in a practical and concrete way—helping this or that actual achievement in art or learning or whatever into being, and then into notice.' Vanderlyn had now turned aside from the path, and was pointing up a steep and stony hillside. 'Can you manage a climb?' he asked.

'Yes, of course.' Shefford remembered how, on his first meeting with the Vanderlyns, he had wanted to discover whether they retained the ability to walk. It was evident that Bernard Vanderlyn did so still.

'Fine. I want you to see the hospital, if only from a distance. It represents one side of what I'd like to do. On the one hand, I want to see my friends on Tyros on a world standard; creating this and that which will be fit to carry wherever culture *is* carried.'

'High culture?'

'That's it.' Vanderlyn's nod showed that he recalled the reference. 'Even things obscurely sited on this small island I want to be like that. For example, I want this general hospital to rank that way. Tyros and this whole group of islands need it badly enough, Lord knows. But I want it to be so that a well-informed man can come from Tokyo or Baltimore, and say at once: "That's efficient—and it's beautiful as well". I want other things to be at that level too. Otherwise, it won't be much of a torch that we light here.'

'I see that.'

'But there's another side to the thing. We have to please ourselves and each other, right here. And not with our second best.'

'I see,' Shefford said—and paused to make sure that he *had* seen. 'You want a small society that will be centripetal as well as the other thing—prepared to apply its best energies to creating itself.'

'Yes.'

'I'd suppose that might be the hard part, really. Plenty of talented people will be ready to come along, and even to do a certain amount of singing for their supper.' Shefford saw no point in not getting down to this. 'You pay—and they'll be sympathetic and co-operative and amusing. But they'll be more likely to have both eyes on that world standard—in the sense of making themselves an international reputation, I mean—than just one eye. People have tried constructing small ideal societies, or even just small sensible societies, often enough. The successes haven't been numerous.'

'Sure,' Vanderlyn said briefly. He had been climbing steadily, and if he paused now it seemed not to recover breath, but to study a crested and brightly plumaged bird which had dropped to a boulder a little way ahead of them.

'One has to be prepared for anything,' he said. 'Do you know about that bird?'

'No, nothing at all.'

'It's a hoopoe. You couldn't have anything more brilliant, but its habits are disgusting. Plenty of what you call talented people incline that way. I won't complain if some of these folk show up as venal, or positively treacherous. But even those that are no more than a shade too self-interested may turn out to be a minority, after all. Anyway, one can but live in hope.'

'Yes,' Shefford said again, and reflected that Vanderlyn was far from being a man unread in human nature. 'It's a handsome bird.' He was looking without much attention at the disgusting hoopoe. 'By the way, where *are* all these folk? Mark said he was one of a crowd. But the crowd doesn't seem to be on parade.'

'We're not an army.' Vanderlyn seemed amused. 'And that's the next thing I wanted to say. It would be foolish to aim at anything rigid, or to begin fancying oneself as a commander-in-chief. You remember those little Italian courts we talked about that night? Nothing like that. Nobody needs to come in and make a deep bow, you know. Of course, there are times when people like these need pulling up, or at least having a line laid down for them. There are occasions when it's no kindness to an artist not to tell him outright he'd better get next to himself.'

'I see.' Shefford found food for thought in this glimpse of a Vanderlyn who hadn't come his way before. 'You might say they're here on a loose rein.'

'I guess so.' Vanderlyn sounded humorously surprised at having to agree to this. 'As for where they all are—well, we've managed to get up a few little villas or chalets here and there, and there will be a few more when the hospital's finished. You'll come across one or two as we walk around. I lend them out—and with services and catering and so on provided as unobtrusively as may be. We have a common table at the monastery every night, and people come along or stay away as they feel inclined. Sometimes there's a lot of talk and music and the rest of it, and sometimes not. There are people who don't show up for weeks on end—and good luck to them, if they behave.'

'But Mark Varley lives with you?'

'Yes.' Vanderlyn seemed to attach no special significance to this. 'It just happened that way—his becoming part of our own household. Gemma is fond of him. And, of course, he's very young still. He has a great future, I guess.' Vanderlyn made his prediction quietly—almost more quietly than Shefford, somehow, cared for.

'There will be a bit of a gathering this evening?'

'There's sure to be. Although, lately, the hospital by day has been almost as much a centre as the monastery by night. We've arrived at the stage where a certain amount of painting and carving is going on. So most people are interested, and I myself have a lot to give decisions about. Well, there it is.'

They had reached the brow of the hill, and a further stretch of Tyros was revealed. As always, there was the encompassing sea, but this time other islands were scattered over its surface. The nearer of these were tiny; farther off, others of greater size faintly glinted, like time-dimmed silver coins thrown down by a giant hand. Immediately beneath them was another fishing village, a good deal smaller than Trianta, like a suburb of the monastery. Beyond this lay a sickle of sand, with at one end of it a jetty which seemed in process of being turned from a temporary to a permanent structure; a faint rumbling and clanking floated up from activities going on there. Beyond this again sprawled a group of hutments apparently run up to house workmen. Behind these, and in the middle of plantations still too rudimentary to screen it from view, stood the hospital. Only—Shefford thought—it couldn't very well be thought of as standing, nor quite as floating either. For the moment its architecture eluded him, and he saw it rather as a sea-bird, caught and held immobile at the moment of touching earth, its wings half-folded with perfect grace.

'Good Lord!' Shefford said. 'Was that designed by that chap Andreas?'

'It certainly was—and why not?' There was nothing

challenging in Vanderlyn's question; it held only the mingling of amusement and warmth that was frequently so attractive in him.

'I'm sure I don't know.' Shefford was a little at a loss. 'Perhaps after his story about that African capital, or perhaps because of some impression of his character——'

'You wouldn't have expected so sensitive and beautiful a thing? I don't think that I should, if I hadn't known Anton Andreas for a long time. But that's the devil about creative folk, Jeremy. You just never *know*, and they're perpetually surprising you. And themselves too, of course —which is why they sometimes need thinking for and acting about, if they're not to be all over the place. I'm learning, you see—although you probably feel I'm too old to get far. As for Anton's character—well, he's the Jaques in this Arden.'

'Shakespeare's Jaques isn't just melancholy and disillusioned. He's rather sinister and corrosive.'

'You're the authority there. I wouldn't call Anton these things. But he's good at the disenchanted view—and so a valuable man to have around.'

'But one of that kind's enough—so I needn't compete.' For some moments Shefford gazed down at the hospital in silence. 'What are you going to call it?' he asked.

'The Louise Vanderlyn Memorial Hospital.'

'Yes—of course,' Shefford murmured, and was silent again. It went without saying that the hospital would be technically tiptop one day: money and a practiced executive drive were all that was needed to secure that. But already, and regardless of whatever painting and carving was yet to do, it was a building to which, for a mark, only the clearest alpha could be given. Its creator—it came to Shefford— however disagreeable, had authority. He turned to Vanderlyn. 'What does Andreas think of Mark?'

'He likes him, I'm sure. Anton has more power of liking people than you'd guess.'

'I don't mean that. What does he think of Mark as a poet?'

'That's another matter. He thinks—I rather gather he thinks—that as a poet Mark will never reach third base.'

For a moment Shefford failed to interpret this. What came to him was the thought that Bernard Vanderlyn, once in the immediate *entourage* of a President, was an expatriate now. It was a condition which, quite unconsciously, he had begun to compensate for. Rather as with his second wife, the daughter of a Greek Ambassador at Washington, his idiom was ceasing to be quite natural. It was as if, every now and then, he took a dip into a dictionary, and produced authentic Americanisms which were yet not—one faintly sensed—appropriate to his character and class. But this was a finical thought—and the sense of Vanderlyn's report didn't really take more than an instant to get clear.

'Would you say,' Shefford asked, 'that Andreas has told Mark himself that that's how he feels?'

'I don't know, but I'd think it likely. No harm in it. There are plenty to believe in Mark. And he's tough, as you've probably discovered.'

Shefford was silent again. He doubted whether there were really all that many people who would stand up to be counted on Mark Varley's behalf; and that Mark was tough wasn't yet, at least, one of his discoveries. He recalled in perplexity his strong persuasion that Vanderlyn was highly perceptive in the matter of young men's feelings and dispositions. He must be a good deal more involved with Mark than he allowed to appear, and the involvement must be of a kind by which blind spots and misreadings can be generated. And it was probably true that, consciously or unconsciously, he was in search of a son. Even his quick response to Shefford himself, his pleasure at his having turned up on Tyros, was not without its shade of something like that. He had, of course, his stepdaughter, and it could be seen that he was devoted to her. Marion's likeness to her mother must represent a constant mingling of pleasure and pain to him. A son, his own son by Louise, would have been something entirely different.

From down by the sea there came a series of small explosions, and like fragments tossed up from some misdirected blast in a marble quarry a flock of gulls rose and wheeled in air. Nobody was shooting at them; the sound had been of an engine firing in an irregular start; a bright red *camion* appeared from behind the jetty and began to trace a zigzag course up to the hospital. Shefford watched it misdoubtingly. In a rather large and imaginative sense, no better site could be conceived of as a place of healing. The prospect from its windows and wide verandahs would be like a perpetual 'get well' card perched before the noses of patients inclined to wonder whether the struggle to hold on to earth's tangible and visible surfaces was worth while. Yet it was oddly remote, and one wondered, after all, about the practical problems it must involve. Vanderlyn was naming this particular venture aptly. It seemed to hold a distinguishable affinity with Schools Afloat; indeed, it was almost a Hospital Afloat. Perhaps it had actually been among the first Mrs Vanderlyn's last idealisms.

'I don't mean that there isn't a certain instability in Mark,' Vanderlyn was saying—again with that touch of extra quietness. 'He has his moods—bad moods, he calls them— and sometimes they last too long. But it's often a penalty that has to be paid, I guess, for the power to achieve what he's going to achieve one day.'

'He needs roots, I think.' Shefford paused to work out what he meant by this. Perhaps he meant nothing at all. His acquaintance with Mark Varley was absurdly short as a basis for making pronouncements on. 'This is marvellous and enchanting, of course. And you're handing him illimitable opportunity——'

'I'm getting an old man, as I said. But he'll never have to wonder about his next dinner. I've fixed all that.'

'I don't know whether that's a good idea, or not—if you mean a kind of endowing Mark for life. But I can see you'd feel you had to. You've transplanted him, haven't you? It can only be called that. And it's my point, rather.' Shefford hesitated, and found Vanderlyn gravely attentive. 'It's not

126

as if he'd been any sort of privileged boy, accustomed to money, travel, a wide society. All he's known is a narrow home—narrower, I suspect, than my own was; and mine couldn't be called spacious. Just that, and then—out of the blue—three months in prison. He has no roots in any sort of command of things, such as comes naturally to you. I'll bet he sometimes desperately wants those he *did* have: the reading room of the public library in some shocking industrial town, a ninepenny seat at the cinema when there happened to be a good film, being taken by an elder brother to see boxing or all-in wrestling, the cake his mother made for Sundays: a host of humble things. If he's to be a poet, it's these things he has to be the poet of.'

'Keats wasn't the poet of the livery stables, was he? Or, for that matter, Shelley exactly the poet of a landed gentry?'

'All right. I express it badly. He just mustn't feel a kind of chasm between all that and his present life. You've done a wonderful thing for him. But his path isn't easy.' Shefford fell abruptly silent. He was rather staggered at having held forth in this way.

'Tyros is certainly an unfamiliar scene to Mark—and I'm afraid we'll never have a movie house on the island, although we might rise to a public library.' Vanderlyn frowned, as if disliking having stumbled on this tone. 'I'm grateful to you for what you've said. It reinforces a thought or two in my own mind. I needn't tell you that Mark isn't here simply because of having gotten into trouble. We have one or two on that straight ticket, but Mark isn't one of them. Still he *did* get into trouble, and it might happen again. It might happen because he felt rootless just as you say. Well, roots must just be found for him, I guess. Does that sound crazy?'

'No, it's what I'm saying. But it's a ticklish sort of horticultural operation.'

'Roots stabilize and nourish. Perhaps something can be done, if one thinks of it that way. Not that Mark's a desperate case. He likes us, I'd say, and is getting attached to

127

Gemma. It's pleasant for her too. After all, he's nearer to her in age than I am.'

Shefford didn't know quite what to make of this last reflection. For one thing, its only truth appeared to be of an order merely chronological. Gemma was certainly much younger than her husband. But they were mature people together, whereas of Mark Varley it could surely be said that he was still busy growing up. Physically, of course, Gemma couldn't yet be called middle-aged and Mark must be described as fully adult. It didn't seem a bond to make much of.

'And Mark's book is coming out,' Vanderlyn said, 'as I'll be surprised if he hasn't told you. Seeing his verse between hard covers should give him confidence.'

'I hope so. It might depend—mightn't it?—on how it's reviewed. And it's tricky with verse. So little is said about it anyway—just half-an-inch here and half-an-inch there—that two or three disagreeable sentences can sound like universal execration.'

'You have a point there.' Vanderlyn looked thoughtful. 'But he has other plans going ahead, you know. He won't let himself be snuffed out by a half-inch article. Shall we walk down the hill again? Mark can't really be called one of a crowd, although he seems to have told you he is. Still, he's not the only pebble on our beach, and there are some other people I'd like you to meet.'

Chapter 7

SHEFFORD SPENT THE rest of the day, and some part of the night, in meeting people. A few were remarkable, but he was later to find that he carried away only a general impression of them, all the same. The citizens of Vanderlyn's kingdom, if indeed they weren't a crowd or an army, were undeniably numerous, and it would have taken leisure to sort them out. As had seemed likely, Vanderlyn's idea of doing things on a moderate scale was conditioned by the general largeness of his background. Probably he didn't think of a venture as of anything but the most modest scope so long as he himself could keep some control of the detail of it.

There were one or two people as young as Mark Varley, or nearly so, but the mean age of the community was rather higher than one might have expected. No doubt Vanderlyn's notion of a world standard was operative here, and a man was to be regarded as young, unknown, and worthy of support so long as he hadn't made such a grade. Even so, there were several people whose names were already familiar to Shefford: two *avant-garde* painters from New York, a young Czech playwright, a late-starting but now well-known English novelist. Behind this set-up one sensed what might perhaps be called a campus prototype: something like a graduate school with eminent visiting persons to associate with and learn from. Certainly in the world of literature and the arts Vanderlyn wasn't baby-snatching. Everybody had got to a stage at which they had, one might say, some sort of diploma to exhibit: a book published, a play or a musical composition performed, a one-man show held. Mark's forthcoming volume would put him in this bracket.

Meanwhile, Mark must be regarded as the tiro of the outfit. Andreas, in fact, called him that: the tiro of Tyros. Shefford thought poorly of this, which sounded like a gibe; but if there was much wrong with the position in itself it lay only in the rather steep pitch of the expectations that Mark had to cope with. Ultimately this must stem from Vanderlyn himself; and Shefford more than once came back to the thought that there was something rash about it. Yet Vanderlyn—so highly intelligent as he must be to have held down the position he did—couldn't but be aware of a danger. Indeed, it seemed apparent that he did—for his hopes of Mark as expressed in confidence to Shefford remained unechoed in anything he said in company. Among his guests—if that was what they were to be called—he accorded Mark no more than a sensible man would accord a member of his family whom he privately hoped to see gain high distinction. So if a disposition to treat Mark as a prodigy was distinguishably abroad it must have percolated from Vanderlyn only through subterraneous and elusive channels. In any case, there was no more than a breath of it. Purposeful people moving through or towards a first artistic maturity were not, fortunately, going to sit gazing at a boy recently down from Oxford, or much to generate the notion that he was a problem of any sort.

The purposefulness made for substance and interest. Dinner when it came—what Vanderlyn had called his common table—wasn't without a touch of formality, so that Shefford even saw why he had been given an early hint of the need to borrow a few clothes. And the long evening that followed it, although it was sometimes disputatious and sometimes gay and boisterous, didn't suggest the Bohemian society of a literary and artistic sort into which he had occasionally dipped in London. There was a basic gravity, a regard for poise, such as really hinted, he thought, Urbino's windy hill.

Vanderlyn's presence was the determining factor here. However little he would have admitted to seeing himself as a patron in the grand tradition, he moved about with an alert courtesy which became him; and if he was attended to it was because he himself had so perfectly the faculty of attention. It was a faculty which had been trained in other fields; and now he had discovered how to bring it into play upon things he had a natural flair for. There was, perhaps, no more to it than that; but even that removed him a long way from the condition of being a benevolently perambulating cheque-book.

'And what is your conclusion, Mr Shefford, on my old friend?'

It was late, and people were drifting away, presumably to those villas and chalets which were all more or less within walking distance of the monastery. Shefford was standing by himself in the ancient refectory which now served as an enormous drawing-room when Andreas came up and murmured this question. It seemed to carry the implication that Shefford had been eyeing Vanderlyn in too considering a way, and he reacted to it stiffly.

'I hardly think a spot judgement on my host is called for. And, anyway, I've enjoyed myself too much for anything of the sort.'

'An admirably discreet reply, my dear young man. But don't think that I am drawing you into a corner to laugh at Bernard. Nor even to weep for him. He requires no sympathy as yet.'

'I'm not sure that I know what you mean.' Shefford found that he didn't want simply to snub Andreas. 'Is he more likely to need it, one day, than you are, or I am?'

'Of course. He is larger and stronger than either of us.'

'But isn't sympathy something we chiefly keep on tap for the small and weak—for a kind of deserving poor?'

'I am sure that you are perfectly right. I have a very poor command of language, and fail to express myself well. Lines and masses, textures and the strength of materials: it is in these I can communicate. Incidentally, I ought to say that it is on a regular professional basis that I have placed my poor command of them at Bernard's service. I will not deny that he has been kind to me. I am a poor devil, and he has. Still, I have designed him a hospital, and he has signed me a cheque. On Tyros, my dear Shefford, you and I are almost unique. We are not Bernard's clients, if that is the word. It is because he has so lavishly equipped himself with persons in that general category that I think he may stand in need of sympathy—support would no doubt be a more masculine word—one day.'

'Perhaps so.' Shefford found that he wasn't liking Andreas any more than he had at their lunch-time encounter. A fellow of indeterminate nationality who could speak English in this way and at the same time natter about a poor command of language seemed to him a tedious proposition. At the same time he felt that Andreas had too much ability

131

to go on talking idly for long. 'I think,' he said, 'that
Vanderlyn has taken on a stiff assignment. But probably
he's done that before. You're an old friend of his. You ought
to know.'

'Is it your habit to drink a little whisky at this hour?
Bernard's is on the table at the other end of the room—
and there is even that pretty child Vangelio, still on duty
and waiting to pour it out for you. But if you can resist
her charms, come with me and drink some of mine.'

'Thank you very much.' Shefford hadn't warmed to this
reference to Vangelio's charms. He thought it vulgar. But
one oughtn't to go round feeling that chaps are not to be
touched with barge-poles—particularly if God has revealed
to one the endless uses of curiosity. 'Shall I say goodnight
to Gemma first? I suppose that would be the thing.'

'I suppose it would. The "thing" is never revealed more
absolutely, I have observed, than to those in whom it is not
quite native.' Andreas delivered himself of this urbane
insult—for it couldn't be called anything else—with the
utmost sweetness of air. 'Yet not invariably so. Our Mark
has no command of the "thing" whatever. And yet'—
Andreas shrugged his shoulders—'*c'est un déclassé, n'est-pas?*'

'We're both jumped-up characters—Mark Varley and I.'
Shefford was trying not to look too astonished. 'If I may
say so, you have a very odd notion of after-dinner conversation.'

'It enables me to tell whether my interlocutor—a hard
English word, Shefford—has the toughness of mind which
alone is agreeable to me. It is something which, despite
your youth, I am disposed to think you possess. Let us go
upstairs.'

They went upstairs. Shefford felt that he could take up to
half-an-hour of talk in this intolerable strain of affectation.
And there were things he wanted to know about Vanderlyn
which he thought Andreas might be able to tell him.

The quarters into which he was led were a surprise. They
must have been chosen by Andreas himself, for they were
remote from the modernised parts of the building, and

devoid of the amenities lavishly built in there. This was a single low and extravagantly long room, roughly plastered, which changed its character as you moved from one end to the other. It began as a drawing office on a substantial scale, as if Andreas had been accustomed to have assistants working there. Then there was the effect of a sitting-room, plainly furnished. Beyond this, surprisingly, were the appurtenances of a small gymnasium. Finally there was a bedroom area, less simple than positively Spartan. The total effect suggested that mediaeval form of staging in which the actors could indicate a change of locality simply by walking from one set of props to another. It made Shefford feel that he hadn't got Andreas in focus at all, since such a *mise en scène* seemed incongruous with so smooth and cosmopolitan a character. But he wasn't terribly interested in Andreas. It was other people he wanted to know about.

'Will malt whisky be all right?' Andreas asked. 'There's bourbon, if you prefer it.'

'Malt, please.'

'I mustn't ask you again what you think of Bernard.' Andreas handed Shefford a glass. 'But at least I can inquire what you think of his venture. Is it what you expected it to be?'

'I didn't expect anything. I'd never heard of it until I ran into Mark Varley by chance this morning. It seems much as he described it—except that I'd have expected rather more people of about his own age.'

'Heaven forbid. Nothing is more boring, surely, than a congregation of the young. I venture to say this, my dear Shefford, since it is evident that you are yourself so courageously advancing upon middle life.'

As this seemed a good long way from being worth framing a reply to, Shefford was silent. It couldn't be conjectured that Andreas had chosen the wrong profession; his creation on the other side of the hill rendered that untenable. But circumstances seemed to have made him an unsuccessful man as well as an unhappy one. Perhaps he was to be explained, Shefford told himself, along these lines.

'Although, to my mind, more young people might be good for the health of the venture. Bernard has a very considerable power of creating personal loyalty. And I suspect that he has carried over into this new way of life on Tyros rather more impulse to direct and even command than he's quite willing should appear. Leopards don't change their spots, you know, and men accustomed to immense authority will never quite lose the impulse to exercise it. So it might be with younger and more malleable people, I say, that something coherent and rather permanent might best be built up. Don't you think?' Andreas was now looking at Shefford quite seriously. 'As it is, the enterprise is likely to turn ragged and disintegrate. The money won't run out, I may say. If you are at all thinking of—adhering, shall I call it?—I can assure you of that.'

'Thank you, but I haven't the slightest notion of adhering. You think these people will drift away?'

'Yes. Others will come. There could never be a question of any shortage of names to inscribe in the pay-roll. But Bernard is a purposeful and courageous man. If the essential idea failed, I think he would call it a day.' Andreas paused. 'What concerns me is the domestic background against which this will happen, if it does happen. His domestic background, past as well as present.'

'I'm not sure that I know what you mean by that.'

'Bernard is convinced that it was his first wife who, in a fashion, launched this venture. She was rather given to launching things in an almost literal sense. She had a project——'

'I know. Schools Afloat.'

'You know more about Louise than I had supposed. If Tyros runs aground—supposing an island can do that— Bernard may feel that it is Louise's argosy that he has brought to grief. I see I preserve my metaphor.'

'Did the first Mrs Vanderlyn project just this?'

'Well, no. I gather that Louise was somehow drawn to do some reading, in Renaissance courtesy-books and the like, which one might remotely hitch on to what we may call the Tyros-image. But her mind was well set in the groove of the lecture-room and the seminar. A Study Centre would have been the conception natural to her. Still, broadly speaking, Bernard is carrying on something that Louise saw. And the break with America was certainly her determination. After the political rumpus—I don't know whether you've learnt about that—she decided on it. Not permanently, perhaps. But for a period of years. Whether she was right or not, I shouldn't like to say.'

'You speak as if she was very much the directing partner.'

'In matters of this sort, yes. But Bernard has a far bolder mind. I conceive that Louise would be a little astonished, could she come alive on Tyros today.'

'Would she be astonished at the second marriage?' Shefford had hesitated before asking this question. It sounded like an invitation to gossip. At the same time he was coming to a perception that beneath the cynicism of Andreas's manner there lay a genuine concern for Bernard Vanderlyn.

'Dear me, no. Louise pretty well arranged it.'

'Arranged it!'

'My dear young man, there is nothing uncommon about that. Good wives—and Louise was a good wife—often urge such a course upon their death-beds. Very sensibly, I should say—so far as marriage is at all intelligible to me. If they are wise, however, they are perhaps not too urgent in positively nominating an individual.'

'You mean that Louise nominated Gemma?'

'I have little doubt of it.' Andreas reached for the whisky and set it down beside Shefford. 'Do you want me to tell you these people's story?'

Chapter 8

'I HAVE SOMETIMES wondered about them.' Shefford had hesitated again, but now plunged on. 'When I met them—

135

it wasn't much more than a couple of years ago—I remember asking myself whether, conceivably, they were on something like their honeymoon.'

'You fascinate me.' Andreas set down his glass abruptly and looked at Shefford in what seemed real astonishment. 'Have you confided to Bernard since that this was the thought that visited you?'

'Of course not. It would be grossly impertinent.'

'So it would. How well Oxford has provided you with all the proper responses! A pity, all the same. When you met them, Bernard and Louise would have been married —let me see—yes, eighteen years. He would be sixty—I have a faculty for figures, Shefford—and she, therefore, would be fifty-five. Their honeymoon—yes. Perhaps you are a most perceptive young man. For who knows that they weren't coming round to it?'

Shefford had an impulse to get to his feet and go away. He ought not to be creeping off to a fellow-guest's room and picking up information on the intimate life of his host in this fashion. And particularly from Andreas, who seemed to give everything he touched a lick with the same ugly brush. Yet he still wasn't certain that he was being fair to Andreas. The ugliness was perhaps no more than a protective mannerism. And there was never anything wrong in knowing about people; the wrongness only came in using the knowledge ill. Having thus tentatively adjusted his conscience to his situation, Shefford sipped his whisky and sat back again.

'You must understand, Shefford, that I knew Louise even before I knew Bernard. When people want to be disagreeable about me—and I am aware they sometimes do—they say that I have a *penchant* for the best people, whether on one side of the Atlantic or the other. Louise's people were certainly that. They exuded the smell of the *Mayflower's* hard-tack, and more than one of her ancestors had been a Signer. All that.'

'A Signer?' Shefford had never heard this word. 'Is that a member of some fanatical religious sect?'

'One of the fifty-six signatories—again you see that figures are at my command—to the Declaration of Independence. Incidentally, you might say that a good deal of the independence had rubbed off on Louise herself. She was a most intransigent young woman. But then she had to be, for her parents were exceptionally conservative—reactionary, rather —in their attitude to the education of women. Louise, who was determined, poor child, to secure the blessings of learning, had to walk out on them, and they then behaved very badly. They didn't let her have a cent. In point of fact, she was an heiress, bound to come into a fortune one day, and even before she was of age she could have raised money without difficulty. Nor can she have remained ignorant of how to set about it. There would have been plenty of interested parties to tell her.'

'She was a woman of principle, I imagine. One could see that straight away.' Shefford said this firmly. 'I met her only once, but I admired her very much.'

'I'm delighted to hear it. Well, Louise set out on her own. At the start, it involved teaching school—and at that time, at least, teaching school was very much at the bottom of a ladder. Later on, she managed to attend some gargantuan institution of the higher education in New York. Columbia University, I suppose it must have been. I used to see her occasionally at that time. She shared with a fellow blue-stocking a high walk-up. Think of that! You know New York, of course.'

'No, I don't.'

'You astonish me. Don't all Oxford dons—do I use the word correctly?—keep dodging in and out of the United States? But that is by the way. Here is Louise, battling her way in the world—or, at least, in the world of learning. And, in recalling her at that time, I would chiefly sound the note of utter inexperience.' Andreas paused. He might have been admiring the phrase he had just struck out.

'What you do mean—inexperience?'

'Well, say that she had not read the ingenious Dr Kinsey's reports. Not, of course, that their riches were then available.

'I don't see that a woman need be called inexperienced just because she hasn't read a lot of stuff like that.'

'No, no—but we must not be of a literal mind. Will you take a little more whisky? It's beside you.'

'No, thank you.'

'I don't know whether Louise ever took time off for affairs of the heart. Probably not. And, if she did, they would have been of the chastest sort. And now I am in a difficulty. Mine, as you can see, is a celibate life, and you must forgive me if I speak inexpertly. I come to unknown ground.'

Andreas, Shefford decided, was certainly not an agreeable man. But it would be stupid to interrupt his narrative now.

'She must have been thirty-three or thirty-four, and teaching in some sadly undistinguished college, when she met Victor Causland.'

'That girl's father? Marion's?'

'Yes, indeed. And they were married within a month or two. She had, shall we say, nobody much to advise her. The child—this Marion—must have been conceived on the wedding night.'

'You mean the chap died?' Shefford looked at Andreas in horror.

'No, no. You must not associate death and the act of sex to that extent, my dear young man. Causland proved impossible. Simply that.'

'Impossible simply in what——?'

'Precisely. It can't, I think, have been merely that he had odd ideas in his head. He must have been pathologically brutal as well. And Louise was innocent, as I have said; she had nothing by which to measure her bridal night. The consequence—psychological, psychosexual—was what they call a trauma. And she had a child in the womb.'

'I've heard of girls made pregnant as a result of rape,' Shefford said slowly. 'It wasn't unlike that.'

'Yes, yes. But now there is a good word to be said for Louise's parents, I am glad to say. They were elderly, but they did pile in. Do I get the expression right?' Andreas waited in vain for a moment to have this linguistic point settled. 'They saw to it that the divorce went through within a week of the child's birth. And Causland, as it happened, was killed in an aeroplane crash only a few months later. Louise had to make a new start. She made it with Bernard Vanderlyn in 1947. He was forty-three, and hadn't been married before.' Andreas paused. 'It was an entirely suitable thing. They were near to one another in years, and Vanderlyn too came of what may be termed a patrician strain in American society. His mother's family, for example, had given three Governors to the State of Connecticut.'

'I see.' Shefford thought briefly of the Milwaukee Can Company. 'Well, that was fine. It all ended happily.'

'Ah! One would like to suppose so. But are we yet out of the wood? I am inclined to doubt it.'

'But they were devoted to each other!' Shefford was staring at Andreas in indignation. 'It was the first thing that struck me. There was a kind of intensity in their relationship. I suppose that was what put the funny idea of a honeymoon in my head.'

'Quite so. But was it a kind of intensity that at all set you thinking?'

Shefford was silent, recalling notions that had passed through his mind on the Ridgeway. And he felt again that it would be a good idea to break off this talk and go to bed. Since he had first become aware of Mark Varley that morning a great deal had been shoved at him about Tyros and its inhabitants. People he'd known only slightly, and people he hadn't known at all, had stacked themselves up in his consciousness, almost as if they were confirmed friends, properly demanding his largest concern. He looked round Andreas's strange room now. Some of the lights had been turned off, and in either direction it faded into mystery. He felt vulnerable in it, as if he were sitting in a Ghost Train that had come to a halt in a squalid sort of tunnel in a fun fair. He knew nothing about Andreas, except that twelve hours ago he had never set eyes on him. And here he was, joined with him in probing into other mysteries—tunnels, perhaps, concealing things that had nothing to do with him. He took up this last thought now.

'Look here,' he said, 'are you starting in to tell me things that Vanderlyn has confided to you as a very old friend? Because, if so——'

'Nothing of the kind. You must be aware that Bernard is a reticent man. It is all observation—observation and inference, my dear Shefford.'

'Does that really improve matters? Should you have grabbed me——'

'I'm not proposing idle gossip.' Andreas produced this with what seemed genuine contempt. 'It's my idea that we might usefully put our heads together.'

'I don't see how. I'll certainly be leaving Tyros quite soon. You mustn't regard me as being in on it at all.'

'*Tant mieux.* What I want to come to is the young man, your former student. I think you are concerned about him.'

'Mark Varley wasn't ever my student, and I had my first conversation with him only this morning.'

'But you like him, I think?' Andreas smiled faintly. 'And feel that there is quite an achievement in that, and that you would be glad to make it a basis of something?'

'That's true. There are things I'd like to help him disentangle, I believe. But I don't see the relevance——'

'In my view, the young man ought not to be here at all. But let me return to Bernard, and to his first marriage. We can take up Master Varley again, when we come to his second.' Andreas paused for a moment, but Shefford didn't speak. Whatever the oddity of what was being said he was resolved to hear it out without further interruption. 'Briefly,' Andreas went on, 'I suspect that Bernard's and Louise's relationship was in certain ways—well, lacking. Victor Causland had done his work well. To put it baldly, Louise never wanted to face a man in bed again.' Andreas produced a small, elegant gesture of resignation. '*Entendons-nous bien, mon ami! C'était un mariage blanc.*'

140

Shefford continued silent. For one thing, the French idiom was unfamiliar to him, and it took a second to work it out. Andreas looked at him speculatively, and then got to his feet, moved to a window, and closed a shutter. There was no chill breeze to exclude, for the night continued warm. Moths, if moths there were on Tyros, appeared un-attracted by Andreas's quarters; none were attempting to fly in. Andreas had employed this gesture by way of placing a small punctuation mark in the middle of this disagreeably developing conversation. When he sat down again, it was to continue it more simply and soberly than he had begun.

'You admired Louise, and in many ways you were right. When she married Bernard, she was still of an age at which she might have borne children——'

'But I don't think that can be right. I remember Vander-lyn telling me——' The interruption died on Shefford's lips. What he had recalled was the voice of Vanderlyn coming to him from the near-darkness of his own car, and saying: 'I have no children. Louise and I married just a little too late for it.' But now he was recalling, too, that some strange quality had attended the utterance of these words. The new and grim meaning they could take on in the context of Andreas's disclosure appalled him, so that he could hardly speak. 'Sorry,' he mumbled. 'I got something wrong. Please go on.'

'She might still have borne children. And she may well not have known how permanent was to be her inability to accept effective sexual experience—if my main conjecture is correct, that is to say. And consider another thing, Shef-ford. She would hardly *know* about sex, except as it had erupted into her life upon a single ghastly occasion. Its depth and urgency would come to her only dimly through books. She belonged to an age in which well brought up women understood that marriage had something called its "sexual side", which it was the business of a civilized couple to play down.'

'In 1947?' Shefford's historical sense was offended. 'I hardly think so. Still, perhaps the idea was still available for people who found it convenient. It may have validity, for all I know.'

'One does well to keep an open mind.' Andreas again spoke quite seriously. 'I am only saying—I am only leading up to the fact that—Louise would consider their childless condition the really serious thing, not their lack of mere sexual congress. And I'll grant you that *that* may have what you call validity too. So we come to Gemma, you see. It's my guess that Louise pretty well wrote Gemma into her will.' As if Shefford were about to interrupt, Andreas raised a staying hand. 'A mere figure of speech; I don't mean that she left Gemma money on condition she took Bernard on. I merely mean that she nominated her—it's your own word—more or less. She was a generous woman. She wanted Bernard, before it was too late, to have what he hadn't had.'

'Children?'

'Children, and whatever pleasure might, for a man, lie in begetting them—for she was a generous woman, as I have said.' Andreas paused for a moment. He had stretched out his arms in front of him, and appeared to be studying the backs of his hands. 'For would you not agree that Gemma is a wildly desirable physical object? I am quite an outsider—but it is my conjecture, for what it is worth.'

'I haven't got round to wildly desiring her myself.' Shefford was about to feel displeased by his own words when he realised that he hadn't intended them flippantly. 'She's extremely beautiful, but rather far from exploiting the fact. I'd say she sees to it that she doesn't have all and sundry tumbling rapidly at her feet. And that's only kindness to animals, really. I feel that if I *did* fall in love with Mrs Vanderlyn—well, I'd be a lost soul in no time.' Shefford paused, suddenly aware of what all this seemed to be leading to. 'Look here—you said that Mark Varley ought not to be on Tyros at all. Do you mean that he's going to make mischief by falling in love with Gemma? Is she going to have to choose between the helpless young poet and the reliable but unglamorous husband, like some woman or other in Bernard Shaw?'

For the first time, and rather surprisingly, Andreas laughed.

'My dear Shefford, not precisely that. In fact, not that at all. Not that I'd put it beyond your precious Mark to fancy making passes—is that right?—at his benefactor's wife. But, of course, he isn't *your* precious Mark. If anybody's he's Bernard's. That's my point. I don't mean anything shocking. A son in a hurry, a disturbing factor, a distraction. That's what Mark is.' Andreas made an impatient gesture. 'Take him away, Shefford. Take him back to Oxford and have them make him another young college tutor like yourself.'

'Mark lacks some technical qualifications there, I'm afraid.'

'Then have him made your Professor of Poetry. No qualifications are needed for *that*.'

'It's an idea.' This time it was Shefford who laughed. 'But isn't it a bit unscrupulous of you to suggest it? I gather you think Mark isn't going to be any sort of poet.'

'Nothing of the kind. But I don't think he's going to be a poet of anything like the size that Bernard has in his head. That's by the way. And you can see what I'm getting at. Look at Gemma's point of view.'

'She's going to be jealous and frustrated over her husband's feeling for Mark? Even do something rash about it?'

'That's a large and hard question. Moreover, she's rather a sealed book to me. She's made this marriage. I think she admires and respects Bernard. She's an artist of sorts, but I don't believe her music is a consuming passion with her. I'd say she has ordinary sensual desires and expectations, including children. She may even see her marriage as making sense chiefly in terms of them. We've decided that that was Louise's idea. The two ladies may even have had a death-bed chat about it.' Andreas paused. His smile seemed to acknowledge a consciousness of the disfavour with which Shefford received this return to his earlier tone. 'Seriously, she probably wants children.'

'She can have them, as far as I can see. Unless you're saying that Vanderlyn is impotent.'

'It's a possibility.' Andreas raised his averting hand. 'But once more we are on territory—are we not?—where we haven't much experience to help us. Begetting offspring seems easy. It's what comes naturally, as some vulgar song says. One sees it happening in the fields; one hears it happening in the next room in one's hotel. And stop thinking that I have a depraved mind, Shefford! I'm being very serious. I'm saying that it can be—simple procreative power can be—rather a subtle affair. Has Bernard at all spoken of himself to you as being an old man?'

'Yes, he has. It disconcerted me a little. What I thought of was that his having given up his public career—his position rather near the top, as it seems to have been— was a little betraying him into an attitude there. Perhaps it goes along with what you were saying about his new way of life here. He misses his former ability to control events, and perhaps even regrets his decision. So he tells himself that he's an old fellow anyway, and that it therefore doesn't matter greatly.'

'You are a satisfactory person to talk to.'

'Thank you very much.'

'Don't think I patronise you, my dear lad. I am merely saying that you can think on your feet. But to be relevant: it is an old man who seeks a son in a hurry—who is entitled to, one might say. But Bernard is barely past sixty. Think of the age to which the wealthy and abstinent and well cared for customarily survive today! He could live to see sons and daughters of his own—and of his wife's—making themselves careers of distinction, surrounded by his grandsons and granddaughters. Instead of which, we are to have your tiresome, talented, neurotic, injured and aggrieved little Mark. For goodness sake—my dear chap—take him right away!'

'I'd take him away if I could.' Shefford spoke soberly, for it seemed to him that Andreas's vehemence had been perfectly genuine. 'Not because of what you have in your mind: indeed, I can't say that your ideas are very clear to me. But if Mark is being expected to turn into somebody's notion of a World-Poet overnight—and I'm beginning to feel Vanderlyn *has* lost a sense of proportion about him— then the climate of Tyros is all wrong for him. All those rather older people I've been glimpsing are all wrong for him. But he won't *come* away. He'd see it as defeat. So we're talking to no purpose. I think, if you'll excuse me, I'll go to bed.'

Andreas rose instantly—and with a measure of apology so politely avoiding excess that Shefford's never very abundant stock of social assurance was shattered. He felt that he had been abrupt and rude.

'Look,' he said at the door, 'I do appreciate your trying to beat all this out with me. But I can't feel that there's a position that's anything like desperate. Isn't there room for Mark Varley as virtually an adopted son—without any number of real sons and daughters being affected? I happen to know that Gemma does already see him as becoming something of a son to Vanderlyn, and she doesn't seem outraged. It's not as if money were a factor.'

'It certainly isn't. *That* sort of birthright isn't in question. What's in my head—if you'll forgive me—is something rather deeper than anything of the sort. Are we sure there will *be* any real sons and daughters? Procreation's a subtle business, I must repeat. And Bernard has a long no-go marriage behind him. How does that affect a man—physically, Shefford? Can you even start imagining it? So what do we know about *this* marriage? What do we know about it in terms of the simple sort of knowledge we might gain by peering through the keyhole? Not that *that* might be definitive. It's subtle, I say, subtle! What if Bernard's thrown up the sponge—without even knowing it? What if—utterly unconsciously, even—he's told himself he's an old man, and not going to wait—but just get a ready-made son, an absorbing pride and joy, off the peg? Is it possible, Shefford, you have to *want* children, if you're to have them—when you'll never be sixty again? *Want* them—not just go through, if you *do* go through, the standard inseminating exercise? Do I shock you?'

'Drop that, Andreas, for Christ's sake! Of course not. Good night.' Shefford turned to go, and then halted. 'I say! There's somebody involved in all this—isn't there?— that we don't seem to think of. Marion. Marion Causland. Why haven't they changed her surname, by the way? It seems monstrous.'

'He was her father.'

'Yes. But what does she know about that father? What does she know about the whole story? They wouldn't pitch it at her. But was that divorce a scandal? Is she bound, somehow, to know?'

'The divorce was as discreet, I imagine, as wealth and legal skill could make it. But I can't answer your real question. How much the child knows, I simply don't know.'

'Oughtn't you to? You're Bernard Vanderlyn's close friend.'

'It's possible *he* doesn't know. A reticent man has reticence returned to him. Shall I see you to your room? No? Then, good night.'

Chapter 9

SHEFFORD WAS TO recall the greater part of the next morning as spent recovering from this nocturnal conference —from that, and from a sense of having been made, with an untoward suddenness, something more than a spectator in a totally strange scene. This feeling of involvement had little rational basis; there was nothing to support it except the passing appeal for action constituted by Andreas's asking him to take Mark Varley away. And that wasn't possible. He couldn't accept Andreas's interpretation of the situation—which was fantastic, after all—to the extent of interfering with Mark's and Vanderlyn's relationship. To speak to Mark in that sense—even if there lurked in Mark's own mind an impulse to beat it out of Tyros—would be interpreted as a lack of faith in him. And it wasn't as if he was a familiar friend of Mark's. It was true that he did almost *feel* that he was one. But you can't put much strain on a relationship that started up only twenty-four hours ago. The strength—as Andreas might say—just wasn't present in the materials.

Anyway, Mark had disappeared this morning. His main diversion, he had told Shefford, was 'taking one of the cars at a bit of a lick round the island'; the degree of danger this could be made to involve—he seemed to imply—was good for inspiration. Perhaps he was thus engaged now. He certainly didn't seem to feel any duty to tote Shefford about. Vanderlyn had gone off to his hospital, and the women weren't visible either. Shefford, who felt glad enough to be alone for a time, wasn't offended. Vanderlyn had handed him a pair of binoculars (he found himself wondering whether they were the same through which the first Mrs Vanderlyn had once vainly sought the Christminster of Jude Fawley) and he had slung them round his neck and wandered off, mildly curious about the topography of Tyros. In addition to Mark's speed-track circling the island, there were minor roads here and there, running either down to the sea or inland to homesteads and hamlets. And one, which looked particularly hazardous, climbed to the summit of Spina, a sizeable mountain round about which the whole island seemed to pivot. It was crowned by a little shrine, which Mark claimed he sometimes drove up to work in.

Tyros, Shefford realised, was even larger than he had supposed, so that Bernard Vanderlyn's position was that of the proprietor of a large estate supporting a scattered peasant population. He had his plans for these people too, it was clear; and he was no doubt as nearly a monarch as made no difference. Here and there there might be a *polismanos* —the weird word actually existed—but apart from that the King of the Hellenes didn't seem to have much concern with the place.

Shefford wandered through a little banana grove, and down to the shore. It was going to be hotter even than the day before, and he planned to find a spot where he could strip and get into the sea; it would be nice to lie naked on a rock afterwards and dry off in the sun. It wasn't like Italy, where in the remotest places solitude turns out not to exist, and there is never a landscape untouched by human movement.

Yet every now and then there were signs of human activity —abandoned, mostly. These islands must be depopulating themselves steadily, and Vanderlyn had his work cut out if he was going to make of one of them a viable proposition so far as an indigenous population was concerned. Here and there one came upon a ruined fisherman's hut, or a tumble-down stony fold once used, presumably, for herding goats. And now he was scrambling along the top of a broken sea-wall whose ancient function it would be hard to guess at. Suddenly he saw that he wasn't, after all, alone. Almost directly below him, a man lay on his stomach on the sand, with a litter of papers under his nose. He was small and emaciated, with a reddish beard, and beside him—ready to put on when it grew too hot—lay a battered straw hat. It was D. H. Lawrence, Shefford told himself idly. Or at least it was one of Vanderlyn's scribbling crowd, though not from among those who had turned up on the previous evening. The scribbling was in evidence now; the man's papers, held down on the sand by pebbles and shells, appeared to be a typescript scrawled all over in pencil and ink. Although close enough to observe this, Shefford had an impulse to pass unnoticed. He did this without difficulty. When he had gone on for about fifty yards, he turned round for another look.

He was in time to see the bearded man scramble to his feet, and extend both his arms upward towards the heavens. The bearded man followed this with a gesture of impatience, dropped his arms to his sides, and at once threw them out-ward again, but this time in a sweeping motion towards the ground. Then he dropped down on the sand, and once more buried his nose in his papers. He must be a playwright or novelist, Shefford supposed, endeavouring to make vivid

148

to himself the capers of his characters. Shefford was surprised to find that the small exhibition antagonised rather than amused him. It was humiliating to have lurking in oneself this philistine dislike of the artistic temperament, particularly when one made one's living by spouting about the products of it.

He walked on, rather depressed. He didn't take another look at the bearded man until the binoculars were necessary in order to do so. There he still was, and it was just possible to see his pen roving here and there over the scattered papers. He must be revising a whole scene, trying to drag it together, something like that. But what chiefly struck Shefford now was the little chap's loneliness: a small sprawl of flesh, intent upon those scrawls and scribblings, under this immense and unflawed Aegean sky. It made him a kind of archetypal figure. If your life was in scrawls and scribblings—or daubs and splashes, or notes and chords— then you *were* lonely, even if you worked in the middle of a crowd. Or at least this was the modern notion of the artist. Yeats in his solitary tower at Ballylee; Joyce armoured within 'silence, exile and cunning'; the fabled Axel of Auersburg in his castle, for that matter: these conformed to the age's notion of an artist of any stature, and only the small fry were allowed to go about in shoals. It was a way of thinking that didn't make any easier a realising of the sort of community Vanderlyn had in mind.

Shefford had sat down in the shade of a spiny and inhospitable-looking shrub, and for a moment he continued to study through his glasses the little bearded man at his literary labour. But the action carried a suggestion of spying, and he swung the lenses round in a wide arc in search of any natural features of the terrain particularly worth looking at. What they came upon—what leapt into almost intimate view—was a further piece of human activity. A small yacht had rounded a headland and glided into the bay beneath him; even as he caught it in the binoculars he heard the faint rattle of its sail coming down and the tiny splash of an anchor dropped into shallow water. There were two young men on board, whom he recognised as Stepho and Dionysios: indeed, this powerful instrument brought them so close that Shefford felt he could stretch out a hand and touch their sun-browned skin. They appeared to be on a fishing expedition. Stepho, in the stern, had already cast a line into the water.

Neither youth was in those tidy and rather oppressively naval-looking clothes; they might have been peasant lads from anywhere round about. The yacht, on the other hand, could belong only to the monastery, for it was a graceful and trim affair. The fishing expedition must be happening on a time-off basis—if, indeed, Stepho and Dionysios ever had very urgently a time-on. Shefford again had a sense of them as occupying, on some deliberate plan of Vanderlyn's, a kind of social no man's land in his household. However that might be, the present spectacle was pleasing, and it could be observed, unlike the bearded man, without any suggestion of invading a privacy. So Shefford turned the binoculars back to the yacht from time to time. He found himself delighted when he caught Stepho landing a fish.

But mostly he tried to see what could be made of the nearer islands. They were, he supposed, the tops of sub-merged mountains, and they were surely more barren above water than below: grey rock, brown rock, here and there faintly shadowed with a deceptive effect of movement, so that one could almost imagine them the emerging mucula-ture, lazily rippling, of some slumbering monster. He looked back at the yacht. A few minutes before, the blue surface of the bay had been absolutely still, and the small craft might have been welded to its own inverted image, keel to keel. Now there was a delicate dance of tiny wavelets, for Dionysios was in the water, swimming and ducking, and from every point at which his fair head broke the surface the slow circles radiated out—circle meeting circle in a sparkling and intricate turbulence. He had a beautiful com-mand of himself in the water; it seemed very much his element. But Stepho, still in the stern, didn't approve. He was waving Dionysios away from his fishing, waving him back to the yacht, shouting some sharp expostulation. Dionysios shouted back at him, rebellious and laughing. But then almost at once he obeyed the summons and scrambled back into the yacht, setting it rocking above its own locked reflection as if it were struggling to get free. Dionysios threw himself down on his back and lay still—gazing, as on the previous day, straight up into the sky.

Shefford continued to watch. The illusion of near-contiguity was so complete that he felt surprised at not being able to hear the boys talking. For they were gossiping now. Or perhaps it was only Dionysios who was gossiping, with the immobile Stepho—he had a strange faculty of immobility—saying little or nothing. It was possible to see the curl returning to Dionysios's rapidly drying hair, and his slightly broken nose and familiar flashing smile were very attractive. He had scrambled to his feet now, and slipped into his shorts; sitting on a thwart close by Stepho, he continued to chatter. Presently his talk became urgent, vehement, and it almost seemed as if, surrounded by sea as they were, he was speaking confidentially into Stepho's ear. Stepho continued to fish; his line was attached to a small float which had his own power of stillness; it looked as if his first fish was going to be his last. And the whole surface of the bay was unruffled again; in Bernard Vanderlyn's powerful binoculars the little tableau hung suspended in an atmosphere of the utmost purity. It was like a marine Arcadia, Shefford thought. It was all the youth of the world in its pristine innocence.

Dionysios, still talking, made a small gesture—uninterpretable but troubling. He made a larger gesture. It was of an obscenity so brutal as to be unmistakable. Stepho fished on.

Shefford let the binoculars drop on his chest. As he did so, he became aware that a new shadow had fallen on the rock beside him. He turned round, and saw that he had been joined by Gemma Vanderlyn and Marion Causland.

At least, with the naked eye, they couldn't have seen that

small ugly thing. And in any case, Shefford assured himself, it was nothing to be particularly shocked at. The
language of gesture is universal in the Mediterranean basin,
and a particular flourish of it has no more significance than
a dirty word. If he had felt revolted it was only because,
seconds earlier, he had been choosing to see as idyllic
the spectacle of these two perfectly commonplace young
men.

But the incident didn't help him to any ease when he
turned to cope with Gemma and Marion now. He had been
hoping that he wouldn't see much of either of them before
he left Tyros—this simply because, thanks to Andreas, he
had learnt more about both than there was any call for him
to know, and he was finding this a situation he didn't at
all enjoy. Curiosity hadn't, it seemed, quite everything to
be said for it, since what it put one in possession of could
be tiresomely embarrassing. Marion Causland, for example,
could only be described as an entire stranger—and yet here
he was, facing her while carrying in his head the most
appalling knowledge about her birth. Or rather about her
conception, which was even worse. As for Gemma, he felt
that Andreas had been inviting him positively to peer
between her sheets. Now he had to make polite conversation
to both of them.

'Are those our Greek boys fishing?' Gemma was asking.

'Yes. And Dionysios has been swimming. I've just been
watching them through these splendid glasses.'

'They have charge of the nautical side of things, but it
doesn't seem to give them a great deal to do.'

'There's all that paint and brass to clean on the launch—
and the yacht there to keep trim, too. That must be something.' Shefford said this very much for want of anything
better to say.

'I think they hire fisher lads to do that,' Gemma said
with an effect of amused tolerance. 'The monastery is a
perch of great grandeur. Old Aphrodite, for example—you
know who I mean?—is regarded as the most important
woman on the island. After Marion and myself, that is.

152

Marion, wouldn't you say?' Gemma paused. This attempt to draw Miss Causland into light conversation achieved no success. 'I think Stepho is often bored. Not that I've any idea of what goes on inside his head. Dionysios, on the other hand, doesn't entirely elude me. He has a very good notion of enjoying himself. He lies on his back, stares at the sky, and sees all sorts of extremely attractive pictures. And, of course, he's rather a splendid young animal. Marion, don't you think?'

Shefford experienced one of his too frequent sensations of discomfort. Gemma's words had scarcely been a legitimate call upon the silent Marion to do her social stuff. And although they hadn't sounded exactly vicious—he didn't believe that Gemma was vicious—they had been a provocative insistence upon something this withdrawn girl was shy of.

'I don't know. I don't think I've noticed.' Marion's confusion was painful. And she seemed to feel that something more must be said. 'Hasn't he,' she added stumblingly, 'something funny about his nose?'

'Then that's something you *have* noticed, Marion.' Gemma sounded affectionately amused. 'It's attractive, I'd say.'

'I think he can be insolent.'

Shefford felt an impulse to applaud. Marion had suddenly spoken with a decision and severity which very much recalled her mother. The first Mrs Vanderlyn hadn't been a woman who would ever let her standards slip.

'I think he sometimes can.' Gemma was instantly accommodating and serious. 'At least once, I've had to call him down. But it's a matter of nationality, to some extent. You must expect from a Greek boy with his manhood growing in him things you won't get from a college professor at a campus tea-party.'

The daughter of the late Ambassador to Washington seemed to be having one of her American turns. Moreover she had been rude, for Shefford was in effect a college professor. And—what was more interesting—she had been rude undesignedly, and wasn't at all pleased with herself as

153

a result. She made amends by offering Shefford a penitent look. He received it as best he could. About these Greek boys Gemma had, for a further moment, held to a note which strained propriety. She might judge Marion Causland unwholesomely inhibited, but it wasn't in the presence of an almost unknown young man that she should let her talk catch just this tone. Moreover—highly evolved as her social manner was—there had been something unconscious and inadvertent at work. He repeated to himself that Gemma certainly wasn't a vicious woman. But somewhere in her an obscure sexual restlessness was stirring. He had told Andreas that a man who really got thinking about the second Mrs Vanderlyn could be driven crazy in no time. It came to him now—and much less as a mere detached observation —that the second Mrs Vanderlyn might at any time get thinking about a man.

'I am so glad we found you.' Gemma's tone had changed again; it was as if she had recollected herself, and was returning to her hostess's manner. 'For I am afraid we have been neglecting a guest. Bernard can hardly be kept from his hospital, at its present stage. And, in the morning, Marion and I usually go round some of our neighbours. Not the writers and artists, you know. The evening's for them. But our own people.'

Shefford managed a murmur of comprehension. Gemma was now less a Greek Ambassador's daughter than an English lady of the manor. It was possible to imagine that she and Marion were bearing burdens of nourishing soups and wholesome advice.

'But Mark,' she went on, 'should be looking after you. I can't think where he's got to.'

'Sometimes he takes out a car. He says it's when he feels reckless.' Marion produced this information instantly. 'And it *is* dangerous. I've asked him——' She broke off, flushing faintly.

'In my opinion Mark can look after himself very well,' Gemma said drily. 'It amuses him to alarm you.'

'But at other times he goes to the ruined fort and reads

until lunch-time.' Marion hesitated. 'Gemma, shall we walk there now?'

'I think we should all three return to the monastery. Soon it will be very hot, and you may feel it. Mr Shefford too.'

Shefford received this concern for his health politely. He would rather have strolled on, leaving the ladies with civil words to their own devices. But this was silly, and as he turned and walked between them he cast about for harmless talk. Yet there had been aspects of this encounter that hadn't escaped him, and it was not quite at random that he chose a topic.

'Mark must be looking forward to the publication of his book,' he said. 'Do you know when it's coming out?'

'On the twenty-fifth of next month. That's in London. And a week later in New York. Bernard's been able to arrange that—although we were dreadfully anxious for a time.' Marion Causland was tumbling this out breathlessly. 'Mark says that New York is far more important than London for books, especially poetry books. His book's going to include the poem that's in this month's *Poetry Now*. And the three translations from Cavafy. I couldn't understand what they're about, but they're said to be very good. And there's to be the one that Mr Valaoritis liked, too. And, I hope, the one they put in *Pali*. That's a very intellectual magazine.' She fell silent. This time, her face was deeply flushed. And then she burst out again. 'But even Mark's early poems are intellectual—the ones he wrote at school. Mr Shefford, do you know what a meson is?'

'A meson?' Shefford found this question wholly strange. 'Something in physics, perhaps. I'm afraid I don't really know.'

'It comes in one of the school poems.' Marion was triumphant. 'A poem Bernard very much likes, because it is about things he had to do with when he was helping the President. And I was silly, because I thought Mark had made a mistake with his French. I tried to correct it, and he laughed at me. It seems that one can have jokes in poems—even the kind of jokes that are called puns. Did you know that, Mr Shefford?'

Shefford nodded. 'Yes,' he said gently, 'I've heard of that.' He was thinking how like—and yet unlike—her mother Miss Causland was. There was the same earnestness of temperament. But Marion would never major even in English Philology.

Gemma Vanderlyn had made no attempt to interrupt. Only she had stooped and picked from the ground a grass which must have been of botanical interest—since she walked on, studying it carefully. She might regard him as an emasculated college professor, Shefford thought, but at least she didn't take him for a fool, even in matters of love. She was aware of his having realised that Marion's rush of words had conveyed information of an order the girl hadn't intended. He remembered how, on their drive to the monastery, he had said to Gemma that Mark as an adoptive son wouldn't be a trouble-free buy. It had been a cheap phrase which didn't please him in the retrospect. But at least it had represented what he thought. And now here was another relation to which he was instantly convinced that the same judgement must apply. It was a hard fate— as college professor and prudent man he could say dispassionately it was a hard fate—to have fallen in love with Mark Varley, if that was what Marion had done. He himself might like Mark surprisingly. Mark might have growing in him all the poetic inches Bernard Vanderlyn swore to. Marion might be dim in everything except this strangely discovered absorption, and he himself might have had no feeling for her at all only five minutes ago. But now he was suddenly sorry for her. And, in an unaccountable way, he was sorry for Mark too. What he had called Mark's hard road suddenly seemed harder.

Whether Marion Causland had felt any consciousness of self-betrayal in this small episode didn't appear. Gemma made smooth conversation until the monastery was in sight.

Chapter 10

It grew hotter after lunch, and Shefford wished he had the trick of going to sleep in the afternoon. But he hadn't, and so he had to take *The Faerie Queene* from the back pocket of his rucksack, and work at it in his room. It got a high rating, he thought, as the world's most unreadable book. He sweated at it doggedly for a time—literally so, he discovered, and he had a go at the shipping-magnate's shower before he went downstairs again.

Gemma was engaged at her piano, and Marion was copying music—presumably Gemma's music. He found he didn't in the least understand what—on this enormous great piano —was evolving itself. He told himself helplessly it wasn't in the least like Spenser's poem, but just as utterly unappealing to his taste. Vanderlyn was closeted somewhere with a newly arrived genius. Mark had disappeared again. Andreas, reading the air-mail edition of *The Times*, looked dangerously prone to drop this papery drug and beckon to further confidences.

Shefford went outside. At about this time on the previous afternoon, he remembered, a breeze had come in from the sea and blown gently until sundown. Somewhere, perhaps in the dry leaves of the little banana grove, he thought he heard it now. He went in search of it in a kind of simple physiological need, rather as a man might go in search of a drink. The banana grove was deceptive; the dry foliage rustled, but seemingly without cause. It was an incongruous place, improbably exotic, like a jungle imagined by the *Douanier* Rousseau, and this effect was enhanced by a row of small windmills in the middle distance: affairs of spidery iron-work and stretched scraps of sailcloth so sketchy as to suggest an existence only within some obstinately childlike mind. He wandered round a further corner of the monastery, and now the breeze was really present—but as a mingling of scents rather than as any cool breath upon his face. There was the smell of the sea itself, and of what he knew was camomile, and of the only flower in bloom near the shore, something which Gemma had told him was the sand lily. He crossed to a rambling cloister, part-ruined or perhaps never more than part-built, and turned into its shade. Here he came upon Mark unexpectedly.

The unexpectedness was a function of some sense of withdrawal, or even of hiding, which Mark's posture contrived to give. He was sunk in a deck-chair which he had set close behind a pillar; his arms were dangling slackly at his sides; beneath his right hand lay a pencil and a blank writing-pad. His first action when he became aware of Shefford was to sweep up these and stuff them down beside him in the taut canvas of the chair. His face was brooding, or perhaps merely sulky; when he looked up and spoke it was without any effect of welcome.

'Oh, hullo,' he said. 'It's fairly cool in here. But you'll find plenty of other cool places as well.'

'I'll stay in this one, I think.' Shefford wasn't going to react to this stupid rudeness. He fetched a second chair—there was a stack of them—and unfolded it. 'I regard you as one of my hosts,' he said. 'It was you who suggested I come over to Tyros in the first place. Still, you needn't make conversation, if you don't want to.'

'It's damned remote, isn't it?' Mark did at least seem to propose to talk. But his unwelcoming expression was unrelaxed. There was an actual physical duskiness about him when he was in this mood—his complexion darkening, as if he were some sort of deep-sea creature with a trick of turning off its electricity during discouragement. The effect was enhanced by his having changed his clothes again: he was very untidy. 'The unplumb'd, salt, estranging sea,' he 'To hell with rotten, cosy Oxford poets! Still, that's it. A queer sort of hole for Bernard's notable exercise.' he paused. 'I suppose you've been about the world a lot?'

'Only Europe. But there, for what it's worth, I've prowled about for a good many years. When I came top in something at school—and I usually managed it in one subject or another, as I bet you did—my father used to give me twenty pounds at the end of the summer term. It's amazing what I managed to do on it.'

'Did he, now?' There was a deliberately false admiration in Mark's tone. 'How nice that was! I wonder if I can take a guess at your father, Jeremy? Yes—I'd say he was a small-time dentist. Like the other Mr Bloom, the pseudo-Bloom, the deutero-Bloom, in *Ulysses*. Perhaps your father was really a Mr Bloom, and took a good, territorial-sounding name by what's-it-called? Deed-poll.'

'Mark, you're the most bloody-minded kid at times. You really are.'

'I'm sorry.' Mark sat up in his chair, and the movement dislodged the writing-pad and pencil. He chucked them down between Shefford and himself in a gesture which—surprisingly—wasn't theatrical at all. 'I mean what I say. I adore Tyros, for most of the time. It's release and security. And then, quite suddenly, it frightens me. For one thing, I'm home-sick. Think of that! Home-sick for small streets and smaller people. Even home-sick for *my* father. Which is incredible.'

'Why should it be incredible, Mark? Tell me about him.'

'I can't tell you any good—not about our relation, I mean. You're only inviting me to be bloody-minded again.'

'Well, why not? Do you good. Quit thinking of me as a don. Imagine I'm a trick-cyclist in a Freudian clinic, and inviting you to unbutton. Go ahead.'

'You're not sufficiently hardened, Jeremy; you'd dissolve in blushes.' Mark smiled quite happily. 'Dangerous, too. I might fall in love with you—what they call a positive trans-ference. You're already my only friend, you know—and gained just a couple of days ago. Think of *that*.'

'Don't be boring, Mark. Tell me about your father.'

'Very well. The indictment begins when I had my first poem in the school magazine. He went and complained to the headmaster. There was something about God in it, so he thought it was blasphemous. If there had been something

159

about sex, he'd have thought it was obscene.' Mark grinned. 'There was, come to think of it.'

'How did the headmaster react?'

'Oh, he supported his clever pupil. He was good enough to say the poem hadn't come off, but showed some talent. My father was furious. I think he'd have tried to whip me, if I hadn't grown as tall as he is by that time.'

'What does he do? Is *he* a small-time dentist?'

'He has a tobacconist's—with newspapers and trashy paperbacks: the kind that have tyings-up and beatings on the covers, or naked couples necking in tropical landscapes. You'd think he might suppose these things to be a little touched by the pleasures of sex themselves. Not a bit of it. That's all by way of trade, which is different. I used to serve in the shop, when my father had gone to choir practice. He's very pious, and has a musical soul.'

'Did you hate it?'

'Of course. But I felt I had to lend a hand. There wasn't too much money; in fact there was none at all. Just some silver and copper in the greasy till. They're finished, low-class little shops like that, and a good thing too. Boys at my school discovered the paperbacks, and used to come in and buy them when I was serving.'

'By way of being friendly—or to jeer?'

'I didn't care a damn which. A bit of each, I suppose. They were just ignorant little bastards. They thought I must know the particularly hot ones. It made me feel I needed a bath.'

'*Did* you know the hot ones?'

'Yes, a bit. But I still needed the bath. A swimmer into cleanness leaping.' Mark put a curious undirected bitterness into this random quotation. 'Remember, I was already reading real books at a great rate. They're the only ones that ever have any sex worth getting your teeth into.'

'I suppose so.' Shefford accepted this image as deliberately revolting. 'Is your mother alive, Mark?'

'As much as she can ever be said to have been. She's

160

harmless enough. Always washing and cooking, poor woman, and doing what she's told. She did what she was told about my having been inside. Never darken the doorstep, and so on. That was my father's actual phrase—like a Victorian parent's to a daughter who's turned tart. He must have read it somewhere, or heard it in a sermon.'

'You mean your parents actually turned you away?'

'Yes, of course. It's a wonderful simplification. I've had parents, and that's it.'

'Do you know, Mark, that you always say "Of course" when it's a question of something particularly negative or dreary?'

'I suppose I do.' Rather unexpectedly, Mark produced his spontaneous smile. It lit up his brooding features strangely —making them more sensitive, Shefford thought, in a manner not common with smiles. 'Don't think I suppose life can't be any good. I'm for it. I'm mad for it, really. Sometimes it's almost as if I knew my lungs were rotted away or something, and I had just a year or two to go, and felt a wild need to clasp things that perhaps aren't there.' The smile turned to a satirical grin. 'But no need to be anxious, Jeremy, about your new friend. I'm disgustingly healthy, as a matter of fact.'

'That's obvious enough.' Shefford was still held by Mark's picture of his parents, and by the air of indifference with which he had painted it. Could anyone, so swiftly aware of things, really quite believe in such a stereotype of lower-middle-class rigidities? Did Mark reflect that his mother at her wash-tub and his father fumbling in his nasty little till were conceivably heartbroken by the strangeness of their son—and no doubt by the disgrace which must bulk so large against their small horizons? Shefford felt an impulse to explore further. 'My own parents,' he said, 'used to find it difficult to understand what I was about. They'd made sacrifices, as the phrase is, and I was grateful to them, but it was sometimes terribly difficult to get along. Before my father died, I had to buy myself rather a large car. He wanted me to be a success; he wanted, in a simple human

161

way, a return for his money. And a big car was the sort of success he understood.'

'It must have been a burden to you, a rather grand car. Still, it was worth it—showing nice feeling like that. Fine, Jeremy, fine.'

'Oh, shut up, Mark.' Shefford wasn't going to be put off by this jibe either. 'I'm only saying parents are naturally a bit difficult, when one's interests get outside their scope. Do you feel that your father really thwarted you—positively got in your way? Wasn't he just a bit bewildered?'

'I don't care what he was. He certainly wanted to push me around. And I won't *be* pushed around. I'm an artist. I won't be given orders. That's flat.'

This time Shefford was silent. He hadn't, he told himself, quite realised before the extent to which Mark Varley was a chip-on-the-shoulder type. And the chip was liable, so to speak, to fly off dangerously in any direction at any time. It was having been in prison, he supposed. Or that had beefed it up, had pumped dangerously high what may have been already a sufficient reservoir of resentment. Random resentment, it might be called. And yet not entirely so. There had been something ominous—there had been surely something ominous, as Bernard Vanderlyn might say—in that last sequence of Mark's ideas.

'They'd have liked me to marry and settle down.' Mark was laughing, and it was a laugh with his alienating touch of the stage. 'Think of that! Oxford had been no good. They could just understand a class-list: First, Second, Third, Fourth. So it was a write-off, and I'd better have another little shop, and a little wife to match. A chapel-crawling girl from next door, with a face like a bun. Me—who could dream of Helen and the topless towers!'

For some reason that he couldn't quite place, Shefford stirred uneasily. Mark, although seemingly so lost in contemplation of himself, caught the movement warily. He might have been recalling that his companion wouldn't be too impressed by rodomontade.

'But think of it!' he said reasonably. 'Actually supposing

they could hand me a wife on a plate, in order to keep me from the haunts of vice. Talking of topless towers, do you know about Marlowe's life?'

'Of course I do. He's my territory, as you know very well. What on earth are you talking about?'

'He was a damned good poet—and when quite young. He might have been better than Shakespeare.'

'Rubbish.'

'Well, he certainly got going quicker, didn't he? So they gave him a raw deal. Had him up in some sort of court— rather like me, Jeremy—and told him it was coming to him. That was it, wasn't it?'

'It's a possible interpretation of such records as survive.'

'And then they bumped him off in a pothouse. With a dagger worth one-and-eightpence, just above the eye. How could you do that? Just above the eye. Think of it!' Mark paused, as if this was an actual invitation, and Shefford remembered that the Marlowe image was potent with young men disposed to see themselves as of anarchic impulse. 'But, Jeremy, he'd had his whack, hadn't he—Marlowe? He'd got back at them, from time to time. Do you remember what they said about him?' For a moment Mark waited for a reply. But Shefford said nothing. He could remember several things they'd said about Marlowe. ' "Sudden privy injuries to men." That's what they credited him with a fancy for. Doesn't it sound magnificently sinister? And I suppose it's what I managed in Grosvenor Square. A sudden privy injury to a man.'

'Come off it, Mark. You got the privy injury, and you were ass enough to slam back with a public one. They clapped you in jug for it. But now you're here on Tyros, with your work to do—and, for the moment, with me to gas at.'

'And play-act before?'

'Yes—but why not? You're casting around, you know. You're threshing around, hunting for the true Mark Varley. You haven't arrived at a proper knowledge of yourself yet. That's the first thing the trick-cyclist has to tell you. Look at your clothes.'

'What do you mean—my clothes?' Mark was suddenly looking juvenile and embarrassed—and also quite good humoured. He didn't really need to be told. And Shefford was confirmed in the view that a certain candour, as if they had actually been undergraduates together for years, was the key to getting along with him usefully.

'All natty one day, Mark, like an elderly English gent strolling in front of his villa at Rapallo. And then a corsair-turn. And then in off-duty clothes you must have borrowed from Dionysi or Stepho.'

'So I have, and I'm in them now. How very acute of you. I scrounged them off Stepho to go fishing, and haven't given them back. It's very significant. I must want to sink to my proper social level again. Or perhaps I identify with Stepho—isn't that the trick-cyclist's word? I get quite thick with him at times. Birds of a feather. Hullo—there they are! Both of them. And very much off-duty, too.'

Chapter 11

MARK HAD POINTED between two of the roughly-squared pillars of the half-ruined cloister in the shade of which they were sitting. Its farther side had crumbled to a low wall. The sea—in the distance a deep blue, and in the nearer shallows emerald shot with lime green—closed a vista framed between Attic pines and carpeted with grass. Here was the side on which lay the domestic offices of the monastery as it now functioned, and this was in fact a large drying-green, sedulously watered in an endeavour to keep down the dust. It looked dull and parched, all the same; between the dark trees it showed like the bottom of a dried-up swimming-pool, faintly greening under some feebly vegetative process. The old woman called Aphrodite was just hobbling away from it like a decrepit magpie, since she had gathered up a bundle of sheets which had been bleaching on the unpromising surface. Certainly it wasn't much of a playground. But on its farther side there had now appeared Dionysios and Stepho, dribbling a football between them. Each was in sea-stained shorts and a ragged T-shirt, such as Mark himself was wearing. On their feet were rope-soled sandals —which didn't prevent their beginning to punt the ball around with vigorous kicks.

'Yes, there they are,' Mark repeated lazily. 'The little victims play. My fellow felons, too.'

'What do you mean—your fellow felons? And what was that rot about birds of a feather?'

'Don't you know, Jeremy? Hasn't anyone told you?' Mark either was, or affected to be, surprised. 'They've both been in trouble, and that's why they're here. Bernard is indefatigable in that sort of do-gooding.'

'No, I didn't know.' Shefford found himself uneasy before this information. What he had seen on the yacht that morning stuck in his head. 'I haven't thought much about them. Only they've struck me as not quite out of one drawer.'

'You're probably right. Dionysi is just a nice boy from the people, like me. Stepho is from a good way higher up. He's had some sort of tumble, I suppose. I've picked up the impression that he got off more lightly than he should. The higher ups do.'

'Do you know just what their trouble was?'

'No, but I'm going to find out. I think Dionysios just did a little good-natured thieving—don't you? But Stepho's is a darker tale. You read it in that still face and smouldering eye. Isn't that right?'

'You're talking rot, I should think. But it's true I have a feeling I shouldn't trust Stepho in some situations.'

'That's right, Jeremy—just as you wouldn't trust me. They don't do badly with that ball. They can head it quite well, too.' Mark had stood up and stepped half into the open. The afternoon was drifting away, and the light had turned low and raking; it cast cones of shadow from the pine trees over the broad expanse of grass where the Greek boys were at play. Shefford wondered whether they had noticed the presence of onlookers. Although, as Mark said, they were rather good, there was a conscious grace about their movements that suggested a ballet rather than a game. 'But they need toughening up,' Mark said. He turned towards Shefford, so that the horizontal light cut through his skimpy clothes and changed him to a stripped silhouette. Shefford found himself recalling the college garden, and reflecting that the body now before him looked much as it had done then. He found himself, too, regarding this as slightly surprising, and he wondered why. Lurking in his mind, perhaps, was the assumption that there was something soft about Tyros, or something inescapably relaxing in Mark's role on the island. As an honest toiler earning one's bread, one was disposed to see as ignobly relaxed anyone sheltering beneath Vanderlyn's ample umbrella. Shefford didn't like stumbling on this reflection, and he would have liked it even less if it hadn't somehow carried with it an awareness of how much, so to speak, he was on Mark's side.

'Yes—toughening up.' Mark had repeated this with a sudden and sharp vigour. 'And why don't they play Rugger? Even if they're almost proles and almost Wogs, why don't they play a gentleman's game?' This demand, which ought merely to have carried on the effect of an edgy and tedious strain in Mark's talk, conveyed instead a rising up of something like joy. 'It's a better game. Let's teach them.'

'Rubbish, Mark. It's still much too hot.' Shefford stared in surprise at his companion. It didn't occur to him to take the suggestion seriously. For one thing, he thought of poets as people characteristically without any sort of athletic inclination. It would even be something suspect in them. There had been Georgian poets who played cricket and wrote verse about it, but the results had been mediocre, and were no longer read. 'Relax,' he said—rather unreasonably, since he had just been reflecting that relaxation was what Tyros put Mark in danger of.

'Come on, you out-of-condition don.' Mark had seized his wrists and yanked him upright with unexpected strength. 'We'll knock the bloody breath out of them.'

For a moment Shefford was going to protest. Then the truth of his years took hold of him, and he found himself on his toes and sprinting into sunshine. If they were to begin with a race, he was going to beat Mark to the field. The ball was sailing high in air towards Dionysios; on a rapid calculation he deflected his course and made for Stepho, hard. And he hadn't forgotten this sort of timing; there the ball was, and he gathered it with a revived dexterity which surprised him from just in front of Stepho's feet. Like the young Rugbeian who first invented this superior form of the game, he tucked it under his arm and ran. Stepho and Dionysios, suitably confounded, uttered cries of indignation, and with large gestures appeared to invoke the interposition of some appropriate saint.

'Tackle him, Dionysi! Go for him!' Still a few yards behind Shefford, Mark was yelling wildly. 'Tackle him low, man, *low*!' Since this was naturally unintelligible, Mark put on a turn of speed and did the job himself, hurling himself at Shefford's knees and bringing him down with a bump such as he hadn't felt for years. To have the hard earth rise up and smack one like that, to have the breath beaten out of one's body only a little less completely than one might expect: these were sensations distantly familiar and instantly exhilarating. Both of them were up again in a moment, hacking at the ball. In a moment, too, the vast new conception seemed to have dawned on the Greek boys, and they came piling in. For a time, indeed, it failed to strike them that it all wasn't simply a fight, and this extended to Stepho's punching Mark hard on the jaw. 'You rotten bastard!' Mark shouted—so that for a second Shefford felt there was to be nothing for it but a free-for-all. But Mark had gone off with the ball, turned on a wide arc, and came charging down on Stepho once more. Stepho waited with clenched fist. At the last moment, Mark's body swayed out of reach, and his free arm, thrust out stiffly, took Stepho's own jaw with a flattened palm. 'You can do *that*!' Mark yelled. 'You're let do that if you can—see?' With flashing and triumphant heels, he was off again.

And so a game of sorts evolved itself—as Helios' chariot incandescent in the west, turned to gold the sky above the invisible stony Pelopponese, the dark Ionian Sea, the distant Ausonian lands beyond. Great bars of shadow from the Attic pines lay across the field, thronging it as if with vast and spectral opponents. There was a smell of dust, a smell of sweat as the boys struggled in a tiny scrum, an aromatic smell released by some unseen herb crushed beneath their pounding feet. Sometimes it was England against Greece. Sometimes, as in an orthodox pick-up, they formed a single three-quarter line, and dashed up and down the field, passing the ball as they threaded their way among the final, slowly-wheeling shafts of sunlight. They had stopped the uninhibited yelling with which they began. As on the most correct of football fields, there were the sounds only of their panting lungs and of the booted or bouncing ball.

At one point, and out of the corner of his eye, Shefford noticed that they had collected an audience. Vanderlyn and Marion Causland had appeared in the cloister. They were watching the game, but they hadn't sat down to do so. The effect was rather as if they had been arrested by some untoward thing. There seemed to be no strong occasion for this. It couldn't be that Vanderlyn disapproved of his guests associating with his servants, since it had become clear that the two Greek youths were positively required to accept a role that cut across such distinctions. Perhaps Rugby football was just one of the things that he hadn't reckoned to introduce to the island of Tyros. Or perhaps—and this was more probably it—the image of his resident poet, dusty, sweaty, and rushing around like a tall, dark demon, was a little outside his conception of the vatic or laureate character.

Shefford hadn't much leisure for these thoughts. As far as this mad game was concerned, he was determined to keep it up at least as long as Mark. He didn't mind if the other two were left in command of the field after his own last breath had left him. They must both be short of twenty still, but not too short of it not to have hardened into an adult physique. They were both more or less actively employed all day. But Mark, who lounged around waiting moodily for inspiration to crystalize on an empty writing-pad, or drove uselessly about in a fast car, he just wasn't going to be beaten by. He began deliberately conserving his energies and calculating his rushes, like a seasoned runner in a race.

It was during a pause prompted by this plan that he took a longer glance at the cloister. The result was a sharp perception that, however, it might be with Vanderlyn, the unruly spectacle had only bewildered Marion Causland. She stood in an attitude of anxious attention—rather like a Vestal Virgin who, suddenly apprised of Goths and Vandals rampaging within the precinct, supposes that some seemly explanation can be arrived at. Under her arm she carried a large book in a red binding, and it was as if the horizontal light, catching and accenting this, pointed the colourlessness of everything else about her. She appeared to have been interrupted in reading, for her spectacles, suspended by some incongruously elderly contrivance round her neck, glinted before her breasts with the effect of an unrealised symbolism. Shefford suddenly recalled the first Mrs Vanderlyn asking 'Is that a fast game?'; imperfectly recalled, too, his sense of her as in some essential particular remote from Piero della Francesca's Eve. But it was simply, of course, that in Marion he was disposed to see Louise Vanderlyn over again, anyway. He turned back to the flying ball, and when he looked again both Vanderlyn and his stepdaughter had departed.

The game was in its last phase. There were no rules, after all, and it had begun to fall apart. Dionysios was finding breath for laughter, as if the Homeric conflict had become a romp. Stepho's features, which had been lively with the passions, took on again the stillness Mark had remarked in them; he had been a dangerous opponent—but it was somehow possible to feel that he could be yet more dangerous when it was all over. They were all four grey with dust; they had managed considerably to clutch and tear such scanty garments as they wore; when they called it a day and ran for the cloister's shade they might have been antique marble statues, freshly dug from earth, and hastily clothed in rags by a prudish posterity. Only Mark, with a graze on the thigh, had one leg gloriously bloodied, like a blazon of gules on a faded argent field. And it amused Mark to carry himself like a knight. Perhaps a *Paynim* knight, Shefford thought, recalling his *Faerie Queene*. Mark's long dark hair, with its long falling lock, showed on his head like a battle-blackened Saracenic helmet.

Both Vanderlyn and Marion had returned. Vanderlyn had even had the pretty maid Vangelio bring a tray of cool drinks, and he handed them to the four youths himself. Stepho and Dionysios sank into chairs without ceremony; they had a quick instinct, in this strange community which had adopted them, for knowing when they should do what. Shefford went to talk to Marion, something which Mark showed no disposition to do.

'Is it a real game?' Marion asked. 'I mean, is there a proper game, with rules, that is played in that way?'

'Oh, yes. But it needs thirty people, not four.'

'Thirty people behaving like that?' She asked the question anxiously, as if it were always a duty to amass accurate information. One felt that presently she would go away and record the facts in some appropriate notebook. 'Mark has hurt himself. He ought to go and wash.' It was half to Mark that she addressed this, as if, although diffident, she was anxious to bring him into the talk. It could have been only social training, learnt from Gemma or in some finishing school. But Shefford, remembering the morning, knew that another current was at work.

'In heroic times,' Vanderlyn said, 'you'd take on the chore yourself, Marion.'

'Should I? Perhaps if we had——' Marion's pale face had flushed faintly, and she broke off without finding anything more to say. Mark, disregarding, curled up further in his chair and deliberately, almost luxuriously, put out his tongue and licked round the grazed place. It was a small boy's action, and one would have supposed that only a small boy could twist his limbs and torso into the position required. Marion watched with what, for a moment, suggested itself as a horrified and eruptive fascination. Then Vanderlyn was on his feet. For the first time that Shefford could remember, there was about him a hint of regretting something he had just said. He murmured that he had promised to walk over to the hospital, and moved away. Marion accompanied him without a word.

For a short time the four young men sat on together. The departure of the others had re-established the fellowship of the game. But—in the limited medium of communication available to them—nothing more was said. As their excitement died out, Stepho and Dionysios seemed to judge it correct to appear a little shy. They made small, formal bows when at length they rose to go away. Shefford wondered whether, when they were round a corner, Dionysios—an archangel with a damaged nose—would find occasion to make that evil gesture again.

Shefford and Mark continued for a while in silence, their blood still faintly racing. The emerald and blue of the sea were both darkening. In the west the whole sky was empty, shading from an opalescent zenith to a horizon of deep rose. There was a single sail on the sea, sharp and dark; it belonged, they knew, to the caique of some sponge-divers strayed from the Dodecanese. And just above the vanished sun floated a single ribbon of cloud, flaring like the note of a trumpet transmuted to incandescent gold.

Mark Varley gazed into this spectacle for a long time. Its light remained constant, yet the reflection of it seemed to be fading from his face.

'Jeremy,' he said abruptly, 'you know, don't you?'

'Know what?'

'That that was happiness.' Mark had made a small gesture towards their late football-ground, now almost vanishing from sight.

'Yes. It was.'

'It always comes unexpectedly. And always it may never come again.'

PART III

Chapter 1

IT WAS THE day of the garden party—that annual garden party in the rain with which Charles Blaine had once been told he would have to content himself as the measure of the year's festivity in a reformed Oxford. But this day, at least, was still full of junketing; the garden party would be merely its most populous occasion; more select affairs of one sort and another were going on from morning to midnight. The university was commemorating anew its founders and benefactors, and doing so with a proper prodigality. The Bodleian Library had closed down ('for this day only' the *University Pocket Diary* told one) and various corporate purses had been opened. The feast of the Encaenia was on. Nor did the rains come down. It was a perfect June day.

Gavin Naylor strolled through the Great Quadrangle, dressed in scarlet. He was returning from the enjoyment of Lord Crewe's Benefaction, a modest side-show, open only to the university's most learned persons, and consisting of a well-conceived mid-morning refection of champagne with strawberries and cream. From this, Jeremy Shefford's obscurantist views on the futility of pursuing higher degrees excluded him. The exclusion was responsible for his present employment, which was leaning out of his sitting-room window and pitching mocking remarks at his friend below.

'Come and have some black coffee,' he called out. 'Sober you up before the speechifying.'

'I'm not going to the speechifying. I'll come up, all the same.'

Shefford got out his coffee-percolator, and had it working by the time Naylor entered the room and scrambled out of his robe.

'You oughtn't to discriminate,' Shefford said. 'If you're content to guzzle strawberries at a kind of children's party for elderly macaws, then you ought to be content to go and listen to the Public Orator.'

'It doesn't follow. I enjoy strawberries. I don't enjoy Latin, or not when it's being so absurdly used. Think of it. Here are a number of chaps being given honorary degrees: politicians, physicists, actors and Lord knows what. Only a minority of them can have as much as opened Caesar's *Gallic Wars*. And this Orator-character gets up and makes a lot of jokes about them of the kind that Cicero might have contrived, had it ever occurred to Cicero to exhibit a sense of humour. All the learned laugh in the right places, and the recipients take their cue from that and manage sickly smiles. It's really too silly—worse than one of those Welsh Eisteddfods. An obsolete tribal rite. No sugar, thank you.'

'Did you run into Bernard Vanderlyn?' Shefford stirred his own coffee. 'I think I told you he remembers you.'

'I only saw him from a little way away. It was my impression that he doesn't look well. Do you think he'll understand the Latin pitched at him?'

'I shouldn't be surprised. I expect his first wife took him through short readings in selected texts daily.'

'I'm astonished you should be flippant about the first Mrs Vanderlyn, Jeremy. You used to have quite a thing about her.'

'Did I? Yes, you're right.' Shefford was serious. 'I did admire her, rather. But one forgets. Vanderlyn, too. He and his affairs interested me a lot—and now it's quite a time since I thought about him. Or about Mark Varley. His *First Poems* was decently received, although some reviewers said bits of it were juvenile. I haven't noticed anything about him since.'

'Do you hear from him?'

'I never have, and it's a year since I was in Tyros. I wrote to him a couple of times, but he didn't reply.'

'It was my impression that you'd chummed up with him.'

'I had in a way. But I was only there, you know, for a

few days. I've heard from Vanderlyn. I wrote to him when I saw that Oxford was going to give him this degree. He sent me a long letter back, but it wasn't very informative about Tyros. He seemed to insist that he's been given the degree here on the strength of his public career, and the Vanderlyn Foundation in New York, and so on—and not because of the Tyros venture, which he continues to regard as private. It seems fair enough. He didn't say anything about not being well.'

'I may have got a wrong impression. You'll see him this afternoon, I suppose. What about his new wife? Does she run around with him to affairs like this?'

'I don't know, but I'd suppose so. Gemma lived in England for a time, and probably likes coming back. Not that she's a simple Anglophile like her predecessor. She's not a *Heaths and Haunts of Thomas Hardy* type.'

'I remember you telling me about that, and about Varley celebrating a black mass——'

'Nonsense. He was invoking the moon. It had to be done naked, but equipped with a bow and arrows.'

'It's much the same thing. He must have been mad. Probably he's mad still.'

'I don't think so. No, I don't think so, at all.' Shefford was frowning. Even a little talk about Mark, he was finding, stirred a sense of responsibility in him. 'But he can do silly things—and wilful ones, like clobbering that policeman.'

'I don't call *that* mad—nor exactly wilful, either.' Sunshine had begun to penetrate the two deep window-embrasures of Shefford's room. The better to enjoy it, each of the young men was now kneeling on a window seat and leaning out with his head and shoulders in open air. It was thus, and across an intervening surface of crumbling grey stone, that they continued their conversation. 'In fact it was quite reasonable,' Naylor went on. 'If one of the coppers did what Varley said he did, that's to say. What would have been unreasonable would have been to propose a boxing-match on gentleman-like terms. No, he did right to find a weapon.'

Naylor paused, as if checking up dispassionately on the validity of these surprising reflections. 'Where he went wrong was in getting nabbed. And in court, you know, he began by lying fluently and resourcefully. Quite right too. But then, when they caught him out, he switched to haughty and passionate defiance. Wrong again. Admirable, to my mind, all the same.'

Shefford made no reply to this. Gavin, he was thinking, hadn't caught a glimpse of the real disaster of having been in prison, or he wouldn't want to talk about Mark Varley's affair at all. For some moments, therefore, and without speaking, he watched what was going on in the quad below. The summer term was over, and the undergraduates had gone away; beside the lodge a last heap of their trunks and suitcases was being hoisted on to a railway van. To-night, when the college held its own celebration, the rooms of these departed young men would pass briefly into the hands of another generation. There would be plenty of fathers and uncles among these old members piously returning to the lost world of their youth; fathers and uncles rather hoping they might be allocated their sons' and nephews' sets. Shefford didn't know whether the spectacle of that sort of continuity was agreeable or not, but at least he could raise no feeling of antagonism to the first preparations going on below. A brightly-coloured canvas awning was being put up along one side of the quad, and beneath it the trestle table from which drinks would be dispensed before dinner. An elderly gardener was giving to a final shaving of the grass the care of a superior barber-surgeon. One of the porters, hazardously perched on a plank straddling the fountain, offered an unnecessary wash and brush-up to the dolphins. From a turret the college flag flew, mysteriously heraldic. Shefford decided that the scene might be approved. It nicely balanced the splendour of an ancient and great foundation with a modestly domestic note.

'It is seducing, isn't it?' Naylor asked, as if similar thoughts had been passing through his own mind. 'The place requires our presence for only half the year, and yet we come to

178

behave as if we were Frenchmen, judging the rest of the world wholly barbarous, or Americans, convinced that it's insanitary.'

'It certainly sells us its own idea of what's important and absorbing.' Shefford's rooms were at the top of his staircase, and from his present perch he could look over the long balustrade crowning the farther side of the quad and survey the tips of Oxford's spires and pinnacled towers against the summer sky. From several of them there was now coming a jangling of bells to mark some mild academic climax in the day's proceedings. Shefford listened for a moment, and then turned to look at Naylor in his window. 'I ought to have gone back to Tyros,' he said with conviction. 'In the Easter Vac.'

'Because of Varley?' Naylor asked, surprised.

'Yes—because of Mark.'

'Even after he hadn't answered your letters?'

'The more so because of that. There's something I owe to him. We played football together.'

'Jeremy, I just don't understand you. Do you mean he comes from your own old school?'

'Nothing of the kind. We played Rugger together on Tyros. With some Greeks.'

'You bewilder me.' Having said this, apparently for form's sake, Naylor added, 'A kind of sacramental Rugger?'

'Gavin, you have a flair for guessing things. Something like that. It sounds silly, of course. However, this afternoon I'll be able——' Shefford broke off. 'There's Charles Blaine. I haven't seen him for weeks. Let's ask him up.'

'Hullo, Charles,' Naylor called out. 'Come up and have some of Jeremy's sherry.' He watched Blaine glance at his watch, give a nod, and disappear into the staircase. 'Jeremy, *have* you any sherry? I don't want it myself. Not after Lord Crewe's orgy.'

Shefford's hunt for sherry, although successful, lasted until Blaine was in the room. Blaine had a robe—differing in its colours from Naylor's but even more gorgeous—over his arm. He tossed it down on a chair.

179

'Hullo,' he said amiably. 'Why aren't you people at the gas-works?'

'Because we don't approve.' Shefford had decided to transfer the sherry to an impressive decanter. 'We think mediaeval stuff of that sort is flummery. Gavin and I are progressive. We know Greek and Latin; we know all about the minor Caroline poets. But we think Oxford should have more and more stinks, and more and more bangs. Even, perhaps, the last great bang of all.'

'Be quiet, and give me a drink.' Blaine dropped into a chair. 'This is a stupid sort of day. I've got to lunch with the Vice-Chancellor. He's another of your progressives, and knows about nothing whatever except Greek Epigraphy. What's Greek Epigraphy?'

'The Writing on the Wall—more or less.' Naylor had usurped the business of pouring the sherry. 'Why go?'

'Why go?' Blaine raised his glass. 'Cheers, chaps. I'm going because I'll be meeting an old friend. Bernard Vanderlyn. Remember him?'

'We were talking about him, as a matter of fact.' Shefford helped himself to sherry. 'I hope to see him this afternoon. Perhaps I never told you that I stayed with him on Tyros. It was just a bit of gate-crashing last summer. But he interested me. I ought to say, impressed me. The whole set-up.'

'Oh, that!' Blaine consulted his glass, so that Shefford remembered how he could give to such a scrutiny the effect of peering into the mysteries of the cosmos. 'Well, I've been there myself since then. Only a few weeks ago. It occurred to me to come back from Russia—there are a lot of sensible chaps *there*—by way of Greece, and to get around a little. So I've seen Tyros too.'

'And what did you think of it?' Shefford asked. 'And how does the venture go?'

'I'm not very qualified to give an opinion.' Blaine said this slowly, as if reluctant to continue with the subject at all. 'I wasn't terribly interested, Jeremy. I felt it to be a kind of obituary visit. Bernard had left us. Do you understand?'

'I suppose I do. But isn't the word unfair? He didn't exactly leave you. He was shoved out. What ought he to have done—joined a sit-down demonstration on the sidewalk outside the White House?'

'I mustn't say that, because I can't claim that it's what I'd have done myself. It's just that I don't understand what he *has* done. Buying an island, and collecting that long-haired crowd! As for how it's going, of course, it's not going too well. How could it? Even the thoroughly sensible things. Did you see the hospital? It's a first-class affair, but not yet off the ground. There are difficulties with some government department about staffing it, I gather. As for the writers and artists and so on: some of them have been packing up. Not that Bernard didn't seem to me to be running the outfit well. His old technique was to let people have their head, and then act decisively, if need be. Perhaps he continues to practise it—both these aspects of it—a little more than his new circumstances warrant. But I wouldn't really know.'

'It doesn't sound too good,' Shefford said. He found himself disturbed by Blaine's report. 'Gavin got a glimpse of Vanderlyn this morning, and says he doesn't look well.'

'Probably he has other things on his plate too.' Blaine shook his head at the offer of a second glass of sherry. 'It's why I want to see something of him today. It's possible I showed myself unsympathetic on Tyros.' He was silent for a moment. 'I think you did once meet his first wife—Louise?'

'Very briefly. But I liked her.'

'Yes. It wasn't a marriage I had the hang of. But it obviously meant more to Bernard than he's ever likely to recover from the loss of. This Gemma—you met her?'

'Yes, I met Gemma.'

'She hasn't come to Oxford with him for this business. Nice manners, perhaps, since it's essentially Louise's husband who's being honoured. But I couldn't help suspecting there's something wrong with the marriage. Wouldn't you say Gemma's an attractive woman?'

'Very much so.' Shefford had been clarifying his mind on this. 'It just wouldn't be safe to let the mind begin to dwell on her fondly.'

'That's a thoroughly moral view of the matter. My feeling is that she'd have Bernard in her pocket by this time, if she was any good. But his main personal preoccupation seems to be fussing over that boy.'

'Mark Varley?'

'That's right—the young poet who was up here. I didn't take to him. And Bernard's practically adopted him. The boy ought to reckon himself lucky, I suppose. Right in the purple. I couldn't help feeling sorry for the young sod, all the same.' Blaine was turning laconic. 'Bernard's obsessed with him. No other word for it. Weren't you aware of it, Jeremy? Hadn't it started when you were there?'

'I'm not sure that it hadn't.' Shefford felt dismayed. 'Charles, did you meet a character called Andreas? He wanted me to fetch Varley away.'

'Yes, I met him. And I'd say he has a nose for things.' Blaine got to his feet. 'But one mustn't exaggerate, and start crying woe. What Bernard wants for Varley is success, and if Varley makes the grade——' He broke off. 'It's your sort of thing, that. *Has* the boy talent?'

'Yes, real talent.' Shefford spoke confidently. 'I don't mean he's going to be an Eliot or a Yeats.'

'Perhaps that's what Bernard expects him to be. I wouldn't know. But I hope he makes some sort of grade, as I said. It might induce Bernard to turn his solicitude elsewhere. And I see the boy has had *some* success. Which is a start.'

'Gavin and I were speaking of that. Varley's book was quite well received.'

'His book?' Blaine was surprised. 'I haven't heard of a book. I mean his winning this prize.'

'A prize? I didn't know he'd won a prize.' Shefford was casting about in his mind for anything that could be meant. 'There are some people in Florence fond of handing things to young European poets——'

'No, no. This university prize. Here in Oxford.'

'The Newdigate? But Varley hasn't won that—and it would mean very little if he had. I think somebody at New College——'

'Not the Newdigate.' Blaine was at the door. 'The other one. You must have seen about it. Don't you read your *University Gazette*?'

'Of course not.'

'I can't understand your not knowing about your own sort of thing.' Blaine was looking at the two devotees of the Humanities in genuine disapproval. 'The poem on a sacred subject. Quite a lot of money in it. And I suppose it's why Bernard has brought young Varley with him to Oxford now. To enjoy his success. See you at the garden party, perhaps.' Blaine gave a casual nod, and left the room.

For a moment the two young men looked at each other in silence. Then Shefford turned and rummaged in a cupboard. Presently he produced a couple of dozen numbers of the *Oxford University Gazette*, and flicked through them. The obscure entry was hard to find.

'Here it is,' he said at length. 'Perfectly true. Mark Varley, B.A.'

'How very odd! What was the subject set?'

'*A Sweet Savour unto the Lord*.' Shefford pushed the disordered file of the *Gazette* away. 'It doesn't make sense. Everybody knows that the poem on a sacred subject is a joke. Something left over from the pieties of the mid-nineteenth century. It's won by awful little clergymen in Wales, or by old women on Boars Hill who were once Oxford Home Students. How could Mark make an ass of himself by competing?'

'The answer's Vanderlyn, I suppose. *He* wouldn't know that this prize has become a kind of joke. And Americans have a different attitude to that sort of thing. Resident poets on the campus, and courses in creative writing. All that. Vanderlyn would take it for granted that by gaining this distinction his *protégé* would be conquering his *alma*

183

mater, after all. So he's brought him in triumph to Oxford now.'

'I suppose that's it.' Shefford had got to his feet, walked to the window, and was staring discontentedly through it. 'It's our own attitude that's absurd, no doubt. But, you see, Mark's such a self-regarding little brute that anything approaching ridicule——'

'He'd dislike it, no doubt. And there is a puzzle, Jeremy, I agree. It may have been Vanderlyn's idea. But what persuaded your precious young friend to play?'

'He was a long way from Oxford, and it didn't seem important. Or he was reluctant to seem to duck a challenge. Or he was feeling cynical. Or it might have been a matter of loyalty, in a queer way. But he can hardly have reckoned on being put on show.'

'He needn't have come to Oxford. After all, there is the business of his having been in prison. If he's as sensitive about this absurd poem-affair as we're supposing, he could have made that a reason for not caring to come. Haven't you told me Vanderlyn has a feeling for the sensibilities of the young? He'd be bound to understand that.'

'Yes.' Shefford came back from the window. 'Unless he's really gone a bit odd. Or Mark may have felt that as he'd begun to play he must go on playing. Or you and I may be imagining things. The whole area may turn out to be one in which Mark has no feelings at all. I think I'll go and look for him. It's the only way to find out.'

Chapter 2

BUT MARK PROVED hard to find, either later that morning or in the early afternoon. This seemed to be because Vanderlyn had him firmly in his train, and he was moving in consequence in what he must be finding awkwardly exalted academic circles.

Still, there was nothing much against this, Shefford told himself. Vanderlyn's wife hadn't been able to come along, and there was no reason why he shouldn't bring, as a guest on the same terms, a young man who was practically in the position of an adopted son. Particularly to the big promiscuous garden party, which was where Mark eventually came in view.

It wasn't an occasion for which Shefford had ever felt enthusiasm. You started off—if you were punctilious—by joining a queue of people waiting to shake hands with the Vice-Chancellor. The men, in bright robes or dark gowns, stood fiddling with their mortar-boards or velvet caps; they were unwontedly jocular—presumably because, as serious persons, they felt uneasy at squandering useful time in this ritual way. Here and there one would see a man staring fixedly ahead of him and grimly silent, as if the ceremony positively offended him; he might actually be a mild and shy person, speculative in habit, who had abandoned the uphill-task of mastering the art of small-talk long ago. The women, if they weren't themselves learned and therefore condemned to be either garishly or sombrely attired, were in their year's new frocks and hats; and every now and then they would bend their bodies sideways out of the queue, as if impelled to perform some old-fashioned Swedish exercise; in fact, they would be trying to catch a better glimpse of a frock and hat in front. Shefford always found himself being wary about these ladies. He nursed a persuasion that they owned daughters approaching marriageable age in North Oxford, and were therefore best to be regarded as dangerous predators. His better reason told him that if they seemed oncoming it was simply because they had been nicely brought up, and were therefore conscious of owing a particular civility to their husbands' junior colleagues. This didn't prevent him from bobbing at them, when required, in what he was conscious of as a sidelong and awkward way.

After the queue for the Vice-Chancellor there was a queue for strawberries. It was a fixed persuasion of the guests, although unsupported by evidence within living memory, that these were likely to run out, so that those in the dusty rear would be fobbed off with tea and cakes. Once provided for, people wandered about, so that groups and coteries formed. The half-dozen or so honorands—like Vanderlyn, mostly foreign—were conducted around by Heads of Houses and others of notable consequence with the vague, untidy formality that attends academic occasions: they would be conscious or unconscious or their stiff new robes according to their individual background and habit. Among the natives and their wives a happy few who joined social to academic distinction kept themselves to themselves, edifying the many by the superior elegance of their comportment. As polite comedy, Shefford thought, it all got a good mark. But it wasn't polite comedy he was looking for now.

At least he had secured his heaped-up strawberries, and it was as he took a first spoonful that he saw Mark in the distance. The young man was standing close to Vanderlyn, and was being engaged in what seemed halting conversation by another of the honorands, an aged professor from the Sorbonne. Mark in this company looked uncomfortably handsome and absurdly young. He had dressed himself more formally than was required, for in addition to a B.A. gown and hood he had put on a wing collar and a white bow tie. There were never many B.A.s at the garden party. They appeared not to rank for it unless—like Shefford himself not many years before—they had precociously achieved some additional academic status. Just at the moment, there wasn't another B.A. in sight.

Shefford moved forward. He expected, as soon as he could distinguish Mark's features, to be treated to an expression of a darkening and sulky order. But this was not so. Mark was pale, and it wasn't difficult to guess that he was wishing himself a hundred miles away. It was also clear that he was trying very hard.

'Good afternoon, Jeremy.' Shefford turned and found that he was being addressed by his colleague Raggett. 'Surely that is our notable young revolutionary—the boy who tried to brain the policeman? Varley, I seem to remember his name is.'

'Yes, that's Mark Varley. But he didn't precisely try to do that. He went for the copper's collar-bone. He says that's what coppers do themselves.'

'Ah, yes. Well, there are no doubt times at which mere half-measures are discreet. But how odd that he should turn up at this jollification! He's doing his best, but he doesn't look to me to be enjoying himself.' Raggett's acute glance turned to Shefford. 'Who has brought him along?'

'Vanderlyn, whom he's standing beside.'

'Dear me! You remember the last honorand to parade a beautiful youth?' Raggett named an eminent French writer. 'It was felt to have its awkward as well as its amusing side.'

'There's nothing of the sort to amuse you now,' Shefford said shortly. 'Varley's quite a good poet, and Vanderlyn is interested in him. He lives with the Vanderlyns on a Greek island, pretty well as a son.'

'Yes, of course. Tyros. I know about it.'

'And so you ought. You had your share in launching it— on the night Vanderlyn dined with us. All that talk about patronage, and how helpful it is to artists to make them your servants.'

'I remember well enough.' Raggett was amused. 'Is Varley a servant? And is he hymning Alderman Bloggs with a will?'

'No, but Vanderlyn rather fusses over him. Bringing him along to all this, for example.'

'Quite so, quite so.' Raggett's interest in Varley was evaporating. Then he remembered something. 'Hasn't the lad won a university prize?' he asked. 'A prize for a poem of some sort?'

'Yes.'

'Excellent. I was glad to notice something about it in the *Gazette*. It should encourage him. A man needs encouragement after being inside. I know. I was once inside myself.'

Raggett nodded and drifted away. He had been a prisoner of war, Shefford remembered, with the Japanese. It was clear that the idea of there being something absurd about the poem on a sacred subject had never entered his head. That would go for most people, no doubt. They would know too little about the matter to have an opinion. But this wouldn't help Mark Varley, whose interest was in people who were interested in poetry.

It was at this moment that Mark saw Shefford. He hesitated, made a little bow to the professor from the Sorbonne, and came hurrying across the lawn, an ill-balanced tea-cup slopping unregarded in his hand.

'Jeremy, how nice! But I never answered your letters. I tried, and the stuff came out like what you'd call play-acting, so I shoved it away.' Mark grinned cheerfully, and then looked hurriedly round him. 'I say!' he said. 'Do you think they all feel it frightfully silly?'

'This garden party?'

'No, no. Just my being at it.'

'Mark, you're the same sort of idiot as ever.' Shefford knew that he must plunge straight back to this degree of companionableness. 'Just look around. There's not one person in a hundred knowing anything about you or giving you a thought.'

'That's true, of course.' Mark managed an emphatic nod. He gave the impression of being desperately resolved to be on his best behaviour. 'Only Bernard, you know, keeps on having me introduced to people. It's embarrassing. The last one was the Professor of Poetry. It was a bit awful. After all, he *is* rather a good poet.'

'And what was he like?'

'He was quite polite. In fact he was very kind.' Mark announced this in a puzzled way—as if he had expected the Professor of Poetry, confronted by one Mark Varley, to have thrown back his magnificent head in peals of scornful laughter.

'Did you have to read a bit of your prize poem at the Encaenia, Mark?' It seemed to Shefford that they had better have *A Sweet Savour unto the Lord* on the carpet—or the grass —at once.

188

'No, thank God! It's the Newdigate chap who has to spout. But, Jeremy, isn't it frightful?' Mark produced what Shefford judged an almost pathetic attempt at an air of fun. 'I didn't mean to do it at all.'

'Then how did it happen?'

'Bernard heard about it, and took it into his head that I should go in. He was rather insistent.' Mark hesitated. 'He used to be accustomed, you know, to give orders in a big way. It's a bad preparation for having to do with artists.'

'There appear to be two possible opinions about that. But go on.'

'Nobody's going to make *me* toe any sort of line.' Mark produced this with a sudden childish petulance which at least seemed to embarrass him. His glance became evasive. 'Of course Bernard's all right. But this directing people does come over him again still. We almost had a row. I was on the verge of asking for my cards.'

'Of walking out on him? Then why didn't you?'

'I had a reason.' Mark's uneasiness had increased. He had ceased to look at Shefford at all. Instead, he was glancing almost fearfully round the garden party. 'I have to do the decent thing by Bernard, after all. I couldn't just quit like a discontented lackey, could I? So I decided that the best thing to do about the prize poem would be to make some sort of joke of it. Write something that would be good in its fashion, but obviously not serious. Bernard likes that sort of thing: something that you might call high-class fun among ourselves on Tyros. You understand?'

'Yes, I think I do.'

'Only, it didn't work out quite like that. Something happened—one day when I was out with Stepho and Dionysios in the yacht. You remember them?'

'Yes, of course.'

'We went fishing, and there was a bit of a storm. In fact, it looked as if we were going to be drowned. It was rather fun.'

'Rubbish, Mark. You mean you were scared stiff.'

'There was that, of course. But the sea was terribly

beautiful—just because it looked as if I was having my last five minutes of it. The sky, too. And all the sounds—and even the wild tossing which was making all three of us bloody sick. Do you know how poems start?'

'In various ways, I suppose.'

'Well, yes. But sometimes something totally unexpected just turns up. And it was like that. This storm, and the business of being about to perish in it, suddenly struck me as declaring what they call the glory of God. Naturally, I don't *believe* in God. But there I was, with this stuff repeating itself inside my head. It was precisely like bits of a sacred poem—an ecstatic one by Christopher Smart. Wasn't that comical? But I was damned silly. I strung the bits together with any rot I could think up, and the thing was pretty well finished by the time we were in harbour again. So far, no harm done. But then I gave it to Bernard, just following this plan to turn his idea of my competing into a harmless joke. And Bernard, you see, thought it all right; thought it *good*.' Suddenly Mark was looking strangely frightened. 'So you can see, Jeremy, that it was difficult. Something has happened to his judgement, I think. At least where I am concerned. Anyway, I had to send the foolish thing in. I thought it would be the end of the matter.'

'I don't suppose there was any other entry,' Shefford said candidly. 'Hunting pots of that kind is one of the things that has been killed by the affluent society. In any case, it's just an odd affair you want to forget. That shouldn't be difficult. Nobody else is going to remember anything about it.'

'Don't you think so?' For the first time, Mark allowed what Shefford remembered as a familiar brooding gloom to hover over his features. 'The whole thing's a mess, Jeremy. I can't tell you how much it's that.' He looked darkly round the aimless eddy of the garden party. 'And we go back tomorrow.'

'To Tyros?'

'Yes. We fly to Athens and go straight down to the Peiraieus. We'll be back in the monastery by dinner-time.'

'Don't go, Mark.'

It was with surprise that Shefford heard himself utter these words. He had been looking past Mark and at Vanderlyn, who was now standing quite close, in conversation with the Vice-Chancellor. He had been reflecting that it was true Vanderlyn didn't look well. He had lost weight; his large frame held the suggestion of a sag or stoop; his eyes seemed in some disconcerting way to have changed their position in his head. But these things didn't add up to any rational occasion for the words Shefford had just spoken.

'Don't go,' he found himself nevertheless repeating. 'Say that you must have a break. Say right out that you must make your way in your *own* way. You can, you know, Mark. As long as you don't get into some disabling mood—or into gaol, for that matter—you're a thoroughly competent person.' Shefford paused. 'Cut and run for it. I'll help.'

'I couldn't do that.' Mark's dark eyes had rounded as he listened to this strange speech. His pallor had increased. He was looking about him almost with the suggestion of a hunted man. 'I've told you that I couldn't possibly let Bernard down. Not now. He's done everything, you know. I told you that, right at the start. Nothing can change it.' Mark looked straight at Shefford. 'But that's not honest, I suppose. It's only a first reason—a first reason why I can't quit Tyros. There's a second.'

'What's that?'

'I can't tell you.'

'Mark, I think that's a stupid thing to say. You'd better tell me.'

'I really can't. You see, Jeremy, you're a reasoning creature. What Keats or somebody calls a consecutive man. You'd say my second reason doesn't square with my first. You'd say I'm mad. And I'm not.'

'For goodness' sake, Mark, don't start nursing dark secrets.'

'All right. I suppose I mustn't forget that you're my oldest friend.' Mark didn't seem to find much relief in this uncomfortable quip. He was scrambling out of his B.A. hood and gown as if at the end of a masquerade that had gone on too long. He had turned even paler than before. 'It's Gemma,' he said, and his voice shook.

'Gemma?' There must have been blank surprise in Shefford's tone.

'Jeremy, can't you *think*? Can't you *imagine*?' Mark made a strange gesture, as of a man suddenly groping in darkness. 'I must go back. I just *must*.'

Chapter 3

WITH SURPRISING SPEED the garden party was thinning and fading out. What was to be eaten had been eaten, and what was to be drunk had been drunk. Many of the male guests had further festivities to face before this massive day should be brought to its close. Many of their wives had kitchens in which evening meals for hungry children had yet to be prepared. The Vice-Chancellor—already perhaps rehearsing an after-dinner speech—was dispensing absent-minded valedictory remarks upon anybody mindful enough to come up and take leave of him. In the marquees and at the damasked and beflowered tables the regardless staffs of catering concerns were scooping up the broken meats. Only the sun, still high above Oxford in a cloudless sky, seemed indisposed to call it a day.

From this dissolving spectacle Shefford turned back to Mark. He did so with a dawning sense of having been remarkably stupid. If he hadn't, like Bernard Vanderlyn, got round positively to fussing about Mark he had managed to think about him a good deal. Yet his thinking had simply missed out a whole aspect of Mark's being. It was an aspect which had never been paraded before him, but it was as certainly and predictably there as was the other side of the moon. Indeed the moon had now, so to speak, revolved, and there was nothing else on view—except, as a sufficiently contrasting background, the disintegrating pageant of the Vice-Chancellor's elderly and composed party.

Shefford was never to know what immediate reply he would have found to Mark's sudden and desperate confession. Somebody had strolled up behind him, and he heard the President's voice.

'Good afternoon, Varley.' The President shook hands with Mark uneffusively but with firm cordiality. 'It's pleasant to see you here. And I congratulate you on your prize.'

'Thank you very much.' The blemish on Mark's cheek had darkened as if flicked by a whip. It was particularly disagreeable to him, Shefford supposed, to have his dramatic avowal of passion interrupted by the cropping up of this offensive topic. Perhaps, too, he was sufficiently at sea to suppose that the President had spoken in irony. Certainly his attempt to be on his best behaviour was over for the afternoon. 'It was a joke,' he said rudely.

'A poem on a sacred subject? Dear me!' The President paused as if to consider. 'Perfectly reasonable, of course,' he said. 'There's thought to be an element of play in all artistic creation. Have you ever read the Bible?'

'Yes.' Shefford could see Mark making a brief hunt for something which should assert the indignity of his lower-class childhood. 'They made me. With a strap.'

'No doubt, no doubt. Take the pentateuch, now. I can't help feeling that Moses himself wrote with his tongue in his cheek from time to time. Or the Holy Ghost, if you take that view of the book's authorship. But you must tell me how you're getting on, Varley.' The President gave Shefford a dismissive nod. 'Yes, Varley and I will walk to the gate together.'

For a moment Shefford thought that Mark was going to rebel. Dignity, however, prevailed in him. He gave his friend no more than a long, mute look, and walked submissively away.

Shefford glanced around for Vanderlyn, to whom this

encounter with Mark had prevented him from paying his respects. He wished he had ventured to approach Vanderlyn among the grandees straight away. The meeting wouldn't then have happened to the accompaniment of his own consciousness that Vanderlyn's *protégé* had taken it into his wanton head to harbour an illicit passion for Vanderlyn's wife. It was a possibility, he remembered, which he had fleetingly envisaged when talking to Andreas. Andreas hadn't been impressed by it, and he himself had ceased to think of it. But now—if Mark wasn't play-acting—it was bang in the picture. And he was sure, on reflection, that Mark *hadn't* been play-acting. Mark was in a genuine predicament, and knew it. Shefford wondered whether Gemma had a notion of his emotional state. Probably she had, however mum Mark had kept about it. But he mightn't have kept mum at all; he might have openly been making passes at Gemma; putting up whatever was his own version of kneeling at a woman's feet. Did Vanderlyn himself know? Shefford couldn't find a likely answer. He realised that he had very little notion of the kind of awareness that Vanderlyn would carry around with him in matters of this sort.

Vanderlyn had departed, and so had everybody else. Shefford himself was actually the last remaining guest at the Vice-Chancellor's party, and at the empty garden's main gate the Vice-Chancellor was now standing in undemonstrative patience. Shefford was appalled. Mark himself couldn't have raised a greater access of self-consciousness in the face of such a situation. And now the Vice-Chancellor, seeing a confused young man proposing to hurry past him with a panicky bow, asserted the claims of courtesy and began to converse. He even contrived to imply that it was by previous arrangement that he and his unknown guest were thus lingering together on the deserted scene. Finally he went away, genially waving his cap.

Shefford walked back to college, displeased with himself. He had been awkward with the Vice-Chancellor. He had been impolite in not making sure of an opportunity to speak to Vanderlyn, whose hospitality he had enjoyed at almost this time in the previous summer. But what chiefly troubled him was something it took an effort to trace and face. When Mark had looked at him and said, 'Can't you *think*? Can't you *imagine*?' he had felt, if only for a moment, the same impulse of straight hostility that he had experienced during that encounter in his own college garden three years before. Both times it had arisen, he supposed, from the perception of something sharply alien to himself. 'I *must* go back', Mark had said—and it had been as if the words were punched out of him by a force which left Shefford at once shocked and envious.

He couldn't believe that he was going to be jealous of Mark—of Mark who, although the younger of the two of them, had through some unfair advantage of temperament been able to advance precociously upon a commanding and searing passion. That would be too silly—as silly as being jealous, so to speak, the other way on. It was true that he had got rather hooked on Mark, and in very much the way that he was inclined to blame Vanderlyn for having got hooked. The prudent man—and it was as a prudent man that Shefford knew he would have received a good word from a mediaeval theologian—the prudent man is always liable to be beguiled by the spectacle of the world's Mark Varleys: creatures of impulse, in one degree or another creatively gifted, and disposed to cry out—the more effectively if mutely or by implication—that they fall upon the thorns of life, they bleed.

The burden of this seemed to be—Shefford told himself as he turned into his own college lodge—that various hazards attend the role of big brother. If he had in any degree really taken on the job in relation to Mark—and honesty obliged him to acknowledge that he had—then there were several directions in which he had to look out for himself. For example, he just mustn't find himself tagging along behind a wayward and incipiently disastrous young man in a feebly expostulatory and even corruptly permissive posture.

Delivering this warning to himself had occupied Shefford as he climbed his staircase. When he entered his room he saw there was a note on his desk, and that it was addressed in Vanderlyn's hand.

Dear Jeremy,
    I have some hope of a word with you at a garden party which I understand I am to attend this afternoon. But the entertainment may not be to your taste, or you may be too busy for it, and even if we do briefly meet I shall be feeling that it would be pleasant to see you other than in a press of people. Tonight's dinner I believe to be a formal affair, and likely to go on for some time. But what about afterwards? If you are not engaged, and it is not too late for you, would it be possible to take another stroll together in your garden? There is, I see, a moon! I have vividly in my mind the account I gave to Louise of our occasion there—and, of course, the strange manner of my first meeting with Mark. I hope you will see something of Mark. And I should like to have a word about him. You will have heard of his prize. His attitude to it has not been without its amusing side. His further plans, however, are not so settled as one would wish.
    Send a note across to me if this suggestion is any good. I can probably cut and run for it a little after eleven. I fancy I know my way to the garden pretty well.

                                        Sincerely yours,

                                        BERNARD VANDERLYN

P.S. Gemma has not come to England with me. Her pregnancy is in an early stage, but she has been advised not to travel.

When Shefford had read this letter he sat down at once and wrote a note confirming the suggested meeting. He took this over to the lodge and arranged for its delivery. When he got back to his rooms he read the letter over again, and found himself wondering whether it was exactly the letter that Vanderlyn would have written three years before. Was there a kind of sentimentality in the rendezvous proposed? At least Vanderlyn didn't intend bringing Mark along as well; his suggestion that Mark was to be talked about seemed to exclude that. Visualised in retrospect—Shefford discovered—his picture of the bow-and-arrow affair now took in his own figure as well as those of Mark and Vanderlyn. There they were, all three: surely a sufficient symbol of the involvement he had come to acknowledge. The moon had grown enormous, and the bits and pieces of garden statuary were extravagantly posed. He remembered having said something stupid to Vanderlyn about a suggestion of opera, but now this scene of his own involuntary recreating was much more like straight ballet; Mark's nudity was even tending to disappear within indecent flesh-coloured tights. Shefford felt the prudent man again rise up in him. What was one to expect of a set of relationships so bizarrely inaugurated? But at least—he told himself—there was satisfaction in the real information Vanderlyn's letter communicated, oddly placed in a postscript though it was. The fact that Gemma was going to have a baby surely put paid to whatever lecherous notions Mark had been heating his imagination with. It also knocked on the head a lot of nonsense that had been talked by Andreas.

In his bath—for he had decided a bath was in order before getting into tails for the final grandeurs of the day—Shefford realised that Vanderlyn would certainly ask him to revisit Tyros that summer. It would hardly be possible to refuse.

Chapter 4

THE GARDEN GLIMMERED in a moonlight less resplendent than three years before, and it was very possible to get the appearances of things wrong. One might have supposed, for instance, that the place had been given over to some modern Pygmalion, operating in a large way. The marble statues and busts seemed more numerous, and every now and then showed signs of animation, advancing upon one another or retreating under the mysterious guidance of small red spots of light. These, however, were simply the glowing tips of cigars, and the moving white figures behind them were gentlemen in evening dress. It was the year in which the most senior group of old members came to dine; their movements were measured and grave; ribbons and medals and stars glinted here and there upon their distinguished persons. The aroma of Havana tobacco was heavy on the still June air. If the scented limes were operating—as they no doubt were—it was without having much of a chance to register.

There wasn't a crowd, since only a scattering of guests had come to wander here at this late hour. But even these perhaps disconcerted Vanderlyn. He was slower off the mark than formerly, and his inquiries about Shefford's fortunes since they had last met went forward with an ambassadorial courtesy which didn't seem to match the rapid approximation to intimacy which they had once seemed to manage. Shefford didn't do too well himself. If a contemporary had confided to him by letter that his wife was expecting a child, he would have known in just what tone to refer to it at a subsequent meeting. But in Vanderlyn's case he was at a loss. He was glad there was going to be a baby, but suspected himself of a subconscious feeling that Vanderlyn was too old to become a father without an effect of indelicacy attending the achievement. When he did say something, what he managed was perhaps no more than an unintelligible mumble. At least Vanderlyn seemed to make no response whatever; when he spoke it was to say something about Louise's frequently having referred, during the last months of her life, to the morning on the Ridgeway. It appeared that she had subsequently corresponded with the author of *Heaths and Haunts of Thomas Hardy* on the vexed question of the Red House near Great Fawley. But no clarification had emerged. Perhaps this was because the author must by then have been in his late nineties. He had written to Louise several times, mentioning certain money matters. Vanderlyn had formed the opinion—which he hadn't communicated to Louise—that the letters came from an institution for senile persons.

This reminiscent vein, although touching, didn't strike Shefford as satisfactory. It was as if Vanderlyn saw his life as having stopped short of his second marriage. It was only when Shefford said something about Mark that his thought seemed to move forward to the present time.

'I can't be sure about Mark and Tyros,' he said. 'Sometimes he loves it, and finds it ideal for his work. But at other times I suspect he would like to be some place else. Has he said anything about it to you, Jeremy?'

'I think that, a year ago, he said something which would cover both these attitudes. But he didn't make a point of it.' Shefford thought of adding lightly, 'I suppose Tyros comes a little short in the way of female society.' But then he told himself that he mustn't tackle this new and disconcerting theme rashly, or in a trivial way.

'I was glad to see you having a talk with him this afternoon. Did he strike you as happy?'

'Reasonably so, I think. There are always clouds drifting about round Mark.' Shefford didn't feel that this reply was honest, and he was disinclined to face anything like a course of inquiry about Mark—whose happiness or unhappiness, and state of mind in general, Vanderlyn had made very much his own business, after all. Perhaps the reluctance made itself evident in his tone, for Vanderlyn ceased to ask questions. But it was still about Mark that he talked.

'Mark's winning the prize,' he said, 'has been very fortunate. It seems that his grades weren't any too good when he was with you, and the success should give him confidence. I've been seeing about getting the poem printed. You haven't read it yet, I imagine, or heard how it came to be written.'

'Mark said something about a fishing expedition, and a bit of a storm.'

'That's to put it mildly. He went out with two of our Greek boys, and they got into serious trouble. The Aegean can be very treacherous at times. They were blown right away from the island. We had an anxious time waiting for them.' Vanderlyn paused, as if taking the measure of some grim memory. 'It got so that the yacht seemed to be foundering, it seems, and they had nothing between them and drowning except a life-preserver apiece. The danger stirred Mark's imagination. Do you remember about John Henry Newman's great hymn, *Lead, kindly light*?'

'I don't think I do.'

'He wrote it during a storm when he was aboard a fishing smack on the Mediterranean. "The night is dark, and I am far from home." It's much better than most hymns.'

'Yes, I suppose it is.' Shefford tried to keep astonishment out of his voice.

'It was rather the same with Mark. He composed some very serious stanzas. They are quite remarkable. Very much more mature than anything he had done before.'

'Religious stanzas, you mean?' It seemed to Shefford that this comparing of Mark Varley and Cardinal Newman would be funny if it were not rather alarming.

'The fear of death can still occasionally lead the mind that way.' Vanderlyn's old note of humour sounded fleetingly in this. 'Of course Mark is still very young, and I won't say that the poem, even in its best parts, isn't derivative. Echoes of Hopkins's *Wreck of the Deutschland* can be found in it.'

'I see,' Shefford said—although he was by no means certain that he did. What had come into his head was the odd notion that Bernard Vanderlyn was taking on something of the character of his first wife. He was certainly sufficiently wrapped up in her. Yet the sense that earnestness was usurping the place of shrewdness in Vanderlyn's assessment of things might be delusory. His view of Mark's unfortunate prize poem, for example, could conceivably be clearer and more honest than Mark's own.

'But of course what this sudden danger and excitement drew out of Mark wasn't too closely related to the subject prescribed by your university. So he cobbled it up with other matter which wasn't inspired and isn't so good. And that offended his sense of artistic rectitude. He was a little letting himself down. He tried to pretend to me that the whole thing was a joke, and that it shouldn't be submitted. I insisted, of course, but not without giving the matter thought. His success has come to mean a lot to me. But he takes handling, as you can guess. And I sometimes feel I'm not too long on tact with him.'

'I don't think I'd worry about *that*,' Shefford said. He spoke with as much emphasis as he thought polite.

'I'm not unaware of what you feel, Jeremy. I cut too solicitous a figure. Isn't that it? Like an anxious parent despatching a child to summer camp for the first time.'

'It's something of that sort that you might most usefully do.' Shefford decided there was nothing for it but to speak out boldly. 'Despatch him—it doesn't much matter where. At least for a time. Let him get up a bit of his own steam. He held out an empty purse to you long ago, in effect— here, in this very garden. You've filled it too damned full. I know about the duty of rich men to help artists along. I know that if they're any good—the rich men, I mean— they'll feel their responsibility doesn't end just with the transfer of pounds or dollars. I respect immensely what you've been trying to do on Tyros. But every case has its individual requirements. It's precisely *that*, surely, that a good patron sees. And Mark's requirement is to be booted out into the world for a bit. I'm sure of it.'

Shefford found that his speech—unpremeditated and therefore sadly unpolished—had fallen into silence. The portly and cigar-smoking gentlemen had thinned out, but a couple of those that lingered were passing close by. He thought he caught a curious glance from one of them. Could he have so far forgotten himself as positively to shout his impertinent speech at Vanderlyn? And was Vanderlyn offended? For the moment, Shefford found that he didn't care. He walked on in silence, with a sense of release attending him.

'Mark has difficulty in working. In fact, he's not working.' Vanderlyn's voice was dispassionate. 'It's a real problem for a poet: what to do while the creative impulse is in abeyance.'

'He'll chop wood, if he has any sense. Or at least he can learn something.'

'That's the teacher speaking, Jeremy.' Vanderlyn's slow smile was just visible. 'Perhaps it's not so clearly the answer today as it was in former times, when the poet saw himself as taking all knowledge for his province. A young man like Mark is impatient with anything that doesn't make some immediate promise to his sensibility.'

'I agree with you there.' It seemed to Shefford that Vanderlyn's perceptions, if patchy, could still be keen enough.

'And you may be right that things have been made too easy for him, lately.'

'That's not what I'm saying. If anything, things have been made difficult. Mark's is in some ways a hard road. I'm not speaking just of material or economic ease.'

This produced another silence, and a longer one. It was as if Vanderlyn had been presented with a new idea at last. Shefford glanced around him. The garden was now almost empty: the cigars finished, the reminiscences exhausted, the elderly gentlemen departed to their unluxurious under-graduate beds. The moon, too, had vanished, much as if it were college property, and had been switched off by a head porter as a hint that festivity was at an end. But most of the stars had disappeared as well. Heavy cloud had arrived unexpectedly over Oxford.

Chapter 5

'Yes,' VANDERLYN WAS saying. 'There's much in that point of view. It brings me back to the feeling that Mark requires responsibilities. He has, of course, one high responsibility. To his own developing genius.'

'I suppose it's his business to give the best he's got.'

'But other responsibilities as well. He needs some sort of sheet-anchor, wouldn't you agree? A fixed point. It has been very much in my mind for some time. Jeremy, I'd be glad if you came out and took another look at us.'

'Of course I'd like to very much.' Shefford found he was saying this quite sincerely. His misgivings about a big brother's role might be abundantly justified. All the same, he couldn't ditch Mark Varley now. Nor Bernard Vanderlyn either, for that matter. What Vanderlyn had just said hadn't pleased or impressed him. It was either vague in a way that Vanderlyn had never been vague before, or it pointed to something so injudicious as to invite disaster. Whether consciously or unconsciously, moreover, it had avoided the real point Shefford was concerned to make: that Mark should for a time be told to go it alone. But all this didn't alter the fact that both Vanderlyn and Mark in some way looked to him. 'It's a good time of year,' he said. 'I've the whole of the Long Vac. before me.'

'But you may have arranged other commitments and expenses, Jeremy. I think I revise my invitation. I impose a condition. You may come to Tyros only if you agree to be my guest from Oxford back to Oxford.'

'Very well—but Economy Class.' Shefford was rather pleased than otherwise that Vanderlyn had thus insisted on putting his hand in his pocket; that it wasn't embarrassing seemed to speak of something satisfactory between them.

'Then it's a bargain—even to the colour of the air-ticket. And come as soon as you can.'

'Any day next week.'

'Jeremy, I'm most grateful to you. Mark probably wouldn't like you to know it, but he has a high regard for you. You could be very valuable to him.'

'I'll do my best.' Shefford felt no sense of resentment at being thus rather naively accorded his place in Vanderlyn's kingdom. 'And I'll very much look forward,' it occurred to him to add politely, 'to seeing Mrs Vanderlyn again.'

'I've kept you up unconscionably, and the moon has very properly deserted us—and all those governing-class Englishmen in their medals and orders as well.' Vanderlyn laughed softly. A certain tension seemed to have left him. It was as if Shefford's promise to visit Tyros had been a material point with him. 'They amuse me. I guess they remind me of old times.'

'Do you find yourself regretting old times?'

'I try not to. At the end, you know, Louise and I were going forward together, and planning a big change in our goal. I feel it would be a kind of disloyalty to have regrets.'

There was nothing to be said to this—and moreover Shefford had to give his attention to making a groping progress from the deserted garden. It struck him that he would be glad to get clear of it. He had been apprehensive that Vanderlyn might make a point of revisiting, rather in the manner of a shrine, the actual spot at which Mark had bobbed up so idiotically as Robin Hood in a nudist camp. Such a prompting would have carried alarming suggestions as to the unconscious basis of the whole Vanderlyn-Varley affair. But nothing of the sort had, of course, occurred. And the first Mrs Vanderlyn—Shefford reminded himself—had been very fond of English gardens.

'There's a difficulty, Jeremy.' Vanderlyn had come to a halt, as if uncertain of his footing. 'If you are coming to Tyros, there is something I ought to tell you. Everything there isn't quite as it should be.'

'The enterprise has run up against difficulty?'

'There certainly is that. For the time being, we are a little in the doldrums. Everybody hasn't seen eye to eye with me.' Vanderlyn paused, but Shefford said nothing. It couldn't have been the original idea, he was thinking, that everybody should see eye to eye with their patron the proprietor of Tyros. Perhaps something disablingly authoritarian had really been seeping up in Vanderlyn—from those old times which he was determined not to regret. 'It's something different,' Vanderlyn said. 'It's something so intimate, Jeremy, that I really have no right to force it upon you as a confidence.'

They had left the garden, and the mass of the New Library impended blackly above their heads. Through the arcading the Great Quadrangle showed like a sombrely conceived theatrical set; only the leaping dolphins at its centre, softly floodlit, seemed to draw an enhanced vivacity from the surrounding dark. Vanderlyn's voice had taken on a constraint that Shefford had never heard before, and the low vaulting under which they stood lent it a curious hollowness of tone.

'You may sometimes have wondered about my second marriage,' Vanderlyn said. He paused as if expecting a reply—an ineptitude which took Shefford by surprise. 'Louise was anxious. And we had both known Gemma for a long time.'

Shefford still didn't manage to say anything. They were out in the open now, but it remained very dark. The few lights showing round the looming perimeter of the high quadrangle made little impression on it. Only the arched cavity beneath the tower, with the great college gates beyond, remained brightly lit, like an inner stage upon which some dramatic episode might at any moment transact itself. They moved towards this. Shefford was once more recalling his conversation with the ironic Andreas. It looked as if Andreas hadn't missed a single trick.

'The marriage made Marion's position more eligible,' Vanderlyn said.

For a moment Shefford made nothing of this; it was as mysterious in substance as it was old-fashioned in expression. Then he remembered Marion Causland as being, as it were, the factor one was always likely to forget. She had never entered his head, for example, when Mark had begun his say about Gemma at the garden party that afternoon. Yet he ought to have thought of her at once. If Mark was in love with Vanderlyn's wife, it surely complicated the Tyros scene that Vanderlyn's stepdaughter was in love with Mark. And she certainly was. Looking back on that moment of Marion's self-betrayal by the sea-shore, Shefford hadn't a doubt of it. It was like the *dramatis personae* of some musty old play: *Mark, enamoured of Gemma;* and *Marion, enamoured of Mark.* Whether Gemma was enamoured of anybody didn't appear. As for Vanderlyn himself, you could call him enamoured of Mark, and moreover he very plainly remained enamoured of his first wife. Indeed, there was a sense in which you would have to say he was enamoured of Marion as well—for what he seemed to be admitting was that he had remarried chiefly to provide her with a suitable female companion. It was all—Shefford found himself thinking again—not his sort of thing. Still, he was committed to renewing his acquaintance with Tyros. He had better listen to anything further that Vanderlyn had to say.

'Our plan envisaged responsibilities which Marion was a little young to shoulder. Indeed, they would never come naturally to her, since she is of a studious and retiring disposition. Yet she has, of course, a great love and understanding of the arts, as her mother had. You must have noticed that?'

'Yes.' Shefford thought he could just square it with his conscience to acquiesce in this large and vague proposition.

'It would be quite contrary to Marion's inclination to have to mingle in an artistic world; to have a *salon*, as they used to say, or to be an active centre for what we are trying to do on Tyros.'

'I'm sure *that's* true.' This time, Shefford allowed himself a firm emphasis.

'But, to an individual artist, a girl at once so sensitive, so well-balanced and so capable of devotion could be of inestimable value. You see that too?'

This time, it was impossible to equivocate. A suspicion

which had earlier crossed Shefford's mind was established as a deplorable fact. The *dramatis personae* had to be revised so as to read: *Mark, enamoured of Gemma and ordered to be enamoured of Marion.* Or that was how it was going to be. The order couldn't yet have been given—or the disposition benevolently made, if one preferred to phrase it that way. But it was coming along. Vanderlyn on his island was like a purblind Prospero. He had discerned that he had a willing Miranda. About Ferdinand he hadn't a clue.

'No,' Shefford said. 'I can't say I *do* see that. At least I don't see anything necessarily valid and desirable to which it leads. You're not dealing, you know, with categories of persons—although I daresay it's just that you *have* been dealing with most of your days. Individuals are different. Just to keep one's hands off them is the good rule, nine times out of ten.'

'Unhappily, there's something more to say.' Vanderlyn had come to a halt just short of the flood of light before them, and his features were lit up clearly. Glancing at them apprehensively—for he felt that he had spoken perhaps more stiffly than was licenced by his years—Shefford saw that his companion had simply not heard what had been said to him. Vanderlyn looked as if he were unaware of either light or darkness, let alone a human voice. A moment of sombre and complete self-absorption had fallen upon him. Yet, almost immediately, he spoke again. 'I mean, of course, about my marriage to Gemma. It seemed reasonable in every way. But it hasn't worked.' As he said this, he took a watch from a pocket, and glanced at it. The act was incongruous and painful. 'I'm afraid they must have been waiting for some time,' he said. 'We're driving straight back to London, you know.'

Shefford said nothing. He wasn't able to, for a porter had emerged from the lodge in order to open the wicket in the big gate. Vanderlyn said good-night to the man, and they both stepped through. The street was deserted and dark, and at the kerb a big car was waiting. It was a Cadillac again, but this time there was a chauffeur. There was also somebody in the back, who could only be Mark but who didn't move. Perhaps he was sulking; perhaps he was only feeling selfconscious and foolish—sitting in this luxurious affair outside his old college.

'I'm terribly sorry about what you say.' Shefford knew he had to get out some such speech as this. 'But I'd hope that the baby——'

Vanderlyn interrupted him with a gesture—perhaps because the chauffeur had got out, whipped his cape off, and opened a back door of the car. Then he spoke in a low voice.

'Jeremy—I don't know who the baby's father is. Come when you said. I'll have them make arrangements. Good-night.'

Shefford watched the car depart. He watched the dark head of the talented author of *A Sweet Savour unto the Lord*, and remarked that it didn't move. He turned back into the lodge, where the porter had something to say about the high success of the college feast. He walked through the dark Great Quadrangle, and expertly up his dark staircase.

Mark, enamoured of Gemma, and the father of her child; ordered to be enamoured of Marion . . .

As Shefford went to bed he told himself that it was useless to dodge the evidence. It pointed only one way. And when he woke up in the small hours it was to find that, this time, he really was jealous of Mark—of Mark who had managed to go to bed with a beautiful woman. What was particularly humiliating in this discovery about himself was his knowing perfectly well that the jealousy was only jealousy-in-the-head—which is a particularly shameful sub-department (he told himself) of sex-in-the-head. Had Gemma Vanderlyn, back on Tyros, suddenly offered herself to *him*, it was quite clear to him that he would have bolted in dismay. For he had to acknowledge that, in some disastrous manner that he didn't at all understand, he had grown up entirely incapable of at least a few forms of common sexual behaviour—one of them being agreeably entertaining one-self with a friend's wife.

It must be a matter of some radical lack of passion, he

assured himself despondently as he went to sleep again. But the next morning, when he was cooking his breakfast and recalled these nocturnal emotions, he discovered they had entirely vanished. He wasn't jealous of Mark at all, and to become so again would require something like a wanton act of the will. But whether to take satisfaction in this mysteriously gained immunity, or to deplore it as unmanly, he just didn't know.

His flight ticket arrived from an Oxford travel agency that afternoon. Vanderlyn—and in so punctilious a man it almost suggested a crack-up—had forgotten the stipulation about its having to be Economy Class.

PART IV

Chapter 1

SOME CHANGE HAD come over the Greek boy with the evocative name of Dionysios, but Shefford didn't know what it was. There was nothing obtrusive about it. Once more Dionysios simply lay on his back on the deck of the launch, staring up into the sky. While waiting for Shefford's ferry-boat he must have been swimming in the harbour, since his curls were wet and flattened on his head. No less strikingly than before, he looked like something recovered from the antique world. One felt that there ought to be vine leaves in his hair; that it could only have been in an authentic bacchanalian fracas that misadventure had befallen his nose. Yet there was nothing overblown about him to suggest habitual revel. Beneath the decorous uniform or near-uniform which he was once again wearing, his limbs were as spare and his tummy as flat as a sprinter's. His observations in the heavens seemed this time to be peculiarly absorbing. Just occasionally he remembered to give Shefford his flashing and encouraging smile.

Stepho appeared not to have changed at all. At least it was plain as he stood at the wheel that his flair for immobility had not deserted him, nor his power to project some perceptibly sinister aura. He was like the figure of Death, Shefford thought, in unnumbered modern ballets: much given to simply standing around, but occasionally remembering to strike a menacing attitude. One never actually saw Stepho throwing up his arms and pointing death-rays at one from his splayed-out fingers, but one did feel that it was something of the sort that was going on inside his head. Yet if Stepho was Thanatos, Dionysios, despite his name, was Eros himself. What Dionysios saw in the sky was a succession of beautiful images of fulfilled desire.

This perception, though it didn't strike Shefford as important, recurred to him once or twice on the passage to

Tyros. It was an uncomfortable passage, although the wind was light and there was no more than a moderate swell on the sea. With the launch to themselves, the two young Greeks seemed disposed to drive it all out—and perhaps they also found it amusing to incommode their passenger if they could. Shefford sat in the stern and made it a matter of pride not to grab at the gunwale; he felt like a lad in some horrible contraption at a fun fair, determined to demonstrate his intrepidity to a girl or to his mates. Tyros appeared every now and then, itself seeming to plunge violently up and down, as if in the grip of a seismic disturbance. Shefford wondered why Mark hadn't come across to meet him. Perhaps he had had enough of the John Henry Newman role on the occasion of composing his sacred poem; perhaps he had quarrelled with these Greek boys, his near-contemporaries; or perhaps he was indulging in his own amusement of driving furiously round and round the island in one of Vanderlyn's cars. But it was possible, also, that Mark had regretted the confidence upon which he had embarked at the garden party, and was going to fight shy of Shefford as much as possible.

From Bernard Vanderlyn, too, there had been a confidence, and the one confidence was far from a comfortable counterpoise to the other. In fact Shefford saw that, with all the speed to be extracted from this powerful engine at full throttle, he was being hurtled into a morally untenable position. He couldn't shuttle to and fro in the monastery, colleaguing with Vanderlyn on Gemma's infidelity to him and with Mark on his adulterous possession of her. He wondered who else knew either of these secrets. It was to be inferred from what Vanderlyn had said that Vanderlyn didn't know Mark's. It was conceivable that Mark didn't know, and that even Gemma didn't know, that Vanderlyn knew what he did. But this would require that Vanderlyn should be sterile but not impotent, should be aware of this as a quite unquestionable fact, and should have married while keeping quiet about it. Did Marion Causland suspect anything at all? One's sense of the probabilities here depended upon whether one took the view that love sharpens or that it clouds the sight. And what about Andreas, supposing he was still on Tyros? He had proclaimed his *métier* to be that of an observer. What had he observed?

Nothing of this was agreeable to Shefford, and after some thought about it he began to wonder whether it was just the sea that was making him sick. He would feel better, he decided, if he could see any honest role for himself; indeed, if he *couldn't* see any such role, he simply ought not to have come. It was his idea that in such a situation as he confronted the least disastrous course might be an immediate airing of the truth. People are often more tolerant of the truth than one would predict. On the other hand the notion that you necessarily improve matters by blurting things out was probably immature and callow. Given a little time, the direst horrors can sometimes evaporate from people's lives, leaving little damage behind. Bucketing over the Aegean, Shefford considered these various possibilities rather in the manner of a man consulting first one and then another volume on a library shelf. He had an idea that events were likely to overtake his deliberations, anyway.

'Perhaps you come to Tyros for the wedding?'

It was Dionysios who had spoken, and Shefford turned to him in astonishment. The words were unexpected in themselves, and equally unexpected was Dionysios's power to utter them. They had come from him with an ease suggesting that he must have been putting in time on English lessons. In the previous summer he and Stepho had both been capable of understanding simple remarks, but neither had ever made an effort to speak other than in Greek.

'The wedding, Dionysios? I don't know anything about a wedding.'

'It is soon, I think.' Dionysios had sat up, with his arms round his knees. 'It is spoken about. We are so pleased. Miss Causland is so very nice a young lady.' There was something about Dionysios's brilliant smile that made Shefford stiffen as he sat. 'Only no tail, yes? And no breasts.' With his hands now raised and cupped outward in front of him, he made

215

the movement of one doing press-ups in a gymnasium. 'Only the little glasses.' Another gesture caught the manner in which Marion carried spectacles dangling on her chest. 'But it does not make any matter, I think? For Mark, *he* has no——'

Most surprisingly at this point, Stepho leant over the wheel and struck Dionysios hard across the mouth. Shefford expected that in an instant the boys would be at one another's throats. He wondered whether they carried knives. He prepared to grab the wheel and control the launch as he could.

But no further violence took place. Dionysios only leant back and smiled again—smiled through the broad red mark left by Stepho's hand. Shefford found this the most shocking part of the incident: that Dionysios, from some position of impregnable strength, could afford to laugh contemptuously at both smart and insult. And when the boy spoke again, it was as if he simply picked up his speech after a few words that had been obliterated by the blow.

'By the *polismanoi*, when Mark was in prison.' Dionysios made another of his horrible gestures; he might have been imitating a man clipping a hedge. 'So sad! But in England always the sport, yes?'

Stepho was immobile again; his own gesture had been made. Shefford wondered whether he himself could successfully thrash Dionysios, and concluded that he couldn't. In any case, his impulse in that direction died quickly away. He found himself recalling the football flying about between Mark and himself and these two boys: the laughing and shouting and the sweat, and then the hard panting slog as they had settled into something like a game. He remembered Mark saying 'That was happiness'. He remembered Stepho and Dionysios as he had seen them through his binoculars on the yacht, and Dionysios's brutal thrusting thumb that seemed in retrospect like the end of innocence. He remembered that Mark had been 'quite thick' with Dionysios, and he realised that the dirty jeer to which he had just been listening could only have originated in some confidence of

Mark's about the calamitous rough house in Grosvenor Square. And if there was really gossip about a marriage between Mark and Marion it was possible that Mark had himself received a first hint of it in other taunting talk by this mysteriously arrogant boy.

The little heliotropic, sun-battered fishing village of Trianta was before them; it shot away as Stepho spun the wheel; they were rounding the promontory on which stood the row of broken columns and the single capital proclaiming to what architectural order a vanished temple had belonged. Soon there would be the forsaken garden, perhaps the dust-coloured Mercedes, certainly the perilous road along the cliffs, the drive through hamlets beginning to betray the touch of wealth and the practical good-sense of Bernard Vanderlyn. Then there would be the monastery.

Dionysios was now, for a change, lying not supine but prone on the deck, and in a pose of complete relaxation, like one who has dropped to sleep. On the dark bronze of his neck the golden hairs glinted, as if a sculptor had there engraved his name with some delicate instrument. It seemed impossible that Dionysios could regard himself as having been other than deliberately and insolently gross, even although what he had said only reproduced his common way of talking among his familiars. And where—Shefford found himself asking—had Dionysios come from, anyway? Where had Stepho come from? They were *protégés* of Vanderlyn's because they had been in trouble—just as, in some degree, Mark was. But, unlike Mark, they had nothing else to recommend them. Or nothing apart from being, as young adult males, easy on the eyes. Mark was that.

Shefford, who had read all the most approved books on psychopathology, tried telling himself that Vanderlyn had become, in the approaches of old age, interested in young men in a fashion it would disturb him to be made aware of. But he saw that this notion was useless; true or untrue, it belonged to an order of statement inadequate to the complexity of real life. What lay buried at the bottom of Vanderlyn's head was no more important than what lay buried at the bottom of Dionysios's. Conduct, after the conscious man had taken stock of himself as he could, was the only relevant thing.

What lay immediately in front of Shefford was the conduct that happened to be going on in Tyros now. If quite a lot of it turned out to be bad, that was no more than was to be expected in a community established upon idealistic and experimental principles. Social history was full of fiascoes that had begun as brave new worlds. On Tyros—and all with the best intentions—Bernard Vanderlyn had been turned into a cuckold, Mark Varley into a traitor, Gemma Vanderlyn into a tart, Marion Causland into a doting girl confronting painful and humiliating discovery, and even these two Greek boys into socially anomalous characters of whom probity was not to be expected. And now—Shefford reflected—here he was himself, being imported as a kind of juvenile sage, relied upon to sort things out all round. At least it was a challenge. At least he'd have a go.

They disembarked. Dionysios was solicitous that Shefford shouldn't get his feet wet; he seemed to derive amusement from behaving as if his passenger was an elderly person of social consequence. Looking round the deserted bay, Shefford remembered being told that when the hospital opened there was to be a helicopter. It would bring in patients from the neighbouring islands at need; and it would also serve to link Vanderlyn's household, and his community at large, with the more populous island, due south, where one caught the ferry boat for the mainland. It would be a big improvement in communications, Shefford thought as he sat once more in the grey Mercedes. At present the monastery's lodge-gates, so to speak, were in Trianta, and from there one had to suffer this intimidating drive across the island. Shefford didn't fancy it the more on the present occasion because he was to be driven by Dionysios. Even Stepho, he felt irrationally, would be more reliable. But Stepho, as seemed customary, stayed behind to potter with the launch. Sometimes, when it was to be used on the following morning, he spent the night in its boat house. More commonly, he returned to the monastery on his motor-cycle.

Something had changed in the configuration of the little rock-encircled beach near the jetties. Shefford wondered whether blasting operations had been in progress, for fragments of rock were lying around, and at the point where a long scree slope impended above the road there was a new tumble of stone which appeared to have arrested itself in violation of the law of gravity. Shefford disliked the look of this. He also disliked the behaviour of Dionysios, who had taken both hands from the wheel in order to make one of his graphic gestures. It wasn't an improper gesture this time. Dionysios was explaining what had happened when there had been a series of small earth tremors on Tyros some weeks before. They weren't regarded as dangerous; the island was far from any earthquake line; but they accounted for the chunks of rock and the movement of the scree. In giving this information Dionysios seemed chiefly concerned to show off his new command of English. At the same time, Shefford supposed that he was trying to make himself agreeable. Probably he regretted his lapse on the launch. Shefford found that he himself didn't judge it any less revolting in retrospect. He wasn't sure that he ought to speak to Dionysios again, but on the other hand silence conveyed to his own mind a rather absurd implication of offended dignity. He compromised by speaking only briefly and with reserve. This wasn't satisfactory either. They drove through the deserted garden.

Dionysios slowed and halted the car. He shut off the engine and raised a finger in air. What Shefford was first aware of was the scent of the gum trees, and its delusive reminiscence of his childhood. Then he realised that Dionysios's gesture was a simple appeal to the ear. As on his first arrival here, a nightingale was singing. On this occasion, the song continued. Although it was broad daylight, the bird was singing like mad.

'It sings of love,' Dionysios said.

This time, Shefford made no reply. He wasn't—not by any devious route—going to be led into a conversation about love with this young blackguard. He wondered whether plebeian Greek boys like Dionysios were taught their country's mythology—and knew, for example, the revolting yarn about Philomela and Procne which all the poets had so assiduously romanticised in their nightingale poems. Whether the bird to which he was now listening owned an aesthetic sense or not, the noises issuing from it were beautiful to a human ear. How odd—he told himself—that the human imagination had associated them with ghastly episodes of rape and mutilation. When Dionysios said 'It sings of love' was he thinking of such transactions, and was Tereus his notion of a lover? It seemed unfair to suppose so, even although a Mark Varley mutilated by a demon *polismanos* had seemed to him an amusing fantasy to conjure up. Yet now, when Dionysios repeated 'It sings of love', and then abruptly flicked the starting switch of the Mercedes, there was something in his tone—something ironic and exultant—which troubled Shefford as he sat. Dionysios possessed some spring of vitality, an animal well-being, by which it was difficult not to be attracted. And he possessed in perfection, and contrary to Shefford's misgivings, the art of driving a motor-car along a dangerous road. He covered the cliff-top stretch at a faster pace than Gemma had done, but so confidently that his passenger found himself in a condition of tolerable nervous ease. Shefford again remembered the afternoon's fun with the football. He remembered watching Dionysios's skill in the water. He didn't propose ever to approve of Dionysios again. But physically he was the finely co-ordinated kind of person to whom it would be agreeable to teach a new game. Squash, say. Or even shove-halfpenny.

The old men faggoting with donkeys and the old women faggoting without them; the children in Vanderlyn's improved playground; the children leading goats: Shefford looked out for them during the drive across the island. If he weren't confronting a mess, he would be enjoying the pleasure of coming back to a place he had an affection for. Even as things stood, he looked forward to his first glimpse of someone familiar from the monastery. He remembered the pretty maid called Vangelio, and spent some unprofitable but agreeable minutes in imagining the beginnings of love-making with her; it was commendable, he hoped, that the awkwardness of affairs on Tyros wasn't driving him to an unwholesome puritanism of mind. Then, as they neared the monastery, he did see someone familiar. It was the little red-bearded man he had dubbed D. H. Lawrence. He still had his big battered hat, and this time he was wearing it, even though he was sitting in the shade of a ruined hovel. He had a portable type-writer on his knees and a couple of files on the ground beside him. He didn't see the car, since he was gazing in a forlorn abstraction into distance. Shefford couldn't help laughing. Here was a sign that the planned course of things on Tyros hadn't miscarried altogether.

'Vangelio,' Dionysios said, much as if he had been reading Shefford's mind of a few minutes before.

They had rounded the monastery, and the Mercedes came to a halt. It was true that Vangelio was in evidence. She had been standing on the terrace as if under orders to await the arriving guest, and now she came running down the steps. In face of the actual girl, Shefford's immodest imaginings went to earth, but he saw that memory had not been unreliable about her. She was nice to look at. He wondered whether either of the Greek boys made love to her. And for a moment it seemed as if Dionysios had been developing feelings of chivalry. Vangelio advanced to take Shefford's suitcase, but Dionysios waved her away and grabbed it himself. A year ago he had shown himself as thinking such a job demeaning. Now he was taking pleasure in it. He mounted the steps two at a time, carrying the suitcase as lightly as if it were a handbag. At the top he turned for a moment and looked down. Van-gelio, deprived of a function, was still standing beside Shef-ford, smiling pleasantly. Dionysios was smiling too, but not in the same way. His glance seemed to sweep Shefford and the girl together as a single amusing and unimportant pheno-menon. Then he walked off. He left Shefford with the sense that there was something mocking and sardonic about his accepting a servant's job.

But now, only a little way along the terrace, Shefford saw

the Vanderlyns. They too were waiting for him. As he moved forward it occurred to him that this was perhaps the first time he had ever thought of them as just that: the Vanderlyns. But there they were, standing side by side, husband and wife.

Chapter 2

'WELCOME BACK TO Tyros,' Bernard Vanderlyn said. 'Your arrival's well timed, Jeremy. For things are looking up.'

'I'm glad to hear it.' It was Shefford's impression that he had been summoned to Tyros because things were looking down. But it was true that Vanderlyn himself appeared less worn than he had done in Oxford. Perhaps his domestic situation had really improved, although it was hard to see how this could fundamentally be so.

Shefford looked warily at Gemma. Her pregnancy was not perceptible, and he could neither see nor sense any other change in her. He still felt a chilliness beneath her social manner—like the chilliness sometimes unaccountably felt by mariners in mild weather, and later identified as the breath of icebergs beyond the horizon. But there was a lodestone, one might say, at the heart of Gemma's iceberg. He would himself always feel its tug now—would feel it though they were sitting in silence at opposite ends of a dark room.

This huddle of imagery didn't much suggest mental ease. Shefford remembered that, upon the occasion of his last arrival at the monastery, he had been obliged to contend with nothing more than ravenous hunger. He was hungry now—although this time it was only noon, and nothing except drinks could be in any immediate prospect. These were in view, laid out on a table at one corner of the terrace: a vine-encinctured nook, with room only for the three chairs placed there, and thus suggesting more intimacy than he found himself caring for. The impossibility of his situation had been accented by Vanderlyn's first words. For how—when one really thought of it—was one conceivably to comport oneself in the presence of a man who, as he poured vermouth for his adulterous wife, could speak of things as looking up? Shefford, however illogically, would have welcomed the arrival even of Mark. But there seemed no likelihood of it. The three of them were going to have a cosy chat.

'For a start,' Vanderlyn said, 'we have just had the news that the hospital will be staffed within a week. There was trouble about having my own doctors, you know, and I'll admit that, in the end, a stiff hint from Washington was required. But all's fair in love and war.'

'That's splendid.' Shefford took refuge in mixing himself a drink with care. The idiom upon which Vanderlyn had fallen was distinctly odd. He was not habitually insensitive to words, and it was almost possible to wonder whether he was right in the head. Yet there had been something in his glance as he spoke that had been far from suggesting madness. Vanderlyn might have been hinting at caution; at a situation in which it was essential to hold one's hand.

'And Bruce Guthrie,' Vanderlyn said. 'I think we stopped by to have a word with him last year? The fellow for whom we managed an out-size studio in the old Turkish barracks.'

'Yes, of course. Those enormous murals—but on canvas or something.'

'Well—believe it or not—Guthrie has been chosen as one of the three painters for the British pavilion at next year's Venice Biennale.'

'Splendid!' It was mechanically that Shefford repeated the word. He could think of nothing else to say.

'We might be a racing stable,' Gemma Vanderlyn commented humorously, 'going all out to train winners. Perhaps we'll even have a Derby winner yet.'

'I hope so,' Shefford said, and again he took a quick look at Gemma. He tried to tell himself that he was surprised at ever having seen her as other than an immoral woman. Confronted by her mask of perfect decorum, he had a horrible impulse to behave like Dionysios; to make some swift,

lewd gesture, unseen by Vanderlyn, and observe what reaction he occasioned. But in an instant he was shocked by
such an idea—and even shocked at supposing that she was
necessarily an immoral woman at all. She might have got
herself where she was only after some appalling emotional
travail. He knew nothing about women. Nothing whatever.
His qualifications as visiting sage were *nil*.

'And Mark,' Vanderlyn said, 'has written a new poem.
Five stanzas.'

This time, 'Splendid' was beyond Shefford's power to
utter. Vanderlyn had given his announcement a kind of
climactic effect. And Shefford couldn't care less. Just at present, Mark's poetic progress, actual or supposed, was of no
importance. Had he in the past week tossed off a worthy
successor to *Paradise Lost*, his deserts would not thereby be
altered a jot. Mark's behaviour had been unspeakable, and
yet it remained clear to Shefford that it was Mark he wanted
to rescue. Mark must be got away from this progressively
bemused elderly man—and from his mistress, the elderly
man's wife.

'But there's something even more important than that. I
think it's going to be all right with Marion. Mark has become
much more attentive to her. I see no reason why they
shouldn't be married soon.'

'It's generally expected, I gather.' Shefford felt that if he
weren't simply to settle in as a spectator, if he hoped to pre-
pare the ground for any sort of effective interposition in the
affair, a plunge must be taken now. For this *was* madness.
He turned to Gemma. 'Mrs Vanderlyn,' he asked, 'do *you*
see any reason why Mark and Marion shouldn't be married
soon?'

'Very little, I suppose.' Gemma was looking at him in cool
surprise. 'Except that it mayn't be so much in Mark's mind
as Bernard supposes it to be. It's in Marion's mind, all right.
You probably discerned that last year. But it takes two to
make a match.' She paused. 'Or sometimes, perhaps, it only
takes one and a fraction.'

'It would be satisfactory that Mark is making himself

agreeable to Marion,' Shefford said, 'if one had much reason to suppose that his intentions were honourable.'

'What an old-fashioned expression!' Gemma was amused.

'I don't mean that Mark may be proposing to seduce her. I can't see that entering his head. Can you, Mrs Vanderlyn?'

'Yes I think I can. I can imagine almost any young man having casual thoughts about seducing almost any young woman, or even some next-to-young women. Bernard, can't you?'

Shefford believed that he had been watching Gemma keenly. But before what seemed the naked brutality of this he dropped his eyes. At least he had got out of Gemma something like proof that her husband wasn't nursing some ghastly delusion. At the moment, Vanderlyn seemed not to be listening. He was gazing out to sea: a strip of sea, today dark blue like an ancient enamel, which was visible from the terrace. He might have been expecting a boat-load of doctors for his hospital, or a freighter which should bear away to Venice the enormous murals of Bruce Guthrie, or even a British cruiser commissioned to bring Mark Varley to Buckingham Palace to receive the Poet Laureateship. Gemma's barb—for surely it was a barb—appeared to have been launched in vain.

'I'm sorry,' Shefford said to her, 'but I can't see Mark as having any thoughts of that kind whatever. Not about Marion. If he's paying her any attention, he must be said just to be trifling with her—which is damnably unfair to her. And he's not even doing it for the hell of it.'

'For the hell of it? I don't understand you.'

'Just for the fun of turning her head. I don't believe he'd do just that. But I'm afraid he'd do what's just as bad.'

'You are quite a moralist in our midst, Mr Shefford.' It looked as if Gemma was angry at last. 'What would be as bad as gratuitous flirting with poor Marion?'

'Giving others the impression that Marion was making headway with him, was really coming to attract him. And giving that impression because he saw it as cunning and politic to do so. He sometimes fancies himself, does Mark, in what he imagines is a Machiavellian role.'

'I don't think you quite remember that Mark is the object of Bernard's particular care and regard.' Gemma's tone was measured as she said this astounding thing. She might have been listening to something incomprehensible which she nevertheless had reason to feel as covertly impertinent, and which she was rebuking with that minimum of fuss which is all a well-bred woman needs to use. She got to her feet. 'No, Mr Shefford. Stay and talk to Bernard, if you please. I have to say a word to Aphrodite about lunch.'

He watched her walk away down the terrace—through bars of sunlight and shadow, so that she looked like a brilliant creature pacing a cage. Perhaps Tyros *was* a cage; perhaps the trouble had started because of that. Perhaps for Mark, too, it had become a cage or a prison. His second prison. One day he might write a book like Pellico's. *Le mie prigioni.*

With nothing better in his head than this, Shefford watched Gemma vanish. He ought, he supposed, at least to be admiring her nerve. He ought even to be taking example from it. For he knew what he ought to do now. He ought to turn to Vanderlyn and say firmly, 'Don't you know it's Mark who's been sleeping with your wife?' He tried out the words on his inner ear—and against a background of silence, since Vanderlyn was still staring absently out to sea. He decided they wouldn't do: partly because they would inflict too hideous a wound; and partly because, until he should himself have seen Mark again, he felt the knowledge was not his to divulge. He even wondered whether, after all, it should never *be* divulged. Let Vanderlyn part with his wife without any further probing of her infidelity. And let Vanderlyn part with Mark simply as a matter of a young man's growing away from an older man who had befriended him for a while. In a word, let it all be hushed up.

Caught between these conflicting impulses, Shefford compromised. He did so in a fashion—he realised too late—that held no promise at all of extricating him from his false position. It was a measure of his discomfort that he found himself boggling over the proper way in which to address Vanderlyn. He wasn't going to call him 'Bernard', as Mark did. To one who addressed him as 'Jeremy', on the other hand, 'Mr Vanderlyn' would have the effect of awkwardly insisting on their mere disparity of years. The same objection applied to 'Sir', which he had had recourse to earlier on. And just to say 'Vanderlyn' would be to insist to an American upon an English usage. There was nothing for it but to stick to one or another purely rhetorical form of vocative.

'Look!' Shefford said. 'I find it hard, as you can imagine, to think of anything except the shocking news you gave me in Oxford last week. Is the position unchanged? I mean'— it was here that he felt himself floundering on the brink of dishonesty—'have you still no idea who . . . who the man is?'

'I don't think I want to know. Not yet.' Vanderlyn had at least returned his gaze from the sea, and he spoke quietly and steadily. Again there seemed nothing unbalanced about him. He might have been debating—as had been his business long ago—some public issue of sufficient gravity to require a completely dispassionate approach. 'Of course there are plenty of men around the place—talented, attractive, and full of an urgent sensuality, no doubt. It's one of the professional risks of a patron that I failed to consider.' For a second Shefford thought he saw the beginning of the slow smile. 'I did consider several risks, but I guess I missed out on that one. Bruce Guthrie, for example—what would you say to him?'

It occurred to Shefford to say, 'Or the little man looking like D. H. Lawrence?' But even if Vanderlyn inclined to a faint, unhappy jocularity, it wouldn't improve matters to follow him into it. So he said nothing.

'Pick a name at random like that,' Vanderlyn said, 'and you see how wrong and futile speculation is.'

'I can see that. But—forgive me—I'd have thought it was up to Gemma not to make a mystery of this thing, even if you yourself ask no questions. There's going to be a child. I'd suppose that the mere business of practical disposi- tions——'

'Yes, Jeremy, I quite agree. You're beginning to think of me, aren't you, as what they used to call a complacent husband? It's the most shameful role of the lot. But don't suppose I don't realise this thing must end. The sooner the better. There must be a divorce, I think, rather than a mere legal separation. Gemma is young enough to want to marry again. I hope she will want to marry the child's father, if he isn't married already. But, at the moment, I don't want the scandal to break. I don't want any further exploration of the matter, even privately. A discovery right now might upset Mark badly.'

Again Shefford remained silent. There was nothing he could say that wouldn't, in effect, be a lie. The irony in Vanderlyn's last remark was of the kind he was accustomed to expound to his pupils as of the tragic or dramatic order. But that was mostly in plays that were hundreds of years old. He didn't like this modern confrontation with the hoary old device a bit.

'And Marion, too,' Vanderlyn went on. 'She is fond of Gemma, and the revelation would distress her acutely. It will come less painfully when she and Mark have each other to rely on.'

'I think you're taking rather a lot for granted.' It seemed to Shefford that he ought to risk attacking at least this illusion. 'What does Mark say to this feeling of yours that he should marry your stepdaughter?'

'My dear Jeremy, of course I haven't mentioned it to him.' Vanderlyn seemed surprised. 'One has to be discreet. Mark isn't to be driven, you know. I've learnt that.'

'But it's being talked about!'

'I heard you say something to that effect. It puzzled me.'

'One of your Greek boys mentioned it to me. Dionysios— the one Mark has been rather thick with.'

'Dionysios?' Vanderlyn was sharply displeased. 'It's not his place to gossip. And I don't think Mark is thick with him, as you call it, now. Mark goes about more with Stepho.'

'For what it's worth, I don't think Dionysios is a very nice young man. But that's beside the point.' Shefford was looking at Vanderlyn in perplexity. He wondered whether Mark himself could conceivably be unaware of his patron's latest luckless design upon him. It was not impossible. Mark's sensitiveness was conditioned in various ways by his self-absorption. He might have failed to see something that Dionysios had seen very well.

'Then what *is* the point?' It was in an almost impatient tone that Vanderlyn asked this. 'I'm afraid I wasn't listening very closely to what you said to Gemma. But if you think that Mark——' He broke off suddenly. 'There!' he said softly.

Shefford turned in the direction of his gaze, and was aware of another stroke that came dramatically pat. Mark had entered smartly on his cue. And he had brought Marion Causland with him. They had not, however, advanced within earshot. They were simply in view. Indeed, they were so much in view that Shefford had an instant conviction that Mark had arranged things that way.

Mark was hot—sweaty, indeed—and dusty: so much so that the fact was observable from fifty yards away. He was carrying in one hand an old-fashioned motoring-cap which he affected on his racing-circuit—as he no doubt thought of it—round the island. His other hand was on Marion's shoulder. He appeared to have picked her up near the ancient granary where the motor-cars were kept, and to have been steering her affectionately to the point at which they now stood—which was in fact at the end of a short vista which Vanderlyn, sipping his *ouzo*, must command every day at this hour. Shefford supposed that Marion, unfortunate enough to suffer tortures of anxiety when Mark went careering about Tyros, had been compelled to hang around near the point of his return. Mark, in consequence, was now able to put on this performance. It was a good performance. That hand on Marion's shoulder was the affectionate hand of a brother, or at least of a young man of instinctive delicacy, who knows just how to make such a gesture to a girl without the faintest suggestion of pawing her. And now, as Vanderlyn and Shefford looked, Mark did an inspired thing. He took his hand from Marion's shoulder, placed the flat of it against her cheek and jaw, and gently pushed her away. It was a motion imported from the Rugger field, and made entirely amusing, made—once again—affectionate, made just short of tender. Mark walked away, laughing. For a moment Marion stood quite still. Then she called out something after Mark as he departed, and as she did so her chin went absurdly, touchingly, up in air.

'You see?' Vanderlyn said.

Shefford thought he did see. But—he told himself—it was no good being shocked, or even revolted. That would be as senseless as being merely amused. If he could get Mark away from such degrading charades—get him a job, say, shoving petrol into cars on the outskirts of some English provincial town—something might yet be made of him. Or rather—for Vanderlyn's mistake had lain just there—Mark might make something of himself.

'Hullo,' Vanderlyn was saying. 'Marion seems to be coming up to the terrace. Why don't you have a word with her, Jeremy? Lunch won't be for half-an-hour.'

Rather surprisingly, he rose and walked away.

Chapter 3

MARION CAUSLAND HESITATED. She had seen Shefford, and it was her instinct to avoid him. He needn't, he knew, feel offended. Vanderlyn had spoken of her as of a retiring disposition, and it was an understatement of a piece with his general failure to see his first wife's daughter quite as she was. No doubt he distinguished more of Louise in her than was actually there. Marion was very far indeed from being the sort of person who could go around agitating for Schools Afloat, or even perhaps climb to the roof of a barn in the tracks of Jude Fawley. Her shyness was extreme. And she certainly wasn't clever.

Shefford knew all this already. Although he hadn't any very lively memory of Marion from a year back it was his impression that conversation with her was largely a matter of being careful not to get outside her range. It was inconceivable that she hadn't been the object of rather ample educational provision; he recalled that there had been a professional person somewhere round the place, engaged in a full-time way on the job. It must have been work requiring patience. But at least Marion was adequate on a social level. At this moment, having seen that she was observed, she had overcome her hesitation and was mounting the steps to the terrace. He noticed that she no longer wore her spectacles in the fashion Dionysios had made fun of. Indeed, she was in a tight-fitting upper garment of fine wool which showed Dionysios to have exaggerated—if not by a great deal—in one of his offensive comments on her. Her face was still flushed from her encounter with Mark. Even her chin was still at that new angle. As Shefford shook hands, he was painfully aware of her as vulnerable and touching. He rehearsed certain things which he was certainly going to say to Mark. He wasn't sure that he'd refrain from saying them to Gemma too.

'Gemma told me you had arrived, Mr Shefford.' Marion sat down. She shook her head at his offer to get her a drink. 'I hope you had a comfortable journey. I hope the boys didn't race the launch.'

'They raced the launch, all right.' Although Marion's solicitude had an air of politeness learnt by rote, Shefford was pleased as well as amused by it. 'It would have been a shame to try to stop them. It's a powerful boat.'

'There are powerful cars, too. Bernard—my stepfather—has an Aston Martin now. It can move extremely fast. Bernard says it is not really suitable for the island. He always likes to have a car which he alone drives.'

'I remember that. In England it's a Cadillac.'

'But now Mark has begun to drive the Aston Martin. I don't think Bernard knows. And Mark drives it so fast and dangerously! I go up to the old fort, and from there I can

231

see long stretches of the coast road. Sometimes I think I ought to tell Bernard. What do you think, Mr Shefford? It worries me very much.'

'*I'll* tell Mr Vanderlyn, if you like. The very first time I see Mark in that particular car. But it mayn't do much good. Doesn't Mr Vanderlyn approve of most things Mark does?'

'Oh, yes—of course.' Marion appeared to feel that Shefford had given the conversation an agreeable turn. 'Wasn't it splendid about Mark's prize? It seems that Lord Tennyson won a prize for a poem too—but at Cambridge, not Oxford. I've read some of his *Idylls of the King*.' Marion paused on this. It was an invitation to converse on a cultural topic, and as such it carried a faint echo of Louise Vanderlyn to Shefford's ear. He was slow, however, to take it up—having been touched, as it were, on the professional side, and having in consequence a sudden vision of Marion's tutor, conducting her conscientiously through the most approved passages of English poetry. Noting his silence, Marion changed the subject, no doubt feeling that Tennyson was only a name to him. She had at least been taught very well the small expertnesses of polite society. 'I am so glad,' she said, 'that you didn't arrive a fortnight ago! The earth shook, and it was very frightening. I don't mean, of course, that *you* would have been frightened, Mr Shefford. Mark wasn't frightened. He made a joke of it—going round with a gong, to scare away the evil spirits. But Gemma and I found it very horrid.'

'I heard about it from Dionysios, as he drove me across the island. But he didn't tell me about Mark and the gong.'

'I don't think he and Mark are such friends as they were. It is with Stepho that Mark goes fishing now. I wish he wouldn't.'

'Don't you like Stepho, Miss Causland?'

'I have bad dreams about him.' As Marion produced this embarrassing information, she looked at Shefford with all her mother's earnest candour. Her tutor, it was to be assumed, had not so far provided any instruction in Freudian psychology. 'Last night I dreamt that Mark and I were sailing together. It was very nice. But Stepho was there as well. And suddenly he pulled out a plug from the bottom of the yacht, and ₜhe water came pouring through the hole. It came like a great snake, a sea-serpent. And Mark had disappeared, although I could hear him laughing somewhere. And there was only Stepho.'

'That must have been rather frightening.'

'I woke up crying out. But when I told Mark about the dream, he only laughed—rather as he laughed *in* the dream. Of course, nothing frightens Mark. I think I could go anywhere with him.' Marion again paused, and Shefford again failed to take a cue. He found these ingenuous revelations ominous. 'But I hope,' Marion said, 'the earth won't shake again.'

'It's not very likely. I gather there's not much record of anything of the sort on Tyros.'

'No—but there are other islands, here in the eastern Mediterranean, where there have been dreadful earthquakes. One whole civilization was destroyed. I heard a very interesting lecture about that by a professor in Paris. There were big palaces. Did you ever read the story of a Greek hero called Theseus? I could lend you the book, if you haven't.'

Shefford said gently that it did happen he'd read about Theseus. He was accustomed to attempting to estimate intellectual capacity on the strength of a couple of sentences, and hadn't, in general, much faith in the validity of the exercise. But here was an instance that was inescapably cogent. He saw that Marion was a girl of even simpler mind than he had supposed. He even wondered whether her simplicity was such that, in a less sheltered situation, she would be in danger of unscrupulous imposition. And then he remembered that Mark's conduct seemed to be approaching close to just that.

'I think we may have it again,' Marion said. 'The thing like an earthquake, I mean. The sunset last night was like the sunset just before it happened.'

'The sunset? In what way?'

'An angry red. It's hard to describe.'

'I don't think there could really be a connection.' It was Shefford's instinct to correct misapprehension when it arose. 'It might be different in a case of volcanic eruption. Strange things can happen to sunsets—at least *after* them. But I doubt whether a small earthquake could be preluded by any sort of atmospheric disturbance.'

'I see.' Marion had listened patiently to these remarks, so that Shefford told himself the poor girl was at least docile. 'I think there will be another, all the same,' she said.

On this small and not unwholesome outcrop of obstinacy the conversation came to a close. It didn't seem to be because small-talk was failing Marion. However limited her intellectual endowment, she didn't seem to lack for that. Nor, somehow, did her silence seem to suggest that her mind was uncivilly wandering—perhaps to Mark. It was simply that she judged it reasonable, and perhaps even pleasant, that she and Shefford should sit together for a short time without talking. He found himself wondering at this composure in her, which he sensed as something new. And suddenly—catching for a moment her quiet gaze, which no longer dropped painfully to the gound—he understood what had happened. Marion's mind moved, no doubt, amid anxieties, but they were no longer the anxieties of longing, uncertainty, a hopeless aim. She had decided—against all modest expectation she had decided—that something unbelievably good was going to happen to her, and she was confident and happy. Even when an incomprehensible dream about Stepho made her cry out in the night, she wasn't really alarmed. She had Mark, after all, to whom she could tell the dream. And as for day-dreams, she no longer had to traffic with them. She wasn't doing so as she sat in this silence now. Mark had ceased to be any sort of dream, and become a fact.

'Good afternoon, my dear Shefford. I've been sent to call you two to lunch.'

Shefford looked up, and found Anton Andreas standing beside him. He had forgotten about the architect of Vanderlyn's hospital, and the first thing he remembered about him now was his being dislikable. He had called him the coelacanth of Tyros—which had been a childish way of expressing the view that he was a cold fish. And at this moment if he didn't look cold he looked cool; he had an air, and a trick of grooming and dressing himself, which would preserve that appearance for him in the middle of a tropical jungle. Shefford felt he ought to dislike Andreas still, particularly as the man was now contriving to look at him with what could only be described as not one offensive expression but two complementary offensive expressions. He was looking at Shefford with amused irony, which is never an agreeable way to be looked at. But he was also looking at him with misgiving. It was almost as if he were reflecting that in Jeremy Shefford his friend Vanderlyn had again gone astray in the tricky field of young men, and that as a visiting sage here was a singularly poor importation.

Shefford would not, perhaps, have disagreed; but he didn't like this hinted estimate, all the same. Then he saw something that gave him pause. Andreas had shifted his gaze to Marion, and irony and misgiving had both died out of it. He was looking at the girl with perfect gravity, so that one forgot that here was a man of acrid mind and cynical speech. Shefford found himself, after all, taking satisfaction in the fact that Andreas was still around. He was dispassionate—at least Shefford supposed he was dispassionate—and there was a certain reassurance in that. It was impossible not to feel that on the ancient stage constituted by the monastery of Tyros some small and muted drama was about to come to its climax and work itself out. Shefford didn't feel that he himself belonged with the *dramatis personae*; but he wasn't clear that he mightn't, in one fashion or another, be coaxed out of the wings. It was comforting, somehow, that Andreas could be pretty well relied on not to budge out of his seat in the stalls.

'Yes,' Andreas said, 'in both senses, lunch is just round the corner. Gemma has persuaded herself there is a breath of air on the other terrace. She has not always been quite well lately.' His glance had returned to Shefford, and it was searching. 'I'm afraid she may find the heat oppressive, as the summer wears on. These islands are overrated, to my mind, at that time of year. Up with you, my dear Marion. I suspect Aphrodite has been labouring for you. Our mortal Aphrodite, that is to say. I glimpsed your favourite *mezedakia*. Shefford, I am glad to see you drinking vermouth, even if you have been pouring gin into it, and not our eternal *ouzo*. Civilization stills exists, after all, and is located no more than one thousand miles west-north-west of us. Do I get my compass-bearing right? Sometimes when the *meltemi* blows— and it is at about this time of year, you know—I can fancy it brings a breath from those blessed regions. Etesian gales, as the ancients said. Shefford, you are a classical man, and the reference is familiar to you. And Marion, too, has made these studies.' Andreas smiled at the girl as he talked this nonsense, and Shefford noted that the teasing did not confuse her. 'So come along, both of you. We must keep up our strength, even if it be on *avgolemono*. A soup, my dear lad— but perhaps you are already familiar with it.'

Shefford followed Andreas and Marion down the terrace. Andreas, who didn't overdo things, had stopped chattering. Only once he offered some remark to Marion, which Shefford didn't catch, but which made her laugh. And then Shefford found himself intercepted by Vangelio, who had been sent by Gemma to show him to his room before he sat down to table. Vangelio—whom Dionysios had deprived of Shefford's suit-case—seemed to take pleasure in having something to do for him, after all. Shefford judged that it was agreeable of Gemma to have arranged it that way. He then reminded himself, rather hastily, that Gemma was a wicked woman. Vangelio walked ahead. He followed her up the broad, shallow stone staircase, hollowed by the sandalled feet—or perhaps it was the bare feet—of generations of bearded monks. At every turn there was a broad landing, and on every landing an object of modern sculpture had been disposed: abstract affairs, for the most part, in which stone or metal had been manipulated to define volumes of empty air. You were bound to collect a lot of junk, Shefford thought, if you were an art-patron in a big way. But he didn't attend much to these things. Vangelio's black dress, not of peasant amplitude, defined her own volumes in a very pleasing detail.

They went through a door. It was the room he had occupied the year before, so it was familiar to him. But Vangelio crossed to a window and drew a curtain against a shaft of sunshine. She went over to the bathroom and opened its door, as if to make sure he didn't remain unaware of it. And then she went away.

He washed quickly. As he did so he realised that, for a modest couple of seconds, Vangelio had paused by the door, still smiling, before she went out and closed it behind her. He ought to have kissed her. Not grabbed her and done anything stupid; simply stolen a kiss (as the Victorian novelists liked to say) before she slipped from the room. He felt depressed, but comforted himself with the reflection that he had acted correctly. He had come to Tyros, after all, to reprobate irregular sexual conduct, and he oughtn't to start off on the wrong foot.

He ran downstairs, knowing these to be idle thoughts, and reflecting that the commerce of the sexes could take on a really bewildering variety of forms and intensities. There was what had existed between Vanderlyn and his first wife. There was what Marion was unlucky enough to be feeling for the unscrupulous Mark now. There was whatever Mark and Gemma contrived to continue to get from one another in bed. And there was this debate about kissing a maid-servant before she began to pass you the *mezedakia* or the *dolmadakia* at lunch.

Shefford passed out to the terrace. The others were waiting for him, and the meal began.

Chapter 4

IT WAS A domestic occasion again, and they sat as they had sat a year before. Shefford was on Gemma's right and Mark on her left. Mark had Marion on his other side and

Shefford had Andreas. Vanderlyn faced his wife across an
ancient marble bowl filled with roses. Shefford noticed that,
before sitting down, he had placed a small parcel in front of
Mark.

The meal was once more simple enough, but Shefford
found himself noticing the perfection—'expensiveness' would
have been a fair enough word—of everything connected with
it. The linen seemed never to have been used before; the
silver was old and beautiful; they drank the common *retsina*
from slender-stemmed modern glasses of exquisite design.
There were a couple of salt-cellars which were probably by
Cellini—although it was unlikely that either of the Vanderlyns would tell him so. He remembered the great house to
which he had driven Bernard Vanderlyn back from Oxford,
and he reflected that his host's life, however purposeful and
devoted, had been lived out against a background filled with
the sort of assumptions that unlimited wealth brings. This
went, no doubt, for Gemma too. And as he listened to the
discreet account of recent events on Tyros which Gemma
was making the subject of her table-talk for his benefit, it
seemed to him that the reflection had continued relevance.

There were people, Gemma recounted, who hadn't liked
the way the project ran, and who had gone away: some of
them delightful and of high talent, so that their defection
had been a regret. On the other hand there were one or two
who hadn't proved agreeable, and whose ideas—to put it
crudely—had been chargeable as parasitic or covertly hostile:
and these poor Bernard had been obliged, much against his
inclination, to sever his connection with. As a consequence
there had been a period of considerable uneasiness—Bernard
had probably mentioned it—and they were only just beginning to bless themselves that they had got out of the wood.
Bruce Guthrie's success had been a great encouragement. It
had quite cheered them up.

'There was a phase when everybody was sick,' Vanderlyn
said humorously, 'and blamed it on the water. Some of them
solved that one by indulging in nothing but wine.' He tapped
the rim of his glass with a finger-nail, and Shefford was

startled to hear it ring out across the table on a clear note. 'We positively had to wrestle with the demon drink.'

'Not really,' Mark said. He was fingering his parcel, but without apparent impulse to open it. 'They'd come in liquored up, but not drunk.' Mark seemed to have picked up Gemma's habit of taking plunges at American idiom. He also seemed to be at pains to catch and follow Vanderlyn's tone. It was almost as if he were becoming frightened of Vanderlyn—on whose continued favour, Shefford thought grimly, depended his access to Vanderlyn's wife. 'Although I did once have to kick out one South American character,' Mark went on, 'who was getting rather more fresh with Marion than was at all polite.' He gave Marion the smile that went just beyond brotherliness; Shefford could see that he was pleased with himself at having perfected it. 'And with Gemma too, perhaps. Gemma, you remember?'

It was the first time Shefford had seen these two look at each other, and it wasn't a look he understood. There was no complicity in it; what it carried, on Mark's side, was rather a hint of desperation. And Gemma's face was a little too hard to be comfortable. Shefford was aware of Andreas, striking in with some smooth remark. There was something odd about the day, Andreas was saying; something exhausting in the air. After lunch they had all better go to sleep. Tyros was in almost every way ideal, but one did have to cope with the afternoon. At least it wasn't as bad as Rome. For a few minutes Andreas talked amusingly about Rome.

Shefford had leisure to look longer at Mark. They had scarcely exchanged a word as yet. He remembered that Mark had seemed almost as anxious as Vanderlyn that he should come back to Tyros. But now he didn't seem too pleased about it. Perhaps he was getting frightened of Shefford too. Mark had always been spare; he was proud of his figure; but now he looked as if he had actually been losing weight. There was something feverish about him, and he was pinched and pale round the mouth. He certainly had no appearance of the happy lover—or only ambiguously, when he put on his revolting just-more-than-a-brother act for Marion. Presumably the strains of parlour adultery were beginning to get him down. And also, perhaps, just the expensiveness Shefford had been remarking. The fatality had been his introduction into Vanderlyn's small household. Mark had belonged, if he belonged anywhere, with the people who got liquored up but not drunk; who were ultimately on Tyros, despite all the graciousness of its patronage, on a simple basis of hire-and-fire. About money and security he was genuinely not a calculating creature, or not in a long-term way. It was the restrictive side of becoming a son of the house that would be vivid to him, and that he would chafe at. What he had been up to with Gemma was basically a wanton reaction, perhaps, to smothered resentment there.

Vanderlyn was talking now. He described Guthrie's last picture to Shefford, and went on to retail some other current activities which Gemma hadn't mentioned. One of these concerned Gemma herself. She was working on a new quartet—for just what instruments, Shefford didn't catch—and when it was perfected there would be the question of having it performed. There were, of course, musicians on Tyros, but it would by no means do to bring four of them together in an impromptu way; an established Quartet must be brought to the island—and it could only be a question of which, absolutely, would be the best. Gemma was in doubt about this; Andreas had informed views; over the coffee the three of them talked it out together. Shefford, who had no technical knowledge here, found the discussion eerie; this planning ahead seemed to take rather far the business of sweeping things under the mat. And he didn't believe, somehow, that the performance would ever take place—or not on Tyros. It seemed to him that Vanderlyn, although so calm and controlled now, yet wasn't going to prove to have all that stamina. His situation was intolerable, and he knew it.

Ceasing to attend to the talk, Shefford tried to get clear where his responsibilities to all these people lay. Mark, who was so much the black sheep of the affair, still came first. Shefford owed something to Vanderlyn, who had been kind, and who had in a fashion made an appeal to him to which

240

he had implicitly undertaken to respond. He also owed something to Vanderlyn because—as his friend Gavin Naylor had discerned—he had that small but definite thing about the first Mrs Vanderlyn, and he would like to honour her memory by a little straightening her husband's road. Marion Causland, again, was touching—so much so, that he almost wished he could himself turn into her Fairy Prince. But as there was nothing of the sort in his heart—a heart, he told himself, which didn't seem to get much beyond Vangelio in its present stage of development—anything of the kind would merely be presenting the unfortunate girl with another deception. And she wouldn't be having any, anyway. It was only in relation to Mark that he could effectively act.

It must be broken to Vanderlyn, it must be borne in upon him, that he was deluding himself about Mark and Marion. Perhaps he could be persuaded that Mark was merely, in a good-hearted way, being kind to her; that if she were to fall very much in love with him Mark's position would become impossible and her own deeply unhappy; and that Mark, therefore, had much better *go*. Along with that, Mark would have to be *persuaded* to go; to break with Gemma, and clear out. After that, Marion's heart must heal as it might, and Vanderlyn and Gemma must settle their own affairs. They were, after all, the grown people in the picture. The rights and wrongs—or rather the balance of advantages—of Vanderlyn's learning or not learning that it was Mark Varley who had been in his bed: this just wasn't for Shefford to pronounce upon.

'The earth moved. I felt it.'

The words, spoken by Marion, brought Shefford back to his surroundings with a jerk. He wasn't, in fact, certain that there hadn't been an actual jerk, and he looked swiftly round the others. They seemed to have been aware of nothing. Vanderlyn was glancing at Marion in concern, and now he put out a hand and touched her reassuringly on the arm. It was clear that the mere thought of the earth-tremors alarmed her.

'I don't think so, Marion,' he said. 'It's only that they

241

have been a little on our minds. And even if they happen again, you know, it is certain that they are quite harmless. All that they do is to bring down a little tumble of rubble here and there. It would take a full-scale earthquake, such as is impossible on Tyros, to damage the monastery. Anton, you didn't feel anything?'

'No—nothing.' The beautifully manicured tips of Andreas's fingers were resting lightly on the table-cloth; he might have been preparing to embark upon a pianoforte passage in Gemma's quartet. 'And, as you say——'

Andreas broke off. He had been interrupted by something like the same musical note that had come from Vanderlyn's wine-glass some time before. Now, it came from Marion's. Her glass—an empty glass, for she had drunk nothing—had given out this single sound, and now lay in fragments before her.

'But I didn't touch it!' Marion cried. She was looking at the shattered glass in bewilderment—not being too quick, Shefford thought, at putting two and two together. 'Anton, surely I didn't?'

Andreas shook his head reassuringly, but made no reply. He had leant across the table, and was gently stirring the shivered crystal with a forefinger. The phenomenon must have interested him. One of his subjects, after all, was the strength of materials.

Chapter 5

THE MONASTERY WAS a place of devious passages. After lunch, Mark took advantage of this to dodge out of sight, carrying Vanderlyn's parcel with him. Shefford, who felt that these evasive tactics had been going on long enough, went in pursuit. The time had come for a show-down. He was clear about this, although not so clear about the form the show-down should take. He rapidly tried out several successive roles in his head: they ranged from unbending moralist to seasoned and discreetly prompting man of the world. He was unable to assure himself that any of them sounded promising.

He had never, during his previous visit to Tyros, penetrated to Mark's quarters, but he had a good idea where they lay. He went upstairs again, and followed a passage lined with small cells on either hand. These had not been worth converting to any modern purpose, and their effect was rather cheerless; Shefford supposed that the original occupants had been an illiterate crowd, and it wasn't easy, somehow, to feel that they had left much odour of sanctity behind them. But at the end of the passage there was a group of larger apartments which had been the lodging of the monastery's top man: the *Hegumen*, he must have been called. Shefford chose the most likely-looking door, and knocked. There was no reply. He opened the door and walked in.

The room was empty, but it was certainly Mark's. It was large, with a large window opening upon a kind of loggia; through the farther arcading of this there was a view of Spina, single dominating peak of Tyros, that topped by its little shrine dedicated—like most such mountain shrines in Greece —to the prophet Elijah. The *Hegumen* must have been able to edify himself with this prospect as he ate his breakfast. Shefford's first impression of the room was of its being sparely and austerely furnished. There were only two pictures. One was a darkly-lustrous ikon and the other a modern portrait. Shefford walked over to look at this. It proved to be an oil-painting of Wyndham Lewis by Augustus John. John had made Lewis very young, very sane, very handsome: he might have been a head prefect with tough views on the use of the rod. Shefford couldn't believe that Mark cared twopence for Wyndham Lewis, and he saw that this portrait was on the wall simply as a suitable embellishment for the room of a young writer. Having seen so much, he saw, too, that the whole room was like that. The plain furniture had been designed, one had to suspect, by somebody brought from

Sweden for the purpose. On a great olive-wood table there stood an electric typewriter.

Shefford surveyed the place uneasily. Mark wasn't here. In no sense was he here. Shefford found the implications of the room depressing, and he left it hastily—so hastily that he bumped into Aphrodite, moving down this corridor on business of her own. She took a token part in all the work of the household, he had observed. In fact, he told himself a shade cynically, she was paid solely to convey the impression that the Vanderlyns lived in this great place in extreme simplicity, ministered to by a single old woman and a girl. It wouldn't be much use trying to converse with Aphrodite, but as she was looking at him with a disagreeable servile suspicion he tried uttering the name of Mr Varley on an interrogative note. She answered in very tolerable French. It was part, one had to feel, of the mild hoax. Aphrodite had probably put in long years as an upper servant with diplomats or other grandees in Athens. Mr Varley—Monsieur Mark, she called him—had another room, not in the monastery at all, but in a building overlooking the miniature harbour where the yacht and some dinghies were kept. There were still two or three fishermen and their families down there, and the young gentleman appeared to enjoy their company. He had this little room where he would repose himself. Having given this information, Aphrodite went on to say something about the earth-tremors. It seemed to be the womenfolk, Shefford thought, who got worried over those ineffective shiverings. He disengaged himself from the ancient creature, and made his way out of the monastery.

It was hot and very still. The breeze imagined by Gemma was non-existent, which made it odd that there was nevertheless the faint sound of a breeze just perceptible to the ear. He realised that the sound came not from the air but from the sea. But the sea, when he had a glimpse of it, was absolutely motionless. In the middle-distance and beyond, it was a uniform deep blue; you felt it to be stretched tight over something, like a membrane. In and around the tiny basin, overhung by its huddle of hovels, the colour was a clear green. All the water here was very shallow; it must be why they didn't bring the big launch, or any larger craft, round to this side of the island. One of the buildings had an outside staircase in wood, with a decayed handrail running up its side and a door at the top. It might have been in an English fishing village. Something told Shefford that this was Mark's hide-out. He mounted the stairs cautiously, tapped at the door, and indicated the general temper of his approach by walking straight in. He had been quite right. Mark was before him.

It was a small, low place, with a long, low window, seemingly unglazed, more or less impending over the anchorage below. The walls were lumpy and shadowed under an uneven plastering, and the plaster had long ago been covered with wallpaper of a hideous design; it would have been called 'contemporary' if bought in Huddersfield or Hull; it looked as if it *had* been bought in one or other of them. Three blown-up photographs had been stuck to it with drawing-pins. One—it was in colour—was of an English woodland scene, the ground smothered in bluebells. Another was of a nuclear explosion of the recognized mushroom-shaped sort. The third was of some black men torturing some other black men with ropes and buckets of water. Mark, clearly, had his own idea of what was pleasing, or at least salutary, in the way of ornament. There was a common wood table with a record-player and a battered portable typewriter, and there were a couple of kitchen chairs. Half the floor was taken up with a tumble of cushions, apparently for sitting or sprawling on, and the other half was littered with paperback books and typescript. There was an oil-stove with a kettle on it, and a shelf with a teapot and some chipped mugs. Mark had made himself a home.

'Oh, hullo!' Mark said. He was standing near the window, with the small parcel still in his hand; he looked as if he had obstinate doubts about opening it. 'I come over here sometimes. It's quiet.'

'I suppose so.' Shefford looked about him again. Mark hadn't managed his rather feeble remark in more than a mumble, and some friendly reply seemed required. 'It's rather nice. It's a sort of room I've been in before.'

'Yes.' Mark, too, looked about him, and his eye fell on the black men misconducting themselves. 'I put up that kind only in a short-term way.' He went over to the wall, tore down the photograph, and crumbled it. 'One should remind oneself of these things from time to time. I'm not a sadist.'

'You're a masochist, I expect.' Shefford thought the kitchen chairs uninviting and the cushions undignified; he walked over to the window and leant on the sill. 'Why don't you open your parcel?'

'Because it's a birthday present. It's an advance birthday present from Bernard.' Mark's brow darkened. 'I'm going to be twenty-three on Friday. It's pretty awful. I haven't done a bloody thing. Nobody's ever heard of me.'

'Open it. It may be something you'll like.' Shefford was aware he wasn't beginning this interview very well. He wondered why he regularly found Mark hard to be stiff with. This time, it was partly the room. Yet the forlorn refuge was only another bit of Mark's posturing, really; if he felt that he'd sold out to a false image of himself on Tyros he ought to make himself scarce, and not set up this mummery within a couple of hundred yards of the monastery. And it suddenly occurred to Shefford that perhaps this was where Gemma came. These grubby cushions were her bank for love to lie and play on. The idea came to him as a swift, concrete image that shocked him; he felt that familiar flare of hostility towards Mark; he swung round and leant out into the open air, as if it would blow away a base jealousy.

'Go on,' he said, casually and without turning round. 'Open your present and have done with it.'

There was no reply from Mark behind him, and Shefford took a more considered look at the outside world. Three women were gossiping in a doorway, and half-a-dozen children were playing some way beyond—silently, except for an occasional shrill, peremptory cry connected with their game. He hadn't realised that there was this substantial little indigenous community within a stone's throw of the monastery. Immediately below him was a boat-house; the bows of a dinghy were emerging from it as he watched; in a moment he saw that it was being poled out by Dionysios. Dionysios seemed to be making some repair—there were a few tools on the stern thwart—and to require a better light, for he was now tying the painter to the little wharf. He was wearing only a pair of shapeless and dirty cotton trousers which seemed too big for him, and out of these his slim torso sprang with a kind of insolent grace. He squatted on the bottom of the dinghy with his back to Shefford; he leant forward to inspect his work, and moving light reflected from the water was at play against the ripple of his muscles and the flexed ridge of his spine. Dionysios's skin was a texture of golden browns, like an ancient map.

There had been a rustling of paper inside the room, and now Mark made a strange sound—a sound so strange that Shefford spun round and stared at him. He had gone so pale that his features seemed almost obliterated; yet Shefford could distinguish them as contorted into an expression he couldn't read. Mark came slowly over to the window, as if he were just aware of it as an oblong of light. He repeated the strange sound—it turned out to be the name of Christ—and then leant out and stared sightlessly down into the pool below. Dionysios, using a pair of dividers, was scratching a circle on the middle thwart of his dinghy.

Shefford turned back into the room. There was wrapping-paper on the floor, and what the parcel had contained now lay on the table beside the typewriter. It was a very slender book, bound in a beautifully tooled leather. He picked it up without ceremony and opened it. An engraved title-page told him that it contained, privately printed, *A Sweet Savour unto the Lord*, by Mark Varley, B.A. (Oxon.).

'You can't tell what he may have done!' Mark was gasping out the words at the window. 'Sent copies to God knows who. He throttles me. I can't take it. I can't bear it.'

Shefford put down the book, and returned to the window. It was so broad that they could both lean out while preserving, so to speak, a proper gazing-distance between them. He recalled himself as believing that Bernard Vanderlyn was particularly responsive to the sensibilities—even the tiresome sensibilities—of young men. And here he was, achieving a kind of *tour de force* of the obtuse.

'I remember Vanderlyn saying something casually about getting it printed.' Shefford strove to sound almost casual himself. 'And he certainly seems to have gone to town on it. But those are his standards, after all. No call for you to start creating about the thing.'

'It's my rotten poem, not his.' Mark's voice sounded genuinely on the brink of strangulation. 'But they've no idea. They haven't a clue. No rich men have. Certainly not Bernard. It's despicable to have no respect for another man's property.'

'Mark, for God's sake don't be such a ghastly little hypocrite.' Shefford, although his own breath had almost been taken away by the extraordinary conclusion of this speech, found that effective utterance had at last come to him. 'Just ask yourself! Could you look Vanderlyn in the eye—and talk about taking another man's property?'

'I don't know what the bloody hell you mean. It's not my fault, is it, if he's always giving me things? He believes I'm going to give it all back—in decent work done one day. I've believed it, too.' Mark's temper flared up. 'If you can only be damned silly, Jeremy, you can bugger off. This room's mine, anyway. I pay an old woman five bob a week for it.'

Shefford felt his own temper rising, and he gave himself a moment before speaking. Dionysios had produced a brace, fitted it with a centre-bit, and begun to bore carefully through the thwart. He had shifted his position, so that he had the brace between his thighs, and was able to glance up at the window. He gave them a brief wave, a brilliant smile, and then returned very seriously to his task.

'Mark, what's the good of a lot of lies? You know very well that Gemma's going to have a child.'

'It's not possible!' In Mark's voice there was a panic which seemed infectious—for Shefford felt something like panic too. But he spoke coldly.

'Isn't it? I suppose precautions do occasionally break down.'

'That's not what I mean. You're mad, Jeremy. You've made some crazy mistake. There's something I oughtn't to tell you, because it's the greatest confidence Bernard has ever made to me. It was only because he wanted to explain why he tends to treat me like a son. He can't have kids. Not any longer—if he ever could. It's only lately that he's found out.'

'Mark, are you going to deny that you've been sleeping with Gemma, and have given her a child? Don't you remember what you told me at that absurd garden party?'

For a moment Mark said nothing. The effect of these questions upon him made itself evident only in purely physiological terms. He ceased simply to look pale, and his complexion took on a hue suggesting the sudden subcutaneous injection of some dark grey fluid. He turned away abruptly, and walked back into the room. Shefford found himself lacking the courage to follow, and he continued to look down on the small Aegean scene. The three women were still talking, rapidly and intently, as if there was some grave matter at issue among them. The children had finished their game and disappeared. Dionysios's brace had now bored deep into the thwart; he seemed to be intending to step a small mast in the dinghy. Without quite knowing why, Shefford continued to watch Dionysios at this employment. Presently he would need to use another tool—perhaps a fine-bladed saw. Already his shoulders were working powerfully as he drove the centre-bit round its deep groove.

'All right. It's true. I have been sleeping with Gemma. And I don't repent it. It's been marvellous.' Mark had returned to the window—although it hardly seemed to be Mark's voice that was speaking. He leant out again, as Shefford was still doing. Shefford had a fleeting recollection of Gavin Naylor and himself, disposed rather like this in his rooms in college, and surveying a scene below. He turned and looked at Mark sideways, rather as he had looked at Gavin. Their glance met. And in a simple and completely definitive moment he knew that Mark had just told him a lie.

249

Chapter 6

WHOEVER HAD BEEN sleeping with Gemma, whoever had been careless about the result, it wasn't Mark. Shefford had got it all wrong, and disastrously wrong at that. For Mark's innocence—it was clear in a flash—wasn't the consequence of any exercise of virtue on his part. He hadn't remotely been a worshipper from afar. He was a rejected lover, and the revelation that somebody else had succeeded where he had failed was a truth his vanity couldn't, at least for the moment, face up to. So he had made this wild claim. It had to be admitted that Shefford had led him to it; that he was only agreeing, in an instant of bewildering discovery, to something which had been thrust at him. It was about the most vulgar false boast a man can manage, all the same.

'All right, Jeremy. I see you know that's not the truth. Forget it.' It appeared to be with an immense effort that Mark managed this scramble out of mere ignominy. 'One doesn't like to be deprived of one's reputation as young Casanova. Incidentally, I never told you a lie before. And this one's been an instant failure.'

'Mark, I'm frightfully sorry. What you said at that party——'

'What I began to say. And *that* was true. It *is* true. I've got so that I can't think of anything but Gemma. It's not like anything else in the world. I couldn't conceive of going away from her. And now somebody——' He broke off, again as if before something he couldn't contemplate. 'Jeremy, could Bernard have come up to the scratch, after all?'

'I don't think so. Vanderlyn seemed very positive about there having to be an unknown father to the child.'

Shefford regretted this speech as soon as he had uttered it. His relief that Mark had not in fact cuckolded Vanderlyn was so great that he had felt the sky as clearing a little. For some moments Mark had struck him as almost out of his mind, and then he had thought he was seeing reason again.

Now he wasn't so sure. Indeed, Mark's face once more filled him with dismay. He found himself not caring to look at it. It was as if the blemish on Mark's cheek had become a point of embarrassment between them. And Mark was so easily overthrown—so easily overthrown in his wretched pride or self-absorption. He had even been squaring up to make a mountain out of the absurd business of the privately-printed sacred poem. And now there was all this.

'But she snubbed me! She turned me down flat. I did try for her, you know. I kept on trying—hard. Women don't dislike me. I've had plenty.' Mark hesitated. 'That's my second lie. Two.'

'I don't care twopence, Mark, about your sleeping with girls—or with married women, either. It's no business of mine. But this was—well, rather a special case. Proposing, I mean, to seduce Vanderlyn's wife.'

'I don't see why.'

It seemed to Shefford that his best course would simply be to go away. For what could you do with somebody who could say a thing like that? But this was perhaps an intolerant view. Moreover he had been brought out to Tyros to do something more effective than just throw up his hands. So he stayed where he was.

'I don't see why,' Mark repeated. 'If Bernard wasn't much good in bed—and why should he be, at his age?—it might have worked out quite well. A stable arrangement, don't you think? Not that one's mind acts like that. Not when one's in deep.' As Mark said this, he behaved in a strange way. The window-sill was less than waist-high. He knelt down, folded his arms on it, and buried his head rather as if he were in church and about to pray. But, instead of praying, he wept. He wept noisily, and this somehow struck Shefford as a crowning horror. Dionysios, pausing in his labours below, looked up in surprise.

'Mark, for goodness' sake pull yourself together. There are other people to be sorry for in this business, besides your blessed self.'

'It was all I had.' Mark had stopped crying with a strange

abruptness. He was looking at Shefford again, but he remained on his knees. 'She was utterly hard to me. I told myself it was because she was chaste. A chaste woman. Diana. Phoebe. It's no good, I told myself, firing your little phallic arrows at the moon.'

Shefford found nothing to say. He didn't care for this reference to that freak of Mark's in the college garden long ago. It was too considered altogether, and suggested that Mark was play-acting again now. But yet Shefford knew this wasn't true. The truth was different, and it was more alarming. Mark was barely listening to himself, and there was more to his perturbation than mere wild and whirling words. Gemma had turned him down, and had then given herself to another man. Perhaps to another man as young as himself. And at some deep level his response to this was of a sort he had no control over. It was an evil response. And the evil might grow.

But at least he had got on his feet again. Shefford, observing this, observed at the same moment that Dionysios had got to his feet too. He was balancing himself easily across the centre-board of his little boat. He was looking up at the window, being still much interested in Mark's behaviour. And as he looked, a flicker of comprehension passed over his face. He still had the brace in his hand. Moving nothing more than his wrist, he created with it a gesture of the simplest and most perfect indecency. Again he glanced up, and Shefford was conscious of his gaze, insolent and enigmatically triumphant, holding Mark's for a long moment. Then he stooped down in apparent unconcern, and with a delicate finger began removing sawdust from the small orifice on which he had been at work.

'It was Dionysios!'

In the instant that Mark said this, Shefford knew that it was the truth. It was even something he had known already, although the knowledge had been of the sort that haunts only the farthest fringe of consciousness. It had taken up its unnoticed station there, perhaps, at the moment when

Dionysios, pausing with Shefford's suitcase on the terrace, had glanced down in a kind of pitying amusement at Vangelio and himself as they stood together, a little awkwardly, beside the Mercedes. Mark, on the other hand, hadn't known; not in any area of his mind had *he* known; he was in the stage of having suffered an instantaneous and terrifying revelation—like a man who, in a flash of lightning, discovers himself to be on the verge of a precipice.

'It was Dionysios,' Mark repeated. 'She turned me down, and she took Dionysios. A servant. A lackey.' He spoke so quietly that Shefford had a sense—instantly realised as delusive—that some relief of tension had taken place. He was even aware of registering mere social comedy in these last contemptuous words as coming from one of Mark's unassuming origin. At the same time, he knew they should be answered.

'I suppose it's to her credit, in a fashion,' he said. 'If she just felt she had to sleep with *somebody*—and there's nothing to be said about that sort of compulsion—she may well have decided it would be intolerably disloyal to choose a person so close to her husband as yourself. But a young servant didn't count—or not in the same degree.' Shefford, although he was filled with dismay, felt a momentary satisfaction in this psychological expertness. 'So she's let Dionysios have her. It's an awful mess. I think myself it's squalid and horrible. You'd better clear out. You can't help in any way—not with this stiff involvement of your own. Even if we're fancying things about Dionysios, that remains true. And I admit that I don't think we are. It's the key to almost everything I've noticed about him since I saw him again.'

'He's got in my way. He always has. Right from the start.'

'Dionysios?'

'Bernard. If he hadn't taken me on in this smothering domestic fashion, Gemma would have felt I was like anybody else on the island.' Mark produced a disturbing grimace. 'Fair game.'

Shefford was baffled. Mark at times had ways of thinking that there just seemed no coping with; it was as if he owned

253

at least an intermittent command of sheer moral anarchy. But that couldn't be helped; it was part of the problem; and what remained essential was to get him away from Tyros. Searching for further argument, Shefford took another plunge. Mark, if the thing could possibly be done, must be made to see how the mischief he was occasioning ramified.

'Listen, Mark. This business about Gemma isn't the whole thing. Think about Marion.'

'Marion?' It was as if Mark had never heard the name. 'What on earth has that girl got to do with it?'

'You damned well know what she has to do with it.' If Shefford spoke in this way, it was because misgiving had assailed him, an alarming suspicion that in this desperate scene he had put foot after foot wrong. But he was committed to the new theme now. 'Just why do you think you've been behaving to Marion as you have? Are you managing to be in love with her too?'

'Jeremy, I won't stand it. I can't. Something will happen.'

'Shut up, Mark, for pity's sake. I know this is horrible for you, but you're not going to improve matters by hysteria. Are you going to tell me you've just been being chummy with her?'

'Chummy? Yes, I suppose so.' Mark seemed really bewildered. 'She's almost an imbecile, but harmless enough. I've had to chat her up a bit. It's something Bernard expects.'

'You've been giving the impression of falling in love with her, just by way of cloaking your designs—your pitifully ineffectual designs—on Gemma.'

'Jeremy, you're cracked. It's all that rubbishing English Literature. You're talking like somebody in a rotten old play.'

'You're acting like somebody in a rotten old play.' Shefford was angry again—angrier than he knew. He had a mounting sense that the situation was forcing him into behaving like a headmaster or a parson, and he didn't like the part a bit. This made him reckless. 'You're fooling the girl— very cruelly. And you're fooling Vanderlyn, who's set his heart on your marrying her.'

'*What ?*'

'If you're not aware of that, it's because you're so wrapped up in yourself that it makes you just plain stupid. Everybody knows it.' Shefford had an extraordinary sensation of trying to restrain his tongue—literally to still its movement in his mouth—and being quite unable to do so. 'This whole fatal island takes it as an arranged thing. And the person who told me about it was that precious Dionysios.'

There was silence in Mark's hide-out. They had both left the window, and were facing each other across the table with the portable typewriter—the instrument, Shefford found himself thinking, of goodness knew what more or less sacred struggles on Mark's part. Mark's complexion had darkened again, as if a cuttle-fish were at work in a pallid pool. His breath was coming quick and short, like that of a man who has been hitting out in some confused affray in the dark, who has been worsted and beaten up, held down to receive ugly blow upon blow. That the Greek boy Dionysios should possess Gemma and that he himself should be judged disposable to Marion Causland: these were outrages which he could not endure—or not without loosing outrage as an answer. When he spoke now, it was in a whisper in which passion quivered like a small intense flame in the depth of a cave. Shefford was overwhelmed by a sense that the whole performance ought to have a purely theatrical quality and had not.

'I could thrash him,' Mark whispered. 'I think I could thrash him. If I took him by surprise, and got the right hold on him first.' He turned and ran to the window as if to vault through it, regardless that it must be twelve feet from the ground. It looked as though the dinghy was going to be the scene of a grotesque struggle: Hamlet and Laertes in Ophelia's grave. Shefford made for the window too—so briskly that they jostled each other as they looked out.

'Gone,' Mark said.

It was true that Dionysios and his little craft had fortunately vanished. And the gossiping women had also departed. The small picturesque scene, brightly lit, might have been waiting, like an empty stage, for the entry of a troupe of persons, equally picturesque, to begin some light entertainment.

'Stepho,' Mark said.

The stage was not quite untenanted, after all. Stepho was there—in the middle distance, leaning against a wall, staring out to sea. If they hadn't noticed him it was because of his habitual immobility. Or it was because of something more than this. His posture, although it suggested lounging, in fact remained unrelaxed; his hips and knees seemed locked; his back made a straight diagonal with the wall behind him. He might have been an inanimate object stacked like that for future use, an implement or even a weapon.

'That girl,' Mark said slowly. 'What am I expected to do about her? I suppose she's Bernard's ward. Go to him and ask him for her hand? I was foolish about the girl next door, you know—my father's choice, the one with the face like a bun. But here's another chance—offered by Bernard, who's being more than a father to me. This time, it's a girl with a face like a crumpet.'

'If you can only talk like a toad, Mark, you'd better shut up. Shut up and think it over. It's my idea that you and I might clear out together—at least for a time.'

'Or this Marion creature and I might clear out. Perhaps that would please Bernard best—and it's my job to suck up to him, isn't it? A spontaneous love-affair, a combustion for which he didn't even have to strike a match. That's it!' Mark's eyes were gleaming; it was as if deep in the cave something was fanning the small flame until it leapt and flared. 'Two burning souls whirled away in a tempest of passion. Ages long ago these lovers fled away into the storm.'

'Look, Mark——'

'Into her dream he melted, as the rose blendeth its odour with the violet. My Marion! sweet dreamer! lovely——' Mark broke off, and stared at Shefford—sightlessly, as if through some dawning conception. 'She *did* have a dream, by the way. She told it to me.'

Certainly there was nothing to do about Mark in a mood like this except leave him. Shefford moved to the door of the little room, but Mark was there before him.

'All right, all right,' Mark said. 'I'll go away and think it over, as you advise. In a spirit of charity and consideration. And I promise not to try and bash Dionysios. He might do the bashing, after all. See you, Jeremy.'

Mark went out, closing the door behind him, and his footsteps could be heard clattering down the wooden staircase. Shefford stayed where he was; it was entirely agreeable to him that Mark should thus make himself scarce for a time. He looked round the room again. It was no longer possible to think of it as a place hired for assignations with Gemma Vanderlyn; there had never been such assignations; he had made an ass of himself in interpreting as he had those few desperate words of Mark's at the garden party. Mark would not be so upset now—would not, in fact, be so ragingly bloody-minded—if there hadn't thus lucklessly been attributed to him an amorous conquest he hadn't made. And the room was just what it seemed to be: the kind of room, with the kind of possessions, that a young man is likely to be able to afford, when he is on his own and determined to be a writer. Unsympathetically viewed, it was a futile make-believe, a gesture as meaningless as taking one's clothes off and playing with a bow and arrows. But it could be viewed in other ways too. Shefford glanced in the direction of the one alien object it contained: the sumptuously bound and tooled poem on a sacred subject. He had no impulse to discover whether he agreed with Vanderlyn that it evinced the influence of Gerard Manley Hopkins. He thought it likely that he would never read Mark's prize composition, and that this was something which Mark would thank him for. So now he looked at a small shelf of books, and then once more at the photographs of the English woodland scene and the exploding bomb. Only when he felt that there had been time for Mark to get well away did he turn to leave the room.

He stood at the head of the wooden staircase, looking at

the narrow cobbled lane below. It ran down from the monastery, took a sharp twist almost beneath his feet, circled the little basin, and then climbed steeply to higher ground and vanished. Nobody was in sight except an old man carrying a couple of empty baskets. Shefford was about to go down the steps when he was arrested by the sound of an engine. An instant later he saw Vanderlyn's Aston Martin, driven by Mark from the direction of the monastery. Mark was alone—so at least, at this moment, it was only Mark himself and the old man who could get killed. Nothing of the sort happened, although the car was travelling at a shocking speed and its mudguard actually brushed one of the old man's baskets as it passed. On the bend beneath Shefford it went into a calculated but hare-brained skid; then it hurtled round the sea-front and disappeared; the roar of the retreating engine increased for some seconds before diminishing, as if Mark were thrusting at the accelerator hard.

It was, no doubt, Mark's way of thinking something over. And of doing so—Shefford remembered—in a spirit of charity and consideration. The old man with the baskets had halted at the side of the lane, seemingly for the purpose of saying a prayer—unless, conceivably, he was calling down a curse upon the projectile which had nearly killed him. Just as the car passed, Shefford had felt the staircase shaking. He wondered whether this had been occasioned—as seemed likely enough—by the brutal wind of Mark's speed, or whether Tyros was rocking on its foundations once more. But the earth-tremors were not, of course, like that. They were slighter than any disturbance one could think of as truly seismic; at the same time there was the suggestion of something organic about them. Shefford had a glimpse of the island as a large and slumbering creature, able through some trick of its muscular fasciae to twitch large areas of its skin. Horses can do it, he thought—but can cows? He couldn't remember. The flies take off in alarm but presently they settle again, and nothing much has happened, after all.

Chapter 7

'AH, WELL MET,' Andreas said. He had encountered Shefford on the terrace some hours later. 'I am charged with a
message to you from Gemma. But come up to my room. It
appears to me not too early for a glass of dry sherry. You will
forgive me if I have the English habit not quite right.'

Shefford had no wish to drink sherry, and he saw no prospect of pleasure in any message from Mrs Vanderlyn. But
he had Andreas in his head as the one person on Tyros who
was both well informed about the state of affairs there and
to be credited with a more or less objective mind. He had
himself not been doing too well as a visiting and juvenile sage.
Perhaps Andreas was doing better as a resident and elderly
one. He wasn't sure that he wanted to confide in Andreas,
and he still found something displeasing in the affectation of
the man's talk. But at least, he thought, he had better go
along.

The enormous room was much as it had been before. In
the part given over to professional activities there seemed
to be an increase rather than decrease in the signs of work
going forward. Perhaps this concerned distant places for
which Andreas had received commissions. Or perhaps on
Tyros itself there was to be further building in a big way.
Vanderlyn might have it in mind to put up a theatre or an
auditorium or a picture gallery. Shefford had to remind
himself, against what he found was his own instinctive persuasion, that the days of the whole heroic venture into
patronage were not necessarily numbered.

'What is it Gemma wants me to know?' The sherry was
before him on a small table; nevertheless it was abruptly
and almost challengingly that he asked this question. He
wondered whether Gemma knew that he *knew*; whether,
through Andreas, there was to be an appeal to him based
on this premise; whether a further stage in the general impossibility of his position was to be arrived at by that road.

He sipped the sherry with an air of appreciation. He didn't want to appear rude.

'Ah, I fear I have made that a mere excuse to gain the pleasure of your company. It is a trifling matter.' Andreas paused for the fraction of a second. 'Nothing in the way of a confidence, you know. It is simply that if you happen to have brought a black tie with you—have I got that idiom correctly?—it will be quite in order to put it on to-night. I am not in favour of dinner-jackets in an Aegean summer myself. But a hostess's wish is law.'

'I've brought a linen one, as a matter of fact.'

'That will be very much the *ton*. We are to have grand company. A Minister has come over from the mainland—in connection with the opening of the hospital, I need hardly say. Bernard, as well as Gemma, seems anxious that things should be done in style. There was a time when a minor member of a Greek cabinet would scarcely have appeared a person of much importance to our distinguished friend. But, as things are now, it will be expedient that this fellow be accorded the *grande entrée*. So we must all be on our best behaviour. Would you say that there is likely to be any difficulty about that?'

'I can't see why there should be.' Shefford glanced warily at Andreas, and felt a reluctance to be drawn. 'Can you?'

'Ah!' Andreas poised a hand over his glass. 'There are these earth-tremors. I have an idea that they affect the nerves more than might be supposed. It is something very primitive that is involved. And we are all primitive creatures. Myself, I feel enormously primitive.'

'If that's all, I don't think we need bother our heads.' Shefford had refused to be entertained by Andreas's last remark. The man certainly had something to say, and this fooling around was irritating. 'The last time we talked, you seemed to feel things weren't shaping too well on Tyros. Do you still feel that now?'

'You have the admirable British frankness and directness. I must take example from you. We must be open, you and I, about these painful matters. And I must not begin by reproaching you.'

'You can reproach me if you want to.' Shefford was impatient. 'But I won't promise to know what you're talking about.'

'You would if I did.' This expresison seemed to amuse Andreas. 'So let me remind you,' he said. 'I did beg you to take away that fatal boy.'

'Is he the fatal boy?' It was as coldly as he could that Shefford asked this question. Mark Varley, after all, although not in fact his oldest friend, was a member of his own college. 'He's barely out of his teens. He's been snatched away from everything familiar to him, and set up as the young poet of Tyros. I think Vanderlyn's motives have been admirable, but I can't think the same of his judgement. Mark ought to be pushing ahead on his own, on bread and lard, if need be: which is said to be remarkably good for the brain. But here he is—and here has been the second Mrs Vanderlyn too, which is what I think we're talking about. And I don't recall that your own sense of the situation was all that accurate. You didn't think Mrs Vanderlyn would be the problem in the least, or not in the way of her being attracted by young men. I admit you were right about something else: Vanderlyn's coming to put in too much time planning for Mark, and thinking to acquire a ready-made son in him. Mark doesn't want another father; he's had one, and he thinks that's enough. Perhaps he's been bad for Vanderlyn, but he scarcely deserves to be called a fatal boy. I agree that he's had ideas in his head. You've guessed at them, I don't doubt, and know that, if they'd come to anything, he'd deserve to be called treacherous and dishonourable. But Mrs Vanderlyn has found her really fatal boy elsewhere. She's found him in the kitchen, more or less. You wouldn't be talking to me now, I think, if you hadn't tumbled to that too?' Shefford paused on this interrogative note.

'I see your point of view.' Andreas, with both hands, made a throwaway gesture. 'The fact remains that Varley should have gone home.'

'He hasn't got a home. Not to speak of. I'm trying to get him away now, all the same.'

'It's too late. The earth is trembling.'

'Look, Andreas—that's the kind of remark I expect to get from Mark himself. Be your years, for Christ's sake. If there's sense to be talked, talk it.'

'My dear Shefford, your own years, if I may say so, are coming to you. We need sense, if we're to be of any use at all.' Andreas had made his odd, recurrent drop into seriousness. 'The Greek lad—of course I've seen it all—is the technically guilty person. If Gemma isn't.'

'Gemma certainly is. And Dionysios has merely taken what's come to him. He's a brutal little creature, and he relishes a kind of vicious triumph——'

'It is my fear that Varley might do that too, if he could contrive such a thing. But proceed.'

'He also possesses—Dionysios, I mean—an animal health or innocence I don't quarrel with. I don't much quarrel with him at all—except to wonder where he came from, and why. And that goes for the other Greek boy too, who sometimes strikes me as a good deal more dangerous. They just oughtn't to be around.'

'I agree. Perhaps, in a peripheral way—is that a possible phrase?—they are sons by a short cut too. Or perhaps they are just young men. There are no doubt areas in Bernard's mind that he has never had much leisure to explore. As for where these young men come from: that's simple. Prison. Which goes, of course, for Varley too. But Varley has a demon that those two lack. It's that, I repeat, that worries me. You know what he's been doing this afternoon?'

'Driving hell-for-leather round Tyros.'

'Well, yes, and in Bernard's car. He's wrecked it, by the way. He told me so, some hours ago.'

'Wrecked it?' Shefford was startled.

'Not very obviously, it seems, but rather drastically, all the same. I came on him in the garage—the old granary, you know—deep in consultation with Stepho. Fathoms deep. It rather struck me, how many fathoms. But I suppose

262

Stepho is a mechanic. Varley confessed to me about the car, but I doubt whether he has confessed to Bernard. He won't do that, so long as the black mood is still upon him. But why, still feeling like that, should he then have put in time spooning with Marion?'

'Spooning!'

'I know the expression is a vulgar one. But so was the thing itself. You have realised that Marion is a simple-minded girl?'

'Yes.'

'Or not so much simple-minded as simple. How long would you say that Varley's demon commonly stays with him?' Andreas paused as if expecting an answer, but Shefford made no reply. 'That affair in London, for example. What is the place called?'

'I suppose you mean Grosvenor Square.'

'Yes, indeed. That was over quite soon, no doubt. But these periods of possession are variable, I imagine, About that policeman, Shefford. Was it the *same* policeman?'

'I don't think so.' Shefford felt the conversation to be taking a turn so frightening that he was surprised he wasn't frightened. Perhaps it was a luxury he felt he mustn't allow himself. 'I fact In know it wasn't. It couldn't be. It was one of the things that counted against him.'

'He had spied a weapon. He deliberately collected it. He returned, and lashed out at *any* policeman?'

'Yes. But one policeman is just like another, in a case like that.'

'No doubt. And what happened immediately afterwards?'

'I don't in the least know. I wasn't there.'

'Well, you are on Tyros now.' Andreas paused. 'You don't know what I mean? It is this. To my mind, that old situation a little reproduces itself. To your friend Mark there has come—quite suddenly today, I don't know precisely how—the same sort of humiliation that was inflicted on him then. You may yourself—again I don't know—have been un-wittingly the instrument of it. You may have exposed some truth to him, one that our own talk has been touching on.

263

It is something people are said to be able to stand very little of—the truth.'

There was a silence. Shefford picked up his sherry glass. As he had taken only a single sip of it, it was still almost full, and he suddenly felt the stuff wet and sticky on the base of his thumb. There was no doubt that Andreas had got him rattled. But Andreas wasn't simply putting in a purposeless half-hour making a young man's flesh creep. He had some genuine sense of crisis. Shefford, for that matter, had it too.

'Andreas, I don't know what you mean. There's no connection——'

'But there is. It's my guess that you yourself have already been aware of it, however obscurely. And I think I know, by the way, what happened afterwards—there in your Grosvenor Square, outside that monstrous architectural presence of our American friends. The demon departed—suddenly, as he had come. And what was left was a rather frightened and appalled English boy. Almost a small boy. Quite a nice and promising boy, really. I don't underrate this Mark. It's all a great shame. I agree with you there.'

'To hell with it's being a great shame. And I repeat I don't see any sense in your saying the situation reproduces itself.'

'The difference is only between the physical and the psychical, if I may express it in a somewhat abstract way. What summoned the demon to your Mark before our friends' imposing Embassy was not the fact that he had been hurt by the bobby—it is the colloquial word, I think?—but that he had been hurt in a particular way.'

'I suppose so. He got it in the groin—or that's how newspapers like to put it.'

'I see that you follow me. And now, on a different plane, his manhood has been assaulted again. Or "slighted" is perhaps an adequate word. To your Mark the evil spirit finds his entrance rather easily. Is it that he has a skin too few for effective defence? Certainly some small thing is lacking in the lad. Something that a greater sinner—such as I believe myself to be, Shefford—may possess almost without noticing it.' Andreas was silent for a moment; his last re-mark hadn't the air of being made for effect. 'But tell me—has our young friend ever expressed to you an interest in, and admiration for, persons given to sudden violence?'

'Yes.'

'But, even more, he is attracted by the notion of stratagem?'

'Yes.' Shefford was gazing at Andreas in horror.

'It is less likely—the subtle Machiavellian thing—to land one in gaol, no doubt. But do not, my dear fellow, credit me with anything of the clairvoyant order. He has entertained me too, you know, with his conversation from time to time.'

'Perhaps one can take Mark's talk too seriously.' Shefford stood up abruptly, possibly because he had heard a lack of conviction in his own voice. 'This is all useless, unless there is something to be done. And you began by saying that it's too late.'

'Not necessarily so.' As once before, Andreas was courte-ously on his feet, and moving towards the door. 'We are a little too much in the dark for effective action at the moment. But at least we can be alert. That is what I would wish our talk to urge upon you. To be prepared for the unknown moment when it comes: that is as much as we can hope. But you are right; it is almost time to put on those dinner-jackets. The Minister, even if of inferior consequence, must not be kept waiting.'

'Damn the Minister.'

'Yes, yes—I abundantly agree. Still, fail not our feast. Now, who said that? My memory deserts me.'

'Shakespeare's Macbeth.'

'To be sure. The quotation is not, perhaps, felicitous. But we shall meet within the hour, and over that eternal *ouzo*. It is my only criticism of Bernard, that on Tyros he insists on drinking those local stuffs. I have no other criticism of him. Remember, please, there may be that moment in which we shall have to act. *Au revoir*.'

Shefford went downstairs. Something prompted him, be-fore dressing, to go out and take a look at Vanderlyn's car. It was a resolution that brought him a glimpse of something else.

The double doors of the great drawing-room were open, and as he walked past them he saw Gemma at work within, arranging a lavish display of flowers. Dionysios, in his best clothes, was standing at a modest distance, holding a big basket of roses. The tableau was of the most perfect propriety. Shefford went on—to pause for a moment before one of the largest of the abstract sculptures on a landing. It suggested a marble cup that had been slashed in half, or the calyx of a gigantic flower, bisected in some botanical interest. Two alabaster balls reposed in it, like mysteriously translucent seeds. Shefford's pause was because he had imagined these to stir and fractionally turn as he looked. He had felt nothing himself, but he supposed that the skin of Tyros had again lazily twitched, as if the slumbering monster the island was were again prompted to flick away the puny creatures come to perch on it. But this time it had been his imagination, for when he looked closely he saw that the beautiful objects, heavy and lustrous, were cemented or perhaps spiked in their place. There was usually a kind of cheating, he thought, in modish affairs of the kind.

He went into the open air. The evening was warm and quite still, with a faint smell of sea-tangle and sun-dried rock-pools in the air. In the west the sky was already flushing to rose, and the sea had begun to glitter. He listened for the curious sound that had seemed to come from the motionless expanse earlier, but heard nothing. Only as he walked round the back of the monastery he caught for some moments a woman's voice: high, scolding, and pouring out words at an incredible pace. That was Aphrodite; he had heard the performance before; she was rebuking some inferior servant. He hoped it wasn't Vangelio, to whom he owed a quick, admiring kiss. He didn't however, feel like anything of that sort now. As he approached the granary he heard the sudden cough and bark of a motor-bike starting up; presently the machine came round a bend, already travelling at a high speed, and with the rider leaning far inwards on the curve. He wore a crash-helmet, large dark goggles, and a black leather jacket inappropriate in this warm air. Shefford recognised

266

Stepho, and Stepho raised a hand to him as he roared past. Turning, Shefford saw that the jacket had a white skull and cross-bones painted on the back. It must be a prized possession obtained from some horrible English shop. It was depressing that such objects should proliferate round the globe. A shrouded rider on a motor-bike was a sinister figure in any case. There was an old film, surely, which made play with that. It had something to do with Jean Cocteau.

The Mercedes and the Aston Martin were parked side by side. The third car usually kept here, a little Fiat *cinquecento* in which Gemma and Marion sometimes ran about, was absent. Shefford looked at the Aston Martin. The near-side wing was crumpled, but seemingly not so as to affect the free movement of the wheel beneath it; there was no visible sign of anything else wrong. Shefford turned away. He had come on this futile inspection, he realised, at the bidding of a general unease now possessing him. There was painful reason for that. But perhaps, in addition, Andreas was right about a sort of subliminal effect of the earth-tremors. They were, after all, to be described as subliminal themselves. *Moving of th'earth brings harmes and feares, Men reckon what it did and meant* . . .

Precisely as this poetic reminiscence passed through Shefford's head, the earth did move. It moved more definitely than it had done before. He recalled having lately let Andreas's sherry slop over on his hand. This tremor would probably have had about the same effect. No more than that, surely—and for a moment he was astonished that he had felt frightened. He found himself looking up to that highest point on Tyros upon which stood the little shrine to the prophet Elijah. It was no doubt what the native inhabitants did when these tiny tokens of the divine displeasure occasionally visited them.

The shrine stood there no longer. It had vanished. In its place, just perceptible above the summit of Spina, was a small cloud of dust.

Chapter 8

By the time Shefford had dressed it was within half-an-hour of dinner, and he knew he ought to go straight to the drawing-room. He had gathered that people no longer came to dine at the monastery as they felt inclined; it was no doubt a sign of the difficulties into which Vanderlyn's enterprise had been running that a more orthodox system of invitations now prevailed. And Gemma's social instincts were conventional, so it was likely that the island's most presentable characters would have been summoned this evening, when an official guest was to be entertained. There might, in the drawing-room where all those flowers had been arranged, be quite a formal prelude to the meal, and introductions to be gone through in consequence.

But at the moment it didn't seem to Shefford that any call to social duty could mean much. If Andreas had intended to scare him he had succeeded. Mark, to put it mildly, was in a disturbed condition and perhaps liable to do something silly. Even if he resented it, he ought to be kept an eye on. Shefford found himself hurrying down the corridor between those depressing monkish cells.

Mark was in his dinner-jacket; he had made his toilet with something like Andreas's care; he offered an air of relaxed well-being which it took Shefford some seconds to begin to dislike. His occupation was also surprising. He was sitting on the lid of an over-filled suitcase, forcing it down.

'Oh, hullo,' Mark said cheerfully, 'did you feel another tremor some time ago?'

'Yes. It didn't seem to come to much down here, but it has caused a shake-up, I think, on top of Spina. Unless somebody has been doing a demolition job up there, the little shrine has been tumbled over by it.'

'Good Lord—poor old Prophitis Ilias!' Mark appeared not greatly interested. 'But just come and sit on this with me, will you? I can't get the damned thing to close.'

They struggled with the suitcase together. It was a companionable occupation which somehow didn't ring quite true. When they had managed to force in both catches, Shefford stood up at once and walked across the room. A cover, he noticed, had been placed over the electric typewriter. There were burnt papers in the fireplace.

'Mark,' he asked, 'what's this in aid of?'

'It's pretty obvious, isn't it?' Mark was looking at him with a smile which Shefford somehow felt could be wiped off with a sponge. 'We're leaving—you and I. I've come to see that you're absolutely right, Jeremy. You always are. It's a way dons have. When they say "alpha" "alpha" is right, and when they say "gamma" "gamma" is right. All experience corroborates this. It's a wonderful thing.'

This speech didn't come to Shefford as entertaining, nor the feeling behind it as amiable. But he told himself that, if Mark was really agreeing to leave Tyros, then Mark was in a sense giving in. And in that case it would be his instinct to salve his pride with equivocal chatter.

'All right,' Shefford said. 'That's fine, and I'm very glad. When would you like to go?'

'We'll go tomorrow morning, before breakfast. We'll drive over to Trianta, and then get somebody to sail us across. It won't be as fast as the launch, but it should be quite fun.' A new thought seemed to cross Mark's mind. 'We might even manage some fishing on the passage.'

'It seems a bit sudden—but then perhaps it's as well that way.' Shefford felt misgiving rise in him. 'Have you told Vanderlyn yet?'

'No. As a matter of fact, I don't think it will be necessary.'

'Good God, Mark, have some decency! It's true, in a way, that the less said the better. But you can't just cut and run for it.'

'Why ever not?'

'Why ever not! Because it would be monstrous. If he finds you vanished tomorrow, he'll be frightfully upset.'

'I don't think so.' Mark's smile appeared to slip oddly on his face; it became his secret smile—the secret smile that was meant to be observed. 'Somehow, I don't think so, at all.'

'I'll have nothing to do with it.' Shefford was alarmed. For some minutes he had taken this Mark for a more or less normal Mark. But it was really the Mark who had raged in his little room earlier who was still the Mark in this big room now. He had simply superimposed upon his fury a disguise which didn't stand up to scrutiny. It was like a pair of improbable dark spectacles, or a false moustache out of a Christmas cracker. Shefford felt anger rise in him. 'As far as I'm concerned,' he said, 'you can't be got out of Tyros too soon. It's been a kind of Circe's Ææa to you, Mark Varley. By which I mean it has precious nearly turned you into a young swine.'

'Thank you very much.' Mark had flushed darkly, but he was also looking apprehensive and placatory. 'I know I talk an awful lot of rot. And of course I'll speak to Bernard, if you think it right. Before we go to bed, perhaps. Please come and talk to him too. I rely on you tremendously, Jeremy. You're my very oldest——'

'If you make that rotten joke again, I think I'll knock you down. I've wanted to be your friend—and at this moment I'm one of the people you're proposing to play some dirty trick on. Don't imagine I'm so thick as not to see that. Well, it won't work, Mark. Your notion that you are a wonderful, invisible Machiavellian schemer and latterday Iago is as stupid as it's vicious. But at least it's just something that comes over you and goes away again. It is, isn't it? And I'm still with you, if you'll come away in decency and order. We'll work something out. And you'll have a damned sight better chance of becoming a good writer in a bed-sitter in Camden Town than tormented by lusts and frustrations in this luckless place. There, Mark! It's an appeal.'

All this time Mark had remained sitting on his suitcase on the floor. Now he rose slowly to his feet—so slowly that he might have been performing a taxing gymnastic exercise, or responding with unnaturally strengthened muscles to a command received under hypnosis. He looked straight at

Shefford, and through what seemed abnormally rounded eyes.

'Jeremy,' he said. 'you're really rather decent.' He was speaking in a changed voice, so that the effect was of something coming from a part of his mind that had gone to sleep. 'Perhaps, after all, we could——'

At this moment the door of Mark's room opened—there might or might not have been a knock—and Andreas stood framed in it. He had judged the coming dinner to remain sufficiently domestic to justify his wearing a smoking-jacket made out of a piece of ancient brocade—flame-coloured for the most part, but with intricate interweavings of turquoise and gold. He might have been a messenger in some mediaeval interlude.

'Ah,' Andreas said, 'both of you.' He looked at the two young men with a swiftly appraising glance. Then he looked at the suitcase, and it was possible to hear him take a deep breath of what might have been relief. 'My dear lads, I haven't positively been sent to summon you. But I have come for something like that purpose, all the same. It's dinner-time, you know—or rather past it. But it isn't only your absence that is holding us up. Gemma may be annoyed with you, but that's merely because we have this tiresome politician from Athens in the house. Bernard, on the other hand, has a real anxiety on his mind.' Andreas wasn't bothering about Shefford now; his gaze was steadily upon Mark. 'Somebody else has failed to turn up, so far.'

'Somebody else?' It was Mark who found it necessary to echo the question. The effect contrived to be like the ring of a false coin on a counter.

'Marion. She seems to have disappeared. And so has the little car, the *cinquecento*. Can either of you throw any light on this? It is perplexing that Marion should have driven off. Particularly while these earth-tremors continue. The poor child is alarmed by them.'

'I think, perhaps, I can help.' Mark had taken a step forward, with the precision of a soldier who hears a word of command on parade—or of an actor, Shefford thought, who has received his cue. 'Yes, I think I can relieve Bernard's mind.' Mark turned towards Shefford, and for a moment frowned like a man who is trying to remember something, to recall the way an interrupted conversation had appeared to go. 'In fact, I have news for him, and for Gemma too. Perhaps it's better put that way.' He made a stagy gesture towards the doorway in which Andreas was still standing. 'Shall we go down?'

They walked, all three, along the corridor in silence. They might themselves have been monks, and under some sort of vow. Rightly or wrongly, Shefford felt that by some hair's-breadth he had suffered defeat. Andreas had put his hands elegantly in the side-pockets of his jacket—elegantly and cautiously, since some centuries must have been at work upon the fabric in which he had encased himself. Mark walked a little ahead of the other two. He descended a stair-case, still like this. He might have been a young prince with courtiers.

There was a murmur of voices. The great double-doors of the drawing-room were before them like a proscenium arch; beyond this, shutters had been closed and curtains drawn; the long and lofty chamber was lit by a line of chandeliers. The company was not perhaps sufficiently numerous to stand up to this splendour. But it was doing its best. It had taken on, Shefford thought, much more the appearance of a diplomatic gathering than of an assemblage of serious artists and writers round their patron. Perhaps the visiting Minister dictated this effect. He was standing beside Gemma at the far end of the room, and he was a person of impressive presence. Vanderlyn was in the act of introducing to him the little red-bearded man who owned the big hat. There were as many as a dozen other people in the room. Being, or having to affect to be, decently gregarious, they were all at some remove from the doorway in which Mark Varley and his two attendants now stood. It wasn't at all proper that from this distance, Mark should begin to speak. But he did, and while standing still, so that all eyes were turned upon him.

'Bernard, are you worried about Marion?'

'Yes, Mark.' Vanderlyn had turned round. He had to speak rather loudly—as Mark had done—to make sure his voice carried the length of the room. For a moment his expression was puzzled, and then there passed across it something Shefford was familiar with. Mark, Vanderlyn was thinking, was behaving nervously and awkwardly in starting this long-distance communication. And what this called up in Vanderlyn was kindness and warmth. It was a response that came to him spontaneously. He never let it become intrusive. But it was with confidence and affection that he was looking down the room at Mark now. 'We have been beginning to wonder,' he said. 'Do you know where she has got to?'

'Oh, yes—and you needn't worry too much.' Mark's voice was steady—although Shefford, standing close beside him, saw something ugly and mysterious beginning to happen round his mouth; it was as if he were making an immense effort to sustain a role upon which the curtain should come down. 'It's only,' Mark said, 'that Marion has gone off with Stepho. A runaway match. They'll have made a rendezvous at Trianta by now. Fair enough, you know. Dionysios has had your wife. So why shouldn't Stepho have your step-daughter?'

It was not to be regarded as surprising that a dead silence succeeded upon these words. The only sound was of Vanderlyn's footsteps going rapidly down the room. He passed Mark without a glance. Mute, the company remained staring at Mark. Pale and drained of passion, Mark stared at them.

Chapter 9

THE CABINET MINISTER must have understood English, for he murmured briefly to Gemma and withdrew by a door immediately behind him. Shefford wondered—even in the

273

middle of this horror he just managed to wonder—how Gemma herself felt, and what she would do. Perhaps, like Lady Macbeth, she would try to keep her banquet going for a time. But this didn't happen. Gemma followed the Minister from the room. He couldn't very well leave the monastery. She probably intended to see that some sort of meal was provided for him elsewhere. It had been a bad moment for Gemma, and at least the theatrical quality of the exposure must have been something she had never expected. She wasn't a woman to crumple, all the same.

Rather unexpectedly, it was the little red-bearded man who took charge at the far end of the room. He went round the remainder of the guests, talking briefly, and with the result that they all simply went away. It was probably the best that could be done. What had happened wasn't of an order to be papered over during a dinner-party from which both host and hostess had departed. Within a couple of minutes the drawing-room was empty.

Mark had gone over to a side-table and poured himself a drink. It looked like a half-tumblerful of *metaxa*. He turned round with it in his hand, but didn't come back across the room. Shefford felt that he was perhaps in some state of dissociation, like a man who eats his breakfast and smokes his cigarette before being taken out and hanged. Not that anybody was going to hang Mark. He hadn't even committed a crime—unless, technically, it was a slander to tell a truth about Mrs Vanderlyn and one of her servants. What he had done was to create a situation in which, among other things, he simply hadn't stopped to view himself: a piece of malign artistry, with its inspired creator standing outside it, paring his finger-nails and chuckling. But he already knew —one had only to look at his face to see it—that no such state of affairs can exist in nature. He was inside the picture, not out of it. Here he was in this drawing-room, a moral being, involved in the consequences of a wicked and wanton freak. He was going to be twenty-three, Shefford remembered, in a few days' time.

'Do you think all these people believed it?' Shefford asked

274

Andreas. It was an unimportant question, and he realised he had taken refuge in it.

'Who knows?' Andreas shrugged his shoulders. 'One part was true, and one part was a lie. Let them believe what they please.'

'Vanderlyn must know that Marion has been tricked in some way?'

'I have no doubt of it.'

'I can't understand in what way.'

'It isn't difficult.' Andreas paused to glance at Mark. It didn't seem significant whether he heard and understood or not. 'Varley has had an even greater ascendancy over the poor girl than we thought. He had only to suggest this romantic thing—that the two of them should make a runaway match from Trianta—and she did as she was told. He'd have persuaded her that Bernard would be surprised but delighted. Varley, is that right?'

Mark made no reply. He gulped *metaxa*. Dimly, he did appear to be listening.

'And he persuaded or bribed Stepho to join in what was to be simply a brutal joke. Marion boards the launch, and instead of Mark there is Stepho. What happens then, I don't pretend to know. But what your friend there is engaged upon is a punitive exercise. Marion is being punished for having presumed to aspire to him. And Bernard is being punished for I can't think what. Marion will be returned to us quite soon, perhaps by a Stepho who affects to regret having misunderstood the matter. The young lady boarded the launch of her own free will. Mr Varley, regrettably, didn't turn up. There may be some hazy idea of such explanation. But it will be given only after a due measure of anguish and anxiety and humiliation and scandal have happened. You see? What a tremendous joke!'

Shefford didn't see—or not clearly. The outlines of the thing were monstrous and wavering, and Andreas was like a *raisonneur* in some extravagant fiction, turned on to credibilize things that simply couldn't take place, that have never occurred to the mind of man.

'Unfortunately, all human action has to be undertaken in darkness and ignorance. Now more closely, now at a slightly farther remove, these things surround everything we do.' As Andreas plunged into these untimely philosophic generalisations, he began to advance across the room towards Mark. Mark had almost finished his brandy. His face offered no clue to his state of mind. The dark lock had fallen between his eyes. The small blemish was livid. He was only a minor devil, Shefford found himself thinking, but he was as handsome as a major one. It seemed unfair. Had Mark's looks been entirely commonplace, many things might not have happened to him.

'Tell me'—Andreas was now speaking to Mark, loudly and slowly, as if to a drugged or drunken man—'do you know about those Greek boys? Do you know their history before they came here?'

Mark shook his head, and for a moment it seemed the only communication he was able, or disposed, to make. But then he spoke—in a kind of thick mumble, like an old man who has suffered a stroke.

'No. I tried to find out once. They were cagey. They wouldn't tell me.'

'Dionysios was a sneak-thief. We must agree that he has continued to vindicate the character—Shefford, one can say that?—very well. The case of Stepho is different. There was not sufficient evidence against him, and he was in prison for only a short time. But what he had done made it impossible for him to live in his own town. The place would have been too hot to hold him. Is that a permissible phrase? So he came to Bernard through a charity organisation. His offence had been rape.' Andreas paused. 'So here was ignorance, darkness. Shefford, you see? Our young friend here was planning more brilliantly than he knew.'

'I didn't know that.' Mark had set down his empty glass with a shaking hand. He seemed to be slowly involving himself again with the situation around him. But his voice was quite flat, as if speaking of some indifferent thing. 'I told him he might be in trouble if he did more than rough her up a bit. Even though her story, you know, could be called a hysterical girl's.'

Shefford became conscious of feeling physically sick, and of wondering whether a first contact with naked evil often took people that way. He was to recall this as the basest moment of the whole affair. He was to remember that at least it had been that.

'But that's not all,' Andreas said. 'You have your own small private demon, Varley. I was saying so to Shefford not long ago. But you have much greater demons, it seems, fighting invisibly on your side. You didn't know about Stepho. And you still don't know the story of Marion's mother, Bernard's first wife. As it happens, she took through life with her the memory of a ghastly and disabling sexual shock, of something as near a crime as makes no matter. Now her daughter is in the hands of a ravisher, who has instructions to do no more than rough her up. Bernard is pursuing them, with these things in his head. Well done, Varley. The melodrama is of the first quality. And yet you get only half the credit, don't you agree? Darkness and ignorance. They place themselves like weapons in our hands.'

Mark, without speaking, reached again for the brandy bottle. He seemed to have withdrawn once more into a seclusion which Shefford suddenly thought might be actual madness. Some minute change in Mark's internal chemistry, some shift of balance in itself as imperceptible as the recent tremors on Tyros had virtually been: this had opened a psychotic gulf into which he had vanished for good. For a moment it seemed not merely a possibility; it was the only plausible explanation of this single day's headlong rush to catastrophe. Yet Mark didn't look mad: not really mad. He looked very close to being what Andreas had predicted he would be once his demon left him: a frightened boy. All that stood between him and that now was a desperate clinging to a less humiliating role, that of the villain of the piece. He might have been preparing to declare that from this time forth he never would speak a word. And from all this it was hard to see anything that could rescue him.

There was a sound at the double doors of the drawing-room. Shefford and Andreas both turned round, and discovered that Dionysios had entered. Or not quite entered, for he was continuing to stand warily on the threshold. There was no doubt about how Dionysios was looking and feeling. He was scared stiff. Mark's exposure of his relations with the *archontissa* had no doubt been overheard by servants and would soon be common knowledge throughout Tyros. He was perhaps not very clear that he mightn't be given a beating. He didn't look as if he would ever again lie on his back in the sun and see voluptuous visions in the heavens. But that was no doubt a mistake. Dionysios would recover, and other ladies would go to bed with him. Meanwhile, his terror made him look even younger than he was. It was an additional horror in this affair, Shefford thought, that a kind of sheer juvenile delinquency bore so large a part in it.

Andreas advanced upon Dionysios. Dionysios said something in Greek. He was in no state to exhibit his English. If Mark understood him, he gave no sign. It seemed that Dionysios had been charged with a message; he certainly wouldn't have come in like this of his own accord; indeed, he had begun to back out cautiously now, but Andreas stopped him with a word. There was another exchange, apparently final, and again Dionysios backed away. Andreas stepped forward, took him by the collar, swung him round with strength Shefford found wholly unexpected, and kicked him through the door. Dionysios yelped, fell, picked himself up, and half-turned as if in headlong attack. It seemed possible there would be murder in the drawing-room. Andreas didn't move. Dionysios's glance dropped, and he turned away again and limped off. It had been a powerful kick.

'I owed him that for Bernard,' Andreas said. 'And it made apparent that the young brute has a menial soul. Otherwise he would not have taken it. I think that is your phrase?'

'Just what had he been sent to say?' It seemed to Shefford no time for Andreas to air his interest in English idiom. 'Did Bernard send him?'

'Yes. Bernard has driven off to Trianta, hoping to be in

278

time to intercept Marion and bring her back. That appears to me unlikely. Our young friend'—he glanced coolly at Mark—'no doubt timed his revelation so as to prevent that.'

Shefford looked at Mark too. Mark had seemed to take no interest in Dionysios's coming, or even in the violent manner of his going. He had poured himself another large allowance of *metaxa*, but had at once knocked over the tumbler and done nothing further about it. Andreas perhaps judged him beyond communicating with, for he now ignored him.

'It is possible that this bad business may not go too far. Varley's influence with Marion has proved itself, but his influence with Stepho may be less than he believes. It is hard to imagine a young man who has only just escaped imprisonment for a stiff term of years, and who is still in possession of his reason, lending himself even to a mere joke of the ugly-looking sort we have here. It is fifty-fifty, to my mind.'

'Fifty-fifty?'

'With luck, the launch will never leave Trianta. Stepho will have reflected about which side his bread is buttered on—right?—and will bring Miss Causland back to the monastery with an absolute correctness.'

'That won't save her from the knowledge that she has been unspeakably treated by a man she believes has come to love her.'

'Perfectly true.' Andreas spoke coldly. 'But the annals of love—I speak purely as an observer—record many such disillusionments. Think of her mother.'

'You needn't tell me to do that. But what's the other side of your fifty-fifty chance?'

'That Stepho—who is too impassive, too secret for my liking—will *not* remain in possession of his reason. The situation will be too much for him, will prompt him too powerfully.'

'Marion isn't——' Shefford broke off, ashamed of what he had been about to say.

'That is true. Yet—forgive me—pathology tells us that the very charmlessness of a woman in such a situation——'

'For God's sake, Andreas, can't we do something?'

'I hope we can. For if the worst happens, it will not be Stepho alone who will go to prison for many years. It will be Varley too. He will not get far by telling a Greek judge that he gave instructions for a mere roughing up.'

Mark was fumbling among the glasses on the table. Perhaps he was fastidious enough to be searching for a clean one. Andreas's words appeared to affect him not at all. They had been aimed at him. Nothing had happened.

'And now I think we had better follow Bernard to Trianta. Whether we can do anything effective or not, we must support him. If you will drive—for it is not an accomplishment of mine—we will go straight over in the other car.'

'Yes, of course.' Shefford was relieved at some prospect of action. 'I suppose I can drive an Aston Martin.'

'No, no. Bernard has gone in that. It is the car, you remember, he reserves for himself. It is the Mercedes that is left in the granary.'

'*No!*'

They swung round. The single word had been wrung from Mark like a cry under torture. He had dropped a glass, and it lay shivered on the floor. The fragments cracked beneath his feet as he stumbled towards them, his face vivid with horror.

'No!' he cried again. 'Not that car. He can't. He mustn't. I wrecked it. I didn't tell him, but I wrecked it. It feels all right, but the steering's gone. It can't possibly stand up to the turns on the cliff. He'll be killed. I'll have killed him. I'll have killed him, I tell you!'

There was a moment's silence, and then Mark turned away from them as from people in whom there is no hope. He ran blindly from the drawing-room, crying out '*Bernard, Bernard!*' as if the desperation of his voice could reach a man now miles away in the swiftly falling Aegean dusk.

Chapter 10

THE MERCEDES WAS no problem; in fact it was the make of car that Shefford had once briefly owned by way of showing his father he had attained a position in the world. But driving any car at high speed and in a treacherous half-light along that eventually dreadful road to Trianta was a different matter, and only crisis would have persuaded him to it. Crisis, however, there was. Indeed, if Mark was right about the steering of the Aston Martin, one of two distinct catastrophes had perhaps occurred already. What might first lie ahead was twisted wreckage.

They hurried from the monastery without meeting anybody. The guests had departed, and the servants seemed to have gone into hiding. Only on the terrace they encountered Aphrodite, who ran after them, crying out. Very frightened, she chattered in a rapid Greek which only Andreas understood. Her French had deserted her, just as his English had deserted Dionysios. She was imploring them not to leave the monastery. The earth-tremors were the reason—not in themselves, but because of what had happened to the shrine of the saint on top of Spina. News of this had spread, and the household was in a panic.

No doubt there had been sacred places on mountains like Spina long before the Prophet Elijah was thought of, and it was natural that the peasantry should be upset. But there was nothing for it but to shake off Aphrodite firmly, since the business on hand was too urgent to admit of talk about omens and portents. Shefford was outside the granary before he realised that Mark had come along too. For a moment it occurred to him to ask Mark to drive, for at least Mark knew every metre of the road. Then he remembered all that *metaxa*, and thought better of it. But if Mark wasn't to be useful there seemed no need of his company; and if Vanderlyn was found unharmed there could be small advantage in immediately confronting him with his singularly unrewarding *protégé*. Shefford turned on Mark and told him to clear out. Mark might have obeyed, since he was in a state of pitiful disorder still. But Andreas, without a word, took his arm and shoved him into the back of the car. Shefford found himself accepting as a rebuke this act of brusque humanity.

The sun had gone down in a flaming western sky, and the first mile of their journey was towards it. Shefford hadn't before seen such a sunset on Tyros; it was as if, just over the horizon, the chariot of the god had crashed in a vast incandescence and would never rise again. He remembered Marion's notion that this angry red was somehow connected with the tremors. It now struck him that this might be true. Although it hadn't been perceptible, a good deal of dust could have been raised by these unimpressive disturbances, rather as when a shaggy-haired animal shakes his coat. If the dust was drifting out to sea, it might very well be affecting the atmosphere. But any fine suspension of the sort wasn't itself visible; it was just that there was this alarming conflagration ahead; in half-an-hour it would be gone.

They climbed, turned south, and ran through the upland valleys—arid ground, patches of poor pasture, smaller patches of precarious cultivation—which would soon be fading on the sight. In the hamlets there was nobody to be seen; perhaps it was the hour of the evening meal, or perhaps the news from Spina had driven people into those tiny churches which no collection of hovels appeared to be without. They passed the place where there was an engineering shop or forge; it was already glowing more brightly than by day. Once Shefford lost the road, and had to back down a rutted track through a stink of manure; he found leisure to wonder where the stuff could come from. They drove in silence. Andreas stared in front of him, as if intent upon what the next bend would reveal—this although they had not yet come to any part of the road that would impose exceptional strain upon a smoothly moving car. Mark, huddled in the back, made no sound either. Shefford hadn't once turned to look at him.

Shefford switched on his side-lights. They would be at Trianta—if they ever got that far—before he would actually need anything to see by. He would be zigzagging down the cliffs in the very worst light of all. But neither there nor here must he drive other than desperately fast. It was conceivable, although it wasn't likely, that they might still overtake Vanderlyn on the road. And there were various situations— he found his imagination active—upon which they might arrive in the nick of time. Not that mere probability wasn't against anything of the sort. For Andreas's fifty-fifty chance appeared an optimistic estimate. It was more likely than not that Stepho and Marion were by now at sea.

Shefford rounded a bend, jammed on his brakes, and came to a halt nose-to-nose with the Fiat *cinquecento*. Stepho was at the wheel, and Marion was beside him.

It was a moment of relief so blinding that for a moment Shefford had a confused notion that the little car's head-lights must be beating full on his face. Then he heard Andreas exclaim softly—he had surely uttered, not profanely, the name of the Blessed Virgin—and saw him leap from the Mercedes. Shefford himself took a long breath, and remained in his seat. Andreas spoke to Marion, spoke to Stepho, spoke to Marion once more. Then he came quickly back.

'She's all right?' Shefford asked.

'In the sense you are thinking of, yes. The poor child is bewildered. At the moment it is chiefly that.'

'Stepho has behaved?'

'He has known that small fact about the side his bread is buttered on. Perhaps a little more. It is not for us to judge. And at least Marion keeps on saying that he has been so kind, so gentle and kind. She appears to have it in her to reproach herself for having disliked and distrusted him. But why she found him waiting in the launch where Varley ought to have been: that, I think, is something of which she has no understanding at all.'

'I don't see how Vanderlyn can have missed them.'

'The next village—Meros. A miserable place. But the road

divides and goes round either side of it. There is nothing else of the sort on the whole route, so it is a hundred-to-one mischance. But it means that Bernard cannot be far ahead. I shall go back to the monastery in the little car. That is essential, however well-behaved Stepho is being. Marion must be handed over to Gemma.'

'Surely——'

'My dear Shefford, you are a man of the world. Gemma is not a monster simply because, in a depressed situation, she has taken a personable if plebeian young lover. And for Marion she is our only resource at the moment. But I waste time. You can edge round the Fiat—the *topolino*, as our Italian friends say. Good luck, Shefford. Pass by.'

Shefford let in the clutch, and passed by. It was, he thought, the only bad shot at an English idiom that he had heard Andreas utter. In the big Mercedes he was perched above the other car. He glanced down as he went past. Marion Causland was sitting quite still. She didn't appear to be weeping. In her lap lay a few flowers: the sand lilies which alone bloomed at this time of year. Shefford didn't imagine that she had herself gathered them in a distraction, like mad Ophelia. They had been given her by Stepho— Stepho who now sat, so characteristically, immobile at a wheel.

The *cinquecento* had vanished before it occurred to him that throughout this episode Mark hadn't come into his head. So now he turned and did look. Mark was still where he had plainly dived the moment the Fiat came into view. However he regarded the collapse of his Machiavellian machination and Marlovian outrage—whether as failure or deliverance—he had been unable to face its immediate consequence, and he had simply gone into hiding on the floor of the Mercedes. The effect was so much that of a child who has dived under the bedclothes and won't come out that Shefford was shocked to find himself laughing aloud. He drove hastily on. The overwhelming need was to overtake Vanderlyn, now at high speed and in a lethally damaged car approaching the hairpins leading down to the forsaken garden, the aromatic eucalypts, the little harbour with its two jetties, the boathouse, that farther promontory on which a ruined temple stood, with a single Corinthian capital still unfolding its intricate acanthus pattern to the sky. Shefford saw it all as he drove. It came to him as a place already habitual and familiar. To reach it, he told himself, was to be safe.

If safety was ahead, danger wheeled now on his right hand and now on his left as he wound the Mercedes down the cliff. But every turn, he realised, increased the chance of Vanderlyn's safety; every twist without evidence of disaster meant that the Aston Martin was holding out. There was one hideous moment when the Mercedes moved sideways under no guidance that was his, and when the sea, far below, seemed to vanish beneath its floor-boards. But that was the only skid. Suddenly and miraculously, they were on level ground. He switched off the engine, and there was silence. Or not quite silence. A murmur was coming from the sea. He had heard it earlier on this ominous day. It seemed not a kind of murmur that a sea normally makes.

The Aston Martin was close at hand—at rest, with nothing amiss. Like Stepho, it had proved a little more resistant than Mark supposed. Beyond it, the track ran on a curve to the nearer jetty, where the launch was moored. On the left of the track, and some twelve feet below, lay the sea. Rising steeply on the right was that tumble of scree which the tremors had of late a little disturbed. Small boulders lay on the track here and there. The light was fading rapidly, but nothing was yet shadowy and insubstantial; the components of the visible scene existed still in the round, although soon they would be reduced to silhouette.

'Vanderlyn!' Shefford said. He spoke without turning his head.

Vanderlyn was walking back from the deserted launch to his car. He moved stiffly, as a very old man might move. But he was a big man, and his figure showed broad and menacing in the dusk.

'*Bernard!*'

285

Mark had cried out, as he had cried out once before. He leapt from the Mercedes—he seemed not to have opened a door—and Shefford had a glimpse of his face as he ran past. It was tear-stained; it was also eager and appallingly young. Mark ran towards Vanderlyn. He looked unnaturally tall and slender in his dark evening clothes, like a Giacometti in lustreless iron.

Vanderlyn had come to a halt on the cry. Now he advanced upon Mark slowly, and Mark continued to run towards him. Mark checked his pace, as if he had seen or remembered something to daunt him; and then in an instant he was running on. Shefford, still in his seat, was groping for any sense of the intent with which these two men were advancing upon each other. He had a momentary vision of something in a romantic mode: repentance and reconciliation achieved upon a single broken word, an overwhelming embrace. He had a counter-vision of duellists measuring their deadly intervening ground. The second of these struck him as the more wholesome of the two—and the more probable as well, at least so far as Vanderlyn was concerned. If Mark had become dear to Vanderlyn it was yet true that Marion, Louise's daughter, was dearer to him still. Mark's offence was not forgivable.

Perhaps they ought to be left alone, but Shefford didn't think so. He tumbled himself out of the Mercedes, and for a moment he thought it had been so precipitately that his balance had deserted him. Then he realised that Tyros was misbehaving again. As usual, the demonstration was an ineffective one. There was a small stirring in front of him and to the right. Pebbles were trickling down the scree, and then little rivers of rubble—and after that, quite suddenly, there were a few boulders, bouncing like tennis balls and travelling fast. Even so, it was seconds before he realised that mere nature had taken the stage; that here in Vanderlyn's kingdom, as once and again in Jude Fawley's Wessex, blind fatality was closing up the scene. The small landslide operated with the precision of a sniper. Only a few yards of the track vanished, but there Vanderlyn had been walking, and

Vanderlyn vanished with it. What must have been less than a cartload of slithering debris had carried him into the sea.

Mark didn't cry out again; he saved his breath for running. His progress almost instantly became a scramble, for he too was involved in a small flowing river of rock. But he reached the point of Vanderlyn's fall, kicked off his shoes, and slipped from the outer garments in which it had been proper to appear before a grandee from Athens. For a moment he stood motionless. He might have been hesitating before the spectacle of the dark water, recently so still, now working in a muddied and sinister turbulence below. But he was choosing his spot. His body curved, then straightened like an arrow as he dived.

Shefford ran forward. But the stony rubbish beneath his own feet was moving too; he fell heavily, and when he rose there was a tearing pain in his right ankle. It was minutes before he got himself into the water. He could swim well enough in spite of his injury. He worked across and across the little bay, quartering it; sometimes he called out; sometimes, where there seemed to be a treacherous snag beneath the surface, he dived and searched as well as he could. It was a surprisingly long time before he was utterly exhausted, and then he found himself unable even to scramble to shore. But by then men had come from Trianta with lanterns, and they hauled him out.

They found nothing more that night. Mark's body was washed ashore in the morning. The action of the sea had stripped him of his few scraps of clothing, and he lay naked in the garden for a few minutes before somebody brought a blanket and covered him. On his neck there were marks which remained a mystery until Vanderlyn's body was recovered on the following day. Vanderlyn's head had been injured; it must have been struck by a falling boulder, so that concussion followed. Had he been fully conscious in the sea, there would scarcely have been a problem. Had he been unconscious, Mark could probably have rescued him. But Vanderlyn had been confused, and there was a struggle in the water. Vanderlyn had strangled Mark, and they had gone down together.

During the remaining days of his stay on Tyros Shefford was not to encounter either Stepho or Dionysios again. The death of the rich foreigner who had begun to set his hand upon the island was a great bewilderment. But it took second place to what had happened on the summit of Spina, and the business of rebuilding the shrine of Prophitis Ilias was undertaken as promptly and with as little apparent need of directing intelligence as might be displayed by some termite community confronted with a similar small disaster. There were, however, stones to be shaped and carried, tubs of mortar to be mixed—and to assist in such tasks both young men, without favour, were despatched by Gemma. It seemed a useful clearing of the stage. Neither of these characters had a meaningful place in the catastrophe.

Shefford was flying back to England before it came to him that this way of thinking was only part of the literary mind. He would be falsifying these deaths if he regarded them as other than senseless. For chance—as he had once told Vanderlyn—is never up to anything morally or even aesthetically acceptable. Had Crass Casualty worked by feet or inches another way, had the slither of rock and the crack of the skull been minutely different, Vanderlyn and Mark between them might have hauled an insensible Shefford from the sea. It is quite blindly that nature sometimes gets round to imitating art.

In Oxford the quadrangles were thronged with tourists; the cine-cameras whirred; the voices of the ciceroni droned on in several languages. Once—it was in a small and superior party—he caught himself imagining that he had glimpsed the figure of the first Mrs Vanderlyn, her serious regard momentarily raised from her guide-book. It was plainly time to go home and work. Bundling *The Faerie Queene* and much else into his car, he departed for the north.